THE PIRATES OF
PACTA SERVANDA

PRAISE FOR THE PILLARS OF REALITY SERIES

"Campbell has created an interesting world... [he] has created his characters in such a meticulous way, I could not help but develop my own feelings for both of them. I have already gotten the second book and will be listening with anticipation."

—Audio Book Reviewer

"I loved *The Hidden Masters of Marandur*...The intense battle and action scenes are one of the places where Campbell's writing really shines. There are a lot of urban and epic fantasy novels that make me cringe when I read their battles, but Campbell's years of military experience help him write realistic battles."

—All Things Urban Fantasy

"I highly recommend this to fantasy lovers, especially if you enjoy reading about young protagonists coming into their own and fighting against a stronger force than themselves. The world building has been strengthened even further giving the reader more history. Along with the characters flight from their pursuers and search for knowledge allowing us to see more of the continent the pace is constant and had me finding excuses to continue the book."

—Not Yet Read

"*The Dragons of Dorcastle*... is the perfect mix of steampunk and fantasy... it has set the bar to high."

—The Arched Doorway

"Quite a bit of fun and I really enjoyed it. . .An excellent sequel and well worth the read!"

—Game Industry

"The Pillars of Reality series continues in THE ASSASSINS OF ALTIS to be a great action filled adventure. . .So many exciting things happen that I can hardly wait for the next book to be released."

–Not Yet Read

"The Pillars of Reality is a series that gets better and better with each new book. . .THE ASSASSINS OF ALTIS is a great addition to a great series and one I recommend to fantasy fans, especially if you like your fantasy with a touch of sci-fi."

–Bookaholic Cat

"Seriously, get this book (and the first two). This one went straight to my favorites shelf."

–Reanne Reads

"[Jack Campbell] took my expectations and completely blew them out of the water, proving yet again that he can seamlessly combine steampunk and epic fantasy into a truly fantastic story. . .I am looking forward to seeing just where Campbell goes with the story next, I'm not sure how I'm going to manage the wait for the next book in the series."

–The Arched Doorway

PRAISE FOR THE LOST FLEET SERIES

"It's the thrilling saga of a nearly-crushed force battling its way home from deep within enemy territory, laced with deadpan satire about modern warfare and neoliberal economics. Like Xenophon's Anabasis – with spaceships."

—The Guardian (UK)

"Black Jack is an excellent character, and this series is the best military SF I've read in some time."

—Wired Magazine

"If you're a fan of character, action, and conflict in a Military SF setting, you would probably be more than pleased by Campbell's offering."

—Tor.com

". . . a fun, quick read, full of action, compelling characters, and deeper issues. Exactly the type of story which attracts readers to military SF in the first place."

—SF Signal

"Rousing military-SF action... it should please many fans of old-fashioned hard SF. And it may be a good starting point for media SF fans looking to expand their SF reading beyond tie-in novels."

—SciFi.com

"Fascinating stuff ... this is military SF where the military and SF parts are both done right."

—SFX Magazine

PRAISE FOR THE LOST FLEET: BEYOND THE FRONTIER SERIES

"Combines the best parts of military sf and grand space opera to launch a new adventure series ... sets the fleet up for plenty of exciting discoveries and escapades."

—Publishers Weekly

"Absorbing...neither series addicts nor newcomers will be disappointed."

—Kirkus Reviews

"Epic space battles, this time with aliens. Fans who enjoyed the earlier books in the Lost Fleet series will be pleased."

—Fantasy Literature

"I loved every minute of it. I've been with these characters through six novels and it felt like returning to an old group of friends."

—Walker of Worlds

"A fast-paced page turner ... the search for answers will keep readers entertained for years to come."

—SF Revu

"Another excellent addition to one of the best military science fiction series on the market. This delivers everything fans expect from Black Jack Geary and more."

—Monsters & Critics

THE PIRATES
OF PACTA
SERVANDA

Pillars of Reality
Book 4

JACK CAMPBELL

JABberwocky Literary Agency, Inc.

To
my niece Megan Englehart

For S, as always

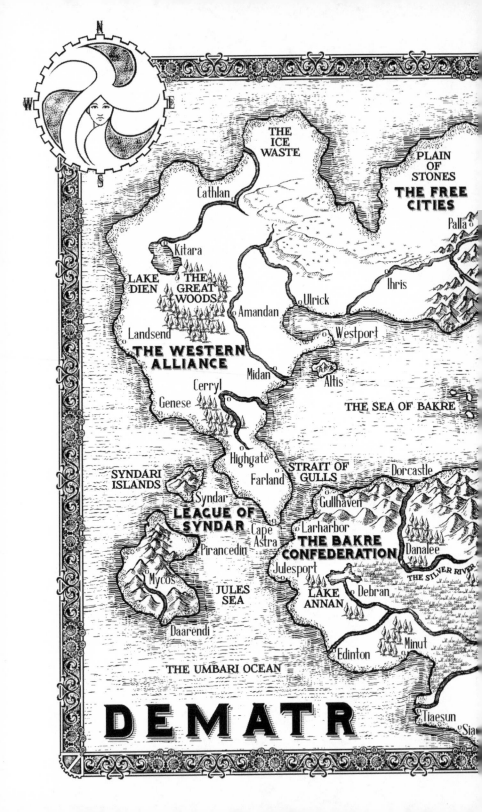

NORTHERN RAMPART
MOUNTAINS

Cristane

Dunlan

Fornadin

LAKE
BELLAD   Beldan

Alexdria

Umburan   Pandin

Severun

Kelsi   Marida

Sandurin

Centin

THE MARAN
EMPIRE

THE SHARR ISLES   OSPREN RIVER   Marandur

Jameston   Caer Lyn   Landfall   Palandur

Jacksport   Alfarin

Longfalls

Emdin

Ringhmon

SOUTHERN
MOUNTAINS   THE
WASTE

Inser

Trefik

THE BROKEN KINGDOM OF TIAE

Awanat

ACKNOWLEDGMENTS

I remain indebted to my agents, Joshua Bilmes and Eddie Schneider, for their long standing support, ever-inspired suggestions and assistance, as well as to Krystyna Lopez and Lisa Rodgers for their work on foreign sales and print editions. Thanks also to Catherine Asaro, Robert Chase, Carolyn Ives Gilman, J.G. (Huck) Huckenpohler, Simcha Kuritzky, Michael LaViolette, Aly Parsons, Bud Sparhawk and Constance A. Warner for their suggestions, comments and recommendations.

CHAPTER ONE

Master Mechanic Mari of Caer Lyn awoke from a nightmare of being pursued by remorseless killers through a maze of city streets, some of them crumbling ruins and others in flames. Those hunting her and her friends wore the black jackets of Mechanics and carried rifles, or were armored Imperial legionaries bearing swords and crossbows, or had the robes and emotionless faces of Mages who held long knives. One by one Mari's friends died until she was trapped, the killers closing in, and behind them a raging mob destroying all in their path, a mob which would soon sweep over her and the killers alike, leaving nothing but death in its wake.

And inside that nightmare, everything was her fault. She had caused all of the deaths, including those of her friends.

She stared at the wooden beams and planks above her bunk, her breath coming in short gasps and her heart pounding. She was alone in the small cabin, but she could hear the clump of boots and the soft thud of sailors' bare feet on the deck overhead.

She controlled her breathing and focused her thoughts. She wasn't in a prison cell, or trapped in the dead city of Marandur, or being chased through the streets of Altis by assassins. She was aboard the small schooner *Gray Lady*, surrounded by her friends, and as safe for the moment as someone being hunted by at least half the world could hope to be.

The safety was only an illusion, though, because if the Mages were right, the mobs which haunted Mari's nightmares would soon arise to smash everything on this world. And the Mages claimed that only she could that stop that from happening.

Her gaze fell on the promise ring on her left hand. The sight of that brought Mari back to full wakefulness. Where was Alain? And why did the *Gray Lady* feel as if the ship were motionless, instead of sailing for whatever brief sanctuary the city of Julesport might offer?

Mari rolled out of the bunk, shrugged into her shoulder holster and ensured that the pistol nestled there was ready for use, pulled on the dark jacket of a Mechanic that she stubbornly continued to wear, and headed out on deck.

Mage Alain of Iris stood at the rail of the *Gray Lady*, peering into the formless world beyond. The harsh and brutal training of a Mage acolyte ensured that his face revealed none of his feelings: not the annoyance at this setback or the fear he felt for Mari, who had changed his world just as she was fated to change this entire world. If she lived.

The morning sun had risen, but the only visible sign of it was a brightening in the white cocoon formed of sea mist, where the *Gray Lady* sat becalmed, her sails hanging limp from their spars and booms. Not even the faintest breeze stirred sky, fog, or the waters on which the *Gray Lady* rode. The air felt heavy and moist, so that each breath required extra labor and conjured up uncomfortable sensations of drowning. Water pooled on every flat surface and formed droplets on every mast, spar and piece of rigging, the drops sliding down the slack canvas of the sails and the rough cordage of the stays, shrouds, halyards, and ratlines, the drops growing as they absorbed other drops until they fell in a fitful rain to add to the wetness on the deck. Sound carried with startling ease, somehow magnified by the moist air, but colors were dimmed, as if the mist were stealing their vibrancy and leaving only pale, washed-out remnants. Those on the *Gray Lady* looked like ghosts to their comrades, looming vaguely out of the mist until they came close enough to be seen clearly.

A world's fate hung on the balance, but they could not move. They had left the burning city of Altis behind less than two weeks ago, riding the breezes south and west out of the Sea of Bakre, dodging warships of the Mechanics Guild and those ships forced to serve the Mage Guild and even more than one Imperial galley forging far afield in pursuit of them. But now not a breath of wind stirred the unusually placid waters of the Jules Sea. Somewhere not far to the east-northeast lay Julesport, a city founded long ago by a pirate and still famously disreputable, but that possible refuge might as well have been a million lances distant.

And their dilemma had just become far more urgent. Alain heard noises of something coming closer under the cloak of the fog. Slow, rhythmic splashing of water and creaking of wood, the soft chant of someone calling cadence to rowers, the occasional rattle of metal on metal which warned of soldiers in armor with swords and shields.

The captain of the *Gray Lady*, a man who had proven to be suspiciously familiar with avoiding those searching for or pursuing his ship, came quickly along the deck, stopping only to whisper brief instructions to sailors who hastened to pass the word to others.

Reaching Alain, the captain bowed. "Sir Mage," he said in a low voice. "I most humbly request that everyone remain as quiet as possible. There is at least one galley out there, and from its movements and attempts to muffle noise I believe it is searching for someone."

Alain nodded once in reply. Despite his outward poise, the captain was not comfortable addressing a Mage, but then no common people were. None of them spoke to Mages if they could help it. Mages were unnerving not only in their ability to show no emotion, and apparently to feel none, but because they possessed mysterious powers that no common wanted employed against him or her on the whim of the Mage. Mages, for their part, rarely bothered to speak to commons unless to issue brief orders. Most Mages, rather, because those who had chosen to follow Mari were slowly learning to regard other people as something other than mere shadows, and Alain had already come far down that path. "Where is the galley from?" Alain asked quietly. "Has the Empire pursued us to the doorstep of Julesport?"

"It's not the Empire, I am certain, Sir Mage. The Imperials don't come out this far. Cities of the Confederation operate few galleys, and the galleys once employed by the broken Kingdom of Tiae are all sunk or foundered now. My guess is, this galley hails from Syndar. I've caught a few words carried through the fog and I believe I recognized the accent." The captain waved briefly toward the west, where the islands of Syndar lay.

"Does the Syndari galley hunt us?" Alain said.

"I cannot be certain, Sir Mage," the captain said. "But I believe that it does. Your Guild, and that of the Lady Mari, have doubtless offered immense rewards for either of you, and from what I have heard of your earlier travels the Imperials as well will pay dearly to have both of you dead."

Alain turned his gaze upon the captain. "You are not tempted by such rewards?"

The captain didn't flinch at the question. He smiled slightly, shaking his head. "No, Sir Mage."

"Why not?"

Taking a deep breath, the captain spoke carefully. "I value freedom, Sir Mage, which is very hard to find in a world where the Great Guilds control everything. The sea has offered the best and sometimes the only refuge in all of Dematr for those seeking liberty. The rewards offered for you and the Lady are no doubt immense, but they dwindle to nothing compared to the chance that she might succeed, that she is the daughter of the prophecy who will overthrow the Great Guilds and grant everyone in this world freedom."

He paused, then added in a rush "I know such as the Imperials will not be free just because the Great Guilds are overthrown. The citizens of the Empire will still have their Emperor or Empress, will still have to deal with Imperial police and Imperial law. And other places will have lesser rulers. Syndar is a nest of petty tyrants and a few colonies of freebooters. But people everywhere will have a chance at freedom, Sir Mage. A chance they now lack. And there is this. The world ashore feels oddly strained, like a line pulled too taut and apt to snap, smashing everything in its path. I've felt that tension growing worse and worse in recent years, and it feels to me far too much like Tiae was before that kingdom came apart and fell into anarchy."

The captain paused again. "My apologies if I have overstepped or misspoken, Sir Mage. But you did ask for my reasons."

"And you did not lie," Alain said. Mages, trained to suppress their own feelings, could easily spot lies told by commons. "You will get us to Julesport?"

"If I can, Sir Mage." The captain gestured again, this time toward the sound of the galley hidden in the fog. "But they can move when we cannot. We need wind. If the fog goes before the wind rises, the galley will see us and close in. Can you…?"

"Raise a wind? No." Alain left it at that. In theory a Mage could create the illusion of the air moving and superimpose that over the illusion of still air that surrounded them, but the amount of power needed far exceeded anything available here. However, commons knew nothing of how Mage arts worked, and so assumed they could do anything.

"I'll prepare my crew to defend the ship if necessary," the captain said, not daring to further question a Mage. He saluted and hurried off.

Right behind the captain came Mari, her eyes searching the fog before coming to rest on Alain.

Alain had been taught to believe that everything he saw was an illusion, that every other person was just a shadow on that illusion, that nothing was real. But every time he saw Mari, he knew how false those teachings were. The world might be an illusion, but she was real.

"What's going on?" she asked Alain, keeping her own voice low. "We're becalmed? Why wasn't I told?"

"You have not slept well since leaving Altis," Alain said. "Your dreams are often troubled, so I decided to let you rest. But I was preparing to wake you now."

"Why?" Mari brushed back an errant strand of her raven-black hair, peering into the fog. "What's that I hear?"

"The captain believes it is a Syndari galley, seeking us for the rewards offered."

"And we can't move." She made it a statement rather than a question, gazing upward into the web of rigging and stays on their ship. "If only this was a steam-powered ship. I can fix a balky boiler. I can't do anything about a lack of wind."

"The captain is preparing his crew to defend this ship if the galley finds us before we can move," Alain said.

"What would our chances be? Did your training in the military arts cover that sort of thing?"

"Some of it," Alain replied. Told that arrogant Mechanics believed they knew everything, he had been surprised upon first meeting Mari to discover that she had no problem with admitting when someone else knew more about any subject. "Our chances would be poor, because a galley has so many rowers who can join in an attack on us. The crew of this ship would be heavily outnumbered."

"But we've got three Mages," Mari said. "You, Mage Asha, and Mage Dav."

"There is not much power here to use," Alain said. "Without that power to draw on, there is little we can do. We also have four Mechanics," he added.

"With rifles," she said, then grimaced. "Four Mechanics firing rifles might not be enough, and our ammunition is limited. I'm worried about the lever action on Alli's rifle. It keeps sticking, and she keeps fixing it, but it might jam again during a fight. And you still have no idea what I'm talking about, do you?"

"No. I understand only that the matter concerns you."

Mari sighed and leaned on the railing, staring outward. "If we ever have time, and if we survive, I need to see if you can learn anything about tools and devices, or if your Mage training makes them total mysteries to you forever. Is your foresight telling you anything?"

"I had a vision last night."

Her gaze switched to him. "What did you see?" she asked anxiously.

"It was another vision of the coming Storm. Armies and mobs raging against each other, cities burning, a terrible sense of urgency, and a second sun appearing in the sky to stand against the Storm."

"Nothing new, then," she grumped, staring back out to sea. "It sounds like my latest nightmare, though that dream didn't have any hopeful sun in it."

"You are that sun. You know this."

She made a face, looking out into the fog. "I know that people believe I can make a difference, and I know that I'm going to do my best."

"My vision confirmed once more that you are the one who can bring the new day, that you alone can stand against the Storm."

"Alain, I am nineteen years old. I am a very good Mechanic trained to fix lots of things. But for some reason my training never included how to fix a world!" She looked over at him, her expression softening, then touched Alain's arm, the sort of gesture that could still startle him after so many years of being taught in the most painful ways not to allow casual human contact. "I'd be lost without you."

"All the world will be lost without you," Alain said.

She gave a brief snort of derisive laughter. "There's my poetic Mage, who doesn't even realize when he's being poetic. You're in love, and while I know that makes you delusional when it comes to me, I don't know why other people so readily believe things like that, why they just accept that I'm…"

"The daughter."

"You promised that you would never call me that!" Mari said, her voice suddenly low and angry.

"I…am…sorry," Alain said, still sometimes having to stumble over the words that had once been literally beaten out of him. "Others have called you that, and you have accepted the title from them."

"You are not others! I need at least one person in this world who sees me as *me*, as Mari. And that person has to be you."

He nodded in agreement, if not entirely in understanding. "Your old friends, the other Mechanics, always appear to see you as Mari."

"That's because if Alli called me the daughter I'd punch her out and she knows it! And Dav and Bev aren't old friends, but they still look at my jacket and see another Mechanic. Besides, Mechanics aren't big on believing Mage prophecies." She laughed, low and full of self-mockery this time. "It's the Mages who look at me like the common folk do. The Mages, who aren't supposed to care about other people at all."

"We are taught that other people are not real," Alain reminded her. "But our foresight, unreliable and imperfect as it is, shows that your shadow is cast wide across this illusion of a world. To Mages, this makes you worthy of notice."

"Thank you so much. Can you sense any other Mages nearby who might consider me worthy of killing?"

"You are using what you call sarcasm again?" Alain asked.

"Yes. And no. Do you sense any Mages on the Syndari galley?"

"Not yet." Alain strained his senses, hearing the creak of oars from somewhere in the fog, followed by the beat of those oars against the water. Then the sound of oars and the splash of water again, along with indistinctly heard orders spoken to someone out there in the formless mist. In between the louder sounds he could hear the soft rushing of a hull cleaving the quiet waters. But he could feel nothing in that extra sense which would warn of other Mages nearby. "If there are Mages with the galley, they are hiding their presence well."

The captain returned, walking with care to prevent the sound of his boots from carrying through the fog. "We are prepared to fight if necessary, Lady," he told Mari, his tone carrying respect and a happiness at odds with their predicament. Alain had noticed it among all of the common people who made up the *Gray Lady*'s crew. Generations of men and women like them had waited for the daughter, and they believed that Mari was she. But, perhaps sensing how little Mari liked being called by that name, they usually addressed her as Lady or Lady Mari.

"That's not a Confederation warship out there?" Mari whispered. "You're certain?"

"No Confederation ship has that sound to it," the captain assured her. "If you've ever heard a Syndari galley bearing down on you under full oars and the drummer beating the chase cadence, you never forget it."

"How close is the galley? From the sound it is as if it were just beyond our sight."

The captain frowned, wiping mist-born moisture from his face. "I cannot tell you, Lady Mari. This fog makes it hard to tell just where the galley lies, how far off and on what bearing. Too close for my comfort, though."

"How much wind do we need to move?" Mari asked, looking up at the slack sails hanging limp.

"Not much," the captain said. "Ships like this are called Balmer Clippers. I never heard tell of anyone named Balmer, but he or she must have been uncommonly gifted at designing ships. These clippers can move like ghosts under a light breeze. That's why they're useful for, uh…smugglers, or, uh…pirates. Or so I have heard. But I wouldn't want to move unless the fog lifts. We're not far from the coast, not far from Julesport. It's too easy to run aground when you can't see any lights, and the bells on the buoys near Julesport are silent with the water this calm. Even the waves hitting the harbor breakwater that would normally give us warning are as silent as mimes today."

Alain looked down at the perfectly smooth patch of water visible below them. "Is a sea this calm unusual?"

"Yes, Sir Mage." The captain gestured out toward the water. "It is rare."

"Then you cannot say how long it might last?"

"Sir Mage, it might last a moment longer or for days. A sailor learns that just when you think you know it the sea will surprise you. Have you heard that the sea is like a woman? There's truth to that. One moment tranquil, the next moment furious, and all men can do is try to read the weather, ride the storm, and hope for the best."

Mari gave the captain a sharp look. "I would guess that women sailors disagree with that comparison?"

"Uh, no, Lady. They tend to agree. A good sailor knows the character of the sea, no matter the character of the sailor." The captain glanced at her, looking apologetic. "Not that I speak of you so, you understand."

"The storms of Lady Mari have, I think, impressed the elders of the Mechanics Guild, the city fathers of Ringhmon, and the Emperor himself," Alain replied, his eyes on the fog again. As he watched it, only half-aware of the captain trying to keep his expression "blank as a Mage," as the saying went, Alain saw a blot on the featureless mist. He stiffened as a black cloud drifted across his vision. His foresight, often undependable, this time was providing a warning. "There." He pointed. "A galley lies there."

The captain stared into the mist where Alain had pointed. "Can you tell me anything else, Sir Mage?"

"Only that you are correct. It is a threat to us."

The captain nodded. "I witnessed what you did to that Mechanics Guild ship at Altis, Sir Mage, and watched the smoke from the burning city for nigh on a day after we left. Can you do the same here?"

"I will do my best," Alain said.

"Then despite the odds against us I feel much comforted. Do you know much of the Syndaris? I've crossed swords with them before. The fighters of Syndar are easily bought, but that does not mean real loyalty has been purchased."

"How hard will they fight?" Alain asked.

"That depends upon the pay, or the reward, Sir Mage." The captain smiled ruefully. "Unfortunately, the reward in your case must be very large. The Syndari galley we hear is risking movement in this fog, so those commanding it must be highly motivated."

"You should know," Alain said to the captain, "that the Empire and the Great Guilds likely do not seek the capture of Lady Mari, but her death."

The captain nodded with obvious determination. "We will not

allow that. Lest you doubt me, Sir Mage, death awaits me and more than one of my crew if the Empire gets its hands on us. Imperial bureaucrats have not been impressed by some of our means of making a living. They would no doubt grant us the promised reward to meet the letter of their law, but then would fine us the same amount for our crimes—alleged crimes, that is—and hang us. I admit that my crew and I are not the type to risk our deaths needlessly. Perhaps we've been more like the Syndaris than we like to admit. But…"

He hesitated, then knelt before Mari, speaking almost bashfully, far from his usual boisterous and confident self. "I long ago stopped believing in anything but what I can hold in these two hands, Lady, and counted those who risk death for no profit as fools. But I have seen you and heard you, and if Lady Mari were to ask life itself of me I would give it. The sea changes in unexpected ways, and so it seems I still can as well."

Mari, looking extremely uncomfortable, beckoned the captain to stand. "I'm sorry. I know you mean well, but I really don't like it when people kneel to me. Please don't do that again. And I very much hope that neither you nor anyone else will have to die because of me. Too many people already have died."

The captain stood up, smiling. "There, you see? We've spent our lives knowing that no Mechanic and no Mage cared the slightest about whether we lived or died, not as long as we were doing what they ordered us to do. We didn't matter, that's all. But we do matter to you. Thank you, Lady. If we can get into Julesport without a fight, I promise it will be done. But if we must fight, we will. I will let my crew know." He saluted with careful formality before departing.

"Great. More people who want to die because of me," Mari grumbled. "If we didn't have to worry about saving those banned Mechanic texts, I'd dive overboard right now and try to swim to shore. But those texts are more important than I am. More important than everyone else on this ship."

"I thought you said—" Alain began.

"I am not more important than anyone else," Mari insisted. "That's what I said. You heard what the hidden librarians we found on Altis told us. Those texts were designed to enable people to rebuild civilization if the worst happened. With them people can recreate the technology that the Mechanics Guild has suppressed for all of these years. I, or somebody else, can use those texts to defeat whatever the Guild throws at us. If we have enough time."

"The Storm approaches," Alain said.

"Well, I wish the Storm would send a breeze ahead of it to help this ship get its butt into Julesport! How much can you and the other Mages do, Alain? Didn't you tell me that while the amount of power Mages can draw on is almost always weak over water, it also varies by location?"

"That is so," Alain said, not surprised that Mari had remembered that. She was always trying to understand Mage skills by using the rules of her Mechanic arts, which usually led to frustration. "There is little power here, as is usual on the sea. Even the elders of the Mage Guild do not claim to know why this is so."

"You managed some spells when we were on the *Queen of the Sea*," Mari pointed out. "That was the Mechanics Guild ship that captured us near the Sharr Isles."

He felt unease at the memory. The large metal ship filled with Mechanic devices had felt strange in a very disquieting way. "That ship was moving fairly quickly, bringing more power available with each distance covered," Alain explained. "Here we sit in the same spot."

"Oh. You were...sort of getting more current by moving along a wire," Mari said. "Yeah. So we have to assume that this time the Mages cannot help?"

That stung in some unaccountable way. "There is a chance," Alain said, "if this ship begins to move even slowly, because I would only need to plant one ball of fire on a galley to eliminate it. But I would have to see that galley coming long enough to create the fire and to aim, and the effort would surely exhaust me."

She was staring at him. "I said that wrong, didn't I? I said it wrong enough to make you show some upset that I could see. I'm sorry. I didn't mean to imply that I was…disappointed. I'm just trying to figure out what weapons we have. And you've done miracles, Alain. I would long since be dead without you. We have four Mechanics and three Mages. What do you think we should do?"

Alain looked about, considering the problem. "We do not know from which direction an enemy might come. I suggest that I take position near the ship's wheel, where I can best view all angles. The Mechanics and the other two Mages can be placed in the middle of the ship, where you can direct the others easily."

"Half facing each way?" Mari asked.

"Half?"

Mari gave that sigh she used when he did not grasp something she had never imagined someone not knowing. "Two Mechanics and one Mage facing port, and two Mechanics and one Mage facing starboard. Alain, you have to learn some math."

"If you know it, why do I need it? I do not ask you to learn how to do Mage tasks."

"Because…" Mari sighed again. "Without realizing it, I keep wanting to remake you into a Mechanic, which would not only be dumb of me but also really conceited. Who you are is what has saved us many times. Um…I need to alert the other Mechanics. You tell the other Mages that we might have a fight on our hands soon. We'll all meet here on deck." Mari brushed back her hair again with her left hand, the still-new promise ring on one finger glinting in the misty light. She noticed it, then looked at Alain, who wore the ring's companion on his own left hand. "I almost forgot to say I love you."

Despite the inhibitions created by years of extremely harsh instruction in avoiding even the appearance of emotion, Alain managed to force out the right answer. "I…love…you."

She smiled despite the worry visible on her. "A lot of other men find it too easy to say those words. Because of your Mage training, you find it very hard, so I know you mean them. I'm going to be counting on you again in this fight, which I know is totally unfair, but I also know I can always count on you. Let's survive another one, my Mage."

She turned to go, then paused and looked back at him, framed by the coils of mist drifting across the deck. "Don't die. You understand? Don't die."

Alain tried to smile reassuringly, knowing that he was probably not doing a very good job of it. "I understand, my Mechanic. You are also not to die."

She forced a grin in reply, then hurried away.

Despite the urgency of his task, Alain stood for a moment watching as Mari walked into the fog, her dark Mechanics jacket standing out. The hatred between the Mage Guild and the Mechanics Guild was long and enduring, constantly reinforced by every contact between Mages and Mechanics—who were mutually certain that the others were conceited frauds. He had been taught to view the dark Mechanics jacket as a sign of the enemy. But despite all that had happened between her and her former Guild, Mari still took great pride in being one of those trained in the Mechanic arts and found comfort in still wearing the familiar garment. And Alain, who had only recently turned eighteen years old, knew that he would never have lived past seventeen if not for the times the young woman wearing that dark jacket had placed it and herself between him and danger.

Even if he had not grown to love her, he would still look fondly upon the dark jacket he had once been trained to hate. Perhaps someday the common folk and other Mages would also look upon the dark jackets of Mechanics without anger and revulsion. Just as Mari had taught some of her fellow Mechanics to see that not all Mages were monsters.

Mari had saved him, and she could save this world.

If he could help get them both past the Syndari galley.

Alain hurried off as well, seeking both Mage Dav and Mage Asha. As he walked softly along the deck, he could hear the sounds of galley oars coming through the fog.

CHAPTER TWO

The *Gray Lady* was a small ship, and Mages tended to keep to themselves, so Alain had no trouble finding Mage Dav and Mage Asha, the short, dumpy male Mage forming an odd contrast with the tall, beautiful female Mage. But his fellow Mages were one and the same in the blankness of their expressions, showing neither surprise nor interest when Alain summoned them to come with him. Within a few moments all three Mages were on deck, looking even more mysterious than usual with the fog swirling around their robes.

Mari soon joined them with her fellow Mechanics, Alli, Bev, and Dav. All four wore the jackets which marked their status as Mechanics, as well as the jeans and boots which, while not identical, seemed as much a part of the Mechanic uniform as the jackets. Only their shirts varied: Mari's a pale white, Alli's bright blue, Bev's a somber gray, and Dav's a darker blue that almost faded into his jacket.

Everyone looked at Mari, waiting to hear what she had to say. "Everybody keep their voices down," she cautioned. "Sound really carries in this fog and there's at least one galley looking for us."

"What's the plan?" Mechanic Alli asked her.

Alain was not surprised by that. Despite Mari's insistence that she and Alain were equals in making decisions, everyone else tended to view her as being in charge. That bothered her every time she realized it was happening, but it did not concern Alain because he knew that Mari really did try to give him an equal voice in their decisions.

Mari gestured toward parts of the ship barely visible through the fog. "Mage Alain on the quarterdeck. He'll use fire if he can get enough power. The rest of us along the deck here, facing each side. Alain, I'd like you, Mage Dav, and Mage Asha to work out which spells each of you can use if it comes to that."

Mage Dav nodded slightly once. Mage Asha merely looked back at Mari. There had been a time when that lack of acknowledgement would have angered Mari, but she had since learned through Alain that the mere fact that the other Mages had accepted her existence was a major concession.

Mari pointed at Mechanic Bev. "Bev, please break out the rifles."

Mechanic Bev nodded as well, but with a quick jerkiness that bespoke tension. "All of them?"

"Yes. All six. That one that Alli has been working on still jams way too easily, and if we're facing a galley of fighters coming at us we'll want to keep shooting and put off reloading as long as we can."

"What exactly are we facing?" Mechanic Dav asked.

"At least one galley out of Syndar. Listen and you'll hear it out there. Alain says it's looking for us."

"Can I ask something?" Bev said. "Seriously. Why not just let your Mage blow up the galley like he did the Mechanic ship in the harbor at Altis?"

"My Mage..." Mari paused and gave Alain a quick, proud smile. He knew that she liked that phrase. "My Mage might not be able to handle it because there's not much power here for him to draw on."

Bev nodded again. Mage powers—abilities that appeared to violate every rule Mechanics had been taught about how the universe worked—were a mystery to Mechanics, but Alain had learned that Mechanics could understand the idea of limited power restricting what could be done. "We don't have a big supply of ammo," she pointed out. "I'm just saying."

"I understand," Mari said. "I don't want to get into a fight if we can help it. I hope we can scare off the galley instead, or at least avoid letting it come to grips. If all of us are shooting we'll have four rifles in use at once, and that is a lot more firepower than commons are used to facing. The Syndari Islands are also more likely to forgive us for frightening off one of their ships than they are if we sink it, and we've already got enough enemies at the moment."

"Why not tell them that you're the daughter?" Alli asked.

Alain saw Mari grimace and look away before answering. "I think they already know, but are chasing big enough rewards that they'll find reasons to believe I'm not really that person."

"They could believe it," Bev pointed out, "and still want you under their control. As long as the commons and Mages believe that you're her, you're like the queen on a chessboard."

Mari gave a scoffing laugh. "Maybe. That's the closest to being a queen that I'll ever be, though. But it doesn't matter exactly why the Syndaris are chasing us. What matters is that they are."

"Fair enough," Alli said. "I bet it still feels weird to be looked at that way, huh? Hey, Bev, let me look at your rifle once we've got them. I want to make sure the ejection mechanism isn't sticking."

"Yes, honored Mechanic," Bev said, making a joke of the phrasing usually required of commons, and hurried off to get the Mechanic weapons.

Alli shook her head at Mari. "Some of these standard-model repeating rifles are over a century old. The parts are so worn the things rattle when you move them."

"Every one of them hand crafted," Mechanic Dav said, looking out into the fog. "Just like the bullets. I had a friend whose aunt suggested some faster methods of fabricating ammo. The aunt disappeared soon afterwards."

"The Mechanics Guild doesn't want a lot of rifles and bullets in circulation," Mari said. "They want just enough to be able to parcel them out one or two at a time where needed to help any commons doing what the Guild tells them to do, or to hurt any commons disobeying the Guild. We're going to change that."

"Is that necessarily a good thing? I mean—more rifles, more ammunition, won't that make wars even worse?"

Mari paused, looking troubled.

Alain answered. "Mechanic Dav, I have already seen many die at point or edge of sword or from a crossbow bolt. I cannot see that it is different from dying as a result of one of the Mechanic weapons. And having seen what was done at Marandur, I think that it is *why* weapons are used or not used that matters, not which weapons are used."

Mechanic Dav gazed at Alain and nodded slowly. "I guess that's true. War is going to be terrible, no matter what. And like Mari says, wars up to now have been all about keeping the Great Guilds in power. At least we're fighting for a better reason than that."

Mage Asha came up to stand near Mechanic Dav, her expression still void of any feeling. "If we are to fight, I will stand here," she said in the emotionless voice of a Mage.

Mechanic Dav looked over at her and smiled. "I'd like that," he said.

Asha inclined her head very slightly toward him, then looked back out to sea.

Mari leaned close to Alain and whispered. "What is that about? What is Asha doing?"

"Mage Asha is showing great interest in Mechanic Dav. I am surprised how blatant she is being."

"She's—" Mari stared at him. "Is Asha flirting with Dav? Is that how Mages flirt?"

"I do not know what flirt means," Alain said. "But her interest in him is obvious."

"Obvious? Seriously?"

"Does this bother you?"

"No. Not really. Not that." She gazed north as if able to see through the fog and the distance. "I'm...nervous, Alain. Not just scared because we're facing another fight, but nervous about how everyone is asking me what to do. Until Altis it was just you and me, and that was bad enough, wondering if some snap decision of mine would end up trapping us. And at Altis I was just responding to events, trying to keep ahead of things, without time to worry. But now we've got three other Mechanics and two other Mages, and they're not only depending on me to make decisions, they're also in major danger just because they're with me. So are the crew of this ship. And how many others, Alain? How many commons are going to die because they believe I am that person they've been waiting for?"

Alain knew that the impassive expression he was trained to project was the wrong thing at a time like this. He tried to show concern, hoping that Mari would see it. "You have heard the commons speak of this, Mari. They have been dying for centuries for no greater purpose than to ensure that the Mechanics Guild and the Mage Guild continue to rule this world. Without you they would still die, and without you almost all of them *will* die."

"I'm under enough pressure already, Alain! Where's that Syndari galley now?"

Perhaps he should have said something else. Or perhaps this was one of those times when nothing said would really help. Alain gazed into the mist and saw nothing but the hanging curtains of off-white fog. "I cannot tell. There are faint noises which say the galley remains in this area, but my foresight is not working now."

Mari exhaled angrily. "Is it because of me? Did your foresight stop working because I'm so tense?"

Alain, who still had to work at revealing his emotions, had no problem in showing surprise. Then he shook his head. "No. That should not be involved."

"You've told me that foresight requires a personal connection to someone else, and if I'm not exactly encouraging close feelings at the moment…"

"Such a connection does not vary so quickly," Alain assured her. "Nor do my feelings vary so much, especially when I know you are under the strain of being responsible for so many things. This is not your fault. Do not blame yourself for my lack of foresight. You know that my gift has always been erratic, Mari."

She leaned on the rail, gloomily looking into the mist. "I know. But somehow I think of it like another machine. A Mechanic device. Something that I can turn on and it'll work when I need it to work. Which is kind of funny, really, because I know plenty of machines that don't always work when they're needed. But this is part of you, and you're always there when I need you."

"Thank you." Those words had grown easier to say. Mages were taught not to use them, not to consider any courtesy. Alain had once forgotten those words and what they meant. But she had reminded him of the simple phrase, far away in the desert waste outside Ringhmon when they had first encountered each other.

"I take you for granted," Mari said. "I know I do. And I yell at you when you don't deserve it."

"We are not living an easy life," Alain noted. "But you often show your love for me. I cannot imagine wishing to be with anyone else, whether in peace or conflict, and especially amid the perils we have faced together."

She reached over and grasped his hand. "And here we are facing danger again, my Mage. At least we're not facing it alone."

Apparently he had said the right thing this time. Alain turned to look along the deck, almost immediately spotting instead a dark blot against one part of the mist. "It is there. The galley lies in that direction."

Mari looked intently where Alain had indicated. "I can't see anything, but your foresight is obviously working again. After I made nice to you, I might add."

"That—" Alain paused, thinking. "That is not supposed to matter. The Mage elders—"

"Lied about a lot of things, Alain. Just like my Senior Mechanics lied to me."

Out of the corner of his eye Alain noticed something else and swung to look off the opposite side of the ship. Another black blot on the fog. That could mean only one thing. "And there is another galley in the direction."

"Two of them? Wonderful."

"Why is that wonderful? I thought wonderful meant—"

"Sarcasm! Never mind! We need to tell the captain we've definitely got two galleys out there now."

Alain pivoted slowly, looking for more warnings from his foresight. He paused as another blotch appeared off the bow of the *Gray Lady*. "There are three. And they surround us."

Mari snagged a passing sailor. "Tell the captain that there are three galleys out there, all looking for us. One in that direction, one out there, and the third over that way somewhere."

The sailor gaped at her, then hastily saluted. "Yes, Lady Mari! I'll tell him immediately!" Rushing off toward the quarterdeck as quickly and quietly as he could move, the sailor vanished into the fog.

More soft footsteps sounded, and the shape of Mechanic Bev came out of the fog. "Did you do something to one of the crew?" she asked.

"I told him that there are three galleys out there hunting us," Mari replied.

"That explains the look of terror on the guy's face. Three? I thought it was one." Bev herself no longer seemed rattled as she handed one of the Mechanic weapons to Mari, then others to Alli and Dav.

But Alain could still sense a tightness in Mechanic Bev. *She hides something,* Alain told himself. *Mechanic Bev hides emotions as a Mage does, but for other reasons than Mages do. There is something she will not reveal to anyone.*

If it is what I think it is, don't ask, Mari had told him. *Bev has been hurt, but if we are loyal to her she'll be loyal to us.*

He had not understood, but now was not the time to pursue the matter of whatever in Mechanic Bev's past had been kept hidden. Not as long as Mari was certain that Bev could be counted on.

Alli scowled as she flipped the object she called a lever action on the rifle. "This thing is just waiting to jam the moment I need it. I can feel it. Bev, set this one aside and let me have that one."

"Sure. If you can't fix it, nobody can."

Mari faced the rail, cradling her weapon. "If a galley runs across us in this fog they'll be right on top of us before we see them, so we won't have much time to deal with them. If you see one, call out fast."

Alli leaned on the rail next to her. "While I was at Danalee some Syndaris tried to place an order with us for a lot of pistols. I gathered that they prefer to capture other ships by coming up fast and flooding them with attackers. That's why the Syndaris wanted to buy pistols from the Guild but weren't interested in rifles. They don't want to fight long-distance battles."

"That's what Alain said. Did the Guild sell them any pistols?" Mari asked.

Alli grinned. "One. And exactly twelve rounds of ammo. You wouldn't believe how much the Syndaris had to pay for that."

Mechanic Dav called softly from the other side of the ship. "They want to capture the ship, you say. What about us? Do they want us alive?"

"Probably not," Mari said. "You know how we've been warned that commons will *accidentally* hit Mechanics during a battle. That's under normal circumstances. This time they know our Guilds want us dead."

"Mage Guild, too?" Dav asked. "All of us dead?" His eyes strayed toward Asha.

"All of us," Alain confirmed.

"Well…that's not going to happen."

Alli grinned. "We made it out of Altis in one piece, which is more than the people trying to catch us there can say."

Mari glared at the fog, her face tight with emotion. Alain could sense what she was thinking, that she and Alain had been through many more such tight situations than the others, and how narrowly the two of them had often survived. "All right," Mari finally said, her voice probably sounding perfectly calm to the other Mechanics even though any Mage could have heard the tension within it. "Ideally, we need to keep the Syndari galleys from getting close enough to board us. That's going to be very hard with visibility this low. If one shows up, everybody start throwing lead at any spot where they try to board."

"Throwing lead?" Mage Dav asked.

"That means firing our rifles," Mari explained. "You Mages will have to do whatever you can to either scare off the galley or stop anyone trying to board us."

"We will cast what spells are possible," Alain cautioned. "And if any Syndaris should reach the deck of this ship we will deal with them." He partly drew the long knife which all Mages carried under their robes, and Mage Dav and Asha did the same.

Mari's eyes met his. "At times like this I wish you could use my pistol."

"It is hard. I could strike someone with it if they came close enough," Alain said.

"And yet you can't use a hammer," Mari muttered, glaring into the fog again.

They stood at the rail, saying little and even then speaking in low voices. Except for the quiet creaking of wood as the *Gray Lady* rode the barely apparent ocean swell, the sailing ship made no sound, a fact for which Alain was grateful. It left the galleys no clue to follow to their location. He frowned very slightly as a thought occurred to him. "Mage Asha and Mage Dav. The galleys seek us here in the fog. They know of our presence in this small part of the sea despite not being able to see us."

Mage Dav nodded without expression. "They must have a Mage with them, one who can sense the presence of you, me, or Asha. Only the dense fog has kept them from finding us before now. I cannot sense this Mage, though."

Asha gazed into the fog, her expression a curious mixture of blankness and intensity. She was, very slowly, following Alain's lead in beginning to show traces of her feelings again. "I sense…" Asha pointed off the stern of the *Gray Lady*, her arm and hand slowly moving forward. "There. It is very hard. He hides himself well. But I know him." She looked at Alain. "Niaro, the Mage who was almost your downfall in Palandur."

"Great," Mari muttered. "Can this Niaro cast fire like Alain?"

"No. His Mage gifts are modest." Asha nodded to Alain. "His envy, I think, feeds his ability to find Alain despite Mage Alain's skill."

Alain saw Mari's jaw tighten and her hands flex upon the weapon she held. Mari did not like shooting at others, often displaying great distress after having to do so, but she would when necessary. Now she looked ready to deal with Niaro. "We need to discourage him," she said. "If I get him in my sights, he's going to have something to worry about besides his own inadequacies as a Mage."

"I believe he was also attracted to me," Asha explained, almost apologetically. "In physical ways, and blamed my rejection on Mage Alain."

Alli smothered a laugh. "He's a man? He saw you? Yeah, he was probably hot for you. What do you think, Dav?"

Mechanic Dav looked uncomfortable, but wisely refrained from replying.

Asha shrugged lightly at Alli's statement, then tapped her robes where the long Mage knife was concealed beneath them. "I am experienced at discouraging those Mages whose attention was not welcome. Niaro did not take that well."

Bev, who had been more distant than the others around Asha, now turned an approving smile on her.

Mari glanced up at the sails, staring at the fog drifting among them. "I thought I felt a breeze."

A sailor came running along the deck, bare feet making little noise, his gaze turned upward where the fog had begun swirling. The masts, spars and booms creaked as the gentle, erratic breeze pushed at the still-limp sails, the sound seeming huge amid the silence on the ship.

Alain concentrated on preparing himself for action as the fog began opening up slightly in small patches. For a moment he could clearly see the quarterdeck of the *Gray Lady* not far from him, then it vanished in the white mist again. "I should go to the quarterdeck as we discussed."

"Let's change that plan. I'd rather you stay here, if you don't mind," Mari said.

Grateful that she had given him a reason not to leave her side, Alain nodded.

More of the sails overhead came into view, then disappeared. The mainsail flapped with a thunderous sound as it caught a freshening wind for a moment before drooping again. Straining his hearing, Alain heard oars splashing, then pausing, as the galleys searched for them.

"Hang on," Bev warned. A large gap had opened in the fog on the *Gray Lady*'s starboard side. Moments later the shape of a galley loomed out of the mist at the far side of the open space, its banks of oars resting unmoving in the water. Crewmembers on the galley spotted the sailing ship, pointing and calling out to the officers on their own quarterdeck. The galley lay low to the water, long and lean with a single mast. A large raised platform at the stern held the ship's wheel and another raised platform at the bow offered a fighting position for lightly armored soldiers carrying crossbows and wearing swords.

Alain heard commands being called on the galley. Now that its presence was known, the drummer keeping cadence for the oars stopped gently tapping and instead began pounding, the sound carrying clearly across the water. The oars rose in unison, an unexpectedly graceful sight as the banks of oars swept up and around to splash into the water as one. The galley jumped forward, curving around slightly to aim straight for the *Gray Lady*, which was still barely moving under the irregular winds flowing past.

Alain felt the power in this area, appalled by how weak it still was. "Mage Asha, Mage Dav, only one of us can hope to cast a spell at one time. I will try this first one, which will likely exhaust me."

Asha drew her long Mage knife, holding the hilt in both hands before her and making a couple of swift practice cuts through the air as she serenely watched the Syndari galley draw closer.

"I cannot hope to create a strong fire spell," Alain told Mari, "and the fog has made all surfaces wet."

"Is there a weak point you can strike at?" Mari asked.

"A what?"

She had her rifle leveled toward the galley and kept her eyes on her target as she answered. "Some spot where applying a little force can produce big results. You've made holes in things. Like…like the mast on the galley. See it? What if part of it at the bottom went away?"

His eyes focused on the base of the galley's mast. Alain concentrated on that spot, trying to block out the uproar around him as the *Gray Lady*'s sailors tried to trim her sails to catch the erratic winds and the Mechanics prepared to fire their weapons. He had to draw to himself the dregs of power available here to augment his own strength, because no Mage could change the world illusion without some outside power added to his or her own. As Alain gathered the power he recited to himself the lessons that every Mage learned, the beliefs that made their arts possible. The illusion which was the world showed him a galley with a tall mast, the sail on it furled as the galley drove forward on its oars. The illusion of a mast stood tall and straight, but that illusion could be changed. Overlay another illusion, one in which the mast had a break in it, a small gap not far above the deck. It required the belief that what he saw was an illusion, and the confidence that he could change that illusion for a brief period.

Alain felt the effort draining his strength but held his concentration as the galley swept down upon the *Gray Lady*. He almost lost his focus as Mari's rifle roared next to him, followed by a series of other explosions as the other Mechanics fired. He barely heard Mechanic Alli calling to the others. "He's a still a bit out of range for these old weapons. The rifling in their barrels is worn almost smooth. Let him get a little closer and then we'll give him another volley!"

Alain heard but did not pay attention to the captain calling out commands, hardly noticed the *Gray Lady* slowly, slowly starting to move and turning as the freshening wind teased at her sails and her rudder bit into the water, saw but did not pause to think about Mari standing at the rail, her rifle still raised and ready. This spell needed everything he could give, and suddenly it was there, the power and his own strength draining as the world illusion changed for a moment.

A portion of the galley's mast just above the deck rippled and most of the base vanished for several moments, leaving the mast supported only by a thin strip on one side. Not a total success, but enough.

Unable to hold the mast, the remaining strip of wood buckled and snapped, the mast swinging against the restraints of the galley's rigging. But those ropes weren't strong enough to hold the mast's full weight. The rigging broke with loud reports sounding like a Mechanic weapon firing, then the top of the mast toppled forward and down, its base crashing upon the deck and the upper portion with the sail striking the water with a mighty splash. The stricken mast served as an anchor on that side, jerking the galley back and over, away from the *Gray Lady*, as the galley's oars flailed in confusion and cries of distress arose from the crew.

Alain fell forward, almost dropping to the deck. Mage Dav caught his arm, holding him up, then nodded with approval.

"You are skilled," Mage Dav said. Then he looked down at where he held Alain's arm, supporting him. "This is help," he announced with the pride of someone who has discovered something new.

"Yes," Alain agreed tiredly, worn out by his effort.

Moments later the slow progress of the *Gray Lady* finally took her back into a deeper area of fog, losing sight of the stricken galley. Mari turned to Alain, gazing at him anxiously. "Are you all right, my love?"

He nodded. "I am only exhausted. I cannot do more anytime soon."

"But you took out a galley."

The captain's voice calling down from the quarterdeck dispelled that idea, though. "That one's not finished. He'll cut the mast free and come after us under oars again."

Alain leaned against the mast, waving off Mage Dav's aid. "Prepare yourself for the next attack. I did not sense Mage Niaro aboard that galley, but my focus was on my spell so he may have been there. Thank you for your help."

"Help," Mage Dav repeated. He nodded, then went to the rail to search the fog.

Mari made sure Alain was securely propped against the nearest mast, then rejoined the other Mechanics and Mages at the rail.

The sails of the *Gray Lady* banged overhead as more gusts of winds came and went. The ship drifted through another slightly open area, where visibility stretched for almost a bow shot in one direction. Rags of fog flew by, merging into another bank that once more reduced sight to less than the length of the ship. Looking up, Alain saw threads of blue sky appearing and disappearing as the fog began shredding above them. A wind steadied, billowing out the sails as the captain bellowed orders to trim them to take best advantage of the breeze.

The *Gray Lady* gathered speed, her clipper-rigged sails seizing the wind and her sleek hull sliding smoothly across the water. The fog parted again with shocking suddenness, leaving Alain staring at the shape of another Syndari galley cruising past in the opposite direction, its oars working steadily. Once again shouts of command could be heard on the galley, once again the drummer began pounding his deep cadence. The oars on one side paused before reversing, and those on the other side swept down hard forward, twisting the galley in a tight turn. At the same time a volley of crossbow bolts flew up from the forward platform of the galley, arcing through the sky toward the *Gray Lady*.

The *Gray Lady's* captain wasn't waiting for either the galley or the bolts to arrive. Yelling his own orders, he brought the sailing ship around to port so hard that the Mechanics and Mages on the deck all staggered to the rail and held on tightly. Several crossbow bolts thudded into the deck, one striking so close to Asha that she stumbled to the side, off balance.

Before she could fall Mechanic Dav had lunged away from the rail and caught her.

Asha gazed at the Mechanic dispassionately. "You help."

"I...I don't want you hurt," Mechanic Dav said. "You're not hurt, are you?"

Alain saw one corner of Asha's lip bend into the tiniest of smiles. "I am well. Back to your duties, Mechanic Dav."

Alain had assumed that Mechanic Dav's interest in Asha was all about her beauty. Certainly from his reactions that was what had first attracted him to her. But now Alain wondered if this Mechanic Dav was wise enough to see the woman within Asha's Mage exterior. The thought cheered him even through his weariness.

Mechanic Dav went back to the rail, where Alli made a low-voiced comment that drew brief, tense laughter from Mari and Bev. Alain wondered what the women found amusing.

The ship kept turning, the spars and booms swinging overhead. The sails rumbled as they lost the breeze then caught it once more. The *Gray Lady* cruised into another heavy bank of fog and lost sight of the pursuing galley.

Alain heard the captain cursing as he jumped down from the quarterdeck and raced forward. Alain managed to get back to his feet and followed, wanting to know what might be needed. The captain reached the bow and grasped some rigging tightly, peering ahead. "Hide and seek, Sir Mage," he explained in a near whisper. "And the rocks of the breakwater not far off, if I'm any judge."

A splashing noise and the wash of water past a hull sounded clearly through the white mist enveloping them. Before anyone could do or say anything, the shape of a galley shot into sight, heading right across their path. "Hard a-starboard!" the captain yelled back to the quarterdeck. "Bring her about!"

The *Gray Lady* had built up enough speed that she heeled far over under the command of her rudder, port side rising up as the starboard side dipped. Her bowsprit swung past the bow of the galley, looking as if it had missed striking the other ship by a matter of a hand's-width. Then the *Gray Lady* was swinging parallel to the galley as it swept past close aboard.

The oars on the near side of the galley had no time to swing up vertical and safe. Still poised out from the galley's hull, they formed a thicket which rushed past the *Gray Lady* as the sailing ship bore away in the other direction. With a series of cracks, crashes, and moans of tortured wood which merged into one long roar, the oars on that side of the galley disintegrated into a flurry of splinters and broken stumps. Over the sound of rending wood, Alain could also hear the screams and yells of the oar handlers being bludgeoned by the impact of the *Gray Lady* against their oars.

Before Alain could grasp what was happening it was over, the two ships losing each other in the fog again, the *Gray Lady* wearing back to port under her captain's commands and the crippled galley wavering as it vanished into the mist. He looked aft and saw Mari staring after the galley, her face bleak. Knowing her, Alain was certain she was tormented by the fading cries of the stricken oar handlers.

The sails rumbled again as the breeze faltered, then the wind swung around to come from another direction. The captain cursed, using a number of words that Alain had not heard before despite his time among soldiers. The meaning of the words was clear enough, however. Nursing the *Gray Lady* onto a new heading, the captain got her speed up again, calling nearly constant commands to the helm to adjust the course and to his crew to trim the sails to make the most of the wandering winds.

They cruised through another clear patch, then another bank of dense fog, then into another open space, this one as large as the grand coliseum in the Imperial capital of Palandur. And in a picture that could have been drawn from one of the coliseum spectacles, a second Syndari galley was angling through the same gap, so close a stone could have been thrown from the deck of the *Gray Lady* to that of the galley.

Mari shouted commands from amidships and the Mechanic weapons thundered. Alain saw splinters flying from the area around the galley's tiller and wondered that none of the officers or sailors there had been hit. Syndari crewmembers dove hastily for cover, abandoning their stations for the moment. Amid the sailors, Alain caught a glimpse of a Mage's robes.

"Niaro!" Asha called across the gap, her voice still lacking emotion but loud enough to carry easily. "Even now you lack strength and skill!" She wagged the blade of her knife derisively at the other Mage. "The Syndaris could not afford a real Mage!"

Alain stared back at Asha, wondering why she was taunting Niaro so. While the other Mage had been able to help find the *Gray Lady* even in the fog, with so little power in this particular spot on the ocean no Mage could hope to manage any major spells alone. But as

Alain looked over at Niaro, he saw that Mage stagger toward the rail of the galley and then collapse.

A moment later, with no hand on the wheel, the Syndari galley swung away, vanishing into the mist again.

"He'll be back," the captain noted, his face grim.

"He will have more difficulty finding us," Asha announced with the closest thing to a satisfied smile Alain had ever seen on her. "Their Mage tried to match you in spell work, Mage Alain, and all his strength drained to nothing. Niaro will give no more aid to the Syndari galleys for some time."

"You mocked him," Alain said. "Like an elder toying with a very young acolyte."

"And Niaro responded as a very young acolyte would," Asha said. "With anger and little control."

Alain nodded to her. "I am fortunate to be your friend, Mage Asha."

"Yes. You are." She nodded back to him.

The crewmembers in the rigging had been calling out to one another now that secrecy was impossible, but the captain shouted a command. "All hands, quiet!"

The Mechanics and Mages, who would normally have ignored the command of a common person, fell silent along with the crew at Mari's gesture. Alain, marveling at her ability to exercise control over both Mechanics and Mages, watched the captain of the *Gray Lady*, who was leaning slightly forward over the rail near the bow, not just staring into the mist but also listening intently. A small smile came to the captain's lips as he heard something. "Oars are very useful, Sir Mage, for making a galley move when wind is lacking, but sails make little noise by comparison, whereas the oars of the galleys splash and creak enough to mask the sounds of other things. And a wise sailor always listens for the sound of danger." He paused, apparently not looking at anything but listening very carefully. "Hold on," he muttered very softly to himself.

The *Gray Lady* shot through a thin sheet of fog, in and out in a flash with the remnants of the mist rapidly dissipating now. Ahead, a low bank of fog still remained, obscuring the sea in their path. Glancing upward at the now-visible sun, Alain saw that the *Gray Lady* was going almost due north.

The third Syndari galley burst out of the fog behind them, its oars sweeping the water to either side like great white wings as the hostile ship bore down on them.. Despite its menace, Alain could not help admiring the beauty of the sight and the pounding menace of the drum. But instead of ordering another immediate course change, the *Gray Lady's* captain watched calmly, still listening. Alain, concentrating, could now catch a sound ahead as well, a murmuring and soft roaring he could not identify.

The galley was closing rapidly, Mari and her fellow Mechanics preparing to open fire again with their Mechanic weapons.

The captain suddenly roared a command back to the helm. "Hard right rudder! Six points to starboard!" Under the strong rudder, the *Gray Lady* yawed heavily, her deck listing at a high angle as the nimble ship swung to the right with an agility the larger, fast-moving galley couldn't match. Alain caught a glimpse of white surf breaking on rocks to port as the *Gray Lady* turned away, realizing that the officers on the galley wouldn't have heard the surf over the noise of its own passage and probably couldn't stop in time.

They didn't. Realizing too late the trap they had been led into, the galley tried to turn away in the *Gray Lady's* wake, her banks of oars halting in the air, then frantically coming down in the opposite direction to try to check the galley's speed. But the oars began clashing and banging against each other as panicky rowers lost discipline, and the smooth rhythm of the oars fell apart. The galley turned partway under the push of its rudder, but it was too late to avoid the rocks.

As the *Gray Lady* showed her stern to the galley, the Syndari ship suddenly shuddered violently. Alain could see oars on the side away from them, the side facing the rocks, bending and cracking. Distant cries of pain from battered oar handlers drifted across the water. The galley, having turned just enough to avoid running hard aground, bounced away from contact with the rocks, staggering like a drunkard from the force of the impact and the damage doubtless done to its hull. As the galley wobbled away from the rocks, Alain could see the bow dipping and guessed enough planks had been stove in by the collision to allow dangerous flooding of the ship.

His attention on the wrecked galley, Alain was shocked when Mechanic Alli slapped his shoulder.

She was laughing. "Don't mess with momentum!"

Mari came up beside them, grinning. "Or momentum will mess with you," she said. Both Mechanics laughed again at some shared joke that was incomprehensible to Alain. He wondered who Momentum was and what he or she had to do with what had just happened.

The laughter of the Mechanics died as another lingering fog bank shredded to reveal the first galley, looking crippled with its mast missing but pivoting nimbly under the push of its oars to charge again at the *Gray Lady*.

CHAPTER THREE

Alli," Mari said, her angry gaze fixed on the galley, "I'm tired of watching the rowers suffer while the bosses on these galleys keep ordering them to come at us. I want whoever is giving the orders on that ship stopped."

"You got it." Alain watched as Mechanic Alli knelt to steady her weapon on the ship's rail. "What about whoever is at the helm?"

"Dav, Bev, and I will target the helm. You take out the officers."

"No problem." Alli squinted along the barrel of her rifle. "There's a guy with a lot of gold on him. Inlaid armor. Very pretty. Hey, tell the captain to hold this ship steady, will you?"

"Captain!" Mari called. "Hold the ship steady!"

The captain looked startled, but passed the order to the helm. The *Gray Lady* stopped turning, cutting smoothly through the still-placid waters of the Jules Sea. The wind had steadied as well, filling the sails and pushing the ship along at an even clip.

Asha came to stand beside Alain. "What do the Mechanics do, Mage Alain?"

"They will use their weapons to kill those in charge on that ship," he explained. "It matters to Mari that only those shadows of the lowest status have been harmed."

"Why?" Asha said.

"She regards each shadow as another like herself," Alain said.

"That is very strange. Yet I recall you saying it was because Mari saw you as one like herself that she saved your life when all she knew of you was that you were a Mage. Do all Mechanics believe this?"

"Many do not," Alain said. He noticed Mechanic Bev tossing a puzzled look at him and Asha and guessed she was baffled that he and Asha could be having such a dispassionate conversation while the enemy galley bore down on them. "But those with Mari follow her ways of thinking."

"Like Mechanic Dav. It is useful to have such companions," Asha concluded, "and such weapons as theirs when the power to use Mage spells is lacking. Though now I sense more power available with each moment."

"It is because we are moving," Alain explained. "I am still weary. Can you cast a spell?"

"It is possible. Where is it needed?"

A weak point, Mari had said. This galley had already lost its mast, and losing a single oar wouldn't harm it much. "Do you see the large wheel that the sailors call a helm? If something were to happen to that, it would hurt the ship."

"I will see what can be done."

The galley was coming toward them, the drum cadence fast, the oars flashing up and down in a quick beat that drove the enemy warship closer at ever-increasing speed. Soldiers packed the forward fighting platform, swords in hand, ready to fight hand-to-hand. "He means to ram us!" the captain called from the quarterdeck, sounding very anxious.

"Hold your course!" Mari called back. She was aiming along her rifle like the other Mechanics, still looking angry. "Why do people make us do this?" she grumbled to Alain. "Why do they have to try to harm others?"

"I do not know," Alain said.

The crash of Mechanic Alli's weapon surprised everyone. There was a pause as Alli worked the lever to load a new bullet, then a figure in grandiose armor staggered backwards on the Syndari quarterdeck and fell.

Alli bent to aim again as chaos erupted on the galley.

"Get the helm!" Mari ordered.

The enemy ship seemed very close indeed as the three other Mechanic weapons boomed almost in unison. Two more figures fell, but the galley kept on.

"Move however you want!" Mari called to the captain of the *Gray Lady*, and a moment later the clipper heeled over hard as she turned away from the charging galley.

The sailors at the galley's helm began turning to stay on a collision course with the *Gray Lady*, but as Alain watched they suddenly staggered back, the wheel free in their hands instead of firmly attached to the post where it had been.

He felt someone slump against him, then Alain and Mage Dav were holding the limp figure of Mage Asha, who had exhausted herself with her spell.

Mechanic Alli fired again, and another grandly dressed figure dropped on the galley. The other Mechanics fired a volley, though with everyone scrambling around on the galley's quarterdeck and falling against each other it was hard to see the effect. What Alain could tell was that the galley was swinging wildly to one side, its earlier turn becoming more and more extreme with no means of controlling the ship's rudder. The drumbeat broke off, the oars trying to stop and instead crashing into each other.

Once again the Mechanic weapons fired, and this time everyone visible on the galley went flat or dove for cover. Its oars in a shambles and the useless wheel sliding unheeded off one side of the quarterdeck into the water, the galley glided past the stern of the *Gray Lady*.

"I think they've had enough," Mechanic Alli commented, standing up and canting her weapon over her shoulder.

"Yeah," Mari agreed. She turned, looking at the other galleys, now visible as the last remnants of the fog dissipated. Both were drifting and showed no signs of wanting to renew the fight. The galley that had hit the rocks had taken on so much water its bow was nearly awash, with most of the crew busy using any available container, including their helmets, to try to bail out the seawater before the galley sank.

"Mage Asha?" A stricken-looking Mechanic Dav was kneeling beside the female Mage, across from the apparently placid Mage Dav.

"She is tired," Mage Dav explained. "Not hurt."

"Back to work, Mechanic," Bev said, helping Mechanic Dav stand. "The job's not completed yet." They walked back to the railing to help keep watch on the galleys.

"Steady!" the captain of the *Gray Lady* called to his helm, grinning. "Those rocks that discomfited one of our enemies are the breakwater for Julesport, Lady Mari! I knew they must be somewhere near. Oars have their place, and I know the Mechanics use their steam, but with all respect for your arts, to me sails are what a proper ship should depend upon."

"You make a strong argument for that," Mari said, smiling with relief. "Jules herself couldn't have done better."

The captain beamed at the praise comparing him to the legendary sailor. "You would know if anyone, daughter of Jules," he declared, bowing low to Mari. "Having you aboard has no doubt brought the favor of Jules to our voyage, and if I may say so, I have never been so glad to have honored Mechanics and honored Mages as passengers!"

Mari laughed, since she knew that commons had never before been glad to have Mechanics and Mages as passengers, though it was not hard for Alain to see her embarrassment at being linked to the famous seafarer. "How far are we from Julesport?" Mari asked.

The captain pointed ahead. There the rocks of the breakwater rose higher and were capped by a stone fortification and lighthouse that seemed designed to withstand any attack and the mightiest of gales. "That marks the entrance to the harbor, Lady! Welcome to Julesport!"

❊ ❊ ❊

Despite the captain's announcement of their arrival, in fact it took quite a while to first wear around the end of the breakwater and then make their way against the wind into the crowded harbor. The *Gray Lady*'s crew was kept busy adjusting and trimming the sails, while the captain kept his attention on the many ships and boats that the clipper had to avoid while threading her way to an anchorage.

That left Mari with nothing to do but lean on the rail and watch the slow progress of the ship into the harbor. They only needed to stay long enough to take on food and water before sailing south toward the one destination no one was likely to suspect, the Broken Kingdom of Tiae.

She had a hard time relaxing after the tension of the recent battle, instead worrying about what other challenges they might face even here at Julesport. The stack of a single steam-powered ship was visible on the far side of the harbor. That would be a Mechanics Guild ship, since no one else was allowed the use of boilers as propulsion. Everything else was under sail, under oars, or at anchor. Every time the wind shifted sails flapped, spars shifted, and booms swung as sailors on dozens of different vessels of widely varying size adjusted to the vagaries of the breezes. To Mari it looked like a huge, complex machine with scores of independently moving parts, each pursuing its own path, yet all in a strange kind of harmony in the service of some greater purpose.

She would have to create something like that if she were to overthrow the Great Guilds. But that would be impossible to do alone. After so long of just barely surviving with just her and Alain seemingly against the world, it was very comforting to know that she had friends here ready to help.

Mari looked around, seeing most of her companions, but noticed that two were missing. "Where are Mage Asha and Mechanic Dav?"

Mechanic Alli looked innocently off to the side, Mechanic Bev rolled her eyes, and Mage Dav, as usual, betrayed no feelings at all even though Asha was his niece. Alain looked around, as if startled to realize the other two were not on deck.

It took Mari a moment to realize what their reactions meant. "You're kidding," she said. "They're together belowdecks? Mage Asha and Mechanic Dav met for the first time in Altis. They're already that close?"

"At the moment they're probably very close to each other," Alli said, grinning.

"And," Bev added dryly, "probably trying to disprove the Exclusion Principle."

Alain looked at the Mechanics. "What is the Exclusion Principle?"

"The law that says no two objects can occupy the same place at the same time," Mari snapped. "Think about it."

"We just won a fight," Alli pointed out. "Don't you feel like celebrating?"

"Not that way! Where are they doing this? Alain and I have been trying to find a private place on this ship since we left Altis! How did they find a private place when Alain and I couldn't?"

"You know how young lovers can be."

"Alain and I are young lovers! We're both younger than Mage Asha or Mechanic Dav!"

"But now you're an old married couple," Alli explained.

"We've only been married for about a month. All right, a month and a half. That's not *old*." Mari gave Alain an accusing look. "Did you know about them?"

"Did I know what about them?" Alain asked.

Sometimes she wondered if Alain were truly that oblivious or if he just pretended to be unaware of human interaction. "Did you know that they were that interested in each other?" Mari asked patiently.

"Not until this day, when Mage Asha made her interest so plain," Alain said. "I recall a time that Asha discussed Mechanic Dav with you."

"She did," Mari conceded. "At least, she asked if Dav was fair game and I said as far as I knew he was. I just hope she doesn't hurt him. I like Asha, but she is still a Mage, taught to believe that other people don't matter."

"Mages are taught that other people do not exist," Alain corrected. "But I believe that Mage Asha…what is the word?"

"I hope you're not looking for the word love!"

"No. Not yet, if I am to judge love by what I feel for you. Something less?"

"She likes him?"

"Yes," Alain said. "I believe that Asha *likes* Mechanic Dav."

"Do she like him or does she *like* him like him?"

Alain stared at Mari, openly conveying confusion. "I have no idea what you are asking."

"Is that because you're a man or because you're a Mage? Never mind. Who Asha takes up with is none of my business, as long as it's not you."

"You know that Asha is not your rival in any way."

Mari shook her head, smiling to let him know she wasn't really worried about Asha. "Alain, she's the most beautiful woman anyone's ever seen. She's a few years older than me and a Mage like you. She's even got a better rear end than I do."

"On that last you are absolutely wrong," Alain said.

"Sure. I'll try to believe that." Mari looked around the harbor again, at the city spreading beside it and up into the low hills beyond, at the forts and walls defending it, and wondered if she really was a descendant of Jules, who according to legend had been the first to see this harbor and who had founded this city. She felt a shiver born of some indefinable sensation and decided it must be nerves.

"Alli and Bev," Mari called. "We'd better shed the jackets so no one can tell we're Mechanics. We need to get the supplies we require and then leave this port without any complications."

She pulled off her own jacket, wondering if the Syndari galleys would notify the city leaders of Julesport about who was riding on the *Gray Lady* in an attempt to claim the rewards, despite failing to capture Mari themselves. Or if the Mechanics Guild Hall and the Mages Guild Hall had taken note of the battle just outside the harbor.

Mari didn't make any comments when Mechanic Dav and Mage Asha eventually reappeared on deck, but both Alli and Bev began pestering Dav with mock concern, asking if he had been hurt in the fight and exactly where he had been and what he had been doing.

By early afternoon the *Gray Lady* had tied up to an anchor buoy only about a thousand lances from the nearest pier. The captain immediately began negotiating with barges that came alongside offering food and water or transport ashore for the crew. The latter left disappointed, since no one planned to leave the *Gray Lady*.

But Mari was quickly reminded that plans were what people made before they found out what the real world had in store for them.

"There's a launch heading this way," the captain called to Mari. "Not normal port tax collection from the look of it. Too fancy. That fellow in the back is not the run-of-the-mill customs inspector, Lady. I'd guess from the cut of his jib that he's a high official of the city guard."

"We'll get under cover," Mari said, beckoning to the other Mechanics and the Mages. "You see what they want, Captain, and hopefully talk our way out of any trouble."

"As you wish, Lady Mari!"

The large launch coming toward the *Gray Lady* flew the flag of Julesport, an official emblem which incongruously boasted the crossed swords of the sometime-pirate Jules. Jules had not just founded this city, but had also been the primary founder of the Confederation. It was from Julesport that she had led a flotilla against an Imperial fleet to win the battle that saved this region from Imperial control and gave Jules the title Hero of the Confederation. Mari was certain that Jules must have received aid from the Mechanics Guild and the Mage Guild in her victory, because neither of the Great Guilds wanted the Empire to grow so powerful it might openly challenge their authority, but she had still been the sort of person whose legend had trouble outpacing reality.

The idea of being linked to such a woman, of being the long-awaited daughter of Jules, was disconcerting for Mari, to put it mildly. But that was who Alain said she was, who the Mage Guild had decided she must be, who the common people saw in her: the person who was prophesized to overthrow the Great Guilds which had ruled Dematr for all of its history. A history that was measured only in centuries, but on Altis Mari had finally learned the reason for that.

Mari gazed through the windows of the stern cabin using her far-seers. The man in the stern sheets of the launch approaching the *Gray Lady* wore an impressive uniform. "That's a dress uniform, isn't it? Not a working outfit."

Mechanic Dav borrowed the far-seers and took a look. "Definitely. It looks like…uh-huh. The oar handlers have knives, and the guy in the fancy uniform has a sword, but there aren't any other weapons in sight. They don't seem to be coming to start a fight." He lowered the far-seers, returning them to Mari with obvious reluctance. Like other Mechanic devices, the far-seers had been deliberately kept too rare and expensive for widespread use. "These are nice. Made in the workshops of the Guild Hall in Palandur?"

"That's right. I took an advance on my first year's Mechanic pay allowance for them." Mari took another look at the official in the launch, then glanced at Alain. "High-ranking, but obviously not one of the leaders of the city. What do you think that means?"

Alain considered the question. "I would guess that it means they suspect that this ship carries not just any passengers, but that they also wish to know more before making any decisions."

"I cannot sense any unusual activity among the Mages in Julesport," Mage Dav said.

"That one steam ship hasn't fired up its boiler," Mechanic Bev offered.

The launch was nearing rapidly under the pull of its oars. Mari looked across the harbor, seeing no other activity that seemed out of the ordinary. Work everywhere within sight had slowed for the afternoon break. "The captain told me that we can't leave without taking on more food and water and then getting official clearance to depart. All we can do is see what that official wants and what questions he asks."

"It is safe to assume that the leaders of all cities are under a great deal of pressure from the Great Guilds to find us," Alain said. "Was not Julesport the site of rioting not long ago?"

"Yes," Mari said. "About the time I went north to find you again. The last I heard, the Mechanics Guild was leaning hard on the city leaders and the city leaders, according to the gossip among commons, were pretending to go along with orders but finding ways to avoid actually complying."

"My experience with commons," Mechanic Dav offered, "is that they are really good at that sort of thing. The Senior Mechanics kept telling me the commons were too stupid to understand what they were told, but it looked to me like they were plenty smart enough."

"That's what I've seen, too. We'll crack the hatch so we can listen while that guy talks to the captain," Mari decided.

The wait for the launch to pull alongside and its passenger to climb up the rope ladder to the *Gray Lady's* deck seemed interminable to Mari, but eventually she saw the official step on deck, looking around casually. The hatch onto the deck was open but a narrow crack. Mari stood slightly back from it, surely invisible to anyone outside, with Alain right beside her and the others clustered farther back.

Alain murmured in her ear. "This official pretends not to be aware, but he is watching everything. There is a worry inside him that he does not show to other commons."

The captain greeted the official with a smile and a salute. "The *Gray Lady*, an honest merchant ship out of Gullhaven, honored sir. Here to pick up provisions and perhaps give the crew a bit of liberty ashore."

The official nodded, smiling politely back, but only for a moment before his face went serious. "Gullhaven? That was your last port?"

"Aye, sir."

"That's odd. We have a report out of Altis that a ship like enough to yours to be her twin left that port under hasty circumstances."

Mari tensed, but the captain of the *Gray Lady* only looked surprised. "Is that so? I've not seen that ship, sir, or I'd have marked it for certain. Much like this one, you say?"

"*Exactly* like this one," the official stated. "Even down to the name."

The captain looked outraged. "They claimed the name of my ship? That's not the work of honest sailors, sir."

"I daresay," the official responded, glancing around again. "The Mechanics Guild gave us the description and the name. The Mechanics Guild said there was a substantial reward for this ship and its occupants. They want this ship very badly."

The *Gray Lady*'s captain looked puzzled. "Why ever for? We're but honest sailors."

"Naturally. But the Mechanics Guild thinks you're carrying someone the Guild wants badly enough to offer that substantial reward for, dead or alive. I might add, preferably dead."

"What!" the captain cried in feigned astonishment. "I'll not deny looking askance at the odd Mechanic, sir, because you know how they can be with their pride and their ill manners, but surely that's not grounds for such a charge. No one on this ship could match such a description, sir. We're all—"

"Honest sailors," the official finished dryly. "The Mage Guild has communicated with us as well, saying that they also seek a ship carrying someone, a young woman, and offering a huge reward for her death."

"No wise person deals with Mages, sir," the captain avowed.

"In that we are in agreement. Do you have any passengers?"

"Passengers? Well, sir, I'm not comfortable with carrying passengers, you see."

"The harbor sentries on the breakwater reported sighting figures on your deck wearing the jackets of Mechanics. They also," the official added, "saw at least one person in the robes of a Mage."

"The fog does funny things to a man's sight, sir. There have been times I've been near to jumping overboard from thinking I saw mermaids beckoning to me."

"You took on three Syndari galleys and bested them," the official said. "That's very impressive. But do not think that you can best the city leaders of Julesport."

The captain held out his hands in earnest entreaty. "I have but one task in Julesport, sir, and that is to take on food and water for my crew. We're bound for other ports, sir. I have no wish to act contrary to the laws of Julesport."

"Which other ports? Where are you bound?"

The captain finally hesitated in his reply. "We were bound for Daarendi, but after that tussle with the Syndari galleys I've been rethinking things, sir."

The official gave the captain a stern look. "You are sailing in very deep waters, whether you realize it or not."

The captain nodded. "I full realize it, sir, but I have my reasons."

"Do you? There are rumors about, Captain. Rumors that someone may be headed this way. Someone important enough to cause both of the Great Guilds to demand her death. Julesport needs to know if that someone is on your ship. Julesport needs to speak with that person. I can promise nothing except this. Your ship will not leave this harbor until we have spoken with her, or until this ship has been searched down to the last nail."

The captain eyed the official. "And if I knew her whereabouts, this person you seek, why would I betray her for any price or in the face of any threat?"

"Your reputation is known," the official said.

"That may be a poor guide in this case. Tell me you mean her no harm, and we'll discuss more."

"You know that we're discussing a woman? A young woman?"

"Aye. And those traveling with her."

"A Mage?" The official waited for some confirmation, but the captain just stood watching him. "I swear by the honor of my mother and my father that if this woman is who she claims to be, there will be no harm done to her."

Alain leaned close again to murmur to Mari. "He does not lie."

"And he already knows too much," Mari said. She sighed, nerved herself, then shoved open the hatch and walked out onto the deck, straight to the official. Alain and the others followed her. "There doesn't seem much point in pretending I'm not aboard."

The official eyed Mari, then Alain standing beside her, then the other Mechanics and Mages. "A young female Mechanic and a young male Mage. And others unknown to me. Are you the Mechanic your Guild seeks, Lady? Master Mechanic Mari of Caer Lyn?"

Mari nodded, trying to keep her face calm and wondering just what the city council of Julesport was up to.

"Are you also…" The official paused, as if finding it hard to ask the next question. "Do you know why your Guild wants you dead?"

"I know exactly why," Mari said. "Why do you want to know?"

"I am one of those responsible for the protection of this city."

She took another look at Alain, who nodded to confirm that the official was once again being honest. "I am no threat to Julesport. I do not intend staying here."

The official stared at her. "Lady, Julesport is on edge. The people have been pushed as far as they can go and are ready to set this city ablaze for no better reason than anger and frustration and fear. If they hear that…someone…is in this city, it may be all the spark that is needed."

Mari took a step closer to the official. "I'm not trying to be a spark. You said it yourself. The people are angry and fearful. They lack hope that things will ever change. What if they could gain such hope again?"

"What if," Alain said, "they had reason to believe that the prophecy is coming true?"

The official rubbed his mouth with one hand as he gazed at Mari. "Hope. Hope will not defeat the Great Guilds, Lady."

"I have other means for accomplishing that," Mari said with confidence she did not entirely feel. "But hope is important. Without hope there is nothing, and without hope there will be no future. Just let us go on our way, and when next you hear of me you will know I spoke the truth."

"Lady, if it were up to me I would do so, but I have orders. Will you accompany me into the city? There are those who must speak with you. I swear that we will not betray you to either of the Great Guilds."

"Yet," Alain said, "simply entering into your city will make her more vulnerable to them."

Mari looked out at Julesport, biting her lip as she thought. "I'll go talk to your leaders. But only if Mage Alain accompanies me."

"I was told to bring only you, Lady."

"The Mage Alain goes where I go," Mari said. "That is not negotiable."

The official saluted her. "Very well. I agree."

"You need this," Alli said, offering Mari her Mechanics jacket.

Mari shook her head. "Hang onto it for me, will you? I don't want to be any more conspicuous than I have to be. You guys stay aboard, keep a low profile, and watch for trouble. If our Guild finds out we're here, they'll try something."

Bev pointed toward the smokestack just barely visible amidst the forest of masts. "If the Guild plans to start anything, they first thing they'll do is order that ship to get steam up. We'll see the smoke and know there's something up."

"If there is an attack on this ship," the official said, "Julesport can officially do nothing. But there will be boats near you, ready to take on… refugees from the fighting and bring them ashore, where a unit of the city militia awaits to protect anyone and take them to a safe location."

"Good," Mari said. "Hopefully it won't come to that. Alain, aren't you going to change out of your Mage robes before we go ashore?"

Before Alain could answer, Mage Dav spoke up. "I would advise that Mage Alain remain garbed. He must show that he is still a Mage in good standing, not a Dark Mage skulking about in the clothes of a common and willing to sell his skills in exchange for money."

Mage Asha nodded. "The advice of my uncle is wise."

Mari wasn't so certain, knowing that they had made it through many dangers only by hiding their guild status, but when Alain nodded in agreement she knew there wasn't much sense in arguing wisdom with three Mages. Arguing with one was usually frustrating enough. "All right. Mage Dav, Mage Asha, will you listen to the… suggestions of Mechanic Alli in my absence?"

Both Mages inclined their heads slightly in agreement.

Mari got close to Alli. "Remember. Suggestions, not orders."

"Right," Alli said. "They're Mages. I'm not too likely to forget that, what with the robes and the deadpan faces and all. If we run into any problems getting along I'll ask Dav for advice, since he seems to be on such good terms with Mage Asha."

"Alli, give the guy a break!"

"Not on your life! Teasing him will be the only entertainment we have to pass the time while waiting for you and Alain to get back from the latest trap you're no doubt walking into."

Mari nodded in reluctant acquiescence. "If the Mages warn you of danger approaching, listen to them. Their warnings may be very vague, but they're probably true."

"Got it. And we'll watch that stack. See you back here soon."

The official bowed courteously as he led them toward the ladder into the launch. "I am Colonel Faron, commander of the Julesport harbor guard. It is an honor to meet you."

The journey to the quay was fast, the rowers bending to their labors and someone in the bow of the launch waving off any boat that threatened to get in the way. Colonel Faron hustled Mari and Alain up another ladder to the top of the quay and along it to a building on the shore. There a large force of soldiers in light armor waited, swords at their hips, some with crossbows at the ready, eyeing Mari with questioning looks and avoiding looking at Alain in the manner of commons around Mages everywhere.

Faron spoke quietly to the commander of the soldiers, who saluted briskly. Most of the soldiers faded back into the building, but two squads fell into place on either side of Mari and Alain as they walked inland along a broad street. The soldiers cleared any pedestrians and wagons out of the way, but Mari felt uncomfortably like a prisoner being marched to confinement. She stole sidewise glances at Alain, seeing that he betrayed no signs of alarm, and felt slightly comforted as a result.

They reached an alley down which Mari and Alain were led by Colonel

Faron as the soldiers formed a solid wall behind them facing the street. The alley ran behind a building that looked imposing even from the rear. Faron entered a back door and led them along several long passages.

"This place looks oddly deserted for this time of day," Mari observed. It called to mind uncomfortable memories of the city hall in Ringhmon.

"Those who normally work here were asked to leave for an emergency drill," Colonel Faron said. "Just a routine test of procedures."

"Of course. Absolutely routine."

Finally, Faron led Mari and Alain up some stairs to a large room dominated by an impressive table with only a few chairs near it. "Please wait here."

Mari could see Alain watching Colonel Faron closely. "Is anything wrong?" he asked.

"No," Colonel Faron said. "I just have to inform certain people that you have arrived."

Alain nodded, and Faron left.

"No warnings yet?" Mari whispered to Alain.

"No. I have seen no signs of deception in him," Alain replied.

Standing in the center of the room, Mari pivoted to look around. "One thing for sure, this isn't a prison cell." The high-ceilinged room was paneled with light woods that had darkened with age. Assorted statuary stood in the corners and a number of paintings adorned the walls, some of them clearly evoking events from the life of Jules herself. Under Mari's feet fine carpets covered the hardwood floor, and the table on one side of the room had been made from one of the rare and exotic woods that had once been exported from Tiae. Various weapons were displayed, including swords, a few crossbows, and some shields. Banners hung along the top of the walls, one of those banners the crossed-swords flag of Jules.

"I wonder if that's a banner that Jules herself flew," Mari commented. "It looks old enough."

"The room lacks windows," Alain said. "That is common for rooms in Mage Guild Halls. Do you find it of concern here?"

"No," Mari said. "When people are talking about secret things, or meeting someone they don't want anyone to know they've met, they want rooms without windows."

The door opened again. Colonel Faron entered, followed by an elderly woman and a middle-aged man and woman. The old woman and the man wore the fine clothes of well-off common people, while the other woman wore a uniform similar to Colonel Faron's.

The old woman walked with difficulty to the table and sat in the largest chair before it. The others took up a standing position on either side of her, while Colonel Faron went back to the door to stand sentry.

Silence stretched as no one said anything. Mari felt growing annoyance. "If you're trying to unnerve us or put us off balance," she finally said, "you should know that we've been to Marandur, and personally faced dragons and trolls. This is just irritating me."

The old woman smiled thinly. "You sound as though you think you should be in charge, Lady Mechanic."

"No, I think that if someone has something to say, they should say it," Mari replied.

"Will you give us your name and title, Lady Mechanic?"

"I am Master Mechanic Mari of Caer Lyn." She turned just enough to indicate Alain. "This is Mage Alain of Ihris."

The woman in uniform studied Mari. "Do you claim any other title, Lady Mechanic?"

Alain answered before Mari could, his voice as Mage cold and unfeeling as it had ever been. That gave it more authority, as if one of the statues had suddenly begun speaking. "She claims nothing. She has been foreseen to be the one foretold, the one known as the daughter. Master Mechanic Mari will bring a new day to this world."

The old woman leaned forward, intent. "The Mages have seen this? She is the one?"

"It has been seen. I have seen it," Alain said.

With a sharp gesture the old woman caused the man to one side of her to produce a document bound between stout panels of wood. "We have the prophecy, Sir Mage. The prophecy as given to Jules herself, recorded in the words of Jules. The Mages have always denied the prophecy existed. We knew otherwise. Why does a Mage now admit to it?"

"Because I have seen it," Alain said.

Colonel Faron spoke from near the door. "The Mage Guild wants her dead, wants it badly enough that they have demanded our assistance in ensuring that happens. I have never before heard of the Mages openly seeking the death of a particular Mechanic."

"Hmmph," the old woman commented wordlessly. She opened the document to read out loud. "The Mage came upon me in the twilight just before night, as rain fell and darkened the world even more. He looked upon me and his eyes widened. I had never seen a Mage show such feelings. He pointed at me and spoke in an odd voice. *A daughter of your blood will someday overthrow the Mage Guild and the Guild of the Mechanics. She will unite Mages, Mechanics, and the common people to save this world and free the common people from their service to the Guilds. Only through her can the new day come and halt the Storm that will otherwise consume all.* After he stopped speaking, the Mage looked frightened and stumbled off through the rainfall. I lost sight of him quickly and hastened back to my ship, which was already preparing to leave port. I told no one, but later learned that the Mage Guild was vigorously seeking a woman seen in Caer Lyn. Some women in Caer Lyn who resembled me were reported to have vanished, though of course the Mage Guild refused to answer any questions about them. I still feel guilt for those innocents who must have died because of their resemblance to me, but I know when the Mage Guild finally learns who I am they will seek to ensure my death and those of any of my children. I will take steps to prevent that, no matter the pain it causes me. This is my sworn account of the prophecy, as I heard it and saw it. Jules of Landfall and Julesport."

Colonel Faron was staring at Mari. "On the ship, she had Mechanics and Mages behind her, following her orders, and the captain and crew were following her as well."

"So." The old woman looked at Alain. "What say you, Sir Mage?"

"I was told the prophecy said what you have told us," Alain said.

"May I ask by whom?"

"A Mage elder."

The old woman tapped her teeth with one fingernail. "Did she tell you of this Storm?"

"She did," Alain said. "And I have seen it, as have many other Mages in recent years. It threatens all, just as the prophecy says."

"What sort of storm?" the woman in uniform asked.

"A Storm born of the built-up frustrations of the common people," Alain said. "They will rise, and destroy. Armies will clash, cities fall, all will be laid waste. Though you seek to hide your knowledge, I can see that you know this Storm approaches as we speak."

The old woman sagged back in her chair, the prophecy lying in her lap. "And now a young woman comes to us. A young woman wearing the dark jacket of a Mechanic, one of those who have enslaved us for time out of mind. With her is a Mage, one of those who have treated us even worse than the Mechanics. And they say they will save us. Would you believe this, Lady Mechanic?"

Mari felt a sudden rush of sympathy for the old woman. "I'm sorry. I can't be anyone other than who I am. I didn't ask for this. I didn't want it. But I am told it is a job given to me, and when I am given a job to do, I get that job done."

The middle-aged man raised his eyebrows in surprise. "You, a Mechanic, apologize to us? Why?"

"Because I believe in doing the right thing," Mari said.

"And she has shown me how to do the right thing," Alain added.

The woman in uniform rubbed one hand across her brow. "You must know what we're facing, Lady Mechanic. If the Mechanics Guild learns of your presence in this city, they will demand that Julesport turn you over or be placed under a Guild interdict and be banned from receiving the service of any Mechanic. The Mage Guild would retaliate in even worse ways. And always the Empire seeks justification for another war on hopes of finally gaining a foothold beyond the Southern Mountains. What do you want from Julesport?"

"Nothing," Mari said. "Except an averted gaze. We need to take on supplies. We'll pay for them. Once we've loaded the food and water we require, we will be gone," she promised. "I do not want Julesport crushed because of me."

"Tell me," the old woman said, "why we should not hand you over to the Great Guilds, who have promised immense rewards for your bodies, alive or dead."

Mari felt anger at the question, but also weariness. Why did it even have to be asked? And yet she knew it would be. "Why not? Because it would mean your continued slavery. You would be selling your chance at freedom. How much is the Mechanics Guild offering? How much is your freedom worth?"

"More than the Great Guilds offer," the old woman said. "More than they have. But you ask us to believe that you can gain us freedom."

"All I can do is ask," Mari said. "And I know that's hard. I'm a Mechanic, and Mechanics have done you great harm in the past. But the fact that the Great Guilds fear me so much, me and Mage Alain, is a sign of what I might be able to do."

"You ask leave to depart Julesport. Where will you go?" the woman in uniform asked.

"If you don't know, you can't be forced to tell," Mari said.

"Were you in Ringhmon this last year?" the old woman asked abruptly.

"Yes," Mari said.

"And Dorcastle?"

"Yes."

"You slew a dragon there."

"Yes."

The old woman took a deep breath. "And then the Northern Ramparts. Another dragon. And great damage to an Imperial legion. And a Mage in your service." She looked keenly at Alain.

"Yes," Mari said. "But he is not in my service. He is my partner."

"The stories we have heard," the middle-aged man said, "claim that you did great service for common soldiers in the Northern Ramparts and refused all payment."

"They needed my help," Mari said.

"And then Marandur?" the old woman continued. "Why Marandur?"

"I cannot tell you," Mari said.

"Jules was in Marandur," Colonel Faron said. "Long ago."

The old woman nodded at him, then looked back at Mari. "You must have heard the rumors the Imperials have been spreading. Rumors about the Dark One, Mara the Undying, who companioned the first emperor, Maran."

Mari flinched. "I've heard them. I think you can see that I don't fit those rumors." Mara was supposedly beautiful as well as deadly.

"You don't look like one who craves the blood of handsome young men, no," the old woman said, smiling very briefly. "But you did escape from Marandur. Then Palandur, rumor has it. An attack by Mages, followed by a battle between Mages and Mechanics in the heart of the Empire. Neither of the Great Guilds has deigned to explain what happened there, and the Empire has done its best to suppress such information."

"Having been to Marandur," Alain said, "we could not remain in Palandur to explain events to Imperial authorities."

"I suppose not, Sir Mage," the old woman said, twisting one corner of her mouth in a sardonic smile. "The Emperor would make your deaths painful, prolonged, and public to ensure no one else attempted to visit the forbidden ruins of Marandur. After that, we have had scattered reports of setbacks for Mechanics, including the pride of the Mechanic fleet nearly sunk, before the city of Altis suffered great damage and a great battle was fought in its harbor that left another Mechanic warship on the bottom. This was you?"

Mari nodded. "Mage Alain helped. We did everything together."

"Why Altis?"

"Again, I cannot yet explain."

"Do you want what happened at Altis to take place at Julesport as well, Lady Mechanic?"

"No," Mari said as firmly as she could. "Altis was badly damaged by Mechanics Guild assassins trying to kill me. I want to leave Julesport quickly so that it won't happen here."

The middle-aged man held up a paper. "We have a report from Altis. A swift ship reached Gullhaven and couriers carried copies throughout the Confederation. This arrived only last night."

"What does it tell you?" Alain asked.

"It tells us you speak the truth." The man paused. "And it tells us that you *are* the daughter."

The woman in uniform spoke sharply. "If the people of this city hear that the daughter is in Julesport, the resulting mayhem will make the riots of last summer look like a minor street celebration."

"What does the report from Altis say?" Alain asked. "Was there rioting there?"

"No, Sir Mage," the old woman said. "Are you going to tell us why? Some Mage spell that compels obedience?"

"If such a spell existed, the Mage elders would use it freely and not depend on fear," Alain said. "It does not. There were no riots in Altis because Lady Mechanic Mari told the people there not to riot, not to rise up, but to wait."

"Why would they listen?" demanded the woman in uniform.

"Because they had hope," Alain said. "They had a reason not to destroy."

"It was not the strong hand of the Mechanics Guild that suppressed any rioting? It was not the work of Mages or fear of the consequences?"

Alain gestured toward the east. "When we were in Palandur, there were riots. An entire district burned, and a legion was called in to restore order. This in the Empire, where order is valued above all else. Have you heard this?"

Colonel Faron nodded. "Mostly rumors, again, but with credible details. You are saying the rioting was born of the same problems we have seen?"

"And the same problems that tore apart the Kingdom of Tiae. We were there in Palandur. We could see it, we could feel it."

"If the empire is starting to feel the rot as well—" began the woman in uniform.

"It's not rot," the middle-aged man argued. "I do not welcome this news, but it does not surprise me. It is despair. You all know it as well as I do. What this Mage says matches our own knowledge. You talked to those arrested after the last round of rioting here and you heard, just as I did, that they had lost hope."

"I remember hope," the old woman commented, gazing into the distance. "When I was very young. Before I learned what the world was like, and what my role must be in serving the will of the Great Guilds. But even the very young today don't know what hope is. It has been too many years of enslavement. The next riots will be worse. I fear whether our police and military will be able to control them, and at what cost to this city. What sign can you give me, Lady Mechanic? Your words are all that they should be, and I want you to be what you claim. But what sign can you show that something that has never existed in this world can now be?"

Mari hesitated. She hated doing this, hated making a show out of something that meant so much to her, but there didn't seem any alternative. Mari slowly raised her left hand, fingers slightly spread. "Do you see this?"

"A promise ring," the old woman said. "Where is your husband?"

"Beside me." Mari reached to take Alain's hand and hold it up enough to reveal the matching ring.

All four of those from Julesport stared in disbelief for several long moments.

The old woman recovered first. "Why would you wed a Mage, Lady Mechanic?"

"He asked me," she said. "Proposed to me, that is. I proposed to him later."

"A political alliance, then? A means to the end of overthrowing the Great Guilds?"

"No!" Mari said with more force than she had intended. "We wed because we were in love, and we would have done it no matter whether it helped or hindered anything else."

"In love?" the old woman asked. "You taught a Mage to love?"

"She did," Alain said. Mari saw him relax his face, let some feeling show, and while it was a small display compared to what non-Mages would reveal, it was nonetheless shocking to see in a Mage. "She gave me back my life, a life that my Guild had taken from me."

The old woman began laughing, drawing startled glances from the others. "The oldest magic of all! And it ensnared both of you, did it? You saw the man beneath a Mage's mask, Lady Mechanic, and helped the Mage see the woman beneath your Mechanics jacket! I would not have believed it. See this!" she told the other three. "Those rings do not mark just the alliance of those two, of Mechanic and Mage. They also mark an alliance with us, for they show that these two believe in the same things that we do. That they believe in something other than power and wealth. That they would risk all for someone and something other than themselves! And that a new day can truly come. What else could you call a world where a Mechanic and a Mage are not enemies, but partners in life, joined by love?"

"But the safety of the city—" the woman in uniform began.

"The daughter is right! Give our people a reason to wait, a belief that the new day is finally coming, and they will wait." The old woman shook her finger at Mari. "Don't make it too long. Wherever you go, do not disappear. Let word come back to us. We will keep it from the Great Guilds as best we can, but our people must know you are pursuing their overthrow."

"I will do that," Mari said.

"General Shi," the old woman said to the woman in uniform. "Your soldiers are already on alert?"

"Yes," Shi confirmed.

"These two," the old woman pointed to Mari and Alain, "do not exist as far as your soldiers are concerned. The soldiers do not see them. The same for the harbor guard, Colonel Faron. They will protect these two, but our soldiers will not see them."

"What about the city council?" the middle-aged man asked. "They need to—"

"The city council," the old woman interrupted, "will be told about this tomorrow, when there is no longer any possibility of them arguing other courses of action to death, or of one of them betraying the presence of our guests before they depart. The daughter should be welcomed in the home of her ancestor, and I would hope in the days and years to come that the daughter would remember the special status of Julesport in her family."

The man nodded reluctantly. "The good wishes of the daughter are of immense value. And it is true that too many secrets have become known to the Mechanics and the Mages."

Mari, uncomfortable from the repeated references to her as the daughter, felt a sudden suspicion. "Your city council chamber. Does it have electric lighting?"

"Mechanic lights, you mean?" the man asked. "Yes. Two large fixtures in the ceiling."

"Can I see them?"

"Why?" the old woman asked, her eyes intent.

"I may be able to do you a service," Mari said, "by finding the means by which the Mechanics Guild has learned your secrets."

The old woman gestured briskly, and with a bow Colonel Faron led the way out of the room and into a long hallway. Mari and Alain followed him, while General Shi and the other man brought up the rear, the old woman staying behind to await their return.

Faron halted before an impressive set of double doors. Opening one side, he looked in, then nodded to Mari and opened his mouth to speak.

Mari silenced him with a strong gesture, then walked into the room. It was perhaps four times the size of the room they had left and much brighter, with a long table along one side and two massive chandeliers hanging from the ceiling. She looked up, studying the lights.

Turning back to the mystified leaders of Julesport, Mari pantomimed the need for a ladder high enough to reach the lights.

It took a few minutes before Colonel Faron himself returned with a ladder and set it up where Mari directed. She climbed up, thinking that the ladder felt way too rickety, then when high enough began looking over the light fixture.

And found nothing but the bulbs and the wiring to them.

Fearing that she might look like an idiot, Mari climbed down and the ladder was moved beneath the second light.

This time she found what she had been looking for.

It wasn't until they were out of the room and the door closed that Mari spoke. "The Mechanics Guild has a far-listener in that second light fixture."

"A what?" General Shi asked.

"A far-listener. It's a device that picks up sounds and transmits them along wires to somewhere else where they can be heard." She pointed upward. "The wires for it are disguised by the wires for the light fixture. The Mechanics Guild has been listening in to everything said in that room."

"Did you— Did you break it?" the middle-aged man asked.

"No. Do you want me to? Because if I do, the Mechanics Guild will immediately know that you have learned of it."

Colonel Faron nodded grimly. "It's like arresting a spy the moment you learn of them. Or leaving the spy in place and feeding that spy only what you want them to know."

"You have done us a great service, Lady Mechanic," General Shi said. "Would the Mechanics have shared the information gained here with the Mages?"

"No," Mari said, almost laughing at the idea. "Alain?"

Alain gestured slightly toward the general. "Mages can learn your secrets by what is said—and by what is not said: by what you reveal in your voice, your face, the way you stand."

"We know Mages can spot lies," Colonel Faron said. "But if we don't voice a lie—"

"It does not matter," Alain said. "A Mage can see that you have not said something, that there is more left which you do not wish to speak, that by silence you seek to mislead. It is easy to read, for a Mage."

Once back in the smaller room, the old woman was told. She lowered her face into one hand for a long moment. "No wonder the Great Guilds have been able to outthink us time and again. We thought we had our secrets, our means of avoiding their tricks, but they only let us believe that. How many men and women have died because the Great Guilds knew our plans even as we made them?"

Mari saw that the middle-aged man looked uncomfortable, and was not surprised when Alain called him on it.

"You are unhappy," Alain said to him. "But not for the same reason as the others."

Everyone looked at the man, who grimaced. "I would be a fool to lie to a Mage. Very well. I will say what is in my heart. I am grateful that the Lady Mechanic has done us this service. But she has done so by betraying the secrets of her Guild. I am concerned that someone willing to betray once may betray again."

Mari held up a hand to halt the outbursts that nearly came from the others. "I understand. Would it make you feel better to know that those secrets never really belonged to my Guild? My former Guild, that is. The Mechanics Guild stole those secrets. They were never supposed to be secrets. They were meant to be shared with everyone. I only gave you what your ancestors should have long ago received."

"If this is so, Lady Mechanic, you have my apologies," the man said.

"How do you know this?" the old woman asked.

"I can't tell you yet," Mari said. "Someday I will be able to tell everyone. But I have seen the evidence. So has Mage Alain. The Mechanics Guild is built on the theft of its secrets from everyone else, and on the lie that commons cannot do the work that Mechanics can do. You can. I have proven it to be so."

"You will turn this world upside-down," General Shi said.

"Better upside-down," Alain replied, "than broken as is Tiae."

"No argument there," the old woman said. "Tell me, daughter, do you know anything of the thinking devices of the Mechanics Guild?" Mari felt a surge of interest. "Yes. I know a lot about them. Why?"

"Julesport has been hampered by the failure of the device we have in this building," the middle-aged man explained. "We have been trying to get the Mechanics Guild Hall to fix it for the last year, but they insist that the repair will cost more than even Julesport can afford."

"That doesn't seem too likely," Mari said. "Why aren't they just offering to replace it, if it's broken that badly? There aren't a lot of them, but in a year's time the Guild could have brought in a spare from Palandur. We're talking a Calculating and Analysis Device, right?"

"Yes, Lady Mechanic."

"I can fix one of those in my sleep," Mari said, for once not having to feign total confidence. It felt almost disorienting to be working within her field as a Mechanic again rather than facing the challenges of the daughter. "Let me take a look at it."

Once again the small group trooped down a long hall, then down some stairs, Colonel Faron going ahead to ensure that no one had returned to the building early.

The room Mari finally entered felt very familiar. The Guild insisted on certain design criteria for rooms holding Calculating and Analysis Devices, and there was really only one design of the CADs, with the ability to add on certain options. The large metal cabinets holding the many relays were as well known to her as the face of an old acquaintance.

Mari checked the room carefully for any far-listener, though she didn't expect to find one. She powered up the device, waiting impatiently as it warmed up and wondering just how long she and Alain had already been away from the *Gray Lady*.

Finally she was able to run a test sequence, which went so badly that Mari had a long tape of data printed out so she could analyze the problem. "They've been cheating you," she finally told General Shi and the middle-aged man. "The unit hasn't been maintained all that well." She suspected from what she saw that she knew the Mechanic who had done it. Why was he working in the field after washing out of the CAD program at the Mechanics Guild Academy? Maybe because there were so few Mechanics qualified for CAD work and the Guild had decided to try to kill one of them, Mari herself. "But the problems you're having are because you've got a badly patched set of thinking ciphers."

"Can you repair it?" General Shi asked.

Mari nodded. "Fixing the ciphers will be easy for me. The hard part is going to be doing the fixes in such a way that the Mechanic who is supposed to keep this CAD working doesn't realize that I've fixed it. If it's the Mechanic I think it is, I can do that, but it'll take a while." She looked at Alain. "Maybe you should go back to the *Gray Lady* and let them know that everything is all right. I'll follow when this is done."

Colonel Faron stuck his head in the room. "We have already sent word to fully provision your ship, daughter."

"Uh, would you mind not calling me that?" Mari asked. "It feels like I'm not me any more when people do that. Just Lady is fine."

"Yes, Lady. We could send them a message from you."

Alain shook his head. "They would not know if the message was from Lady Mari. I should carry the message, but I am reluctant to leave here without you," he told Mari.

Mari looked up from her work, brushing hair from her face. "The army of Julesport is guarding me, Alain. I'll be fine. And you can still tell where I am, right?"

He nodded. "The thread."

"Right," Mari repeated. The idea of the invisible, insubstantial thread that connected her to Alain still felt sort of weird to her, but also sort of romantic, and it had saved her a couple of times already.

Reassured, Alain reached out to her. "Be careful."

She got up and kissed him. "Don't worry."

It wasn't until Mari bent back to her work that she wondered how the Julesport officials had taken seeing someone kiss a Mage. That wasn't something one saw every day. In fact, it was doubtful that anyone had ever willingly kissed a Mage before she and Alain had grown together.

None of the fixes were complicated, but doing them in a way that didn't look like fixes took a long time. Mari finally stood up, stretching out her back and wincing. "That's got it. It'll work fine for you. If the Mechanics Guild asks how that happened, tell them you have no idea, that it just started working all right again. CADs do that sometimes."

"In truth," the middle-aged man said, "I have no idea what you did, but we are all very grateful. How much?"

"How much what?"

"Uh…how much is the cost of your services?"

Mari took a moment to understand. "We didn't negotiate a contract. And Julesport is helping us, or at least not hindering us. And if the prophecy is right, I guess I sort of do have a special obligation to the city that Jules founded. So let's call that even."

"Even?" General Shi asked with obvious disbelief. "You are charging nothing? The repair of these devices is one of the most expensive contracts the Mechanics Guild offers."

"Yeah. There aren't that many Mechanics trained to fix them," Mari explained. "But I'm not with the Guild anymore."

"You must accept—"

Seeing that the officials would not accept her services without recompense, Mari offered a compromise. "I'll take something to help pay for the supplies the *Gray Lady* took on, all right? Is that enough?"

"If that is all you will take," the middle-aged man said. He began to say something else, but turned as a messenger rushed up to Colonel Faron. "What is this?"

Faron turned a worried face to them. "The guards who accompanied Mage Alain to the *Gray Lady* have been found in an alley, all dead. My aide checked with the launch at the landing and Mage Alain has not returned."

Mari's sense of satisfaction, her pride in her work, turned instantly to ashes.

CHAPTER FOUR

W e'll begin searching the entire city," General Shi said.
"With the entire army looking—"

"We must be dealing with Mages," the middle-aged
man interrupted. "They captured another Mage and killed your soldiers without creating enough disturbance to be noticed."

"There have been no reports of unusual activity at the Mage Guild,"
Shi insisted.

"Dark Mages," Mari said. "It might be Dark Mages."

"It might," the man agreed. "Your Mage must still be alive, or they
would have left his body with those of the soldiers. How can we find
your Mage without a lengthy search that would give warning to those
who hold him? They might kill him if they know we seek him."

Mari buried her face in both hands, trying to think. If only that
damned thread ran both ways... "Maybe it does," she whispered.

"Lady?"

"I need to get back to my ship as quickly as possible. One of the
Mages there might be able to locate Mage Alain."

They rushed through hallways and down stairs, emerging into the
open where General Shi flagged down a cavalry unit standing guard.
"Two of you dismount and give your horses to Colonel Faron and this
lady. Escort them to the waterfront. Do not delay and move as quickly
as you can."

Mari hoisted herself into the saddle of a cavalry mount, torn between her admiration of the fine horse and her discomfort at riding. The group thundered down the streets of Julesport, pedestrians and wagons dashing to clear the path and sometimes barely getting out of the way. A road blocked by heavy traffic caused the column to veer into an alley, gallop through a series of turns as they vaulted piles of trash, and finally come out beyond the stoppage. Fortunately, Mari didn't have to guide her mount, which kept up with its fellow horses. She was fully occupied with trying to stay in the saddle.

At one point they raced past a corner where two Mechanics stood. Mari saw their faces only as blurs, impossible to recognize, but she thought one of the Mechanics looked indifferent to whatever emergency was causing commons to rush about. The other, though, seemed to gaze toward Mari as she and the cavalry passed by.

The column came to a halt at the quay, the horses blowing with exertion. Colonel Faron came to assist Mari, but she dropped from the saddle without help. As the cavalry milled about, Mari and Faron raced to the waiting launch. This time the rowers bent even harder to their task than before, the launch leaping across the water to the small clipper ship.

Mari jumped onto the ladder still hanging down the side of the *Gray Lady* and scrambled up it as fast as she could.

All of the Mechanics and Mages were waiting and watching her with visible alarm. "What's up? Where's Alain?" Alli asked as Mari caught her breath.

"He was taken," Mari finally gasped out. "By Mages. Maybe Dark Mages. Mage Asha, is my beacon still there?"

Asha was actually betraying enough concern for Mari to see it. "It has never faded. But you do not wish me to speak of it."

"Now I do. There's a…Alain calls it a thread that connects him and me. He's been able to use it to tell where I am. Can you sense that?" Mari asked desperately. "Can you track Alain through me?"

Asha paused for long enough that Mari felt like screaming in frustration. Then Asha said, "Try, yourself, to sense that thread, to feel where Alain is."

"I don't know how." But Mari tried, pretending she could see the thread, thinking feverishly of Alain.

"I…sense something," Asha said. She pivoted slowly, pointing into the city. "That way. It…feels like Mage Alain."

Colonel Faron pointed in another direction. "The Mage Guild Hall in Julesport lies that way."

"That is well," Mage Dav said. "Any attempt to assault a Mage Guild Hall by those of us here would be futile. But if Mage Alain is held elsewhere, there is a chance."

Faron pointed again, this time in a different direction. "That's about where the Mechanics Guild Hall is. So he's not there, either."

"Let's go," Mari said. "Now." She grabbed the Mechanics jacket that Alli offered, shrugging into it and then taking an offered rifle.

"Lady—" Colonel Faron began, alarmed.

Mari spun to face him. "I know. I also know that there's likely to be some kind of fight when we find Alain. And a fight could spark the sort of unrest in this city that none of us want. But if the people of Julesport see that it is Mechanics and Mages involved, they won't think it has anything to do with them."

"Lady, if they see Mechanics and Mages working together they will know that only one person could be responsible!"

"Then…that should calm them, too, right?" Mari didn't wait for an answer. "Who's coming?" she asked the others.

Mechanics Alli, Bev, and Dav were already carrying rifles. Mage Asha and Mage Dav stood by the railing, clearly waiting to leave.

"Thank you," Mari said. She spun toward the side of the ship, pausing as she finally noticed the captain of the Gray Lady standing not far away. "Get all the supplies you need aboard and do it as fast as you can. We may be leaving very quickly when we return."

The captain nodded, as if hasty departures from port were routine for his ship. Then he spoke reluctantly. "There's the matter of funds—"

"No, there isn't!" Mari snapped. "It's taken care of. Any supplies you need that haven't shown up already should be here soon."

With a resigned look, Colonel Faron led the way back down the ladder. The launch was slightly overloaded with everyone aboard, but made it to the quay without incident. "How could they have surprised Alain?" Bev asked. "He's pretty sharp."

"Concealment spells," Mari said. "Mages can make themselves invisible to everyone."

"Except other Mages," Mage Dav advised. "We can see a Mage using such a spell. Not as the person they are, but as a pillar of light being reflected from the Mage. Mage Alain should have sensed another Mage using such a spell near him."

"Maybe he got knocked out," Mechanic Dav said, "before the guards were killed."

"That would require one of the guards to have betrayed us," Colonel Faron said, his mouth a thin, angry line. "But it is the best explanation we have at this time."

As she pulled herself quickly up the ladder and stood on the quay again, Mari remembered something and gazed out across the harbor. "Has there been any extra smoke from that stack, Alli?"

"Not yet. The Senior Mechanics must still be oblivious."

Colonel Faron was issuing orders to some of the cavalry, who dashed off in a rattle of hooves. "Some of the other shipping in the harbor is about to reposition," he said. "The other ships will block the movement of that Mechanic ship if it tries to get underway."

"Won't that cause the Mechanics Guild to target you?" Mari asked as they walked quickly toward land.

Faron looked regretful. "For what? We're just dumb, foolish commons who can't do anything right."

They paused at the place where the quay joined land, nearly a full troop of cavalry jostling nearby, the tips of their lances flashing red from the rays of the setting sun.

Mage Asha stopped and looked around. "I must focus," she told Mari, the Mage voice sounding so strange in its lack of feeling. "We must walk."

"Fine," Mari said. "Let's walk."

Asha started off a fast pace that startled Mari. She caught up and tried to match Mage Asha, but after two weeks of idleness on the ship Mari found herself straining to keep up. For her part, Mage Asha walked without any sign of exertion.

Alli caught up as well. "She's in really good shape," Alli puffed.

"All Mages are like that," Mari said, most of her attention focused on thinking of Alain. "Their training as acolytes is extremely physically punishing."

"Keep your thoughts centered on Mage Alain," Asha told Mari.

"I am!"

They were walking up a broad avenue leading into the city, a detachment of cavalry riding a little ways ahead and contriving to clear the road without revealing who they were clearing it for. Citizens of Julesport were pausing to look, puzzled by the sight of Mechanics jackets and Mage robes together. Mari tried to block out awareness of the growing buzz of conversation, keeping her mind centered on Alain.

The sun set off to the west, plunging the city streets into gloom that was partially dispelled as lamplighters began their work.

Asha came to a stop, then turned herself slowly, as if, Mari thought, she was an antenna trying to pick up a faint signal. She pointed to the right. "They are trying to block his presence, but he lies this way." She turned abruptly onto a side street, leaving the cavalry racing to get ahead again. The small group of Mechanics and Mages moved through the crowds of common folk who would have made way for members of the Great Guilds anyway but were particularly eager to avoid the grim-faced Mechanics carrying rifles as well as the impassive menace of the Mages walking with them.

As Mari checked her rifle again, she heard amidst the crowds the words she had been fearing to hear.

"...daughter..."

"...must be..."

"...it's true..."

But then Asha turned quickly once more. The street they were on now was much narrower, barely wide enough for two carts to pass each other. People were lined up along the sides, staring at Mari's group, further reducing the space available.

"The elders at the Mage Guild Hall will hear of this," Mage Dav said.

"The Senior Mechanics will, too," Mechanic Bev added.

Mari just nodded, keeping her focus tightly on thoughts of Alain.

"If I know my Senior Mechanics," Alli said, "they'll hold a meeting to decide what to do, and then likely call to Guild Headquarters in Palandur for guidance before acting. That should give us a few hours."

Asha came to a sudden halt before a three-story structure that stood slightly apart from a similar building on one side, a narrow alley separating them. A vacant lot with only an old foundation overgrown with weeds was on the other side.

Colonel Faron rode up next to Mari. "It's a former hotel. Now a place of ill-repute. You! Over here!"

The police officer summoned by Faron came running over, holding his helmet on with one hand and a hardwood club in the other. Like most police, he wore only a lacquered leather chest plate as armor over his uniform. "Yes, sir?"

"What can you tell me of this place?"

"We make arrests outside of it nearly every night but haven't been able to prove anything against the owner."

"The owner is paying off the police," Mage Dav said, the coldly emotionless voice of a Mage even more intimidating than usual. "This shadow reveals it."

"I...I..." Terrified to be the focus of a Mage's attention, the police officer backed away.

Faron looked at Mari. "There are laws in Julesport. We would need a warrant to get that door open."

"I don't need a warrant," Mari said. "I've got Mechanic Alli."

"But—"

"You don't see me, right? Aren't those your orders?"

Colonel Faron paused, then smiled. "And I must follow my orders."

"Alli, we need a door down," Mari said, looking at the door barring entry to the building. It was made of heavy planks reinforced with metal straps, the sort of barrier that could require some time to force.

"Right here," Alli announced, sounding cheerful. She had a small lump of something in one hand and was poking what looked like a large stick into it. "Stand back."

Everyone pushed away from the door as Alli pressed the explosives against the lock, did something to the fuse, and then ran back to rejoin the others. "How did you know I'd have some explosives with me?" she asked Mari.

"Seriously?" Mari said. "Mage Asha, are you sure that Mage Alain is inside there?"

Asha nodded.

"Four, three, two…" Alli counted down.

The explosion wasn't large, but it was enough to leave the heavy door sagging on its hinges. Mechanics Dav and Bev hit the door with their shoulders, knocking it open. Mari found herself pushed aside by Mages Dav and Asha as they followed the Mechanics, long knives out.

She rushed after them to find a tall, thin man standing in the center of the room, his mouth agape. "How— How dare you!"

Asha was turning, her gaze sweeping the room. She stopped, eyes intent, then stepped forward, her long knife swinging in a fast, vicious arc. It rebounded from something unseen with a clang of metal on metal, but Asha whipped her knife around in a reverse circle that ended when the knife stopped in mid-air.

A man appeared, his mouth open as he grunted with pain from a deep cut in his side. A knife fell from his own hand as he staggered back.

Mage Asha pulled back her knife for another slash, but before she could strike again Mechanic Dav stepped forward and swung his rifle butt against the man's head.

"This is no Dark Mage," Mage Dav said as the injured man collapsed. "It is Mage Niaro. But there is another here."

Both Mages swung to face another corner of the room. "Another hides there."

Bev took two steps, leveling her rifle at the apparently vacant corner. "Should I just kill him?"

An older man appeared where nothing had been, his face a strange mix of Mage impassivity and terror, dropping to his knees with hands upheld in supplication. "No! I will not resist! I have money! You can have it all!"

"See if you can buy off Colonel Faron after you killed his soldiers!" Mari snarled. "Asha! Where is Alain?"

Asha swung slowly again, then pointed up a flight of stairs on one side of the room. Mari took the stairs two at a time until she reached the top and a locked door there.

She swung the butt of the rifle against the lock with all of her strength, shattering the wood around it. The door slammed open, Mari dashing inside so fast she barely stayed clear of it.

The sparsely furnished room was dominated by a bed. Mari faltered for a moment as she saw Alain lying on it face up, apparently unrestrained and wearing almost nothing. Standing next to him was a woman much older than Mari, who had obviously been startled in the act of undressing Alain. "Get away from my husband, you witch!" Mari yelled, her mind flaring red with rage at the unexpected scene.

"Dark Mage!" Asha warned as she entered after Mari, but Mari didn't hesitate, rushing forward and slamming the barrel of her rifle against the Dark Mage's head.

The force of the blow hurled the Dark Mage against the wall, where she fell to lie unconscious. Mari, all of her fears and angers of this day concentrated on the Dark Mage before her, brought her rifle up and centered it on the woman.

A strong hand grasped the barrel and pushed it to one side, holding it there while Mari tried to bring the weapon to bear again. "Alli! Let go!"

Alli shook her head, maintaining her grip. "Mari. You don't want to do this."

"Yes, I do! Let go!" Mari struggled, but couldn't shake Alli's hold.

"Mari," Alli said in a voice strong enough to penetrate through

Mari's anger. "Remember what you said to me? About how you were afraid you'd change? That you would become someone else because of everything that was happening?"

Mari stopped struggling, gazing back at Alli. "Yes," she panted, suddenly short of breath.

"Would Mari shoot a helpless woman? Even a Dark Mage? You put a bullet in her and you'll feel good for maybe five seconds. Then you'll hate yourself for the rest of your life."

Mari stared at her friend, took a deep breath, then stepped back as Alli finally let go of the barrel of the rifle. "Thank you."

"That's what friends are for," Alli said. "I'll take care of—"

"Let me," Mage Asha said. She walked over to the unconscious Dark Mage, who was lying against the outer wall. Asha tensed as she cast a spell, and a section of that wall disappeared, leaving an opening about the size of a person. Asha placed one foot on the Dark Mage and pushed, rolling her out of the opening.

Mari heard the thud of the Dark Mage hitting the ground as the opening vanished, leaving a once-again solid wall in its wake.

"That's gonna hurt," Alli said with a grin.

"Mage Alain is my friend," Asha said.

"Are you guys all right up there?" Bev called from below.

"We're fine," Mari yelled back, then raced to the bed to look at Alain. His hands were tied but he wasn't fighting the bonds, instead lying limply, his eyes partially open.

Alli leaned close. "Drugged?"

Asha nodded. "It is one of the weapons of dark Mages. They sought to discredit and humiliate Mage Alain, altering his mind by physical abuse so that he would become feeble and irrational. They must have been hired by the Mage Guild here to strike at him. It is not enough that Mage Alain die. The elders want him shown to be a weak Mage before then."

"Let's get him dressed and get out of here," Mari said, grabbing Alain's shirt from where it lay beside the bed.

Alli grunted with frustration as she tried to help. "I can't get his arm through this sleeve. He's got his fist clenched and I can't budge it."

"Why would his fist—?" Mari looked. "It's his left hand." She felt tears starting. "Even when drugged he clenched his fist to keep them from taking his promise ring!" Her voice broke on the last two words.

Alli rolled her eyes. "Seriously? Even when one of you is unconscious, you two are still nauseating."

"It's love, Alli!"

"I know what love is. I just think you two go a little overboard on the whole thing."

"Jealous," Mari said, her heart still pounding from recent events. "We'll just get Alain into his robes. That shouldn't be too hard." She realized that it should have felt weird to have two other women helping her to dress her husband, but at the moment Asha and Alli felt a lot more like sisters.

Once his robes were on, the three women hoisted Alain and began carrying him out of the room. "Wow," Alli commented, looking at Asha as they headed for the stairs. "You've got some muscle hidden under those robes."

"All Mages prepare for any physical demands," Asha said, impassive even while helping to maneuver Alain's limp body down the stairs. "All physical effort must be as nothing."

They paused to adjust the load at the bottom of the stairs, Asha maneuvering Alain's head so that his eyes were pointed toward the Mage who had been injured. "Mage Niaro, working with Dark Mages. You see, Alain," she told him even though he showed no sign of being aware. "That is how the Mages found you in this city."

Mari stared at the fallen Mage, whose blood was forming a widening pool. "Shouldn't we help him? He'll die."

"He is nothing," Asha said.

"No. Nobody is nothing. Not even this Niaro."

Bev knelt down, looking over Niaro. "Well, this guy is nothing now. He just died. Hey, Dav, help me drag him out of here."

Together the two Mechanics pulled Niaro's body through the door as the others got Alain out as well. Bev laid out Niaro straight, his arms folded across his chest, as if he were anyone else who had died and needed to be laid out properly. She dug in one pocket and pulled out a coin, placing it on Niaro's chest in the old ritual.

"Why are you doing that for him?" Mechanic Dav asked.

"I'm doing it for me," Bev said. "So that I know I'm not like he was."

Mari saw that the Dark Mage who had surrendered was standing blank-faced, his arms bound, amidst Colonel Faron's soldiers. Some other soldiers were busy binding up the woman Mari had knocked unconscious.

The owner of the building followed them out, shouting angrily. "You will pay! This was illegal!"

"Hold on a second," Bev said. She brought her rifle to her shoulder, causing the owner to stagger back and cover his head, but her shot went into the building and resulting in a tinkle of breaking glass. "Darn. My weapon went off and hit that oil lamp."

"Did you do that for you, too?" Mechanic Dav asked.

"Nah. I did that for Mari."

Firelight was already flickering within the doorway as Colonel Faron turned to a detachment of police officers who had just arrived. "It is unfortunate that you won't be able to save this building."

"If the fire wardens get here quickly enough—" one of the officers began saying.

"*You won't be able to save this building*," Faron repeated in a way that made it clear no more argument was allowed. "Don't let the fire spread to any other buildings, though."

Mari, suddenly feeling very tired, blinked at an empty, open-topped carriage sitting in the street.

"My unit is supposed to take this carriage down to the quay," Colonel Faron said as if talking to the air.

"Get in," Mari told everyone. It took some work to get Alain up and inside, but he was soon sitting limply between Mari and Asha.

Only then did Mari notice how crowded the streets were, how many people were there, all of them gazing silently toward the Mechanics and the Mages. A low buzz of conversation started among the crowd, and Colonel Faron turned a pleading glance her way.

"What do they want?" Mechanic Dav asked, glancing around worriedly and fingering his rifle even though the weapon would be useless against so many.

"They want me," Mari said. She stood up carefully in the carriage and looked out on the crowds, feeling a chill at their numbers and their watchfulness. And all of them were watching her.

The fire inside the building grew in intensity with a sudden whoosh, the light spilling out to illuminate Mari. The buzz of the crowd grew in volume, and their eyes glittered at her like thousands of candles.

How did she even begin to address these people?

That dilemma was resolved as someone finally called out a loud question. "Who are you?"

In the silence that followed that call, a silence broken only by the distant ringing of bells as fire wardens sounded alarms and the crackling of flames greedily devouring the building, Mari's voice had no trouble carrying. "You know who I am. I have come from Altis. Before that I was in the Empire, and in the Northern Ramparts, and at Dorcastle. I came to Julesport to…to ask you to wait a little while longer. I know you have stopped believing that things could ever change. But they will! It is not yet time. The Great Guilds are very powerful. But they will be overthrown!"

The answering roar from the crowd felt like a physical force beating at Mari. She raised her arms, gesturing for silence, and for a wonder the crowd fell quiet again. "Do not act yet! It is not time! I do not want what the Great Guilds did at Altis to happen here. You will hear from me, and of me, I promise you. But do not risk yourselves and your city by acting before I am ready. You all have a lot to live for. Never forget that."

A shrill voice yelled at her. "You're a Mechanic! Liar! *She* would never be one of them!"

Part of Mari quailed at the accusation, knowing what would happen to her and her friends if this crowd turned into a mob. But part of her got angry. This was all hard enough. Too hard. Why did she have to argue with the people who should be helping her? "Jules was on officer of the Empire before she became something else. Have you forgotten that? Who am I? Ask the people of Altis!" Mari yelled back. "Ask the leaders of the Mechanics Guild, who have placed a high price on my head and already tried to kill me many times! Ask the Mages, who have told me I am that person, and the elders of the Mage Guild who also want me dead!"

Asha stood up beside her, the cowl of her robes back, her beauty making her look spectral in the light of the fire. "She is the daughter. It has been foreseen." The Mage voice, loud but completely unfeeling, echoed among the suddenly silent crowd.

And in that silence a single person could be heard sobbing, crying softly. "At last. At last."

Mari tried to sound calm and determined. "I have to go now. I have to leave Julesport in order to protect you. The days of the Great Guilds are numbered. Believe that because it is true. Together we will bring a new day to this world. Stay safe until then!"

Judging the moment right, Colonel Faron spurred his mount forward, the cavalry with him taking position around the carriage as its driver flicked the reins at the two horses hitched to it. The carriage began rolling toward the nearest edge of the crowd, which reluctantly gave way, everyone straining to see Mari as she sat down again. Mari held her hand before her, staring at how badly it was shaking.

Colonel Faron leaned down to speak to her. "I've sent for healers to meet us at the quay for the injured Mage Alain. There are reports that Mechanics are vanishing from the streets of the city, all withdrawing into their Guild Hall."

"Wh—" Mari swallowed and managed to speak again. "What about the Mages?"

"There are small groups of them out. They don't seem to be converging on any point. They're just out."

Mage Dav went to the edge of the carriage. "I will seek some of them."

"Is that not dangerous?" Mage Asha asked.

"Yes."

Mage Dav stepped down from the slow-moving carriage, vanishing almost immediately into the crowd, while Alli, Bev, and Mechanic Dav stared after him. "You Mages take some getting used to," Alli finally said. "No offense."

"Why should I care what you say?" Asha asked.

Alli's mouth dropped open for a moment, then she looked at Mari. "Tell me again just how you got to know Alain?"

"We were running for our lives," she said, holding Alain with one arm while she tried to suppress the nervous shakes that still shivered through her. "We didn't have any choice. And yes, if the circumstances had been any different, it would have been very hard to get to know him enough to understand why he said things like that. It's not an insult. Mage Asha isn't trying to make you upset or angry. She's just asking why she should be upset by anything you say, and that's literally all she means by it."

"If you say so." Alli looked at the crowds on either side of the carriage. "Just how did Mage Asha help us find Alain anyway?"

"It's my…beacon," Mari admitted.

"Oh, yeah. You haven't talked about that since Altis."

"I don't want to ever talk about it," Mari mumbled.

Asha spoke again. "When Mari developed feelings for Mage Alain, and I learned to see Mari as not just a shadow, I began to sense her presence from afar. Whenever she thinks of Mage Alain, it is as if a distant bonfire lights for me."

Alli didn't answer, and when Mari looked at her she saw that Alli was trying desperately not to laugh. "That must be…really…embarrassing," she finally got out.

"It is," Mari said, trying to sound as cold as a Mage.

Mechanic Dav was giving her a funny look. "Does that happen every time a Mechanic and a Mage, uh…"

"You'll have to let me know," Mari said, which at least shut down further questions from Mechanic Dav.

The crowds were thinning as they reached the edges of the throng, the carriage horses trotting along streets where more and more soldiers were in evidence. As the carriage neared the quay, a cavalry soldier came riding up and saluted. "Colonel," she called. "There is a group of Mechanics down there. They claim to be friends of the daughter."

Faron turned a questioning look on Mari.

"Did they give any names?" Mari asked.

The soldier shook her head. "One of them said to tell Master Mechanic Mari that the next time she is in a blizzard to remember that nothing is real."

"What?" Colonel Faron demanded. "What does that mean?"

"I know what it means," Mari said, laughing with relief. "Alli, you might want to run ahead and meet those guys."

"Why?" Alli asked. "Hold on. Blizzard. Isn't that when you met—?"

"Sure was," Mari said, smiling.

"Wooo!" Alli jumped out of the carriage and ran ahead.

"I guess it is all right," Faron said, motioning the carriage to move on. "Lady, may I ask a question before you take leave of us?"

"Sure," Mari said, feeling totally worn out again and wondering just how much longer this day and night could last.

"What reward do you seek?"

Mari looked at the colonel. "Reward?"

"Yes. What will you gain?"

"Everyone will be free. The Storm won't come. The Great Guilds will no longer control this world."

"But, for *you*," Colonel Faron pressed.

"I…" Mari spread her hands in confusion. "I have Alain. I'll be able to practice my Mechanic skills freely. My friends will be free. Isn't that enough?"

"I would think so," Faron said. "Good luck, Lady. I must go to ensure your ship has a clear path out of the harbor." He flicked his reins and rode away, quickly vanishing into the dusk.

The carriage rumbled to a halt and Mari roused herself to get Alain out, feeling an irrational resentment that he wasn't helping more.

"Four more Mechanics," Bev commented. "No, wait. Five. Alli is glued to one of them so it looked like they were just one."

"Hi, Calu," Mari called, realizing her hail sounded breathless.

What looked like the silhouette of one broad Mechanic separated into two, Alli leading Mechanic Calu. "Hey, Mari. Still causing trouble, huh?" He spotted Alain as the others tried to get him down from the carriage. "Alain's hurt?"

Calu rushed to help, talking as he did so. "I've got four friends with me. When the Guild Hall supervisor ordered everyone into the Hall for a lockdown, we were outside and figured it was time to make a break. We planned to try to find you, but you were a lot closer than we expected. So you're the daughter now, huh?"

"She's already power-mad," Alli commented to Calu as they got Alain down. "That's why we had to rescue this guy. Alain is the only one who can control her."

"He's a better man than I am, then," Calu observed with a grin. But the grin faded into a look of concern. "What's the matter with him?"

"Drugs, we think," Mari reassured Calu. "He'll be all right," she added, trying to convince herself.

"There are a couple of healers here. I guess they got sent to help him." Calu tried to take more of Alain's weight on his own shoulder. "Can I take over here? You must be beat."

"I am beat," Mari admitted, "but Mage Asha and I will get him the rest of the way."

"Mage Asha? Another Mage?" Calu glanced at her, then his eyes widened as Asha's beauty struck home. "Wow. I mean—"

Alli intervened, punching Calu in the shoulder. "We know what you mean. Behave yourself. She's a Mage and she's got a knife."

"And I've already got a girl," Calu said. "I've got to fill you guys in on what's been happening."

"Later," Mari gasped as some of the rowers from the launch helped lower Alain into the boat. "Right now we have to get out of town fast."

"It should be two trips with this many people," the boat officer suggested.

"All right. I'll…" Mari hesitated, torn between wanting to go to the ship with Alain and her sense of duty that she remain on the quay until everyone else was clear.

"You'll go," Alli said. "I can supervise things here for a few minutes."

Mari nodded, grateful that Alli had stepped in. "Thanks. Mage Asha…Mage Dav! We can't leave Mage Dav!"

Asha shook her head. "If Mage Dav means to accompany us, he will be here. If he does not meet us here, he will find us at some later time."

Bev was gazing out over the harbor. "Sparks and smoke, people. That stack is showing signs that someone is trying to get a boiler lit and online really fast."

"Move it!" Mari ordered, scrambling down the ladder into the launch. She sat in the back, pillowing Alain's head on her lap, trying not to burst into tears over how sick he looked.

Bev joined them, as did two common folk with the snake and staff badges of healers, then three of the Mechanics who had accompanied Calu and Calu himself, hustled down the ladder by an insistent Alli.

The launch shoved off and began threading its way through the crowded harbor back to the Gray Lady. "I guess Alli and I are going to be trying to keep you out of trouble again," Calu commented.

Mari couldn't helping smiling. "Yeah. Just like old times."

"These guys are Rob of Larharbor—" one of the new Mechanics nodded to Mari—"and Tess of Emdin and Amal of Farland."

Mari saw how closely Rob was sitting to one of the healers, a woman about his age. "And you're healers?"

The woman nodded. "Cas and Pol of Julesport. Brother and sister. We'll do all we can for, uh…"

"My Mage," Mari said.

"And then can we come with you?" She reached for the hand of Mechanic Rob. "My brother just wants to help you, but Rob and I have wanted to get married for years. The Guild blocked it."

"They're cracking down on any relationships with commons," Rob explained.

"It's gotten even crazier lately," Calu agreed. "You've really got them scared, Mari."

"I haven't done all that much," she said. "Alain and I have mostly just tried to stay alive."

"And get your hands on forbidden Mechanic texts," Bev added.

"Well, yeah, that, too."

The other Mechanics stared at her. "Forbidden texts?" Amal asked. "From the Guild vaults?"

Despite her fatigue, Mari perked up a little at the topic. "Yes. There is some amazing stuff in there. Wait until you see it."

"We'll all get to see the texts?"

"Everyone will," Mari said. She knew they wouldn't think she meant literally everyone. They would assume that she only intended other Mechanics. But she was too tired at the moment to explain, and argue, that the texts should be seen by commons and even by Mages as well.

She was surprised when the hull of the *Gray Lady* loomed above them, the masts of the ship rising skyward like angular trees shorn of leaves. A barge lay next to the ship, its open deck laden with crates, boxes and barrels which were being hoisted up and onto the *Gray Lady* using lines that ran through tackle on some of the spars. The crew, who didn't seem to find the need to haul a limp body aboard the least bit unusual, brought over one of the lines being used as a hoist, passing a large loop over Alain's head and arms and using it to pull him up to the deck. "They're familiar enough with it," the captain explained to Mari. "In every port one or two sailors takes on way too much booze and needs a bit of help up the side."

Mari stood on deck, trying to decide what to do as the healers and some of the crew carried Alain into the cabin. Once again she was torn by conflicting responsibilities. She finally went to the rail, watching as the rest came aboard and the launch headed back for the quay. "Captain, we need to be ready to leave as soon as the launch returns and the people it carries get aboard."

The captain looked at the sky. "Lady, it's not the best night for sneaking out of a harbor. A bit too bright and clear, with a nearly full moon."

"Make the best of it," Mari ordered. "The Mage Guild is not going to be happy when they realize we got Mage Alain away from the Dark Mages."

"The Mage Guild?" The captain blew out a long breath. "I once saw a leviathan turn a bigger ship than this to matchsticks. What about the Mechanics Guild?"

"You can see they're trying to get steam up on their ship. That's going to take a little while, but we want to have disappeared before they can start chasing us. Did we get all of the supplies that we need?"

"Aye," the captain said. "Better quality than we usually have, as well, and I was told it was all paid for."

"All of it? I didn't—" Mari exhaled heavily. "It's too late to argue now."

"How many more are coming, may I ask, Lady?"

"Four or five, I think. It depends if Mage Dav makes it back."

She looked over to where the Mechanic ship was working to get up steam, smoke gushing from its stack visible even against the night sky. "What are they doing?" she asked Bev. "There's way too much smoke."

"I'm not a steam specialist," Bev said, "but I'd guess they're trying to get the boiler going as fast as possible."

"They'll crack the bricks lining the boiler if they're not careful," Mari said. "Why do I think that there's a Senior Mechanic standing over the captain of that Mechanic ship demanding they move faster?"

"Rules are for regular Mechanics," Bev said. "How are you going to run things once the Guild is gone?"

"What?" Mari turned a baffled gaze on her.

"Once the Mechanics Guild is overthrown, somebody is going to have to make new rules. Somebody is going to have to set up some way of running things if the Senior Mechanics are out of the picture. I know Alli and Dav are just sort of assuming you'll be that somebody, and I bet everyone else will, too."

Mari stared at the waters of the harbor, aghast. "Oh, no."

"You can't do worse than the Senior Mechanics have," Bev said, a sudden dark edge entering her voice. "They—" She struggled to control herself. "They've got a lot to answer for," she finally got out.

"Bev, I'm sorry. Whatever it was."

Bev pointed over the side, changing the subject. "Here comes the launch. Looks like Mage Dav collected a few friends."

Mari stared. There were five figures in Mage robes among the others. Mage Dav and Mage Asha made two. Who were the other three?

Mage Asha was first on deck, looking as unconcerned as ever.

"Asha," Mari said, "who are those other Mages?"

"Mage Dav found some who sought us," Asha said. "They seek different wisdom."

"He's sure they can be trusted?"

"Mage Dav would not have brought them along if he was not certain." Asha turned her gaze on Mari. "My uncle...likes...you. Is that the right word?"

"I don't know," Mari said, startled. "Why does he like me?"

"He is a Mage, and one of no great standing, but you treat him with the same courtesy and concern you grant Mechanics. Your trust is also welcome and unexpected, for Mage Dav knows how Mages are seen by others." She paused, her face shadowed. "That has always been difficult for Mage Dav, to know he was seen as a monster."

"It was hard for Alain, too," Mari said. "I hated knowing how the commons looked at me behind my back. Oh, they're very respectful to Mechanics to their faces, but if you turned around quickly enough you'd see their true feelings. And I couldn't blame the commons, seeing how some of my fellow Mechanics treated them."

"Mages have always treated shadows as nothing," Asha said.

"They don't have to be nothing, Asha. Alain is a Mage and he sees me as real, and I think he's seeing a lot of other people that way, too."

"I watch and I listen," Asha said. "I learn."

Mage Dav came up the ladder, followed by the three other Mages with their faces concealed under the hoods of their robes. Mage Dav nodded to Mari and led the other Mages to a spot on deck where they would be least in the way. There all four sat down facing each other in a tight circle.

"Are those…safe Mages?" the captain asked in a worried voice.

"Mage Dav vouches for them," Mari said. "If they can't behave themselves they won't stay. For now, try to work around them. How soon can we get underway?"

"We're taking in the line to the anchor buoy now."

Mari looked over the side, seeing that Alli, Mechanic Dav and the fourth new Mechanic were all coming up the ladder. The launch was just pushing off, the boat officer and the rowers pausing to wave enthusiastic farewells.

Waving back, Mari felt the *Gray Lady* begin moving as her sails unfurled and began catching the wind.

"We have the tide with us," the captain said, "but it's a long ways out of the harbor. Hopefully any galleys outside the harbor will be caught napping when we leave."

"Whoa!" Bev said loudly enough to cause everyone to look at her, and then at what she was looking at.

Mari saw the cloud of smoke from the Mechanic ship was now lit from beneath by showers of sparks and a few actual flames coming from the stack. "They split their boiler. Lucky it happened before they had pressure up, or half this harbor would have felt the explosion."

"Think they'll lose the ship?" Alli asked, coming up to Mari. "I hope it was all right to let Mage Dav bring those other Mages with us."

"Yeah. I trust Mage Dav." Mari took another look toward the stricken steamship. "The flames seem to be subsiding. I think they'll save the ship, but it's not going to be going anywhere soon. Alli, we have to keep everyone alert and ready until we clear this harbor. Get the other two rifles distributed. I'll give mine to Calu since I have my pistol."

"Got it."

Mari leaned on the rail, feeling exhausted, grateful that she could depend on Alli to manage the other Mechanics. Calu could do it, too, for that matter. "Mage Asha, can you tell if any Mages are working on big spells?"

Asha shook her head. "I do not sense such activity near the harbor. The elders have no doubt been surprised. But it would not be wise to give them time to overcome their surprise."

As badly as she wanted to run into the cabin to find out how the healers were doing with Alain, Mari held herself at the rail, watching the dark shapes of anchored ships slide by with increasing speed as the *Gray Lady* tacked through the harbor. They were so close to getting out of Julesport in one piece.

The *Gray Lady* glided gently toward the exit from the harbor, her sails drawing well on the light breeze. Of necessity, her course was bringing the *Gray Lady* close by the largest Confederation warship in the harbor, a three-masted frigate mounting two big ballistae on her deck. Looking like giant crossbows, the ballistae could be pivoted to fire off either side. But Mari saw no reason to be worried about the Confederation warship. She kept her eyes forward, searching for any signs of Syndari galleys near the harbor mouth.

Her complacency was rudely shattered by a hail from the Confederation warship. "Ahoy the clipper! Shorten your sails!"

Mari spun to look at the warship, seeing crewmembers running along the deck and up the rigging while others rushed to the ballistae. "I don't believe it. Why is the Confederation moving against us?"

Alli was standing beside her again. "Alain's still out cold, isn't he?"

"As far as I know."

"Can any of the other Mages do that fire thing?"

"Asha?"

"No," Asha said, her lack of emotion making the single word sound oddly complacent.

Mari ran through options in her mind and didn't find any good ones. Without Alain, their ability to defeat the big warship was pretty much nonexistent. "Alli, get our Mechanics lined up and ready to fire. Mage Asha, if you or the other Mages can disable that ship somehow, let me know."

"We are on the water. There is little power here."

"Of course," Mari grumbled. "Captain! Tell that warship that we've got clearance to leave this harbor! Colonel Faron gave us clearance!"

The captain of the *Gray Lady* complied, raising his speaking trumpet. "Ahoy the warship! We've got clearance to leave! Courtesy of Colonel Faron of Julesport!"

Mari watched the crew of the warship continue their frantic activity, bringing up the anchor and loosing sails. Others were swinging out the ballistae. Mari saw her small group of Mechanics at the rail of the Gray Lady, measured them against the number of sailors on the warship, and knew even six Mechanic rifles couldn't hope to deal with this threat.

"Ahoy the clipper!" the hail from the warship came again. "Shorten sail now!"

CHAPTER FIVE

The captain of the *Gray Lady* shook his head, looking at Mari. "Unless you've a miracle handy, Lady, I'd recommend doing as they say."

My miracle is still unconscious in a bunk, Mari thought bitterly. "If we don't comply and that warship opens fire at this range, we'll be ripped apart. At the least, we need to buy time. Do it!" she yelled at the captain.

The captain shouted the necessary orders and his sailors raced aloft to pull in the *Gray Lady*'s sails, reducing the amount of area the wind could strike and therefore causing the small clipper's speed to fall off. The captain raised his speaking trumpet again. "We're shortening sail."

"Thank you!" the warship called back.

Alli looked back at Mari. "Thank you?"

Mari stared at the warship, then gave the *Gray Lady*'s captain a perplexed look. "Are Confederation warships normally that polite when they're trying to intercept other ships?"

The captain looked equally baffled. "Not in my experience. Not polite at all."

The voice from the warship called again. "Shorten sail more! You'll be too far ahead!"

"I thought that was the idea," Bev complained. "Aren't we trying to escape? What's going on?"

Once again the captain shook his head to indicate he didn't know. Mari hit her limit. "I can't fight people when I don't even know if they're trying to fight me!" She strode aft and took the speaking trumpet from the captain. "On the warship! Why are you asking us to slow down?"

After a brief pause, the warship called back. "Weren't you told?"

Mari glared around the deck of the *Gray Lady*. "Was anybody told anything?" Blank stares met her question. She raised the speaking trumpet again. "No! What should we have been told?"

"The Confederation is tired of the Syndaris harassing shipping. At the request of the Julesport city council, Confederation warships *Intrepid* and *Gallant* have been ordered to leave the harbor immediately and prevent any Syndari galleys from interfering with free commerce."

"I'll be damned," the captain said, for once at a loss for other words.

"You're escorting us out of the harbor?" Mari called back.

"No! We do not see any ships leaving the harbor at this time! There is only open water off of our port side! Whiskey whiskey, nora nora. Please shorten sail more so you don't get too far ahead of us!"

Mari lowered the speaking trumpet and looked at the captain. "Whiskey whiskey, nora nora?"

The captain grinned. "That stands for wink wink, nudge nudge. Sailor talk. They're pretending we're not here."

"But…why?"

"Because the Great Guilds would take it very badly if the Confederation rendered aid to you, Lady. But if the Confederation just happens to decide to get tough with the Syndaris at the same time as you're escaping from Julesport? How could anyone have known that was happening? So sorry, Great Guilds, we didn't mean it and we'll never do it again." The captain's smile shone in the moonlight. "But as for us, the only ones who have to fear that warship this morning are any Syndari galleys waiting outside the harbor."

"This morning?" Mari looked around at the dark sky and the bright moon above.

"It's well past midnight, Lady. A new day, if you'll pardon the term."

Mari heard cheering and stared blankly down the length of the ship. All of the crew and all of the Mechanics were looking at her and applauding.

"Nice," Alli approved as she walked up to Mari.

"What are you talking about?"

"This." Alli waved around. "We get in to harbor safe, we get our supplies, we rescue Alain, we pick up some new friends including Calu—and do I ever owe you for that—and now we just got out this mess without a shot being fired!"

"I did not—" Mari tried to gather her thoughts. "I didn't do any of that. No. I led the rescue of Alain. But not the rest."

"Mari, you're the most modest friend I've got," Alli said with a laugh, "as well as the most brilliant. Accept the praise. You earned it."

"You are all out of your minds," Mari complained.

❊   ❊   ❊

All lights extinguished, the *Gray Lady* kept to the lee of the two Confederation warships as they charged out at four Syndari galleys drifting near the entrance to the harbor. As the galleys scattered to avoid the frigates, the *Gray Lady* slipped past unseen and sailed due west until the lights of Julesport, the frigates, and the galleys all vanished beneath the horizon.

Only then, alone in the wide expanse of the Jules Sea, did the *Gray Lady* turn south. The sun rising off the port side gilded the masts and sails of the clipper ship as she rode before a freshening breeze that sang through the rigging, cleaving the waters en route the broad, clear reaches of the great Umbari Ocean.

Mari, staggering with weariness, finally felt free to head down to the cabin. The *Gray Lady* had begun rolling in the choppy seas, which made her progress even more difficult, but Mari refused to ask anyone for help. She knew she was being stubborn, but she was going to get through this day even if it killed her.

Holding onto the cabin door for dear life, Mari made it inside, where the two healers were still with Alain.

She made it to the bunk and sat down on the edge, brushing his forehead with one hand. Alain's face, relaxed in sleep, looked as young as it had the first time they had met. Her mind, half-delirious with fatigue, generated a powerful vision of that moment, when a panicky Mari had through pure reflexive distrust almost put a bullet into the Mage coming toward her out of the dust clouds. "We've certainly come a long way from that caravan in the Waste outside of Ringhmon, haven't we, my Mage?" she asked.

Someone cleared his throat and Mari, with a guilty start, looked at the healers. "I'm sorry. Is he going to be all right?"

The woman named Cas smiled. "Yes. Probably weak, and he may be in pain when he awakens, not only because of the after-effects of the drug but because of this." She gently raised Alain's head to indicate a bandaged area.

"He hit his head?" Mari asked.

"Something hit his head," Pol corrected. He looked tired, too, but satisfied. "It looks like the sort of injury caused by a sap arrow."

"A what?"

"A sap arrow," Pol explained. "A sap is a leather-covered weight that's used by thieves and kidnappers to knock out their prey. There's a special arrow for small crossbows that has a sap instead of a point and is fired with less force than a lethal arrow. Only criminals use it. We were told Dark Mages did this?"

"That's right," Mari said. "I mean, it looks like the Mage Guild Hall in Julesport hired some Dark Mages to do it."

"Slime-sucking bottom-dwellers," Cas muttered angrily. "We've dealt with the results of their work before. You're lucky you found him quickly."

There was something else important, something that she needed to ask about. What was it? "The drug. Is that going to cause any problems?"

"Doubtful," Cas replied. "There's always a little concern that even someone young and strong could be thrown into addiction after only a single dose of a drug like that, but it's very rare. It usually takes frequent use to develop addiction and create physical problems. Assuming Mages are like other people, I think it more likely he'll have developed a physical aversion to this drug based on this experience."

Pol nodded in agreement. "Is he...like other people, Lady? We couldn't find any differences, but Mages—well, you know."

Mari almost laughed, but she couldn't muster the strength. "Alain is like everyone else, and like no one else. He is the most amazing, important..." Her voice faltered. "Thank you so much. I'm sorry. It's been...a...very...long...day."

She had the vague sensation of being helped into another bunk, then fell fast asleep, aware only of the smile on her lips. Alain was all right.

Mage Alain awoke to find himself in a bunk aboard a ship that was plainly at sea, rolling as it cut through swells. Alain puzzled over that. He knew he was a Mage, but for the moment nothing else came clear to him. He had no memories of a ship leaving port, or of getting aboard a ship. He had been walking down a street in...Julesport. A group of common soldiers about him? Worrying about...Mari. And—

Mari? Who was—?

For a moment he was surrounded by dust, hearing the crashing of strange weapons, the blood of commons spattering his robes, the caravan destroyed around him, ready to die but walking as if in a dream toward the last wagon where someone might survive, seeing a figure in a dark jacket appear before him—

Mari.

Everything flooded back into him, memories and feelings and emotions that left Alain gasping. A vast emptiness that once had been all he had was suddenly full once more, full because of her, and he felt a sudden rush of worry. What had happened to him? Where was Mari?

He twisted to look, almost wincing at a sudden pain on the back of his head. But he could see the other bunk, and Mari lashed into it so she couldn't be tossed out by the ship's motion.

This was the *Gray Lady*. Mari was safe, a trace of a smile on her face.

Alain sat up cautiously, feeling the back of his head. A bandage. That explained the pain there. But he also felt odd, a roiling of the stomach and an aching of his arms and legs that felt like the after-effects of eating spoiled food.

What had happened? Alain looked at Mari, guessing that she would know, but tracing with his eyes the great weariness that held her deeply asleep. He had seen her like this before, when Mari had pushed herself too far and too long because she thought she must, because others needed her, because she would not leave anyone behind. If he woke her now she would abandon sleep and get back to whatever tasks awaited. He knew that, and so Alain stood cautiously and moved toward the cabin door as quietly as he could.

He stepped outside, slightly dizzy and grateful for the door's support before he closed it.

"Alain! You're all right!"

Alain blinked in confusion at the Mechanic standing before him. He knew that face from somewhere. Somewhere cold. "Mechanic Calu? Friend of Mari?"

"That's me." Calu studied him, looking worried. "Take it easy. You still look a little beat up."

"Apparently I have been beat up." Alain indicated the bandage on the back of his head. "Do you know how?"

"Only what I was told." Calu helped Alain sit down on a barrel lashed to the front of the cabin. "You got knocked out by some Dark Mages. Mari led a rescue and found you with Mage Asha's help."

"How was that possible?" Alain wondered. "I will have to ask Mage Asha. Wait. How did you come to be here? You were in Umburan."

"Sure was," Calu agreed. He leaned against the cabin next to Alain, his Mechanics jacket dark against the wood. "But the Mechanics Guild has gotten even more worried about Mari. You remember I got sent to Umburan because the Guild was trying to break up Mari's old gang? Which wasn't really a gang, but anyway. The Senior Mechanics have been moving people between Guild Halls a lot more, trying to keep any gangs from forming. That's how I ended up in Julesport. That's the official reason, anyway. I suspect the Guild thought Mari might go to Julesport and figured that if I was there she'd try to contact me. They've been watching me pretty close, but what they didn't know was that two of the Mechanics supposedly keeping an eye on me were just as eager to join Mari as I was."

"Mechanic Alli was worried about you," Alain said, still gathering his thoughts.

"He needs to be watched or he gets into trouble," Alli said, coming up and putting one arm around Calu. "How are you doing, Alain? You looked pretty bad when we carried you out of that Dark Mage den. The healers said you might be hurting. Are you in any pain?"

"It is nothing," Alain said.

"Is everything nothing with you Mages?" Alli asked. "There's some pain medication you are supposed to take if you need it."

Alain shook his head. "I do not need it. I have endured far worse pain than this."

Alli shook her head in turn, then looked at Calu. "Mari has been telling me some things about the training Mages get when they're—not apprentices…acolytes. It is seriously ugly. Take a look sometime and you'll see all of the Mages, even Asha, have lots of scars."

"I didn't think you wanted me looking at Mage Asha," Calu said. "Scars? I saw them on you before, Alain, and I thought maybe they were from that fight in the desert or at Dorcastle. I'm really sorry."

"Why?" Alain asked.

"Because it must have been pretty tough on you, and on the other Mages."

"Oh." He still had trouble grasping the way shadows thought, of how they could care for others while also doing things that harmed others. How could someone like Alli see others as real and yet also be able to point a Mechanic weapon at them? Mari could do the same, but he knew it caused her great distress. Perhaps Alli hid her distress the way a Mage would. "We are heading for Tiae?"

"Yes," Alli said. "Though Calu and I have been talking about something that might alter that a bit. We'll talk to you when we've argued it out. In the meantime, you might want to check out our other new friends."

He saw some anxiety in her and looked where Alli indicated. Sitting in a circle on the deck were five Mages, not two as he would have expected.

"Mage Asha and Mage Dav have been with them, but otherwise they haven't interacted with anybody," Alli added. "Those three act like regular Mages and—well, it's a little difficult."

"I will speak with them," Alain said. "You are worried that they might harm someone?"

"Yeah. Mage Dav says they're all right, but, uh…"

"I understand." The reputation of Mages—that they treated others as merely playthings—was well established and, Alain knew, well earned. Why care about the lives and well-being of shadows? But he had learned otherwise and so must these new Mages. Alain stood up carefully, still feeling weak.

Calu immediately offered a steadying hand. "Take it easy. Let us know if you need anything."

"Mari may be out cold, but we've got your back," Alli said.

It made no sense, did not comport with the wisdom taught to Mages, but Alain felt stronger at that moment. Strong enough to manage a small smile of reassurance and then walk steadily to where the other Mages sat.

Asha looked up as Alain approached, one corner of her mouth twitching slightly in the way of a Mage who had not yet relearned how to smile. She moved aside in the tight circle so that Alain could seat himself next to her.

Alain looked around the tight circle of hooded figures. Mage Asha was next to him, and next to her Mage Dav. Then a male Mage who bore the marks of advanced age, another male Mage not much older than Alain, and a female Mage of middle years. All looked back at him in the way of Mages, barely acknowledging his presence and giving no sign of how they felt about it.

"Mage Alain," Alain said, introducing himself to the eldest first.

"Mage Hiro," the old man said.

"Elder Hiro," Mage Dav corrected.

"No longer." Mage Hiro's voice and face gave no clue as to whether he felt regret over that. "I have known the wisdom I was taught is lacking. I seek new wisdom."

The young man spoke next. "Mage Dimitri. I cannot see all as shadows, yet I have some power. The elders could not explain, but they could punish."

Then the woman. "Mage Tana. Like Mage Hiro, I have had questions, and no longer will keep silent."

Mage Hiro gestured slightly at Alain. "Mage Dav says you see one other as real?"

"This is so," Alain admitted, realizing that his own face and voice were growing as impassive as the other Mages'. He let it happen, knowing it would help them believe his words. "Master Mechanic Mari. She is real."

"Yet you have power? Show us."

Mage Asha indicated Alain's bandage. "He has been injured."

"I see this," Hiro said. "I feel how little power there is here. I would know what Mage Alain can do when injured, with little outside himself to draw on."

It was the sort of test that elders would demand to judge the abilities of younger Mages. Alain nodded once, seeing out of the corner of his eye that Mechanics Alli and Calu were watching the group from a distance. Watching him. Because Mari cared for him, they did also.

It gave him a confidence and a strength that had been lacking. Alain wrapped himself in the spell that granted invisibility, causing the illusion that light itself bent around him. He held it, feeling his strength draining quickly, then finally dropped the spell.

Mage Tana measured Alain with her gaze. "One who could manage that under such conditions is not weak."

"But he was taken by the Dark Mages," the young Mage said.

Hiro dismissed the comment with another sharp gesture. "See the bandage. A blow from behind. The smallest illusion can defeat the one thing that is real. The mightiest Mage can be felled by a single rock. You know this."

"I do not question that wisdom."

"Has your art changed?" Hiro asked Alain. "Because you see the Mechanic as real?"

"No. The means by which I place a smaller illusion over the greater illusion of the world has not changed. My art has only grown more powerful," Alain said, drawing some barely visible reaction from the three new Mages.

"She accepts your wisdom?" Mage Tana asked. "This Mari?"

"She does," Alain said, swinging his hand slightly to include Alli and Calu. "As do other Mechanics who follow her. They do not understand our wisdom, they strive to see how it works and cannot, but unlike their Guild they accept that it is valid."

"And their tricks?" Hiro said. "The Mechanic toys? You have seen them?"

"They work also," Alain said.

"This is a conflict," Tana observed. "Wisdom says the world illusion cannot be changed so by other illusions."

Alain paused to think, to put into words ideas that he had only slowly been developing. "There is more than one wisdom," he finally said. "More than one path. The wisdom of Mages does things that of Mechanics cannot. Mari says many Mechanics cannot accept this and so deny it. But the wisdom of Mechanics can do things to the world illusion that the arts of the Mages cannot. I have seen this, and so cannot deny it."

"There was a heresy," Mage Hiro said. "Two generations gone. It held that more than one wisdom can coexist, that there were different ways of seeing the world illusion that could produce very different arts. The heresy was suppressed, but if the Mechanic arts can work, it may offer a wisdom that explains it."

"But to see others as real," Mage Tana objected. "Can other Mages accept this and still have power?"

Mage Asha spoke. "I have begun to see one other as real. He…does not harm my power. He gives me a new way to see my wisdom."

"Why did you take this risk?"

"Because I saw Mage Alain and Mechanic Mari, and I knew Mage Alain had not lost in any way. I wanted to share what they had."

"With them?" Mage Tana pressed. "Do they take you into their sharing?"

"Not in that way," Asha said. "They share their reality only with each other. But they offer something else to friends."

"Friends," Mage Dimitri whispered. "I remember friends."

"You may remember again," Mage Dav said. "It is not forbidden among us. Mechanic Mari calls me friend. She saved me from dying where another would have left me."

"Mechanic Mari," Mage Hiro said. "I have seen this one, when we came on this ship. You were the Mage who declared her the daughter of the prophecy?" he asked Alain.

"I was the first who saw her so," Alain said.

"You are not the only. I see her and see the same. If she lives, she has a chance to fulfill the prophecy."

Alain managed to suppress the fear that statement created inside him. *If she lives.*

Hiro kept speaking. "There was another. When I was only a boy, barely become an acolyte. A daughter born in the southern lands."

"I have not heard of this," Mage Dimitri said.

"You are young," Hiro said. "And you have not had access to the secrets of the Mage Guild as an elder does. The Guild denies that the prophecy exists even as it hunts those who might fulfill it."

"What became of that daughter?" Alain asked.

"She died. The records are vague as to who saw her and who betrayed her, but in the end she was alone and slain. Thus did the Mage Guild seek to ensure the prophecy would never come true."

"Could there have been others?" Mage Asha asked.

"There could have been," Mage Hiro replied. "It has been long since the prophecy was made, and the Mage Guild has sought to end its threat ever since."

"The Mechanics Guild does the same," Alain said. "They sought to kill Master Mechanic Mari even before I met her. They would have succeeded, if not for me." He did not say it as a boast, but as a statement of what had been, and knew the others would see it that way as well.

"So? This daughter, this shadow, is not alone." Hiro looked intently at Alain. "She has recognized wisdom and held it close to her. It has saved her, and she has helped you see new wisdom."

"She has lived because of that," Alain agreed. "As have I. Alone, I would have died."

"Alone, both would have died." Hiro pondered that, his eyes hooded.

"I am thinking," Mage Dav said, "that this wisdom is an old one, a wisdom forgotten by the Guild. We are taught that only the one is real, that only each of us should matter to each of us. Yet see the strength in Mage Alain, who has survived where older and wiser Mages would not have. He has lived because added to his strength and wisdom is the strength and wisdom of Master Mechanic Mari. Together there is something greater than each can claim alone."

A flicker of pain flashed across the face of Mage Tana. "I once— There was a time, Mage Dav, when I had a chance at such wisdom."

"You are not the only," Mage Hiro said. "Perhaps all who see such a chance realize the faults in the wisdom of the Guild. Perhaps not."

"We all follow the words of shadows," Mage Dav said. "For if what the elders of the Mage Guild teach is the only truth, then they are shadows to us. If all wisdom comes from the illusion that surrounds us, how can the sole reality which is me be the only source of wisdom?

Is wisdom but the echo of my own thought, or is there something outside to which I must listen?"

The others looked at Mage Dav with visible respect. "We will follow Mage Alain, and Mage Dav, and learn," Mage Hiro said.

Mage Tana and Mage Dimitri nodded in agreement.

"Master Mechanic Mari requires that all who follow her treat others as real," Alain cautioned. "You need not attempt to think of them as real, but they cannot be treated as only shadows."

"It is odd, but not difficult," Mage Tana observed. "One of discipline can act as they will, not as habit dictates."

"Just so," Mage Dav agreed.

"Excuse me, Mage Alain." Alain turned to see that Mechanic Alli had approached them. She crouched down so that her eyes were on a level with Alain's. "I'm not sure how long your talk is going to last, and there is something we need your approval on. Yours or Mari's, and none of us want to wake her up."

"What is this something?" Alain asked, aware of how the other Mages were observing without giving outward signs of doing so.

"Calu says the day before we got into Julesport, a Mechanics Guild ship left carrying a lot of Mechanics. It's a three-masted ship, the *Pride of Longfalls*. They were headed for Edinton. But it's being used as a prison ship, collecting and transporting Mechanics to exile. Most of the Mechanics aboard are the sort of people who would likely join with Mari."

Alain considered that. "Mari needs more Mechanic followers?"

"Yes," Alli said. "We're going to Tiae to fix the Broken Kingdom, right? That's not going to be easy, even if we find enough common soldiers to deal with the warlords and bandits that have made Tiae a living nightmare. A lot of stuff needs to be done by people. Hands-on work to build things, and Mechanics know how to do that. The more Mechanics we have with us, the more we can get done and the faster we can do it. So if we can overtake that ship, the *Pride*, and free those Mechanics, it might help a lot."

"We would have to defeat the guards," Alain said. "Capture the ship."

"Right. It's not risk-free. But the captain of the *Gray Lady* says the *Pride* is, uh, square-rigged, and will have to tack back and forth a lot in these winds to head for Edinton. The *Lady* is square-rigged and fore-and-aft rigged, so she can sail a lot straighter, which means we could probably overtake the *Pride* in a couple of days."

"I do not know what square means," Alain said. "But the captain of the *Gray Lady* has his own wisdom. I have not seen him err in matters of the sea. If we seek to find the Mechanic ship *Pride*, does it force us to fight that ship?"

Alli shook her head. "No. It will just put us in a position to do something if Mari decides to. But the captain doesn't want to alter course to do that unless Mari says so, or unless you say Mari would be all right with it."

"Tell the captain that Mage Alain agrees with the wisdom of what you wish to do," Alain said.

"Great. Thanks." Alli straightened with a grin that changed to an uncertain look as she nodded to the other Mages and walked aft again.

Mage Tana spoke softly. "The Mechanic spoke to you as an elder. She sought your approval and accepted your authority."

"Mechanic Alli helped save Mage Alain from the Dark Mages," Mage Asha said. "She is…different, but she has a wisdom of her own. She will return in kind whatever is given her."

"Given?" Tana puzzled over that. "There is much to think on."

Alain spent much of the day regaining his strength and thinking, sitting on deck with his back against the door to the cabin where Mari still slept the sleep of exhaustion. While the Mechanics he could see and hear were clearly happy, and the other Mages remained in deep discussion or meditation, Alain's thoughts were dark.

If she lives.

There was another…she died.

He remembered Mari's face when he told her that she was the daughter. What had she said? Something about her life being worth only dust because of all those who would want the daughter dead. He had felt awful then, but mainly because of how his words had distressed Mari. He had not wanted to think too much about the fact that her words were also true.

But it was getting difficult to ignore. Mari's dreams were often troubled now, and when she would speak of them she would talk of assassins and death stalking her and her friends. How much comfort could he offer when those dreams were not fantasies but a reflection of the dangers Mari and her friends actually faced?

He could change small parts of the world illusion for short times, but he could not change that.

"Are you all right?"

Alain looked up to see Mechanic Bev nearby. He had long been able to tell that Bev held some secret inside, some pain that she would not share with others. But now she stood eyeing him with concern.

"I am...all right," Alain said.

"You know," she said, "there are a lot of jokes about how much Mages lie, but I never actually caught one at it before. What is it? Is Mari all right?"

"Mari is well. Just tired. And worried."

"Do you mind?" Bev sat down beside him, looking out across the deck. "Mari spends most of her time worrying about the rest of us, and you, and how she's supposed to make this prophecy come true before the world blows up. Every once in a while she stops to think about what might happen to her personally and she gets really scared. I can see it. I don't blame her. I couldn't handle it if it was me. But she's got you. So it worries me a bit when I see you looking scared."

"You saw—?"

"I could tell. I doubt anyone else could. Maybe another one of you Mages." Bev sighed. "It's easy to be scared. To be so scared you don't know how to face it. I know. But you have to keep going."

"I know this," Alain said. "Sometimes it is hard."

"Sometimes it is very hard," Bev said. "You need to be honest with Mari when it is. She thinks you're built of the finest steel alloy and can't crack. But nobody is that strong."

"You are right," Alain said. "Nobody can stand alone."

"Nobody," Bev whispered. "Here I am giving you good advice that I can't follow myself. There's something I can't talk about to people. Not even Mari. But maybe I really sat down here because I have to say something to somebody. I've heard about the kind of hell you went through when you were an acolyte. So maybe you'd understand."

Alain simply nodded, waiting.

"The Senior Mechanics run the Mechanics Guild," Bev said in a very low voice, her eyes on the deck now. "They make the rules and they're supposed to enforce the rules. Maybe you've already heard how much they abuse that power. At the Guild Hall in Emdin where I was an apprentice…" She paused for a long moment. "They lost control of themselves. Completely lost control. They started—"

Bev paused again, swallowing. "It was physical, you know? Not just beatings. I could handle that. Other stuff. And being told it was our duty as apprentices to do everything we were told, to keep quiet about it, to just submit."

"They did this not to teach, but to harm?" Alain asked.

"Oh, they were teaching us stuff," Bev said. "Stuff about how little we mattered, how we were just toys for them, how the people in charge could do anything they wanted and we had to go along with it."

"Mechanic Alli said something about Emdin."

"Yeah. Rumors got out eventually, and then three apprentices committed suicide. Not one by one but all at once. That got the attention of the Guild Headquarters at Palandur, which had somehow avoided seeing anything before that. They had to do something, and there are some Senior Mechanics who aren't monsters. They pushed for an investigation."

Alain waited.

"So," Bev continued, her eyes still on the deck, "investigators came and talked to us and heard everything. And then some of the Senior Mechanics at Emdin were sent to other Guild Halls, and some of the apprentices were sent to other Guild Halls, and all of us were sworn to secrecy and told that if we ever said anything then every single detail would come out and we wouldn't want that, would we? For everyone to know everything that had been done to us?"

"There was no punishment of the elders, of the Senior Mechanics?" said Alain.

"No. For the good of the Guild. Had to keep it quiet. What would the Mage Guild have done? Does that sort of thing happen there?"

Alain shook his head. "No. Not the same. The elders and the Mages who teach acolytes would beat us. They would inflict harm, and with-hold food and water, and leave us to stand freezing in the winter. To enable us to ignore the world illusion, you see. It had a purpose. Sometimes an elder or a Mage would be…too enthusiastic. They would beat and harm in ways that could cause permanent damage. That was not allowed, and they would be sent away, not allowed to teach anymore."

"But what about other stuff? Did acolytes ever get abused?"

"It is different," Alain said, trying to find the words to explain. "Mages are taught that physical relations do not matter except that they are distractions from wisdom. They should be satisfied as quickly and efficiently as possible. And then move on and focus once again on the wisdom that says others do not matter."

"There's no power in it," Bev said. "Your elders and Mages couldn't get any thrills out of that kind of power trip, could they? Because I knew it was about power, mostly. Some of them hurt you in ways that did satisfy their power thrills, but abusing you wasn't one of them because you were all being taught it didn't matter. Did thinking that way make you happy?"

Alain shook his head again. "Happy did not exist. Happy was an illusion. After enough time, we all believed that."

"They stole something else from you," Bev whispered.

"What they stole, I was able to find again," Alain said. "I wish…I wish I could change the illusion so that you had not been hurt. Mari reminded me that the shadows around me feel pain just as I do. But there is so little I can do to stop that pain. It is easier to think of them just as shadows. But Mari never does the easy thing."

"And she won't let you, either, huh?" Bev blew out a long breath. "Thanks for wanting to make it go away, but it never will. Do you hate the elders who hurt you?"

"No. They could not make me into what they desired. They failed. I feel...contempt? I do not care about them. They are as nothing, even as other shadows become something." Alain shrugged. "That is what I tell myself. Mage Asha suffered worse than I did. I used to wonder at how strong in wisdom she was. But she rarely talks of those times."

"That's easy for me to understand. You know, I worried that you could tell about me. That being a Mage could let you see something." Bev shut her eyes tightly. "I worry that everyone can look at me and tell, but Mages mostly."

"I saw nothing except pain," Alain said. "No Mage could see more than that, and no Mage would guess the cause."

"Mages lie all the time," Bev said. "Why do I believe you?"

"Mari would not like it if I caused you more hurt, and I would not like it if I caused you more hurt."

"Um...thanks. Don't tell Mari any of this, all right? Except, tell her I'm all right when it comes to doing things. I won't lose it, I won't go crazy, I won't let her down. She can count on that." Bev paused. "So can you. Thanks, Mage Alain. Just for listening. I had to tell somebody."

Alain felt a helpless sensation. "I can do nothing, though."

"You listened. You didn't judge. You won't tell others. That's more than I could ask of anyone else. Thanks." Bev got up, nodded at him, then walked off slowly.

Alain got up as well, opened the door to the cabin very quietly, and walked inside.

Mari was still deeply asleep, snoring lightly. He sat down on the other bunk, watching her, remembering that she had asked whether she snored while they waited to enter Marandur. They had survived Marandur. Perhaps—

And in that moment, his foresight came upon him again.

Overlaid on his sight of Mari was a vision of her. In the vision, Mari was also lying down, but on a surface of dressed stone blocks, the sort that made up stout outdoor structures. Her face and mouth were slack, not with tiredness, but with the shadow of death upon them, a shadow hovering very near, and something red and wet stained her dark Mechanics jacket.

As Alain stared, horrified, the vision faded. Mari was sleeping, her expression untroubled for the moment.

But he could not forget what he had seen.

And he had not been in that vision. If he had been, it would have meant the vision was of something that might happen. But he had seen Mari only.

Which meant this was something that would happen.

CHAPTER SIX

Mari was not dead?" Mage Asha spoke softly, just as Alain had spoken to her. She was upset enough to betray the emotion and so both of them were at a rail, facing out to sea.

"She was dying," Alain managed to choke out.

"But not dead."

"No."

"Then she is fated to be badly hurt, but you did not see her dead." Asha locked eyes with him. "That means even if this comes to pass, you can make a difference."

"What difference is possible?" Alain asked. "You know as well as I that no Mage can directly affect a shadow. None of our spells can change a shadow in any way, for good or ill. Healing is impossible."

"Then find a way, Mage Alain! You were not in the vision. That must matter."

"How?"

"Perhaps if you are there, it will change things. If you are beside her, what you saw *will not be*."

Alain stopped to think, breathing deeply. "Mage Asha, that offers hope. But how can I learn a wisdom that has evaded all Mages before this?"

"That is something you must discover," Asha said. "How did Mari look? Was she older?"

"I could not tell," Alain said.

"It may have been something that will not happen for years."

"Not too many years," Alain said. "Mari looked as I know her."

"Listen," Asha said with an intensity that Alain had never heard from her. "If it is known that Mari is to be so badly injured, it will harm what she seeks to do. Mari will be terrified to act, and those who would follow her will hold back for fear she will fail. You must not speak of this to anyone else."

"I must tell Mari—"

"To what purpose?" Asha demanded. "Mage Alain, she is already haunted by fears. Will you now wave a bloody vision before her?"

"She deserves to know," Alain said.

"And if such knowing causes her to fail? If such knowing causes Mari to hold back at a moment when she must leap forward? If such knowing causes the Storm to triumph and all to be lost because her fears of failure make the failure come to pass?"

Alain stared out at the sea, where countless whitecaps appeared and disappeared in endless array. "I do not know."

"Ask yourself this," Asha said. "If it were Mari who had this vision of you, lying with death on your brow, would you want her to tell you?"

He had to think a long time about that, his thoughts circling around and avoiding the answer. "No," Alain finally admitted.

"What would Mari do?"

"She would work to...to change things. To fix things so that I would not die, regardless of what the vision shows. That is what she does."

"Then you do the same," Asha insisted. "Mage Alain, you are here for a reason, and that reason is not to bear helpless witness to the death of Mari. You are here to ensure that she succeeds in her task, and that she lives through every peril that task places in her path! I do not have foresight, but still I know this!"

Alain shook his head. "All is illusion. I cannot change so much."

"All cast shadows on the illusion, and such as Mari are fated to cast shadows that change the illusion itself," Asha said. "Your shadow is intertwined with that of Mari. Your fates are joined, just as your shadows are joined."

"I feel you are right," Alain said. "But it will be very hard not to tell Mari."

"And it would be easy to tell her," Asha said. "Easy to drop the burden of this foresight upon her even though she could do nothing with the knowledge but let it break her resolve. Should you do what is easy for you, or what is hard?"

"Hard," Alain said. "Mari would understand." He hoped that was so. "Your advice is good, Asha. Thank you. I did not know where else to turn."

"You are welcome," Asha said with the precision of someone who had just relearned the phrase. "Alain, you would have been my friend had either of us remembered what a friend was. Mari reached out to me when I could see only a shadow before me, and she showed me that I could regain so much I had lost. You and I are friends now because of Mari, and there is a chance that I will become more than a friend with Mechanic Dav because of Mari. I would not advise you in ways that I thought would hurt her, and if the worst comes to pass my grief will be second only to yours. But we will work to ensure the worst does not happen. Mari cannot bear every burden of being the daughter. This part of it must be ours."

He was sitting on the bunk in the cabin, watching her again, the setting sun low enough in the sky to slant through the windows looking out over the stern, when Mari finally woke up. She yawned hugely, then looked over at him. "Good morning. Is it morning?"

"Almost evening," Alain said.

"You look worried. Is anything wrong?"

"I am worried about you," Alain said, feeling bad speaking a half-truth to someone he never wanted to lie to.

"About me?" Mari sat up, wincing at the effort. "I think I pulled several muscles getting you back to this ship. I'll remind you that I wasn't the one who got kidnapped by Dark Mages. Where are we? And is there anything to eat?"

Alain produced a platter of meat, cheese, and bread. "The cook prepared this for you. Do you want wine or water?"

"Watered wine," Mari said around a mouthful of beef. "I see we're still heading south."

"There has been a slight change." Alain explained what Alli had told him about the Mechanic ship *Pride of Longfalls*.

"Good decision," she said. "We've still got about a day to think about it? Even better. Are you sure you're all right?"

"I am fine," Alain said.

"Do you remember anything?"

"Very little," Alain said. "I was on the street with the soldiers, then I recall nothing until I awoke aboard the ship. As this day has gone on I have had a few blurred memories, if that is what they are and not products of the drug I was told they used on me. There are a few images of a dark street crowded with people, and a woman."

"A woman?" Mari asked.

"Yes. I felt she was undressing me, which I do not understand."

"But you did remember it," Mari said, her voice growing sharp. "Men! Anything else?"

"No," Alain said. "My head has hurt some, and so has my hand." He flexed the fingers of his left hand. "The healers explained about my head, but I do not know what caused my hand to ache so."

Mari's attitude softened as swiftly as it had hardened a moment earlier. "Your left hand hurts because you are the most wonderful man who ever lived."

"I...what?"

She stood up carefully, both because of the rolling of the ship and because of the low overhead in the cabin. They had both knocked their heads on the wooden beams more than once. "I think we both deserve a hug. Actually, I need a hug."

"Then you will have one." Alain held her, trying not to tighten his grasp too much as the dark image from his foresight came to mind.

"I should get out on deck at least once before sunset," Mari said with a sigh. "Everybody is going to think I'm lazy."

"I have heard no one suggest such a thing. The crew have been careful to be as quiet as possible all day to avoid disturbing you."

"Oh, great. So I've messed up their day?"

"That's not what I—"

Mari was already headed for the door, chewing a last hunk of bread. She stepped out into a gathering that seemed to include every Mechanic on the ship, the group breaking into smiles as they saw her.

"Great timing as usual," Mechanic Alli said.

"Why?" Mari asked. "What's happening?"

"We just raised your banner!"

"My—?" Mari looked up, her jaw dropping.

Alain followed, seeing that at the top of the mainmast a new flag flew. It was simple as flags went, just a golden sun with many points centered on a field of light blue.

"It represents the new day," Mechanic Calu said. "You needed a banner, so—"

"Why did I need a banner?" Mari asked. "A banner? For me? Like I'm some empress or the queen of Tiae?"

"Jules had a banner," Alli pointed out.

"I'm not Jules! Guys, I really appreciate this, but how is this going to make me look?" Mari demanded. "Like I think I'm so great? Like I need to have my own *flag*?"

"Mari," Alain began.

"Did you know about this? Because you should have told them it was really nice but not a good idea."

"Mari," Alain said. "I did not know, but I believe it is a good idea. For two reasons."

She crossed her arms and narrowed her eyes at him. "The first reason being?"

"Your friends are right. You need an emblem that reveals whether someone supports you, or your enemies." Alain pointed at the group in their Mechanic jackets. "How do you know these Mechanics are your friends?"

"Because I recognize them," Mari said. "Well, most of them."

"And if we have a hundred Mechanics? If we stop in a city and the Mechanics there are of different loyalties, how do you know which are loyal to you?"

"All right," Mari said, "first of all, nobody should be loyal to *me*."

"To Master Mechanic Mari or to the daughter," Bev said. "Whatever you call it. Like it or not, that's what it comes down to. Are they taking orders from the Senior Mechanics of the Guild, or the elders of the Mage Guild, or some local lord from Syndar, or from you?"

Mari hesitated. "I'm sure there's a good answer for that which doesn't require having my own banner. I just need to think of it. Besides, everyone isn't going to run around carrying my banner. That would be ridiculous."

"That is the other reason," Alain said. "Do you remember my vision in Dorcastle?"

She gave him a sidelong look. "The one about the battle we were going to be in? How could I forget that?"

"I told you that in that vision, you and I were wearing armbands of a strange design."

"Armbands?" Mari's eyes widened in dismay and she looked upwards again.

"Yes. That was the design, Mari. We were wearing your banner."

"Then this is your fault," she said, looking accusingly at Alain.

"Hold on," Calu said. "Are you saying that you knew we were going to make a banner with this design?" he asked Alain.

"I saw this design," Alain said. "Several months ago, in a vision I had on the walls of Dorcastle. I did not know what the design meant. Not until now."

"Do I get any say in my own life?" Mari demanded. "You see us wearing some design and I end up with a banner showing that. You see us married and we end up married. You—"

"Huh?" Alli broke in. "Alain predicted that you two would be married?"

"Guys do that," Calu said.

"*Most* guys don't see visions where you are both wearing promise rings and then months later ask you what the rings mean!" Mari said.

"Is that why you married him?" Alli asked doubtfully.

"No! How can you even ask that? My point is, things keep happening whether I want them to happen or not! Are all of my decisions already carved in stone somewhere and I'm just some puppet living out the script?"

That quieted everyone.

Alain shook his head. "That is not so. Your decisions brought us here. Fate gives us choices to make. There are many points at which different things could have been done, different choices made, and those choices dictate the next set of choices. Had you not chosen to rejoin me in the Northern Ramparts, I would have died there and your actions these last several months would have been much different. My vision was of something that might be. So far, your choices have kept us on that path. But they might change our path at any time."

"But not all foresight is like that, right?" Mari asked. "If you don't see yourself in the vision, it's something that will definitely happen, right?"

Alain wondered if the guilt and sorrow her question triggered showed on his face. "No."

"No?" Mari looked doubtful. "I was sure you had said—"

"Much remains unknown and uncertain about foresight because the Mage Guild elders have discouraged study of it. I believe that any vision represents only something that might be, and that if we try hard enough we can change what comes to pass." Truth might not exist, as the elders of the Mage Guild taught, but surely what he said was not false. And the elders had always insisted that any aspect of the world illusion could be changed by a Mage of sufficient skill and wisdom.

Mari bit her lip. "I don't want to end up fighting in some huge battle at Dorcastle, Alain. I don't want to fight any battles. I want to build things and fix things. And that banner sort of means there will be battles."

"Mari, the warlords in Tiae aren't going to just surrender, and the Senior Mechanics everywhere aren't going to give up without a fight," Alli said. "They'll fight as hard as they can to keep anything from changing, right up until the moment when everything falls apart. Unless we can stop them before then."

"We." Mari looked up again. "It's not really my banner, is it? It's *our* banner. It's about what we're all fighting for." She seemed to be comforted by that.

"Symbols are important," said Mechanic Rob, who had joined them at Julesport. "And I think you're right that it's important this symbol be about what everyone wants to happen and not about you personally. The Senior Mechanics are already claiming you just want to set yourself up as the sole leader of a new Guild."

"There!" Mari said. "See? Someone gets it! Wait. What are the Senior Mechanics saying?"

"That this is just about you wanting to be in charge, becoming some sort of queen of the Guild," Rob said.

"The banner works against that," Calu said. "It makes it clear that you and all of us are fighting for something much bigger than some power grab involving the Mechanics Guild."

"It's your banner," Alli said, "but it's not about you. We could fix that, though. Put a crown on it. A big one with Mari Queen Of Everything stenciled on it."

"Don't you dare!"

Alain and Mari found the captain of the *Gray Lady* in good spirits. "I am confident we'll run down that Mechanic ship, Lady," he told Mari. "Not tonight. We may catch sight of her upper masts before the sun sets tomorrow, and we'll catch her fair before the sun rises on the day after."

"We're considering trying to take that ship," Mari said. "Do you know anything about sneaking up on a ship at night and getting people aboard it?"

The captain scratched his head. "Well, now, I may have heard a few things about that. Just idle talk in the portside bars, you know. But I think I may remember enough to help you out, Lady."

Alain could easily see the deception in the man, who showed every sign of being extremely familiar with the matters discussed. "The moon will still be bright."

"That depends on what time we make our approach, Sir Mage. If no clouds come along to aid our concealment in the night, we can move in between the time the moon sinks and the sun rises." The captain paused, eyeing Mari. "I do feel obligated to point out, Lady, that the matter we are discussing is commonly referred to as piracy."

"That may be the one crime I have not yet been accused of," Mari said. "We'll make some plans tomorrow."

"Aye, Lady. That will also give my crew time to sew the armbands your Mechanics have asked for."

"Armbands." She gave Alain an aggravated look.

"It's not a problem, Lady," the captain assured her. "All sailors know some sewing. There aren't any tailors out on the water to mend rips in clothes, and sometimes the sails themselves require some repairs."

"Thank you, Captain," Mari said. "I'll talk to you tomorrow about the plans."

Alain could see that she was dogged by weariness, but Mari circulated about the ship, talking not only to her fellow Mechanics but also to the common members of the crew, the healers Cas and Pol, and even the new Mages. Her stubbornly determined attempts to converse with the Mages Hiro, Tana, and Dimitri were getting nowhere, though, until Mage Dav intervened and began presenting questions of wisdom to her. His inquiries were posed in terms that Mari couldn't grasp, so she didn't realize their purpose. But she gave Alain a look that told him she assumed Mage Dav was acting for a reason, and after a few rounds of questions all three new Mages inclined their heads towards her. "We accept your wisdom, elder," Mage Hiro said.

Mari's jaw dropped, and even Alain had trouble hiding his reaction. "Elder?" she asked.

"An elder," Mage Hiro said in his emotionless voice, "is one who teaches wisdom, or a new wisdom. You have shown a new wisdom to Mage Alain, Mage Asha, and Mage Dav. You will be Elder Mari to us now."

As Mari and Alain walked back to the small cabin, she turned a baffled look on him. "Elder? I'm nineteen years old."

"Yes, Elder," Alain said, unable to resist the impulse.

She glared at him. "You just lost a chance at a warm, happy night, Sir Mage."

"I…am…sorry?"

"I'll bet you are." Mari reached the cabin, looking over the main deck of the Gray Lady. The last vestiges of daylight were fading in the west, the sea a great, dark expanse stretching uninterrupted on all sides, the stars already shining brightly in the vast bowl of the heavens.

"Look up there," Mari whispered. "One of those stars is the one our people came from. And somewhere the remains of the great ship are still above this world. Do you think it could be one of the twins that follow the moon?"

"Did you not say you could look?"

"My far-seers aren't powerful enough to tell," Mari said. "And I can't divert the efforts of the Mechanics to making a big far-seer just to satisfy my curiosity as soon as possible. That's not a hard decision to make."

She fell silent, gazing out over the water. After a long time, she spoke in a wistful way. "I've been thinking about what you said, Alain. About how my choices were still driving us toward that battle in Dorcastle, and that I could make other choices if I really wanted to change that. And I remembered the western continent. You and I know where that is now. I could tell the captain of the Gray Lady to point this ship toward it, and I'm sure we could make it, and then we could just stay there. We have plenty of men and women. We would be safe from the

Storm. We could just build something new there, and I'd never have to face that battle in Dorcastle."

She fell silent again, this time for so long that Alain felt the need to prod her. "But you have not done that."

"No." Mari looked at him, both sad and determined. "Because what about everyone else? What about all of those people we saw in Altis, and in Julesport? The fathers and mothers and children. Did you see the babies in Julesport? They wouldn't have a chance. How could I just abandon them to that fate? It's a choice I have, but it's a choice I can't make. I have to keep trying. I have to keep trying to fix things, even if my choices lead us to that battle, and…"

She bit her lip, staring into his eyes. "Even if I lead us into that battle and we don't come out of it. As long as we win."

"Mari—" Alain began, once again feeling wracked by guilt.

"No. That doesn't mean I want to die," Mari said. "I intend doing my best *not* to die. And my best to ensure that you don't die. Because if I lived and lost you then the greatest victory would still feel like a defeat to me. But I need to accept the possibility, or I'll be so scared of what might happen that I won't be able to do what we have to do."

"You know that my foresight shows things," Alain began, his resolve wavering.

"Yes. We— Do you mean it might show something else? Something…bad? About you or me?" Mari inhaled abruptly, a deep and shuddering intake of breath. "But then we could try to change it, right?"

"Yes." If he had ever believed in anything, he now believed in that.

"But if you did—" A deeper darkness passed across her face. "If you did."

"Mari?"

"Alain, don't die! Do you understand?"

"You have told me before that I am not allowed to die," Alain said. He was still struggling to figure out what Mari wanted. "I will die, though, if it is the only way to save you."

"We have been over this!" Mari said in a low growl, pointing her forefinger at him. "You don't do something stupid in the name of saving me! You especially do not die in the name of saving me! And if your foresight, which I am really beginning to hate, shows you or me or someone else we really care about being badly hurt or…or dying, then we change that. We do not accept it. Am I clear on that?"

"You are," Alain said. "Do you trust my decisions?"

She held his eyes with her own. "Yes. I may be the Mechanic, the one trained to fix things, but you, Sir Mage, are very good at fixing things as well. I hope you understand how much I trust you. There will be times when we can't ask each other for input or advice. Like what happened in Julesport. I just had to act. There may be times when you have to do the same thing. I *know* you'll decide well."

"Thank you," Alain said, the words coming easily this time. He was still uneasy about not telling Mari, but it seemed to be clear that Asha had been right. Mari would not want that information, and she trusted him to decide what to do. "I have known from the first day we met that you make wise decisions."

"Oh, sure." She laughed. "Like when I led us into the desert waste? Or went into Ringhmon City Hall all by myself and ended up in the dungeon?"

"Sometimes the choices available to us are not good," Alain said.

"You don't have to remind me of that." Mari sighed and leaned against him, wrapping her arm around his waist. "But I had a choice to save a Mage or think only of myself, and saving someone else was the right decision. I assume that you agree."

"Yes."

"Let's go to bed. Keep acting nice and we may find out if two people can fit into one of those bunks."

"You always make wise decisions," Alain repeated.

She laughed as she led him inside.

❀ ❀ ❀

"Hey, Alain."

Alain nodded in greeting. Mages were not supposed to notice or care about the weather. But along with reminding him of feelings, Mari had shown him how nice a morning like this could feel, with the ship bounding along over following seas and a warm sun and the blue sky merging into the blue water all around. "Hey, Calu," he said, proud to be able to display what Mari called "social skills."

The Mechanic sat down next to him, looking up at the sails. "Mari told us to let you rest today since we might need you at full strength tonight. I wanted to see if you needed anything, though. The blow to your head wasn't that long ago."

"I need nothing," Alain said. "Mari will not rest," he added.

"No. Right now she's grilling the captain of the *Gray Lady* on every little aspect of tonight's fun and games." Calu smiled at Alain. "Mari's always been like that. It's one of the reasons I've always liked her. She'll see that something needs doing and then she'll go talk to everyone she can find who knows something about it so she can figure out exactly what to do. Mari doesn't just accept that something that is wrong or broken has to stay that way, and she doesn't assume she knows enough on her own to decide what to do. Like she's doing right now, learning all about what's going to happen tonight. By the time we meet up with the *Pride of Longfalls*, Mari will understand enough about what is happening and what should happen that if anything unexpected occurs or goes wrong she'll be able to know what to do or tell others to do. Did she ever tell you about the time she saved several Mechanics at Caer Lyn?"

"No," Alain said. "I will ask her."

"Don't bother. She'll wave off the question and say it was no big deal. What happened was that the governor on a lathe was going bad, but the Senior Mechanic in charge of that shop didn't want to report it because the shop was already behind on a work order."

Alain nodded, grasping that something had been going wrong but not much more than that.

"Mari," Calu continued, "stopped by to check on an apprentice she knew. Mari never worked with lathes much but she can tell when a piece of equipment is making a noise that says *Run, you fools!* She heard that lathe making that kind of sound and declared a safety emergency and ordered everybody else out of the shop. The Senior Mechanic showed up pretty soon, mad as could be that Mari had interrupted the work. He walked over, activated the lathe, and the governor failed. The lathe over-powered so much that it blew apart and filled that shop with as much shrapnel as a high-explosive shell. Somehow the Senior Mechanic survived, but if Mari hadn't done what she did somebody would have died, maybe several people."

Something bad had happened, but Mari had kept anyone from dying. Alain understood that much. "Did Mari get praise for her wisdom?"

"Nah." Calu's grin this time was crooked. "Admitting that she'd saved lives would mean the Senior Mechanics admitting that one of their own had put those lives at risk. Officially, the Guild reprimanded the Mechanic in charge of keeping that lathe working, even though that Mechanic had been warning about the danger for weeks and been ignored."

Alain felt a concern crystallizing inside, but did not know how to ask about it. Lacking whatever social skill was needed, he fell back on his Mage training. "Mechanic Calu, this one has questions."

"What?" Calu gave him a confused glance. "Um, sure. What is it?"

"Your description of Mari's actions. I know she did something important. I know she saved the lives of others. But beyond that I have no idea what happened or why."

"That's no big deal, Alain. It's not like you're going to be tested on Mechanic knowledge. There aren't any commons in the world who would understand it any better than you would."

"But it reminds me that Mari and I have so many differences."

"I guess you do," Calu said with a laugh. "But lots of people do. Take Alli and me. We're both Mechanics, but I'm a basic skills Mechanic at most things. I'd never gain Master Mechanic status at anything, because nothing hands-on clicks for me. I'm a theory guy, and I'm really good at that. But Alli is one of the best hands-on Mechanics out there. She'd have been a Master Mechanic by now if the Senior Mechanics weren't worried about her knowing Mari. Alli just has to look at a piece of gear and she knows how to fix it and maybe make it better."

"This is a big difference between you?" Alain asked.

"Huge," Calu assured him. "The hands-on types think the theory types—and there aren't very many of us, just enough to keep the knowledge alive—are pretty useless. And my theory instructors tried to convince me that the hands-on Mechanics were just hammer-pounders. That could come between us. But it doesn't. Oh, we don't always see eye-to-eye. That's just life. But we know what we've got in each other." Calu looked at Alain. "You do know what you've got in Mari, right?"

"Yes," Alain said. "But she must know how flawed I am."

"Everybody has flaws. Mari has her faults, too, Alain. She can be a little short-tempered—"

"More than a little, sometimes," Alain said.

"Yeah. And she's pretty stubborn, and impulsive at times. So she's not perfect. But she is absolutely loyal. If you're sitting there thinking *Mari's so wonderful that she'll leave me for someone better*, you can relax. In her eyes there is no one better, and the only person who could convince her otherwise is you, if you start acting wrong to her."

"I may have to marry you," Alli said.

Alain looked up and saw that Mechanic Alli had approached as they talked.

Calu covered his face, embarrassed. "How much of that did you hear?"

"Enough," Alli said. "What do you say? I was going to wait, but we're about to go on another one of Mari's death-defying missions, so why not get it done? And we're on a ship, which means we've got a ship's captain to do the legal stuff."

"You mean get married today?" Calu asked.

"I mean right now, if we can get Mari to leave off pestering the captain long enough for him to sign the document." Alli pulled a folded paper from her jacket. "Which I happen to have been carrying around for a while, just in case."

Calu grinned and pulled a similar paper from his own jacket. "If you hadn't had that, we could have used the one I've been carrying around. We're already on our honeymoon cruise, so why not? We need a witness, though."

"Alain's not busy. Come on, Sir Mage. Hey, Calu, we'll be the first in history to have a Mage as the witness at our marriage!"

Calu helped Alain stand. "I'm afraid this won't be as glamorous as whatever Mari managed for your wedding, Alain."

"I did not even know our wedding was happening," Alain said as he walked with them to the quarterdeck.

Alli gave him a delighted grin. "Oh, I have got to hear that story. No wonder Mari has refused to talk about it much! Hey, Lady Mari, your daughterness! We need to borrow the captain for a couple of minutes."

"What for?" Mari asked, brushing hair from her eyes and turning away from the captain. "And the daughter thing isn't funny."

"Excuse me! The captain just has to sign this." Alli offered the paper and a pen to the captain. "Oh, you too, Calu. And you, Alain."

The captain was gazing at the paper, nonplussed.

"Is something wrong?" Calu asked. "You do have legal authority under the laws of Dematr to sign that."

"Yes," the captain admitted. "But I've never actually done it before! I guess my ship hasn't been sought out by young lovers prior to this."

"Young lovers?" Mari bent to look at the paper. "Alli? You and Calu?"

"It's not exactly a rush decision, Mari," Alli said. "Calu and I would have gotten married a couple of years ago if the Guild hadn't kept us apart."

"I know! It's easy to forget that you two are a little older than I am. I just…with everything going on…are you sure this a good time?"

Alli reached out to tap Mari's promise ring with one finger. "Are *you* seriously asking us that?"

"Uh…" Mari shrugged, looking uncomfortable. "I guess that would be a little hypocritical of me, wouldn't it?"

"Just a little."

Alain watched as Alli and Calu looked at the signed paper, then embraced.

"We'll get to celebrate our honeymoon by attacking a Mechanics

Guild ship," Calu commented as Alli and Mari wiped tears from their eyes and also hugged.

"Yeah," Alli agreed. "Nice wedding present, Mari!"

It had taken Alain some time to realize what a joke was, and then more time to recognize one when it was being made, something he still was not good at. He had been confused at first by the way that Mari, and then her friends when he met them, would make jokes before doing dangerous things. But looking at Alli and Calu, he saw the tension in them, and realized finally that the jokes were their means of coping with their fears. Mages were supposed to deny all fear, not even to admit it existed, but Mechanics dealt with it differently.

And of what his fears? He could not joke, but looking at the deck beneath his feet, Alain realized he could deal with them. His vision of Mari lying on a floor made of stone blocks had been very clear. He would know if he saw the type of stone and the shape of the blocks again. And if he did, he would be able to stop that vision from happening.

"Mast sighted!" the lookout called down from high above. "Two points to starboard!"

The captain grinned. "Just about where our prey ought to be. We'll run in a little closer to be sure he has three masts, and then we'll know he's our target. After that, we'll hold course and gain on him as he has to tack with the wind. By midnight we'll be ahead of him and well positioned to come over and manage a little meet-up in the darkness before dawn."

Mari stood near the rail of the *Gray Lady*, Mechanics jacket on, her pistol ready and snapped into its holster under her shoulder and her right arm wrapped about the end of a rope that rose up and away to meet the end of one of the great spars holding the largest square sails on the ship. The moon had set some time before and a layer of thin clouds scudding not far overhead dimmed the light of the stars, making the darkness thick enough to feel as though she could reach out and close her free fist over a patch of it.

The only break in the surrounding dark was a light visible just to starboard. Ships, Mari had been told, were required to show lights at night in order to avoid collision. One lantern at the stern, one high up and forward, and two colored lanterns at the sides, red for port and green for starboard. The *Pride of Longfalls* was following that rule, but from this angle only the stern light could be seen. The *Gray Lady* was using it to spot the exact position of her prey.

The *Lady* herself wasn't showing any lights, and everyone moved with great care in order to make no noise. Aside from a slight sigh of wind in the rigging and the murmur of water flowing along her hull, the *Lady* was both dark and silent as she swept down on the *Pride*.

Mari tightened her grip on the rope and looked over at Alli, who grasped a similar rope leading up to another spar. Alli had worked with the sailors to knot line into something she called slings, which were tied to the Mechanic rifles. One of those rifles now rested on Alli's back, the sling across her chest.

"I feel ridiculous," Mari whispered to Alli.

"Ridiculous?" Alli whispered back. "We're doing the whole pirate thing, Mari. Black of night and swinging over the water and knives in our teeth. This is so great!"

"Well, yeah," Mari admitted. She couldn't help smiling. "It's dangerous! Why does it feel like fun? I'm not Jules!"

"Every kid dreams of being Jules," Alli said. "Then we grow up and realize Jules is long gone and we have to put on our jackets and be adults every day." She grinned at Mari. "But not this day!"

Mari looked forward again, her smile fading. Everyone had been very nice to her. No one had berated her for making such a serious mistake in Julesport. She never should have spent time working on the Calculating device there, never should have let herself be separated from Alain. But she had wanted to be back inside that safe bubble again, that place where her training had led her, where she knew everything that needed to be done and exactly how to do it. She had wanted to be just Master Mechanic Mari again, so badly that she had wasted precious time, put Alain at serious risk, and forced the others, Asha and Alli and Dav and Bev, to risk themselves as well to rescue him.

Maybe they all understood that they didn't have to say anything. Maybe they already knew how much Mari had disappointed herself.

Alain had been a little odd the last couple of days. Probably just an after-effect of the drug the Dark Mages had used. Surely he didn't blame her for what had happened. He would have had every right to, though.

And his blasted foresight! As useful as that had been at times, Mari found herself wishing that it would disappear as mysteriously as it had manifested so that she and Alain could stumble through life not knowing what was coming, just like everybody else.

"Stand ready, Lady," a crewmember whispered near her ear, jerking Mari out of her reverie. She nodded, then looked back to where the others waited. Those of the *Gray Lady*'s spars that angled out in the right direction could support sending only four over at a time, so the first group would be her, Alli, Mechanic Dav, and one of the crew. The second group would include Calu, Bev, Mechanic Rob, and another crewmember. Hopefully the third group including the other two new Mechanics and a couple more crewmembers would make it as well.

Alain stood slightly to one side, watching her. She knew how unhappy he was that she was leading this attack without him. But he had accepted that if the Mechanics on the *Pride* saw any Mages they would refuse to surrender. He would have to wait until the others had seized control of the ship.

Or do his best to help the others escape back to the *Lady*, if everything went to pieces.

"Coming up," the sailor whispered.

Mari could see the *Pride* as a darker blot against the night sky, the only sure mark the lantern glowing on the stern. That lantern was growing closer with unnerving speed as the *Lady* cut silently across the stern of the *Pride*.

"Now!" the sailor said.

Mari nerved herself and leaped into space.

CHAPTER SEVEN

Hurtling into the darkness, Mari felt herself dropping and swinging forward as the rope tightened with a jerk that almost popped her arm. Her stomach insisted that she was doing a lot more falling than swinging, the sea's surface just barely visible below. Mari fearfully wondered whether the sailors had accurately estimated the lowest swing of the rope. How far down was the bottom of the ocean here? If she fell into it and couldn't resurface, how far would she sink before reaching the dark and silent mud far below?

The thoughts occupied barely an instant. A moment later, the rope reached the bottom of the swing and began yanking her upward as well as forward.

Part of her was exhilarated by the thrill of it. Part of her was terrified. She tried to ignore both and focus on trying to spot something to grab onto.

The black wall of the *Pride*'s stern suddenly gained detail as Mari neared the farthest edge of the rope's swing. The stern rail of the other ship appeared before her and just above. Mari swung out her free hand to grab on, frantically fighting to maintain the hold as the weight of the rope began trying to drag her back. If she didn't get rid of that rope very quickly, it would pull her off the *Pride* as the *Gray Lady* kept going.

She spun the rope off of her arm, unable to do anything for a moment but hang there, suspended by one hand from the stern rail, nothing beneath her feet but the wake of the *Pride*.

Mari finally thought to look over and saw Alli clinging nearby, also hanging from the rail, though by both hands.

"Did you hear something?"

Mari looked upwards as the low voice came clearly to her from the *Pride*'s quarterdeck.

"Like a thump?" someone answered. "Yeah. Do you think somebody fell overboard?"

"Nobody is supposed to be out on deck at night except the watch and the sentries. But I better check."

Mari thrust her free hand into her jacket, scrabbling for her pistol. She got the weapon out and the safety off, raising the pistol just as someone looked over the rail directly above her.

"Not one sound," she whispered as quietly as possible, her pistol almost touching the Mechanic's nose. "Don't move."

From the corner of her eye Mari could see that Alli was using both hands to silently pull herself up high enough to get over the rail. Once on deck, Alli brought the sling over her head and grasped her rifle.

She surveyed the situation, then stepped over to place her rifle barrel against the head of the Mechanic being threatened by Mari. That allowed Mari to reholster the pistol, edge sideways a little, and employ both hands to get over the rail.

Two Apprentices were standing on the quarterdeck, one holding the big wheel that controlled the rudder of the *Pride* and the other beside her. Both were looking forward, oblivious to those boarding the ship behind them.

Mari looked to the side and saw Mechanic Dav, the crewmember from the *Lady* beside him, giving her a thumbs up as he also readied his rifle.

A swoosh of wind and rush of water noise heralded the return of the *Lady*. Mari leaned out to grab Calu's hand as he swung over, helping him up.

"I heard something again," said one of the Apprentices, beginning to turn. "Mechanic—?"

She stopped speaking as she saw Mechanic Dav pointing his rifle at her and raising one finger to his lips.

Mari made sure that Calu was up, saw that Bev, Mechanic Rob, and the other crewmember were making their way over the railing, and then took some swift steps to the helm, trying to walk without making noise. She had her pistol out again as she swung into the line of vision of the Apprentice at the wheel. "Shhh. Let's keep it quiet and nobody gets hurt."

The first crewmember from the *Lady* took over the wheel, and Mari hustled the two Apprentices back to where the captured Mechanic was glaring in silent bafflement. His expression suddenly cleared, though. "It's a drill, isn't it?" he whispered.

"Riiiiight," Alli said, turning over guard duty on the three to Rob. "Surprise safety drill. But it's not over yet. You're all supposed to simulate having been killed, so lie face down and stay silent."

Accustomed to following orders, the three did as they were told, except that one Apprentice excitedly whispered to the other, "Do you think they'll be able to take out both sentries on the main deck?"

"Shut up!" the captured Mechanic growled. "You were told to be silent!"

"Two sentries on the main deck," Mari commented to Alli as they walked to the front of the raised quarterdeck and looked down at the main deck before them. "There's one. The group up here were all unarmed, but that sentry has a rifle. How do we sneak up on them?"

"By being obvious," Alli said. "Hey, Calu, snuggle up."

The last group of four was coming over the stern as Alli and Calu held each other in a one-armed hug, their rifles held in their free hands and concealed between their bodies. The dark shape of the *Gray Lady* faded back, having lost enough speed in her repeated course changes to be unable to keep up with the *Pride* for the moment.

Mari watched nervously as Alli and Calu sauntered across the deck, giggling softly to each other.

The nearest sentry reacted. "What the blazes are you two doing?" he demanded.

"We're just looking for a little privacy," Alli said in a lighthearted voice.

"You idiots know that no one is allowed on deck at night except sentries and watch standers!"

The other sentry had come from a bit farther forward, wandering closer to see what was happening.

"Cut us a break," Calu said.

"I'll cut you something, you idiot! Is that you, Judi? I told you what I'd do if I saw you with another guy!"

The two guards were close enough by then for Calu to twist and raise his weapon to cover the second guard. Alli brought her rifle up too, but in a hard blow against the head of the sentry who had almost reached her. That Mechanic staggered back, Alli taking his rifle from a slack hand. "You are really lucky I'm not Judi," Alli said. "Or I would have hit you a lot harder."

Mari came down the stairs from the quarterdeck, looked at the stern cabin, and paused. Instead of one door leading to where the captain slept, there were two doors equally spaced. The stern cabin must have been subdivided. Which side did she want, and who was in the other side?

Bev and Mechanic Dav were coming down the stairs as well when Mari's dilemma was resolved by one of the doors beginning to open. The man who stepped out was the second that night to find Mari's pistol pointed straight at his nose.

He was an older Mechanic, with dark hair and a mustache both bearing enough grey that it could be seen even in the darkness. Age had given him enough wisdom that he said and did nothing.

"We're taking this ship," Mari said. "Hopefully without anyone getting hurt. That's entirely up to you. Surrender it and no one gets hurt. Fight, and it could get ugly."

The eyes of the older Mechanic went to one side, looking over Bev and Dav with their rifles and Alli and Calu standing over the two chastened sentries. He looked upwards enough to see Mechanic Amal from Julesport, rifle also in hand, standing by the front rail of the quarterdeck. "My surrender would seem to be a mere formality, but why am I surrendering to a fellow Mechanic? Who are you?"

"Master Mechanic Mari of Caer Lyn," she said.

After a pause, the Mechanic nodded. "I see. We were warned that you might try something in port, but you do tend to exceed expectations, don't you, Master Mechanic?"

"Who told you that?" Mari asked, thinking it sounded oddly like praise.

"One of my passengers on an earlier voyage. I have an obligation to the passengers' safety, Master Mechanic. As well as to the safety of my crew. Do you swear you mean them no harm?"

"I swear," Mari said. "I understand that your passengers are actually prisoners."

"Your understanding is correct." The Mechanic's voice clearly conveyed his distaste for his role as a jailor.

"I'm going to set them free and give them the option of joining me. Anyone who doesn't want to will be put off in your ship's boats with enough food and water and guidance to reach shore."

Another pause, longer this time, then the Mechanic nodded again. "I surrender my ship to you. I am Mechanic Captain Banda of Marida. At your service."

Mari lowered her pistol, grateful since her arm was beginning to ache. "I would appreciate your assistance in assuring I take the rest captive without harming anyone," she said.

"You need those two first," Banda said, gesturing toward the other door to the stern cabin. "The two Senior Mechanics who are actually in charge of this work detail."

"Are they armed?"

"Yes and no. The extra weapons are locked up in there, but those two don't routinely carry them. Denz might have a pistol, since he liked parading around with one stuck in his belt. He's the man. Gina's the woman, and before you go in there I feel obligated to say that she has done her best by us during this voyage. I would not have been surprised if she had ended up among the so-called passengers on the next trip because of her insufficiently zealous attitude toward the Guild's instructions."

"Bev, Dav, you heard him. Go in there. If the guy twitches wrong, don't take any chances. Club him."

Bev's smile held no humor. "I can't shoot him?"

"No. I promised no one hurt, Bev."

"Yes, Lady Master Mechanic." Bev tried the door handle, found it locked, and knocked gently. Waited. Knocked again. Waited. Began knocking lightly but continuously.

Mari heard the lock being unlatched, then a very angry man stuck his head out. "Who dares to—?"

The question ended when Bev stuck the barrel of her rifle under his chin. "I do. I'm Mechanic Bev of Emdin. I was an Apprentice at Emdin. Do you want to see how little it would take to make me blow off the head of a Senior Mechanic?"

Keeping the barrel right under his chin, Bev led the Senior Mechanic, who was wearing only his trousers, out on deck while Dav dashed inside. He reemerged quickly, leading a woman in shirt and trousers who looked around in disbelief.

"The key to the weapons," Mari asked, extending her hand for it.

The woman looked for guidance not at her fellow Senior Mechanic but at Banda, who nodded. She pulled out a key on a chain and dropped it into Mari's hand.

"Traitor!" the other Senior Mechanic got out before the barrel of Bev's rifle jerked upward and slammed his jaw shut.

Mari gave Bev a worried look, but she returned a controlled expression that conveyed she wasn't losing it. And Alain had made a special effort to tell her that Bev could be trusted in a tough situation. He must have had a reason for that.

"She wouldn't have had any trouble picking the lock," Senior Mechanic Gina told Denz. "Didn't you read her file?"

Mari paused to think. She had the top deck of the ship, but most of the men and women aboard were belowdecks. "Captain Banda, I assume the passengers are locked down?"

"You assume correctly."

"What about your crew? Do I have to worry about them?"

"My crew will follow my orders," Banda said. "I will tell them not to resist so as to limit any chance of anyone being harmed. For the good of the Guild," he added, sounding almost sincere as he parroted the standard justification for any Guild action.

But then Captain Banda visibly hesitated, as if trying to tip off Mari. Taking his cue, she raised her pistol again toward him. "What did you leave out?"

"The guard force sent along by the Guild. They are in forward berthing."

"Are these two examples of them?" Alli called in a low voice, indicating the disarmed sentries.

"Those two are part of the guard force," Banda confirmed.

"That's bad news, Mari. From what Calu and I have seen of them, these two are hard core."

"The guards were selected to be reliable," Senior Mechanic Gina said. "And to be willing to use whatever force was necessary. I personally think they are overly eager to use force."

Senior Mechanic Denz apparently tried to interject some comment, but couldn't speak with Bev's rifle barrel holding his jaw shut from beneath.

"Are they armed?" Mari asked.

"Most have knives. A couple have personal pistols," Banda added. "Standard Guild revolvers, not semi-automatics like yours. Yours is only the second of those I've ever seen."

"They were only intended for bodyguards of the Guild Master," Alli commented. "Mari, we need to get those goons up on deck a few at a time. And someone needs to give me some line so I can tie up these two and gag them until we've got the whole batch under guard. Otherwise they might yell a warning when others come up."

One of the *Lady's* sailors ran up to Alli with a length of line and began expertly tying the arms and legs of the two guards. Finishing there, Mari directed him to do the same to Senior Mechanic Denz. "How many of these guards are there?" Mari asked Banda.

"Twenty."

"We've already got two, so that leaves eighteen. Which of you will help me get those guards up in small batches?" she asked Banda and Gina, who exchanged glances.

"You're asking us to participate in an action that is likely to lead to the injury of fellow Mechanics," Senior Mechanic Gina said.

"You mean like the Guild did when it imprisoned your fellow Mechanics and assigned those guards over them?" Mari asked angrily.

"I am uncomfortable with the idea of actively assisting you as well," Captain Banda said, "but it does not matter because they will not obey orders from me."

"So I have to do the dirty work? Fine!" Mari looked around. The two former sentries and Senior Mechanic Denz were trussed up, the sailor in the final act of putting gags in their mouths and being none too gentle about it. She thought about telling him to ease up, but she was in a bad mood about once again having to deal with people who resisted being helped. "Alli, Calu, Bev, come with me. Dav, you and Amal cover the deck and our current crop of prisoners. How are Rob and the others doing up there?"

"No problems," Amal called.

"Will you at least point out the right hatch?" Mari asked Banda, who looked unhappy with himself. He gestured toward one of the forward hatches.

Mari led the other three Mechanics to the hatch, which was open for ventilation and led to a stairway, or ladder, as the sailors called stairs on ships. "Calu, can you imitate that oaf that Alli slugged?"

"I can try," he said.

"When we first reached the ship, the Mechanic on the quarter-deck thought someone might have fallen overboard. That gives me an idea. The ship would have to do a muster if they thought they'd lost someone, right? Like those bed checks when the Guild Halls try to catch Apprentices who aren't where they're supposed to be. Call down, sound annoyed but not scared, and say someone might have fallen overboard and that everyone has to come up for a muster."

"Got it."

"Anybody who comes up with a weapon on them gets pulled aside and knocked out," Mari ordered. "If they aren't armed, they get hustled over there. Bev, you'll cover that group. If everything goes to blazes, our goal is to hold as many of the guards as possible up here and keep them from doing anything."

"Do we open fire if we think we have to, or wait for you to say?" Alli asked.

Mari hesitated, swallowing at the thought of giving that order. She suddenly realized how Captain Banda had felt. "I know you guys. I trust you guys not to fire unless you have to." Mari made sure to look at Bev so that she would know she was included in that statement. "If you think you have to, do it without asking for permission."

Feeling sick to her stomach, Mari checked her pistol while the other three ensured their rifles were ready, then nodded to Calu.

He leaned over the hatch and called down in a loud, gruff voice. "Hey! Everybody up here! They think someone might have fallen off the ship and we need to do a muster!"

Groans and curses echoed up from below. "Says who?" someone yelled back.

"Senior Mechanic Denz!" Calu yelled back.

The grumbling subsided, but there remained a low rumble of discontent. Mari braced herself as the clomp of angry feet on the ladder sounded.

Two women came up first, scowling and disheveled from sleep. Alli met them with a leveled rifle and gestured them to move to the side fast. Surprised and mentally off balance, the women stumbled over to where Alli directed to find themselves facing Bev's steely gaze and leveled weapon.

Then came a big man with an angry glower and a holstered pistol at his hip. As he cleared the ladder, Calu swung his rifle butt so that it connected with the Mechanic's head and knocked him over to the side.

"What was that?" someone still coming up the ladder complained. "Tripped," Calu called back. "Watch your feet, you idiots!"

"Who the blazes are you?" another Mechanic said as he reached the deck along with two others.

"Special duty," Calu said, keeping his voice in the low, angry tones of a Mechanic who was bullying someone. Mari wasn't surprised that Calu could mimic it so easily. They had all heard that sound too often in their time with the Guild.

Seeing the rifles, the three let themselves be herded over with the first two.

Mari lost count after that, as they tried to keep the line moving while keeping anyone from realizing what was going on. A female Mechanic wearing a holstered revolver managed to jerk back and avoid Calu and Alli, but found Mari's pistol barrel pressed against the back of her neck as Mari reached forward to seize the revolver.

There had to be twelve or even fifteen on deck already, Mari thought, but the line out of the hatch was backing up as the Mechanic guards on deck reacted too slowly to silent orders to move.

"Get out of the way!" someone still on the ladder bellowed, and a small group shoved their way onto the deck, sending those just ahead of them stumbling in all directions.

For a moment, Mari could not see Alli or Calu.

"Everyone freeze!" she yelled, surprised to hear how deep and intimidating her voice sounded.

On the other side of the crowd, a rifle shot sounded.

Mari waited, her pistol on the dazed Mechanics facing her, wondering how many more shots would erupt.

"That one went into the deck on purpose. The next one goes into whoever I think looks ugliest," Mari heard Bev say.

"All of you get over there!" Alli shouted.

"Move!" Calu added.

The crowd shifted, moving back and to the side. Most of them looked scared, and all of them looked confused. That had been their best weapon, Mari realized, to make things happen too quickly for the Mechanic guards to have time to understand what was going on. But it had also been their greatest risk, since moving so fast had meant little time to react if the Mechanic guards had gathered their wits in time and charged as a group.

Mari moved to the side to be in line with Alli and Calu, all three of their weapons pointed at the Mechanic guards. She could see Bev slightly off to the side, her rifle also leveled.

"Who—?" another angry voice began demanding from near Mari. She pivoted to cover the woman coming up from another hatch. "—are you?" Mari finished for the suddenly silent Mechanic.

"Mechanic Deni of Farland," she said, raising her hands. "Ship's crew. I heard a shot."

"Good," Mari said, trying to get her breathing and her heart rate back under control. "Your captain has surrendered the ship to us. He said you would follow his orders."

"Captain?" Mechanic Deni called.

"Follow the orders of Master Mechanic Mari! Pass the word to the rest of the crew," Captain Banda's answer came back. "She is the master of this ship."

As Banda's words soaked in, the faces of the Mechanic guards twisted into almost comical expressions of anger, disbelief, and fear.

Mari faced them again, stepping back from the hatch where Mechanic Deni stood. "First off, no one will be harmed as long as no one tries anything. Secondly, anyone who tries anything *will* be harmed. You're also being covered by rifles from other parts of the ship, so don't do anything stupid."

It took a while to get the rest of the *Pride*'s crew on deck and for Captain Banda to assure them that Mari had control of the ship. Banda suggested to Mari that an improvised barrier be set up to confine the guards, who were gradually coming to grips with their situation and muttering among themselves in a way that Mari did not like at all. She had the two sentries and Senior Mechanic Denz added to the group but left them tied up for now.

The crew set to with a will to rig a large net so that it hung from some of the spars overhead and completely confined the Mechanic guards against part of the starboard rail. "They've endured their share of abuse from that group," Banda commented to Mari. "You've made my crew prisoners and happy in the same day."

A small group of guards began to move forward as the last section of the net was raised, but found themselves facing Bev's rifle again. Something in her face convinced them to stop and back up. "You can untie your friends and the Senior Mechanic now," Bev told them.

Mari finally relaxed a little as the barrier settled into place. It wasn't impossible to get over, but to do so would require a lot of awkward climbing for the guards. "I guess now we can deal with your passengers, Captain. Do you have the keys to where they're held?"

"No," said Banda, shaking his head, "you do. It's on the same ring as the key to the weapons. That one there."

Mari twisted the key free and handed it to Banda. "Then please do me the favor of releasing them and getting the passengers up on deck, Captain."

"Please?" Banda asked. "And the use of my title? Why so polite, Master Mechanic, when you rule this ship?"

"It's what I do," Mari said. "I have no reason to treat you with anything but respect, Captain."

"I hope you will always feel that way," Banda said, smiling, and walked toward one of the aft hatches.

A short distance off to port, the *Gray Lady* raced along next to the *Pride of Longfalls*, the first rays of the morning sign highlighting the blue and gold banner flying from her mast. The rising sun turned the sky to shades of coral and turquoise as Banda led the bewildered passengers onto the deck. One of them laid eyes on Mari and began laughing. "Master Mechanic Mari of Caer Lyn! I should have known when I heard gunshots and cursing that the Senior Mechanics were trying to deal with you!"

Mari broke into a smile. "Mechanic Ken! I haven't seen you since I left the Guild Hall at Caer Lyn for the Academy at Palandur!"

Ken, well into middle age, walked over to her, oblivious to the rifles held by Mari's friends. He grasped her forearm, still grinning. "And now a Master Mechanic! Well done, Mari!"

Alli smiled too. "Hey, Ken."

"Alli! And Calu? That's great. I guess what the Guild tried to keep asunder, Mari brought together."

"That's why we're here," Calu said. "Why are you here, sir?"

Ken waved away the honorific. "We're all Mechanics now, Calu. Why am I here? Because I was one of the Mechanics who taught and sponsored a certain Apprentice Mari of Caer Lyn. Given how she turned out, I was accused of not doing any of that well."

"Given how she turned out, I'd say the question is still open," someone else said.

Mari turned to look. "Master Mechanic Lukas. You?"

"Me." Lukas was considerably older, and wasn't smiling. "Under suspicion as someone who once advised you, but I'm here because I protested too strongly that we had to change practices or lose more of the Guild's technology. What now, Mari? I always told you to think three steps ahead. What's the point of this? Freeing us is well intentioned, but life as a refugee among the commons isn't likely to be much of an improvement over life as a prisoner of the Guild."

"Why don't I tell everyone?" Mari said, feeling more nervous than she had just before swinging into the dark. She waited as the freed passengers gathered on the port side and the crew near the bow, then stood before them all, her friends arrayed behind her. There were twenty guards, plus Senior Mechanic Denz. The crew consisted of another twenty-five, with Banda and four other Mechanics, five Apprentices, and fifteen common sailors. Plus thirty-one passengers.

"Tell Alain and Asha to swing over from the *Gray Lady*," she asked Mechanic Dav. "You and Bev help them get aboard."

Turning back to the eyes upon her, some hostile, some curious, Mari took a deep breath. "I'm going to start off by saying that anyone who does not want to join me will be free to leave this ship. They will be put off in one of the ship's boats, with sufficient food and water to reach land. All I ask is that you listen to me before you decide."

"Don't listen!" Senior Mechanic Denz yelled. "You are all already in great trouble, and this will surely get you all branded as traitors, just like that delusional, arrogant young fool!"

Bev smiled and raised her weapon. "If you say anything else without first raising your hand and then being called upon," she told Denz, using the old schoolroom rule for young Apprentices, "I will shoot you."

Mari waited, but no one else said anything and Denz appeared to have been quelled by Bev's threat. "Let me say a few things that you all know are true. The technology the Mechanics Guild uses is failing. Everyone knows it, but the Senior Mechanics refuse to make any changes. Mages can actually do things. Many of you have seen that, and you have all been told not to speak of it. The commons hate us, and even though they supposedly do as the Mechanics Guild and Mage Guild order, they actually find ways to sabotage us at every turn."

No one interrupted, so Mari continued. "Here's what you may not know. I committed no crime against the Guild before it tried to have me killed. I was loyal and doing my job as best I could, and I was set up to be killed by commons."

"How do you know that?" one of the passengers asked.

"I was told it by a Master Mechanic who had personal knowledge of the matter," Mari said.

"What she says is true," an older male Mechanic among the passengers said. "I was one of those in Palandur who learned of it and tried to bring about an accounting. Instead, we were ordered to be silent about it."

"Here's another thing," Mari added. "Something you all may have felt. The commons have been slaves of the Great Guilds for centuries. They're like a belt under greater and greater tension, and they're about to snap. The rioting, the sudden, random attacks on Mechanics and Mages, the blind defiance we've all been seeing is getting worse at an accelerating rate, and soon it will pass a point of no return. When it does, this entire world will go the way of the Kingdom of Tiae. Only much worse. Tiae isn't an anomaly. Tiae is a warning sign."

"I have felt the tension you speak of," a male Mechanic said. "But how can you be sure this isn't just a temporary problem, part of a cycle of resistance and acceptance?"

A deeper silence fell before Mari could reply. She turned enough to see that Alain and Mage Asha had joined her group, standing out in their robes. "Partly because of them," Mari said, indicating the two and knowing how badly the Mechanics she was speaking to would take that. "And partly from being among the commons."

"Do they work for you?" someone demanded.

Before Mari could answer, Mage Asha did, her emotionless voice carrying clearly and eerily in the stillness of dawn. "Master Mechanic Mari has shown us new ways of wisdom. We follow her to learn more, and to aid her when called upon."

"You're teaching them to be Mechanics?"

"No," Mari said, "I'm teaching them to be human! A lot of you may be wondering how I have managed to stay alive with both of the Great Guilds and the Empire trying to kill me. That Mage," she said, pointing at Alain, "is the reason. In places where my Mechanic skills would have failed or been insufficient, his Mage skills made the difference."

"That's hard to believe," another passenger commented. "Mages?"

"Believe this," Senior Mechanic Gina said from where she stood with the passengers. "I was briefed on her before this job, told everything the Guild knew. Master Mechanic Mari should have been dead a dozen times already. She keeps getting out of impossible-to-get-away-from situations, including escaping from the *Queen of the Seas* with just one companion and disabling the ship in the process. According to the updates we received just before sailing from Julesport, at Altis she not only avoided being killed by the Special Missions Mechanic force but also did substantial damage to Guild assets, including sinking a ship comparable to this one. The Guild keeps blaming our failures on incompetence, but the Special Missions goons never fail. Until Altis.

Either the Mages have made a big difference, or Master Mechanic Mari is personally unstoppable and unkillable."

After a few moments spent thinking, another passenger nodded. "No offense, Master Mechanic Mari, but I do find it more believable that the Mages made a difference."

"There's still something else going on," another insisted. "Why did these Mages even listen to you? You've got commons on that ship following you, and according to the Guild you're close to stirring up rebellion by all the commons. What are they seeing?"

"They listen to me," Mari said, not sure how the full truth would be received. "Because I listen to them."

"She's insane!" Senior Mechanic Denz yelled, ducking back behind the other guards to shield himself from Bev. "She thinks she's the daughter of Jules!"

"She is the daughter," Mage Asha said. "It has been seen."

The commons among the *Pride*'s crew turned shocked glances toward the sailors from the *Lady* who were aboard. Those sailors hoisted their fists high and shouted answers to the unspoken questions. "It is her!" "She's the one!" "The daughter has come at last!"

Mari braced herself for the reaction from the Mechanics, but instead of mockery and contempt she saw thoughtfulness changing to admiration and looks of shared amusement. What did that mean?

"Smart," Master Mechanic Lukas murmured.

She finally got it. These other Mechanics thought that Mari was working a scam on the Mages and the commons, posing so successfully as the legendary daughter that she could get them to do as she wanted.

"What's your plan?" Lukas asked.

"To set Mechanics free," Mari said, determined not to disclose too much while people who were certain not to join her, like the guards and Senior Mechanic Denz, were in earshot. "Free to do new things, to innovate, to change. Learn what we can from the Mages and accept what skills they can bring. And give the commons freedom. Why are Mechanics ruling the commons? We're engineers. Let the commons rule themselves and come to us for the technology and the tools they need."

"If the commons rule themselves," one of the passengers said in a worried voice, "everything could go to blazes."

"It's already been going to blazes," Mechanic Ken commented. "There are almost always wars and raids and attacks going on, and look at Tiae. The Guild has always claimed it can rule the commons, but the Guild ended up abandoning Tiae. That's not a sign of superior strength or wisdom."

"It's Tiae that makes me believe her the most," another Mechanic said. "That and my experience with far-talkers. I was on a task force working on the portable far-talkers being constructed now. We were told to use the same design, but some of the components being turned out either don't work or are bigger, heavier, and less efficient than they're supposed to be. Something is being allowed to change, but only in one direction, and that's downhill."

Captain Banda pointed back to the stern cabin. "One-half of that used to house a far-talker. But over time the big far-talkers have been pulled off most Mechanics Guild ships to be used for parts to try to keep the far-talkers on a few other ships and those in the Guild Halls still working.

"I've been like the rest of you," Banda continued. "Trying to do my best, trying to do my job, but coming under suspicion by the Guild because I wasn't willing to watch everything fall apart without saying or trying something. I'll admit I've had it easier than many of you. Once the big far-talkers came off of these ships we gained a degree of freedom from the Guild whenever we went to sea. But we always had to come back into port sometime. And you are all examples of what is happening: how any dissent, any questioning, is taken as disloyalty. Too many Mechanics are disappearing, too many are being arrested and sent off to exile, while the rest of us wait for an alternative that we don't think exists."

Banda pointed to Mari. "Now we've got an alternative. I'd rather die trying to make something work than die in a prison cell because

I wasn't *allowed* to try. This Master Mechanic has given me a choice. When is the last time you were offered a choice? When is the last time you were treated with respect? Master Mechanic Mari treated me better as her prisoner than the Senior Mechanics have treated me. I'm going to follow Master Mechanic Mari."

"Me, too," said Senior Mechanic Gina, stepping forward. "You're going to need someone who understands administrative functions. I can help."

"We don't need the Senior Mechanics running everything!" an angry voice rose among the passengers.

"I don't want to run anything!" Gina insisted. "I want to help things run. You need administrative talent. It's like the grease that keeps a machine moving. The problem with the Mechanics Guild isn't because the grease is part of the system, it's because the grease has decided it's the reason for the machine's existence."

Mari saw Alain give her a slight nod. Both Banda and Gina were telling the truth. And with that she realized how to resolve her worries about whether anyone else was being truthful. "Stay next to me," she told Alain in a low voice, then spoke loudly again. "Welcome to both of you," she said to the captain and the senior mechanic. "For everyone else who wants to stay, I would like you to come up here, one by one, and tell me you want to work with me."

"No vows of obedience?" a sarcastic voice called.

"No. Just say you want to work with me. We'll start with the crew."

Unsurprisingly, all of the commons and the Mechanics among the *Pride*'s crew agreed, as did all but one of the Apprentices. That boy came close to Mari and Banda to speak quietly. "Mechanic Captain, sir, I truly want to stay with you, but my parents and my little sister live in the Guild Hall at Amandan. If I am seen to be a traitor to the Guild—"

"I wouldn't ask you to risk your family," Mari said.

"But we need a stronger reason for your refusal," Banda added. "Something that will protect you." His voice rose. "I am surprised," he said, his tone growing colder. "I expected better of you than blind loyalty to the Guild. Go, then. You belong among those who think as you do."

The Apprentice quickly hid a relieved smile, tried to look abashed but determined, and walked to stand next to the net cage holding the guards.

Then came the Mechanics who had been passengers. The first several came up without incident, but then a woman approached. "I wish to work with you," she said in a businesslike manner.

Alain's hand came up in a warding gesture. "She is lying."

The female Mechanic flicked a quick glance at Alain. Mari saw a knife appear in her hand with shocking suddenness, then the female Mechanic lunged at her from only a lance away.

CHAPTER EIGHT

Mari had barely begun to shift position in an attempt to meet the attack, knowing that she had too little time to save herself, when she heard a gasp of exertion from Alain. A section of deck just forward of Mari's toes vanished, leaving an opening gaping down to the next deck below. Her attacker, unable to react in time, stepped onto open air and fell forward through the opening.

The female Mechanic swung the knife at Mari as she fell, coming close enough to her that Mari easily felt the wind of the knife's passage.

Mari stepped back into a defensive crouch, pivoting enough to grab hold of Alain as he slumped with exhaustion. She heard the impact of the female Mechanic on the deck below, accompanied by a sound like a broomstick snapping and a cry of pain. A moment later the opening was gone, the deck as solid as ever, and Mari was trying to keep Alain from collapsing while everyone stared at her.

Asha moved to help hold Alain, freeing Mari to stand upright again. Mari looked around at the shocked expressions and somehow managed to speak in a clear voice despite the pounding of her heart as adrenaline belatedly tried to shock her system into readiness for the already-passed emergency. "You just saw two reasons why I keep Mages with me. They can tell when someone lies. And they can do that."

She pointed at the deck where the opening had briefly existed.

Captain Banda shook his head like one coming out of a dream. "Mechanic Deni. Take a couple of our people, and one of Master Mechanic Mari's people, down and take custody of that viper. Mind the knife, but she shouldn't give you much trouble. That was the sound of a leg breaking, unless I'm much mistaken."

"Is he hurt?" Mechanic Ken pointed at Alain as Mechanic Deni led her group down to the next deck.

"He used up his strength to manage that spell," Mari said. "He's all right, but worn out in an instant's time."

"Then it's not…magic? It requires energy?"

"Yes," Mari said, not wanting to explain any more while the former guards and Senior Mechanic Denz could hear.

Mechanic Deni came back up the nearest ladder, she and her helpers hauling along a very angry female Mechanic whose arms had been trussed. The would-be killer's legs were still free, but it wasn't hard to see why. A shard of bone protruded from her trousers and blood dripped from her pants leg.

Mari looked over and spotted the healer Cas, who had come across from the *Gray Lady* and was standing with Mechanic Rob. "Help her out," Mari ordered.

The female Mechanic was being held down by of the *Pride*'s crew and was swearing steadily, screaming nonstop obscenities at Mechanic Deni and Mari. As healer Cas knelt by the injured woman's leg, Deni threw out one arm, grabbing a long, hard belaying pin from its stand. She brought the pin against the injured Mechanic's head hard enough to knock her out and cease the yelling. "You might want to check her for a concussion, too," Deni told Cas as the stunned healer looked on.

Deni noticed Mari looking at her. "Sorry, Master Mechanic, but she got on my nerves. If someone is going to swear in front of a sailor, they should be creative and fluent. This one just kept repeating the same old things in a very uninspired way. It offended my sailor's sense of the art of obscenity."

"All…right," Mari said. She was secretly grateful that Deni had silenced the woman, but didn't feel that she should openly admit to it.

"Remind me not to swear in front of the sailors anymore," Mari heard Alli murmur to Calu.

"Let's get this done," Mari said, gesturing to the next passenger in line.

The process proceeded without any problems until near the end, when the turn came of a personable young Mechanic. He walked up to Mari with a smile on his face, declaring "I want to work with you" with enthusiasm.

But Mage Asha, and Alain who had recovered somewhat by then, both halted him. "He lies," Asha said, the passionless voice with which she voiced the statement making it sound even more damning.

The Mechanic's smile faded, but he shook his head as Bev, Calu and some other Mechanics closed in on him. "No. Really. I mean it."

"He lies," Asha repeated.

"Let's search him," Calu suggested.

It was Mechanic Ken who found a small concealed pocket on the inside of the young man's Mechanic jacket. He extracted a folded piece of paper, looked it over with his eyebrows rising, then passed it to Mari.

She scanned the document quickly. "This is a letter from the Guild Master introducing you to the Guild Hall Supervisor at Edinton. The Guild Master says you're a very capable undercover agent for the Guild." Mari looked at the young man. "Did you think your eagerness to work with me so you could spy on me would fool my Mages?"

His smile completely gone now, the young man didn't resist as he was shoved over to join the former guards.

The last couple of Mechanics passed without any problem. Mari looked over to see three of the passengers still standing some distance away. "The choice is yours," Mari said. "But you won't get a second chance today. If you are certain that you want to remain with the Guild, then go join that group."

None of the three appeared enthusiastic as they walked to join the former guards. Mari suspected their reasons were similar to that of the

Apprentice. But she didn't want to question them for fear of seeming to try to bully them into changing their minds.

"Twenty-seven leaving us, then," Captain Banda observed. "We'll have to give up two of the boats from the *Pride*." Banda didn't look happy at giving up two of the four boats hanging from davits aft.

"Make it happen, please, Captain," Mari directed.

The crew went to work with considerable enthusiasm, showing every sign of being eager to be free of the former guards and Senior Mechanic Denz. Both the *Pride* and the *Gray Lady* brought in most of their sails so that their speed was cut to something safe for launching boats. By early afternoon the boats had been stocked with food and water and lowered to the waves, and those who wished to remain loyal to the Guild descended a rope ladder into them. The would-be assassin with the broken leg was let down by rope, once again awake and cursing loudly until the crew "accidentally" dropped her the last lance-length into the boat. "You have the necessary navigational instruments," Captain Banda called down to the Apprentice from his crew. "And directions back to Julesport. You should make it easily in a little more than a week's time, assuming the wind holds."

Mari looked down on the boats. The faces turned up toward her were hard, angry, and hostile, but she still felt badly about setting people adrift in the ocean. "They really will be all right?" she asked Captain Banda.

"The only worry they should face is sunburn," Banda said with a dismissive wave of his hand. "Or if the fools refuse to listen to Apprentice Tan. But even Senior Mechanic Denz knows that sailing east is going to bring them ashore somewhere in the Confederation. He'll want to go back to Julesport, though, mark my words."

"He's not going to want to wash ashore someplace where he'd be at the mercy of the commons," Calu agreed. "What if he decides to head for Edinton?"

"Trying to beat against these winds in those boats? Maybe two weeks. He could do it, but they'll have to stretch their food and water very carefully."

"Good," Mari said. "Let's get going, then."

"Where to?" Captain Banda asked.

"For now, keep heading for Edinton." She called across the water to the *Gray Lady*. "We're going to speed up! Stay with us!"

Not long later Mari sat on the deck, in the inner circle of several rows making up most of those aboard the *Pride*. Next to her was Alain, and right behind Alain was Asha. Clustered close by were the rest of Mari's original group, Mechanics Alli, Calu, Dav, and Bev. Only Mage Dav, still aboard the *Gray Lady*, was not present.

Mari could feel the eyes of Mechanics, Apprentices, and the common sailors upon her. Before she could say anything, Master Mechanic Lukas spoke up, seated facing her across a small open area in the center of the group. "Master Mechanic Mari, my experience with you is that you work out details before deciding on actions. I didn't question the vagueness of what you've told us so far because I could understand your reasons for withholding the details while hostile ears could hear. I think most of us would like to hear more now."

"And you will," Mari said, once more trying to sound totally in control. She was getting better at that, she realized. And that was good, since Master Mechanic Lukas's words could be taken as a challenge as well as a request for more information.

Alain reached into his robes and produced the text she had asked him to bring from the *Gray Lady*, handing it to Mari. She had wanted that done in full view of the Mechanics. "This is a big detail," she said, holding up the text, then passing it carefully to Master Mechanic Lukas. "Texts containing technology banned by the Mechanics Guild."

"Banned technology?" The Mechanics around the circle were straining to look, their eyes filled with wonder, as Lukas took the text and began looking through it. "Communications," he commented.

"Look at that!" a Mechanic behind him gasped, pointing. "We could do that! It would improve our portable far-talkers."

"But what's that?" another Mechanic asked, staring. "It's…all right. I get it. But can we build that?"

"If we can't yet, we'll find a way," Lukas said. He nodded to Mari. "This is huge. How many do you have?"

"Quite a few more," Mari said. "Including medical, and armaments, and mass production."

"Mass production?"

"Making things fast. Making a lot of things fast," Mari added.

"The Guild wouldn't like that," Mechanic Ken said. "According to them, the Mechanic arts involve hand-crafted work for everything. No wonder the Guild would have kept that banned for centuries." He peered at the text that Lukas held. "That paper doesn't look ancient."

"These are copies of the originals," Mari said.

"Who gets to see these?" an eager voice cried.

"Everybody," Mari said.

"She means it," Alli said. "We've been looking over the texts on the *Gray Lady*."

Lukas was frowning at the text he held. "Mari, this is amazing. In the long run, it will let us build some of the things we've only dreamed of. In the long run. But we may not have a long run. I don't know where you're planning to set up shop, but a few dozen Mechanics and Apprentices who have to build their basic tools before they can even start on these things won't be able to get very far before the Guild locates us and destroys us."

"The Mage Guild wants Master Mechanic Mari dead, too," said Senior Mechanic Gina. "They'll come after us as well, which I wouldn't have worried about as much before what I read today."

"We need tools and we need more workers," Lukas summed up.

Mari took a deep breath, knowing that her next statements would have to be said just right. "We can get workers. We can get a lot of workers." She pointed to the common sailors listening to the discussion. "Commons can do basic Mechanic work."

Utter silence fell.

"I've proven it," Mari said. "They can use our tools. They can operate a boiler. If given proper instruction and supervision. They can build things, if we show them what to build and how to do it."

"Are you saying," Lukas said slowly, "that the commons are Mechanics, too?"

"No," Mari said. "We're better at it all. The lie the Mechanics Guild has told all these years is that we're the only ones who *can* do it. What we are, are the people who are *best* at it. When I was working with the commons, what to me was easy came harder to them. I don't believe this was just because it was new to them. We Mechanics will remain the leaders, the teachers, the skilled practitioners of our arts. But we don't have to keep them secret anymore."

Calu nodded. "We can design, we can innovate, we can supervise, we can be engineers. The Guild has pretty much told us we have to dig every ditch because commons can't use shovels. But the commons can. They can do basic production and operation tasks. Which frees us up to do, well, the stuff we like to do."

"Commons mess up a lot," someone commented.

"They mess up," Captain Banda said, "when they're treated poorly. When they're treated with respect, they do a fine job. My sailors are skilled, reliable workers."

"Let me be clear," Mari said, acutely aware of the commons listening. "I'm not talking about the same deal the Guild has been running on Dematr, where the Mechanics are in charge of everything. The Mechanics should be in charge of Mechanic tasks. In charge of their workshops and manufacturing and design areas and the places that teach people how to be Mechanics or how to do jobs like operating boilers. But we shouldn't be telling the commons what to do. I meant what I said earlier about freedom. The commons should rule themselves. We have to stop treating the commons as slaves to Mechanics. They are people, like us, and just as we deserve freedom and respect, so do they."

A low rumble sounded among the Mechanics as they took that in. It didn't sound like a happy rumble.

Alain stood up, attracting everyone's attention. "I am a Mage," he said. "The elders of my Guild taught me that everyone else was only a shadow. What happened to those others did not matter in any way. Mari showed me that others do matter. That Mechanics do matter, as do common people."

Mechanic Alli stood up, too. "All of us have been unhappy with the way we've been treated by the Senior Mechanics. Right? They've ordered us around, and told us we can't do things, and forced us to do things, and generally made our lives miserable because they wanted to control everything. You, and me, and every Mechanic haven't been the rulers of Demätr. That's what we were told, but it's not true. It's the Guild that has ruled this world. We've been the servants of the Guild. One step higher up the ladder than the commons, but still servants."

"Everybody has to be free," Mari said, giving her words more force and more volume. "Everybody. Mechanic. Mage. Common folk. Because it is going to take everybody to beat the Mechanics Guild and the Mage Guild. It is going to take everybody to change this world. We work together, and we all win. We try to keep things the same, and we all lose."

She had chosen those words carefully, and could see the reaction they caused. Especially the last sentence. She didn't have to underline that keeping things the same had been the primary governing rule for the Guild since its founding. And everyone here had bloodied themselves against the wall of inertia that rule had created.

"Do you really think," Master Mechanic Lukas asked, "that you can get Mechanics, Mages, and commons to work together that way?"

"I already have," Mari said.

Several moments of silence followed. Lukas looked at Mage Alain and Mage Asha, then around at the common sailors. He smiled slightly. "I'm looking forward to learning more about that, Master Mechanic Mari. All right. It's your project. Does anyone disagree?" None of the Mechanics spoke up this time. "Now tell me where we're going to get tools."

Mari grinned. "We know where to get tools. A Guild Hall. We're heading for one right now."

"Edinton?" Mechanic Ken asked incredulously. "I won't deny that Edinton has a lousy reputation and is probably riddled with dissent, but that doesn't get you through the door, Mari."

"The front entrances have been reinforced even more in the last year," Senior Mechanic Gina said. "And additional guard procedures put into place. You would need an army to break through the front door."

"Why do you seek ways to overcome the defenses at the front entrance?" Alain asked, drawing looks from all of the Mechanics. Only Mari knew that she had prepared him to ask that question after he had been the one to suggest to her not only attacking the Guild Hall but how to get in.

"Because that's the way inside," Master Mechanic Lukas said gruffly.

"But my training in military matters advises that when faced with strong defenses, it is better to go around them than to strike them head-on."

Lukas paused before answering. "There is merit in that. In theory. If you want to break something you aim for a weak point instead of hammering where it is strongest. But there isn't any way to go around the defenses at the front. The other entrances to the Guild Hall are heavily armored and routinely locked, barred, and alarmed. I doubt with the materials available to us we could even blow our way through them."

"There are other ways to make openings where none exist," Alain said.

Master Mechanic Lukas froze with his mouth half-open.

"You mean like when you made that opening in the deck?" Mechanic Ken asked eagerly, leaning in toward Alain. "Can you do that for a longer time?"

"Yes," Alain said. "On land there will be much more power to draw on. And the other Mages who follow Mari can also perform this spell."

"We've seen it," Alli said. "It's a solid wall, then the Mages do their thing, and there's an opening big enough to walk through."

"How can they make openings in walls?" Lukas asked. "I've seen it, but how do they do it?"

Alain answered. "Mages do not make openings. We create the illusion of an opening in the illusion of a wall. The illusion lasts as long as our power can sustain it, and then the illusion of the wall returns to its former appearance."

Mari laughed. "I've had this conversation before! Everyone, Alain is not messing with you. That is how the Mages think. It's how they do something that we can't explain. And Alain was the one who proposed this plan. Unlike me, or probably any of the Mechanics here, he actually has some training in how to conduct military operations."

"If we can get inside the Guild Hall somewhere far from the front entrance," Calu said, "then we'd just be more Mechanics walking around. We could get access to things like the armory—"

"That's heavily alarmed and locked," someone cautioned.

"Why can't a Mage make an opening in the armory?" Ken asked, looking around.

"Bring a Mage inside a Mechanics Guild Hall?"

"Why not?"

"What happens when they kill somebody?"

"Why would we kill anyone?" Alain asked. "Would that be necessary?"

"No," Mari said. "And if it did prove to be necessary, Mechanics would do it. We can handle our own. The Mages will not harm anyone if I tell them not to."

"They aren't like other Mages, then," someone scoffed.

"This one is talking to us," Master Mechanic Lukas pointed out. "I can even spot some feeling in his voice at times. No, he's not like other Mages. And neither is the Lady Mage there. While we were pounding our heads against the front entrance fortification problem, this Mage thought of a way around it. Why haven't Mages broken into Mechanics Guild Halls that way before this, Sir Mage?"

"Why would Mages want to?" Alain asked.

"Don't Mages hate us?"

"Mages hate no one. Mages do not care about anyone. That does not mean they will never harm them," Alain added. "It means Mages do not care whether others are hurt or killed, because they do not believe others are real. Why attack the Mechanics unless they first attack the Mages?"

"Which I understand did happen in the past," Mari said. "Maybe our Guild decided in part to leave the Mages alone because the Mages did break into Guild Halls in the way Alain has suggested."

"Your...work," Mechanic Ken asked. "It can't be detected by alarm systems?"

"It can be," Alli offered. "If a Mage makes a hole that breaks an alarm wire, that sets off an alarm just as if someone cut it. But if we tell the Mages where to make the holes—I mean, if Mari tells them where to do it—they should be able to avoid setting off alarms. There's about thirty of us. Counting the weapons we still have on the *Gray Lady*, we've got a dozen rifles and four pistols. That's already a lot, but Edinton's armory should have ten or twelve more rifles and a couple of revolvers."

"We go in at night," Mari said. "We know where the security patrols travel and what their schedules are because we've all walked those patrols and the Guild never changes them. We know the exact layout of the Guild Hall at Edinton because the Guild builds every Hall using the same plan. I don't know where all the alarm wiring runs but I bet some of the others of you do. We surprise everyone, we get all the weapons under our control, and when the Senior Mechanics at Edinton wake up, we'll be in control of that Guild Hall."

"I've always wanted to loot a Guild Hall," Bev said. "To get my hands on some of the stuff the Senior Mechanics have hidden away for only their use."

"I've wanted that longer than you have," Lukas said.

"Do we get a vote on this plan?" another Mechanic asked.

Mari could see Alain's head move very slightly to left and right in a tiny shake of disapproval. They had discussed this, too, and Alain had been very firm that while voting might be a good idea under other circumstances, it was no way to run an army.

And while this was a very small army, it was going to attack a Guild Hall.

"No," Mari said. "We can discuss long term policy issues, but when it comes to a project like this, we need someone in charge."

"Why is that someone you?"

Calu laughed. "Are the Mages going to listen to you?" he called to the dissenting Mechanic. "Are the commons going to do what you say? How many Mechanics in Edinton are going to look to you as someone to follow?"

Mechanic Ken glared at the objector. "You are just like me and the others here. All except Master Mechanic Mari. We sat around as the years went by and things got worse and worse. We complained and said something ought to be done, and watched our friends get shipped off to exile or prison, and waited for someone to do something. Why follow Mari? Because she's willing to lead! And you know what the best measures are of how good she is at that? The fact that the Guild has worked so hard to kill her, and the fact that she not only is still alive but has hit the Guild harder than we ever dreamed possible."

Ken pointed to the banned technology text that Lukas still held. "Anybody else who has managed to get their hands on that can present themselves as a candidate to lead us."

"We should have an organized group in charge," Senior Mechanic Gina said cautiously. "But when dealing with issues of Mages and commons, there is only one person who can give orders."

"I just don't want her setting herself up as the only one in charge," the dissenter complained.

"I don't want that, either," Mari said. "Believe me. I want to build things and fix things, and when this is over that's what I'm going to do. Anybody who tries to haul me into a Guild Master's job is going to face a very nasty fight."

"That settles it," Lukas said. "None of us would have been interested in joining—if you'll forgive me, Mari—a mindless act of rebellion by a girl barely out of school. But the Guild has already made it clear how much they fear your ability to inspire other Mechanics, and it is obvious that you have put a lot of thinking and preparation into this. We've been looking for a leader, and we've found one. A leader with plans and the means to carry them out. That leaves only the question of where we're going to take all of the equipment we will hopefully get from Edinton."

"I want to avoid saying that until we leave Edinton," Mari said. "There is a place, but since we have a chance of losing someone at Edinton I don't want to tell everyone yet and risk the Guild learning right away."

As the meeting broke up, Mari turned to her friends. "Thanks, guys. Alain and I should stay aboard the *Pride* to keep an eye on this bunch."

"It's a good thing Master Mechanic Lukas backed you," Calu commented. "He deliberately brought up issues others might use to try to undermine you so you could address them up front."

"Yeah," Alli said, "but he was also testing her. I worked with Lukas enough to be able to spot that. If Mari hadn't passed, he would have challenged her. Hey, Mari, as long as you're staying here, maybe Calu and I should go back to the *Gray Lady*."

"You just want to be alone in that rear cabin," Mari teased, feeling giddy with relief that she had made it through the meeting so well.

"Stars above, yes! Calu and I got married yesterday, remember? And we didn't get to spend last night alone."

"We did get to spend it playing pirate," Calu said.

"Yeah, we did." Alli giggled. "That will make a great story for our kids. Playing pirate on our honeymoon night."

"They probably won't want to hear about that," Captain Banda said, approaching. "Master Mechanic Mari, my sailors and those from the *Gray Lady* who are still aboard this ship wish to present you with a gift."

"What? A gift?" She turned to see the commons gathered nearby, one from the *Gray Lady* in front.

That sailor stepped forward and offered Mari something.

She stared at the object in the sailor's hands. "A knife?" Mari picked it up carefully, turning it to examine the weapon. It was a sailor's knife, with a short, broad, heavy blade designed to handle dozens of tasks. The handle, gleaming hardwood inlaid with mother-of-pearl from seashells, contrasted with the dark metal of the blade. Folded into the handle was a curved spike that could be swung out for use. "It's beautiful. Why are you giving it to me?"

"It is traditional, Lady Mari," the sailor said. "To gift a knife whenever someone is initiated into the fellowship of Jules."

"He means the pirates," Captain Banda explained. "You can be certain that most new pirates don't get a knife nearly that nice."

"Most new pirates aren't the daughter herself," the sailor said. "Any doubts anyone had disappeared when we saw you take this ship like Jules would have. Her blood is in you."

"Thank you," said Mari, looking down at the knife, simultaneously feeling proud of the gift and embarrassed by it and the praise. "I will do my best to, uh…" *Be a good pirate* didn't sound right. "Live up to the example of Jules."

The sailors backed away, smiling and nodding.

"Put the knife in your teeth," Alli suggested. "Let's see how piratical you look."

"Weren't you and Calu going back to the *Gray Lady*?" Mari asked pointedly. "You're going to need your rest. How many days until we reach Edinton, Captain Banda?"

"If these winds hold, about three days," Banda said.

"Three days?" Alli said. "What do you think, Calu? Are you up for three days of serious *resting* on our honeymoon?"

Mari tried to keep a straight face as she shook her head at Alli. "Over the next three days you're not supposed to be *resting* nonstop, wench, you're supposed to be helping plan our attack on the Guild Hall!"

"I am not a wench!" Alli said as Calu led her away. "I'm your armaments expert! And don't you forget it, your daughterness!"

"Don't call me that!"

Mari noticed Captain Banda smiling at her. "Your friends must be a great comfort in times of stress," he said.

"I don't know if they're always a comfort," Mari said. "But they do help me keep my head on straight. And help keep my head from exploding when the pressure gets too high." She indicated Alain. "But by far the most important is Mage Alain. Without him, I couldn't do this."

Banda studied Alain. "It's real, then? I've noticed the promise rings but didn't wish to pry."

"It's real," Mari said, putting her arm through Alain's.

"You were wise not to make too much of that while convincing the others," Banda said. "They've had enough to take on as it is. We'll clean out the half of the main cabin that was occupied by the Senior Mechanics so you'll have a place to stay on the ship. I don't think any of the Mechanics you've freed will begrudge you a little more space and privacy for the next few days."

Alain woke just before dawn two days later. Mari sat in a chair before the window looking out over the stern of the *Pride*. He got up as well. "More nightmares?"

She shook her head, keeping her gaze fixed on the water. "Just very restless. We should reach Edinton tonight, and so many details of our plan have to wait on exactly what we find there."

"There is something else," Alain said, walking to stand beside her.

Mari sighed. "Serves me right for trying to lie to a Mage. Alain, I'm worried about what might happen. If I mess up in Edinton as badly as I did at Julesport, we could have a disaster on our hands."

"You messed up at Julesport?"

"Don't pretend otherwise," she said unhappily. "You've been very nice, you and everyone else, not to bring up my mistakes. But I still made them, and things could easily have ended up a lot worse because of that."

Alain moved to be able to see Mari's face. "Mistakes?"

She glared at him. "You do remember that you were kidnapped, right? Because I wanted to play Master Mechanic and ignored my larger responsibilities? Including my responsibilities to you?"

"This has been bothering you?" Alain sat down on the small ledge running just inside the stern window.

"Of course it's been bothering me! Alain, if I hadn't sent you off alone, you wouldn't have been kidnapped."

"I was not alone," Alain pointed out. "I had soldiers of Julesport with me."

"That's sort of irrelevant, isn't it? They couldn't protect you and I wasn't there and they died and you got kidnapped," Mari finished, sounding both miserable and angry with herself. "I messed that up so badly. And now we're going into Edinton and if I mess up again like that dozens of people could die."

Alain paused to think his words through. "I understand your worries, but do not blame yourself for Julesport. Mari, you know I was knocked unconscious, and the soldiers were killed by Mages using spells to conceal themselves."

"Yes. So?"

"The two Dark Mages we found and Mage Niaro could not have so quickly and silently killed that many soldiers. They must have had help. I have discussed this with the other Mages, and they agree that the Mage Guild must have assisted in my kidnapping, using at least several other Mages, then turned me over to the Dark Mages for degradation and humiliation."

Mari frowned, then gave him a demanding look. "Why haven't you mentioned that to me before now?"

"Because it has been clear that you did not wish to discuss events in Julesport."

"All right, but so what? How does that change anything?"

"It means," Alain explained, "that if you had been with me, you would have been killed along with the soldiers. You could not have defended yourself against opponents you could not see. Perhaps the Mage Guild intended that and were frustrated by you not being there. Perhaps they would simply have taken advantage of the opportunity to kill you. But had we both left the city hall in Julesport at the same time, I would still have been kidnapped, and you would have died."

Mari stared at him, her mouth partway open. Finally recovering, she shook her head at him. "You're saying that my unthinking and selfish decision saved my life?"

"And mine," Alain said. "For without you, Mage Asha could not have led the others to me."

She fell silent, looking past him at the waves. "All right. But even if it is true that I made the right decision for the wrong reasons, the fact remains that I had no idea it would be the right decision."

"Perhaps you did," Alain said. "You stayed to fix that Mechanic device, which is of value to the commons in Julesport. That was not selfish. It placed them in your debt. Perhaps that unselfish act is what led them to ask the Confederation warships to protect our departure from the harbor."

Mari finally smiled slightly. "I don't know if I believe you, but… It's nice to think I may have at least made good mistakes." Her smile vanished. "But Alain, everyone will be counting on me in Edinton. What if my mistakes there are all bad ones?"

"Then you will do something to fix them," Alain said. "That is what you do, is it not? Fix things?"

That earned him another brief smile. "Why do they trust me, Alain? I'm not somebody like General Flyn. I'm just me. Yet they're letting me make the big decisions about Edinton, including attacking the Guild Hall."

"Master Mechanic Lukas did not simply accept you as a leader," Alain said. "Not until you had passed the tests he asked of you. And if anything goes wrong in Edinton, they know you have proven the ability to make decisions quickly under great stress."

"You mean like in Altis, where my great decisions trapped us in a warehouse?" Mari said.

Alain shook his head at her. "Your decisions were not wrong. They should have worked. You did not know we were being perceived by that Mechanic device that betrayed our location. I will remind you that you kept making decisions despite the situation getting more and more desperate. You did not freeze in terror or indecision."

"I came awful close, Alain," Mari admitted.

"But you did not. You kept thinking and you kept acting." Alain reached to rest one hand on hers where it lay in her lap. "You have two more important qualifications. One is that those who follow you believe in you. That confidence is no small thing in battle. Call it pure illusion if you will. You know almost as well as I the power that such an illusion can wield."

Mari grimaced but nodded. "What's the second thing?"

"You listen to those who know more and are willing to accept their advice, just as you have listened to me and are willing to accept that perhaps you are not so awful a leader as you fear. Perhaps you are even very good at it."

This time her smile lingered. "What did I do to deserve you?"

"You did not kill me when first we met."

"I'm never going to live that down, am I?" Mari closed her eyes and sighed. "I should try to get a little sleep. Would you mind lying down with me? When you're holding me, it's easier to keep the nightmares at bay."

"I could be convinced to lie down with you and hold you," Alain said.

"I'll bet you could!" She smiled at him. "Thank you. Sometimes I think too much."

"You will never be someone who thinks too little," Alain said.

"That's true. Every time I think you're totally deluded about me and just seeing some perfect illusion of me, you say something that helps me realize you do know me." She nodded to him. "Whatever happens in Edinton, I'll do my best."

The *Gray Lady* and the *Pride of Longfalls*, both flying the flag of the Mechanics Guild, entered the harbor of Edinton just before midnight. A harbor police boat rowed up to the *Pride*, but before those aboard could issue any instructions Captain Banda called down to them in the arrogant and assured tones of a Mechanic. "Guild business!"

That was all it took to get past the harbor defenses, which had been strongly admonished not to interfere in any way with Mechanics Guild shipping.

Leaving behind the unhappy occupants of the harbor police boat, the *Pride* led the way through the harbor, past a variety of large sailing ships which carried out trade all over the Sea of Jules and into the Sea of Bakre as well as many smaller ships whose size, oars, and sails were suited for short voyages up and down the coast. Reaching an anchorage as close to the main quay as possible, the *Pride* tied up to the buoy and passed a line over to the *Gray Lady* so the smaller ship could tether to the larger one.

The boat from the *Gray Lady* and two much larger longboats from the *Pride of Longfalls* came alongside the boat landing a short time later. Crewmembers tied up the boats as thirty-one Mechanics disembarked displaying widely varying degrees of physical skill and agility. Alli arranged the armed Mechanics in front of the group, which produced an intimidating image. "We have as many rifles as two or three Imperial legions," she commented to Mari.

A few city guards at the landing, previously bored as they endured the tedium of duty during a period of the day when little ever happened, were gaping at the Mechanics. Their officer came forward, looking as nervous as could be expected. "Honored Mechanics, may I request—"

Mari held up her hand to forestall questions she wasn't going to answer. "This is an internal Mechanics Guild matter," she said. "Neither the city of Edinton nor the Bakre Confederation is involved. Stay clear of us, do not interfere, and do not sound any alarms. No harm will come to your city."

"But—" The officer's eyes came to rest on the six Mages accompanying the Mechanics as the Mages walked into the light of the guard post lantern, and her jaw dropped. "I must...I must inform my superiors, Lady Mechanic."

"Of course you must," Mari agreed. "Feel free to notify your superiors. Just don't sound any alarms and don't get in our way."

The officer's gaze had shifted and was now locked on Mari. "Lady? Are you…?"

"Don't do anything," Mari said, giving the words all of the force that she could. "Tell the city leaders, tell your commanders, that they should not do anything. I will speak with them before I leave this city."

"Lady, I must know. Have you come from Julesport?"

"Yes."

The officer saluted, then hastily moved to one side. Mari waved her force onward and they walked past the common soldiers, who gazed at the procession with rapt expressions.

"A couple of those soldiers ran off once we were past," Calu told Mari. "Taking the news to their bosses, I'm sure. A lot of commons in this city will be getting early wakeups this morning."

"Just as long as none of the Mechanics hear about it," Mari replied.

It was a long slog from the waterfront to the vast open plaza that surrounded the Mechanics Guild Hall of Edinton. Mari's force labored along nearly deserted streets, the Mechanics soon feeling the exertion required to maintain the speed necessary to reach the Guild Hall in the hour before dawn. Edinton was pretty far south on the continent, and even at this hour the Mechanics grew uncomfortably warm in their jackets. But none of them would remove those signs of their status and their knowledge.

The Mages, wearing their robes, walked as if they could hold the same pace for days without pausing. As far as Mari could tell, none of the Mages had even broken a sweat. She wondered why she gained an impression of smugness even though they were revealing no feelings at all.

The few commons they encountered hastily sought shelter in the nearest open building or side street. Whatever an armed group of Mechanics was doing at this predawn hour was not anything any smart common would want to get involved in. And if the commons spotted the Mages among the Mechanic jackets, that only offered further grounds for avoiding the group.

"We are being paced," Alain said to Mari. "Cavalry and some soldiers on foot."

Mari glanced over as they passed a side street, seeing a couple of mounted soldiers a block down riding parallel to the progress of the Mechanics. "What do you think they're doing?"

"Watching," Alain said. "There are far too few to threaten us. The city leaders of Edinton are taking the wise course of waiting to see what we do."

"Good." She cast an annoyed look at him. "Why are you keeping your eyes on the street so much? You're looking down as though you expect to see something."

"I am studying the surface," Alain said.

That was an ambiguous statement at best, but she remembered Alain telling her that Mages needed to know the details of the "illusion" of the world so they could effectively change that illusion in the ways they wanted. "All right. Sorry. I'm nervous," she half-explained, half-apologized.

"The other Mechanics are far more nervous than you are," Alain said, keeping his voice low. "They have far less experience with risking their lives."

Mage Asha walked a little faster to catch up with Mari, Mechanic Dav staying right by her side. "I sense a Mage in that direction," she told Mari and Alain, indicating a low hill crowned by the trees, shrubs, and ornamental structures of a small park that loomed off to their left. "I feel that she is aware of us, but only watches for now."

It was a very odd feeling to be walking down the empty streets knowing that so many hidden eyes were observing your progress. Mari had to suppress an urge to shout at those concealed watchers. But she was growing more worried as time went on. Edinton was the southernmost large city in the Confederation, and thus the closest to what had once been the Kingdom of Tiae. The closest to the place where the Storm had already begun unraveling the fabric of civilization. Mari had spent a few months in Edinton, but almost all of that time inside the Mechanic Guild Hall or at work sites. She had gained little sense of the stability of the commons here. Would the attack on the Guild Hall trigger some larger disturbance that would threaten everyone?

Consumed by those concerns, Mari was startled when they finally reached the large plaza that separated the Guild Hall from the surrounding common buildings. The group, still concealed from the Hall by those buildings, stopped to rest while Mari studied the familiar lines of the Guild Hall with new eyes.

From the outside, the first floors of the Guild Hall presented the walls and slit windows of a fortress. Mari knew those walls were thick and strong.

"Has anyone ever broken into a Guild Hall before?" Mechanic Dav asked.

"Yes," Mari said. "At Marandur."

"Oh, yeah, of course. What was that like? The Guild Hall, I mean."

Mari paused at the memory. "Haunted. Everything collapsed on top of everything else. Rusted tools and equipment, spilled chemicals. Old, broken bones. Dead. It was pretty awful, Dav."

"I wonder if my ancestor died at the Guild Hall?" Dav said, crouching to look across the plaza. "Or somewhere else in Marandur during the battle?"

"Somewhere else," Mari said.

Dav turned a surprised look on her. "How do you know?"

"I saw his grave, Dav. I'm sorry I haven't been able to tell you much, but someday I will. I will tell you, right now, that he was a hero, and an ancestor you can be very proud of."

"Thanks," Dav said with a smile. "Do you think he would approve of what we're doing?"

"I know he would." Mari looked at Alain. "Any warning?"

Alain shook his head. "My foresight provides no warning. Which does not mean there is no danger, given how unreliable foresight is."

Mari pointed at the windows of the Guild Hall. "The guards posted inside the front entrance can't see us from this angle, but the security watches that rove through the building are supposed to look out the windows as they pass and make sure no one is on the plaza during the night," she explained to Alain and the other Mages.

"Five minutes," Alli said, checking her watch. "Right, everybody? The roving watches should pass by this side and give us a small period of time when it's unlikely anyone will see us coming."

"If they're following the routines," Master Mechanic Lukas cautioned. Sweat was still running down his face from the long, fast walk. "But this is Edinton. They might have increased their alert status. Or they might have let the roving watches get sloppy."

"Maybe," Mari agreed. "We've all walked those watches when we were Apprentices. At this moment, every one of those on duty will be thinking about how tired they are and how much they wish they were back in bed, how they've got more than an hour left before being relieved, what they'll have for breakfast—"

"Everything but their watch responsibilities," Lukas agreed dryly. "It's still a substantial risk to go out there. Even a single Mechanic spotted on that plaza would be grounds for a roving watch to sound the alarm."

"Then we'll have to hope that doesn't happen." Mari looked at Alli. "How much longer?"

"One minute. Let's get ready to head out, everyone."

At Alli's signal, they began walking again. Mari had considered running, to minimize the time they were out on the plaza, but running Mechanics would certainly signal trouble to anyone who saw them. Whereas walking Mechanics might look like an unusual but not threatening group arriving to check in at Guild Hall at an odd hour.

Hopefully. Mari put one hand on her pistol as she walked, trying to breathe steadily, watching the windows of the Guild Hall as they approached it, wondering whether someone would look out at any moment and see them, whether weapons inside were already being pointed toward her and the others.

She had never realized just how wide this blasted plaza was.

CHAPTER NINE

I swear that Guild Hall is receding from us as we try to get closer," Alli muttered, fingering the rifle she held in both hands.

"It's not much farther," Mari encouraged everyone.

The group finally reached the outside wall of the Guild Hall, everyone pushing up against it to minimize the chance of being seen from any windows overhead. "I can't hear any alarms sounding inside," Calu commented.

Several of the Mechanics studied the wall they were at, looking up and around to orient themselves, using their hands to trace lines on the blank surface. "The alarm line should run along here, right?"

"A little higher."

"There ought to be a junction about…there."

"Where's the internal floor level?"

"There's a dividing wall inside. Is that…no…here. Right?"

Eventually, one of the Mechanics looked at Mari. "This is where we need a door, Master Mechanic."

"Trace it for Mage Alain," Mari said.

The Mechanic ran his forefinger along the wall, outlining a squat rectangle.

"Any problem?" Mari asked Alain.

"It should not be," Alain said. "But once I use this spell, and the other Mages with us begin using spells as well, the Mages in Edinton will know we are here and may be able to identify some of us."

Alain took on the intense concentration familiar to Mari, while most of the Mechanics looked on skeptically.

The opening appeared. "Do not take too long," Alain said, keeping his eyes on the spot.

Mari and her friends hustled the rest of the Mechanics inside, everyone ducking to get through the low opening, while Mage Dav ensured that the Mages entered. The walls here at the base were so thick that the opening was much more of a tunnel than a door. Alain came last, relaxing once he was inside and slumping back against the once-more solid wall. "Are you all right?" Mari murmured.

"Tired," Alain said. "Is it what you call ironic that the area around us has a good supply of power to use?"

"Power for Mages around the Mechanics Guild Hall? Yes, that is ironic." Mari looked around. With the illusion of a hole in the illusion of the wall gone, the group was crowding a hallway so dark it took a few moments for their eyes to adjust. "Are we where we're supposed to be?"

"We need light," someone complained.

Mari brought out her portable light, as did Bev and a few other Mechanics. As they switched on, Mage Hiro moved close to Mechanic Ken and gazed closely at the light. "How is this done? You are changing the illusion of dark to that of light, but there is no power being used."

"We're using power," Ken assured Hiro. "These have batteries."

"Different power," Mari told Ken. "It's so different from what the Mages use that they can't sense it."

"That makes me feel better," Ken said. "Sir Mage, after seeing one of you Mages make an instant tunnel through more than a lance-length of reinforced concrete and masonry, it's nice to know that some of our Mechanic skills impress you."

"This one is…interested…" Mage Hiro said without feeling or expression. "Not…impressed."

"He means that well," Mari whispered to Ken. Then, more loudly but still quietly, "Isn't this hallway on the roving watch route?"

"Sure is." Alli checked the time. "But the watch won't be by here for half an hour."

"The armory is this way," another Mechanic said. They went down one of the narrow hallways that ran next to the outer wall, passing an armored emergency exit with thick steel bars locked in place across it to protect against anyone breaking in. "We need to go up to the next corner, then left."

Just short of that corner, Bev held up a warning hand. "Hold it! I heard something."

The group shuffled to an irregular halt. Once they did, the sound of footsteps became clear. Whoever was walking didn't seem to be in any hurry, but was coming their way. "I know that slow, dispirited shuffle," Calu commented in a whisper. "That's an Apprentice on roving watch."

"Either they're off-schedule or the schedule here at Edinton has changed!" Alli whispered back.

Mari realized that everyone was looking at her, waiting for her to tell them what to do. Could she convince the Apprentice that this was just some routine group of Mechanics who were out at an odd time?

"Wait," she murmured. "If we were a regular group of Mechanics…"

"Mari?" Alli questioned.

"Everybody else stay here." Mari gestured the others back, then came around the corner.

Partway down the hall, an Apprentice was making his rounds, meandering along in the bored fashion Mari remembered from her own days having to fulfill such duties. Despite the fact that he was supposed to be watching for trouble of any kind, the teenage Apprentice took a while to notice Mari wearing her dark jacket in the dim hallway. Finally he did, stumbling to a sudden halt.

Mari saw that unlike the security patrols she was used to, this Apprentice was equipped with a pistol in a holster on one hip. She beckoned imperiously, adopting the worst kind of Master Mechanic attitude. "Get over here."

Even in the dimly lit hallway she could see the Apprentice's worry as he doubtless wondered what this full Mechanic was about to chew him out for. He hastened up to Mari. "My pardon, Lady Mechanic, I was—"

"Never mind that," Mari interrupted harshly. "Let me see that revolver."

"Lady Mechanic, my instructions are not to remove the revolver from the holster unless—"

"Did I ask you what your instructions were?" Mari broke in, letting her voice grow even harsher. "Don't you think I already know what your instructions are? Hand me that weapon for inspection!"

The Apprentice hastily removed the pistol from the holster and handed it to Mari.

She looked it over. "Five chambers loaded. Safety on. Very good. Where is your alarm signal?"

"Here, Lady Mechanic." The Apprentice pulled a large whistle from one of his pockets.

"Give it to me."

"Yes, Lady Mechanic." As the Apprentice did so, the first traces of a different kind of worry crossed his face. "Lady Mechanic, I was told not to—"

"Relax." Mari smiled reassuringly at him. "It's a drill," she said, remembering what the Apprentices aboard the *Pride* had thought. "Pretend you're a prisoner."

"Y-yes, Lady Mechanic." The Apprentice stared as the rest of Mari's group came around the corner. "M-m-m-mages? Lady Mechanic, why are some of them dressed as Mages?"

"You're not questioning your instructions, are you?" Mari asked as one of the other Mechanics took custody of the young man. "Now, quiet. You're a prisoner, remember?"

"Yes, Lady Mechanic. Are you going to take Mechanic Ilya prisoner too?"

"Mechanic Ilya?" Mari heard more footsteps approaching.

"My watch partner. He was just resting for a moment."

"Watch partner?" Calu asked. "They've teamed full Mechanics on the roving watches with Apprentices? I'll bet that hasn't helped morale in the Guild Hall any."

"You didn't know—?" the Apprentice began with a puzzled expression.

Mechanic Ilya came around the turn, huffing slightly from trying to catch up. "Who's talk—?"

"Shhh," Alli said, pointing her rifle at him.

Ilya, facing at least four rifles, stopped and held his hands up. "Wha—?"

"It's a drill," the Apprentice said.

"You idiot! This isn't—"

"Shhh," Alli said again, walking forward to pull the Mechanic's revolver from his holster. "Noise makes me nervous," she said, holding her rifle with the barrel in Ilya's face, "and my finger twitches when I get nervous."

Not resisting, Mechanic Ilya stared over Alli's shoulder. "Master Mechanic Mari? I remember you from when you were here early last year. What are you doing back in Edinton? The Senior Mechanics have a shoot-on-sight order out on you."

"I know. I want to have some words with the Senior Mechanics," Mari said. "How is Mechanic Abad?"

"He got sent to Debran. After you left and word got out that you'd been ordered into Tiae, there was all kinds of hate and discontent here. Even more than before, that is. They sent off anybody considered a dissident, and then shipped in a lot of other people considered dissidents who were internally exiled to here."

"Brilliant," Calu said.

"But now—" Mechanic Ilya looked over the group before him. "You're really doing it, aren't you? You really are. Give me back my revolver and I'll help!"

"He speaks the truth," Alain said.

"Why," Master Mechanic Lukas demanded, "did the Senior Mechanics put someone like you, who was sympathetic to Mari, on a security watch?"

"To punish me!" Ilya said. "For my bad attitude!"

"Just when you think the Senior Mechanics can't get any more stupid," Alli observed, "they prove you wrong again. Putting people with questionable loyalty on security watches to punish them. That's just awesomely dumb."

"We're on our way to get more weapons," Mari said.

"The armory? That's on our roving watch route. You shouldn't run into anyone else at this hour."

"Mechanic Ilya?" the bewildered Apprentice asked.

"These Mechanics are all right," Ilya assured him.

They hurried, Mari checking the time remaining until the official day would begin in the Guild Hall and the Mechanics and Apprentices would begin waking up. Everything needed to be done before then.

The entry to the armory loomed before them, a steel door set into a steel frame with multiple massive steel locks set through heavy steel hasps.

A female Mechanic knelt to one side of the door. "All of the walls are alarmed," she said. "Except for this spot." She traced an area low on the wall. "I've been telling the Senior Mechanics for fifteen years that they needed to run an alarm wire across here, and for fifteen years they've sent my every report back with demands for further justification for deviating from established design. Open this up like you did the outside wall, and I can get in and disarm the alarms from the inside."

"Mage Asha, will you do this?" Alain asked.

"I will," Asha said.

"Mechanic Dav," Mari added, "you and Asha go inside as well in case your assistance is needed in getting the door open from the inside."

The female Mechanic's eyes widened as the area she had outlined vanished. She slid through the hole, followed by Mechanic Dav and then Mage Asha.

The hole vanished.

"What did I just see?" Mechanic Ilya asked, sounding fascinated as well as horrified.

"You'll get used to it," Alli told him. "Well, actually you won't get used to it. You just won't worry about it as much."

A rapid tapping sounded on the inside of the door. "Mage Dav?" Alain said.

"With your assistance, Mage Hiro," Dav said, pointing to the locks, "I will cause the illusion of the top half of this one to be replaced by nothing."

"I will do the same to the other," Hiro said.

The upper halves of both heavy locks vanished, leaving them to thud to the floor with a noise that made Mari wince and berate herself.

The massive door swung open on its hinges under the pull of Mechanic Dav and the female Mechanic. "You are not going to believe this," she said.

Mari crowded forward, her eyes widening in shock. Instead of the ten or twelve rifles she had expected to see, there were piles of rifles below the racked weapons. "How many are there?"

"About fifty, I think. And nearly twenty revolvers. Plus a whole lot of ammunition."

"Tiae," Master Mechanic Lukas said as he surveyed the weapons. "I remember seeing the orders when the Guild pulled out of the Guild Halls in Tiae. They were told to bring anything that could be easily moved and destroy everything else."

"And rifles could be easily moved," Alli said. "The Guild must have stacked them all here instead of distributing them elsewhere. Ugh. Look at some of these. It's going to take some work to get the rust off. But we've got at least thirty immediately usable weapons. Mari?"

"Pass them out," Mari said.

The Mechanics quickly took one rifle or pistol each, only the captured Apprentice remaining unarmed. With a few weapons left, Alli moved to give a rifle to Asha, who stared back blankly.

"She has no idea how to use that," Mari said.

"She can point it," Alli said.

"No. Not consistently. Don't give guns to the Mages, Alli. They're dangerous enough without them." Mari looked around, knowing that she was about to give another critical order, one that would no longer allow her to exercise direct control of everyone else. But she either trusted these others to be able to do their assigned tasks, or she didn't. "It's time to split up. You've all got assigned targets, and those of you who might encounter locked doors will have Mages with your groups. The Mages have agreed to listen to *requests* for their assistance from the Mechanics they know. Mechanic Dav, stay with Mage Asha. Bev, stay with Mage Hiro. Alli, keep Mage Tana with you. Calu, you stick with the group including Mage Dav and Mage Dimitri. Mage Alain will stay with my group to help take the front entry."

"They've got six people on guard at the front," Mechanic Iyla cautioned. "Two Apprentices and four Mechanics."

"Do any of them have bad attitudes?" Mari asked.

"At the front? No. The Apprentices are…Apprentices. Regular watch rotation. But the Mechanics aren't the sort just to give up."

"You come with me, Ilya. Everybody else, remember to send a runner to the front to let me know when you've taken your objectives. We're running low on time, so don't waste any of it!"

She took off at a run, hearing others doing the same. The group split and split again, going up stairs and down hallways as each section headed for its assigned objective.

If she allowed herself time to think, it felt bizarre. To be running through the empty passageways of the Guild Hall, a pistol in her hand, a Mage alongside her, knowing that others under her command were doing to same. Not simply to defy the Senior Mechanics, but to defeat them in this one place and time. It would not topple the Mechanics Guild. It would only begin that process. But it was a beginning.

It was a long way through silent, darkened hallways from the armory to the main entry of the Guild Hall. Mari led her group unerringly in the right direction, her pistol held in a ready position. Thanks to the identical floor plan of Guild Halls everywhere she knew every corridor, every stair and every turn, yet there were differences in furnishings and decorative items that made the way seem familiar and strange at the same time. At one moment she might have been back at the Guild Hall in Caer Lyn, while a moment later Mari saw something that clearly said this was Edinton.

Mari slowed down as the small group still with her approached the front entry. "There will be an Apprentice sitting at a panel of alarms on the, uh, right side as we get to the entrance," she told Alain. "The Apprentice can't be allowed to touch anything. No one should touch anything on that panel."

"Can you deceive this Apprentice as you did the one near the armory?" Alain asked.

"No," Mari said, grateful that Alain's Mage training made him impassive at times like this. He appeared to be totally unconcerned, which helped keep her own worries under control. "The front entry will be lighted. The Mechanics at the entry will probably recognize me the moment I stick my head in there."

"I will stop the Apprentice from touching anything," Alain said.

"Without hurting the Apprentice?"

"Without hurting the Apprentice," Alain agreed. "Pause here." He took several deep breaths, then vanished.

Mari waited, pretending not to notice the shock on the faces of her fellow Mechanics. After she guessed that Alain must have reached the Apprentice at the alarm panel, she led the others forward.

They stepped into the light of the front entry. It was set for night levels, lower than during the day but the open space still felt bright after the dimness elsewhere in the Guild Hall. Mari saw four Mechanics lounging to the side, two of them playing cards, while one Apprentice stood watch at the port that gave a view of the plaza outside and the other sat next to the alarm panel.

Alerted by the sound of her footsteps, the four Mechanics were already scrambling to their feet, rifles in hand. The two Apprentices turned their heads to look towards Mari.

She was leveling her pistol at the Mechanics when the first shout rang out. "It's her! Sound top alert!"

"Freeze!" Mari shouted in return, but the Apprentice at the alarm panel quickly raised her arm to slap the top alert switch.

And hit instead Alain's chest. He had dropped the concealment spell and stood between the Apprentice and the alarm panel.

The Apprentice felt the unexpected barrier, turned to look, and fell backwards away from Alain, her eyes wide and mouth wider.

The Mechanic on the far left levered a round into his rifle, ready to fire at Mari from the waist.

She saw the metal of the rifle suddenly glow red and the Mechanic dropped it with a yelp.

Mari waited for a long moment to see if the heat would make the ammunition in the rifle explode, but as the rifle rapidly cooled she spoke with deadly seriousness, her pistol backed by the rifles of the three Mechanics with her. "That was a warning. The only one you'll get. Drop your weapons."

"You'll never get away with this," one of the Mechanics on guard said.

"Then there isn't any sense in you dying to try to stop me, is there?" Mari said.

First one, then the other Mechanics put down their rifles. The fourth was blowing on his slightly burnt hands.

Mari checked over the two Apprentices, but neither had pistols. Both were watching Mari with expressions of horror.

Mari couldn't help sighing. She remembered tales of famous outlaws who had gloried in being recognized and the fear such recognition generated in others. As far as Mari was concerned, there was nothing pleasant about bringing fear to anyone who figured out who she was.

"How can you do this?" the male Apprentice asked as the four Mechanics were tied up one by one by Mechanic Ilya, who was apparently enjoying the task.

"Maybe I'm not doing what you've been told I'm doing," Mari said.

"You're trying to destroy the Guild!"

"*That* I am doing," Mari admitted. "For some very good reasons, which can be summarized for the moment by saying that aside from your technical training, just about everything else the Guild has ever told you is a lie." Ensuring that all of the alarms had been silenced, she had one of her Mechanics open the front entrance and wave a signal to the sailors who had been watching. They came across the plaza, accompanied by the healers Cas and Pol. "Notify Captain Banda that so far everything is going all right," she told one of the sailors.

"I'm afraid we have little for you to do," she advised the healers.

"That's not a bad thing," Pol said, looking around curiously. "I've never been even this far inside a Mechanic Guild Hall. Are your Mechanic lights everywhere inside?"

"You mean electric lights? Yes." Mari moved to cover the main hallway leading to the front entrance as running steps sounded from the interior of the hall. To her relief, it was one of her Mechanics, easily identified thanks to the armband with the sign of the new day on it. She would have *to apologize, again, for doubting that would be needed,* Mari thought.

"We have control of the kitchens and the dining hall," the Mechanic reported. "All of the Mechanics and Apprentices are being brought to the dining hall to be held under guard."

"Good," Mari said. "Make sure they know that no one will be harmed unless they try to harm one of us. And as long as you're heading back that way, help one of my guys escort the four Mechanics who were on guard here back to the dining hall."

She had barely finished saying that when Mage Asha and Mechanic Dav showed up. "We've got the far-talker," Dav reported cheerfully. "No warnings or alerts got sent before we gained control."

"Outstanding. You and Mage Asha stay here in case I need to send reinforcements somewhere."

The two captive Apprentices had been seated on the long bench that spanned part of the back wall of the entry area. Asha walked over and sat down right next to the female Apprentice, who tried to shrink back but was stopped by the presence of the male Apprentice on her other side.

Asha looked at the female Apprentice. "What is your name?"

"A…A…A…A…" The Apprentice managed to swallow. "Apprentice Haru of Dorcastle."

"I have not been to Dorcastle." Her stock of social skills apparently exhausted, Asha lapsed into silence.

"Are you guys all right?" Mechanic Dav asked the two Apprentices. "Don't be scared of Mage Asha. She's nice."

"Nice?" Apprentice Haru glanced sidelong at Asha. "A Mage?"

Asha managed a small but real smile. "Thank you, Mechanic Dav."

More runners arrived, bringing news of more areas successfully seized and more surprised Mechanics taken prisoner.

By the time Mari saw the sun rising over the buildings to the east, the final reports had come in. "You control this Guild Hall, Master Mechanic Mari."

"I should go check things out in person," Mari said. "Dav, can you handle being in charge here at the entrance?"

"No problem," Dav said. "Lady Mage Asha and I can handle anything!"

"Alain, why don't you stay—"

"I will come with you," Alain said.

"I'll be fine, Alain, and you'd be better employed helping to protect this entrance."

"I will come with you," he repeated.

Mari gave him an exasperated look. She knew when Alain went all Mage-impassive on her that he wouldn't give in on an argument. "Fine. Let's go."

With the occupants of the Guild Hall held prisoner in various areas, the hallways were oddly vacant at an hour when there should be increasing levels of traffic. Mari went to the dining hall first, concerned about the place where the great majority of the Edinton Mechanics were being held.

She found Master Mechanic Lukas at the entrance and raucous sounds coming from the dining hall. "What's going on?"

"About two-thirds of the men and woman in there are celebrating being captured by you," Lukas said, smiling at Mari. "The other third are keeping very quiet. Is what I heard right? No one was injured?"

"Only a few burnt fingers," Mari said.

"You've more than proven your right to be in charge, Master Mechanic. My apologies for doubting you."

"You questioned me," Mari said. "If I can't handle that, I don't deserve to be giving orders."

"She said you'd feel that way," Lukas observed.

"She?"

An older woman in a well-worn Mechanics jacket stepped out of the dining hall. "Is there any chance of parole, Mari?"

"Professor S'san!" Mari embraced her old instructor, feeling tears start. "I was worried about you. We had to leave you at Severun and I was so afraid of what the Guild might have done."

"Oh, hush," S'san said, waving off Mari's concerns. "All the Guild did was place me under Hall arrest and send me here. I think they planned on using me as a hostage to influence you. But even I never expected you to show up at Edinton and take over the Guild Hall. As long as you're here, and apparently still fixed on changing the world, can you use any more help?"

"I would be honored to have your help," Mari said. "And you won't have to take orders from Senior Mechanics anymore."

"Speaking of which, the Senior Mechanics are being held in their main conference room, as you ordered," Lukas told Mari.

"Good. Mechanic Ken is leading teams to evaluate how much equipment we can, uh, borrow from this Guild Hall if we use the Mages' help to create larger openings to the outside. If any of the Mechanics we captured are eager to help, let me know so I can have them vetted by the Mages." Feeling a little awkward at having given orders to someone of Lukas's age and seniority, Mari dug in one of the pockets of her jacket and pulled out a spare armband. "Would you wear this, Professor?"

S'san frowned at the golden star on light blue. "Why is this your symbol, Mari?"

"It's not my symbol. It's the image of the new day. What we're fighting for."

"I doubt your followers see it in the same light." S'san pulled the band over one sleeve of her jacket. "You were always very practical and down-to-earth , Mari. And correspondingly weak on symbolism. Who convinced you that an emblem of the new day would be a good thing?"

"My friends made it," Mari admitted. "Alain convinced me it was a good idea to use the image on banners and armbands."

"They were right, if my opinion still matters to you. So, Lukas here tells me that you have access to banned technology texts. How did you manage that?"

"I can't tell you yet, Professor, and your opinion will always be very important to me. Master Mechanic Lukas, I'm going back to check things at the front entrance and then drop in on the Senior Mechanics." Mari led her old teacher through the hallways, Alain following.

"I see the Mage is still with you," S'san added, looking at Alain.

"He'll always be with me," Mari said, holding up her left hand so that the promise ring showed clearly. "I've got five more Mages with me now as well."

"Five more?" S'san walked alongside Mari, shaking her head. "You don't believe in changing the world slowly, do you, Mari?"

"We truly do not have time to move slowly, Professor."

S'san shot a keen glance at Mari. "According to the Senior Mechanics, you're also doing your best to get the commons to revolt."

Mari had to laugh scornfully at that. "The truth is the opposite. I'm telling the commons to wait. Not to act until things are ready. If they rose up now, cities would be destroyed while the Great Guilds fought back, and the loss of life would be awful."

"And they are listening to you? Are they so easily convinced?"

"She is the daughter," Alain said. "The commons can tell."

"Alain," Mari said, her voice sharpening. "I'm talking sense to them.

They can tell that." She felt relieved to reach the entry again, where all of the Mages were now gathered along with a few of her Mechanics. "You're all right?" she asked the Mages. "None of you were hurt?"

To her surprise, not just Mage Dav and Mage Asha but the three newer Mages all acknowledged her question. "There is one concern," Mage Dav said. "None of us can sense any activity from other Mages in this city. Our spells must have told the Mages and the elders here that we are present, but nothing is happening."

"They must be preparing," Alain said.

"Or deciding to prepare," Mage Dav said. "We will continue to rest and watch for signs of spells elsewhere."

"Thank you," Mari said. As she, Professor S'san, and Alain walked quickly toward the Senior Mechanics' main conference room, Mari gave Alain a worried look. "What do you think the Edinton Mages are doing?"

"It is likely the elders are trying to learn what is happening. If it is seen as merely a dispute among Mechanics, the elders will do nothing. But if they hear that the daughter is in Edinton, and present at this Hall, they will act."

"Can they…sense me?" Mari asked.

"As if you were a Mage?" Alain said. "No. A Mage must see you to know that you are the daughter. The elders will not want to attack a Mechanics Guild Hall based on the rumors of shadows. They will seek other confirmation."

"That should give us more time, which we need. Getting that heavy equipment down to the docks is going to take some work, even with the Mages helping."

"Did the Mages help you penetrate the vaults at Mechanics Guild Headquarters and remove banned technology texts?" S'san asked.

"That's not exactly what happened," Mari said. "When we get somewhere where I don't have to worry about being overheard, I can tell you the truth of where Alain and I got the texts. Somebody else should know in case something happens to me and Alain, but to everyone else it still has to be a secret."

"I can understand your reasons for that," S'san said. "I have only one regret at this moment: that I won't be able to see the faces of the Senior Mechanics and the Guild Master at Guild Headquarters when they hear what you've done here."

"You'll be able to see the Senior Mechanics here. Is Senior Mechanic Vilma still the Guild Hall Supervisor?"

"Oh, Vilma got sacked months ago, for letting a certain Master Mechanic slip through her fingers instead of ensuring you were safely dead in the service of the Guild. We've had Senior Mechanic Tam lording it over us since then. His leadership skills are poor even for a Senior Mechanic, which is saying something. Who are these people?"

They had nearly reached the Senior Mechanics' conference room, but the hallway was blocked by a group of several Mechanics, two wearing Mari's armbands and the others apparently new captives. "Master Mechanic!" one of Mari's Mechanics cried. "We need your instructions. These Mechanics want to help, to join with us, and we need their skills."

Mari paused in front of the group. "Mage Alain?"

Alain looked over the five Mechanics from Edinton as Mari had them recite the statement about wanting to work with her.

"Hold on!" Mari said as the last of the five came up to her, grinning. "Gayl? Gayl of Daarendi?"

"That's right," Gayl said. "Fernan said you'd do something some day!"

"I knew Gayl and Fernan at the Guild Academy," Mari explained to Alain and Professor S'san. "Where is Fernan? Is he all right?"

Gayl's smile slipped. "I think he's all right. He was sent to the Guild Hall in Palla, to break us up."

"My fault again." Mari sighed.

"Not this time. A Senior Mechanic took a very close interest in me and thought that if Fernan got sent far, far away I could be convinced to fall in love with someone else." Gayl's lip curled. "It didn't work, so I got sent to Edinton."

"None of them are lying," Alain said.

"Welcome to all of you," Mari said. "Stay with my Mechanics until you get armbands of your own. I very much appreciate your assistance, and it is great to see you again, Gayl. We'll get word to Fernan so he can join us where we're going after this."

"I don't know everything that you want to do," Gayl said. "Aside from finally breaking the hold of the Senior Mechanics on us all. But you've already done the impossible. Tell us what you want and where to go, and we'll follow you!"

"I'm nothing without people like you," Mari said, hoping that she didn't look too embarrassed.

They paused outside the door to the Senior Mechanics' conference room, which was next to the Guild Hall Supervisor's office. During her time of exile in Edinton she had been called on the carpet in that office more than once for trivial matters. If she had been the sort to want to settle scores, there would have been plenty of them to deal with here in Edinton.

She felt an habitual urge to knock and await permission. It took a moment to overcome her training and walk in as if she ran the Hall. Which, in fact, she did at the moment. More than a dozen Senior Mechanics were lined up against one wall of the large room along with several other high-ranking Mechanics, two of Mari's Mechanics standing guard over them all with rifles at ready. Mari came to a halt in front of them, running her eyes over the group, recognizing several of them from the weeks she had spent in Edinton. "Are there any Senior Mechanics missing?" she asked S'san.

"No, Mari, you got them all." S'san seemed to be quite pleased about that.

Mari's eyes came to a rest on another familiar figure. "Professor T'mos," she murmured.

Professor S'san leaned closer to her and murmured back. "He hasn't been here long. The Guild leadership took it very poorly when Professor T'mos allowed you to slip through his fingers in Palandur. They accused him of either deliberately aiding you or of being too dense to realize you had fooled him."

Mari couldn't help a twisted smile. "He didn't deliberately aid me."

"I myself thought the second option was more in keeping with dear, prideful T'mos. But he got sent here anyway, either because he was suspect or because he was punished. Maybe both. We haven't spoken all that much since he arrived, but then we never did."

"You should have warned me more about his controlling paternalism," Mari said, aware that the senior Mechanics were watching her with hostile and angry expressions. She raised her voice. "For anyone who doesn't already know," she announced, "I am Master Mechanic Mari—"

"Your title was taken from you! Do not sully it!" a Senior Mechanic Mari vaguely recognized yelled at her.

Mari gave the woman a flat, hard stare. "Don't interrupt me again." Saying that felt good. Over the years there had been any number of Senior Mechanics she had wanted to say that to, and now she finally got to do it. "If I were you, I'd be spending my time thinking up explanations for how you let this Hall be captured. I imagine the Guild is not going to be pleased with you. Maybe you'll finally be called to account for your inability to do anything but yell at Mechanics junior to you in the Guild hierarchy."

Professor T'mos, looking outraged, spoke in the firm tones of a teacher admonishing a recalcitrant student. "Mari, you must cease this immediately. You can't get away with it. If you throw yourself on the mercy of the Guild—"

Mari felt a surge of anger. She held up one hand, palm out, her expression so foreboding that even someone as self-assured as T'mos stopped in mid-sentence. "I've learned all about the mercy of the Guild and the gratitude of the Guild and the morals of the Guild. The Guild that disregarded my loyalty and used me as bait against Ringhmon, hoping that commons would kill me. The Guild that tried to murder me by sending me to Tiae. The Guild who beat me and threatened to turn me over to the Emperor's tender mercies. The Guild whose assassins I barely escaped in Altis. And of course the Guild that has systematically lied about so much to everyone on Dematr for centuries.

The Guild was built on a foundation of lies. That flawed foundation is finally cracking. The Mechanics Guild will fall, and anyone who continues to back it will fall with it."

"The Guild fall?" another Senior Mechanic blurted out. "You're insane, girl! Just as the Guild has warned us! Absolutely insane! The Guild has always been here and always will be!"

Mari shook her head. "No. The Guild's days are numbered. I have no wish for bloodshed, unlike the Senior Mechanics who keep trying to kill me, but I will break the hold of the Mechanics Guild on this world. Believe it or not, I'm doing you a favor. If the Guild succeeded in keeping Dematr in chains, that victory would last a very short time before the commons finally rose and drowned everything in blood and fire." She didn't think these Senior Mechanics could be convinced, didn't think they would believe her or join her, but they would report what was said, and many eyes would see those reports. Some of those eyes might become future allies.

"How would you know such a thing?" Senior Mechanic Tam asked contemptuously.

"The Mages have seen it—"

"Mages!"

"And I would say that any fool who walks among the commons can feel it, but you obviously haven't." Mari paused while Tam purpled with rage. "This world will be free. Mechanics will be free as well, and everything you have tried to control will slip through your fingers."

"Nothing will change except that you will die," another Senior Mechanic said in a very cold voice. "And your lies will die with you."

Mari managed to smile despite the tightness in her gut at the threat. "I don't think so. Things are already in motion that will survive even if I don't. I have a job to do, and I'm going to see it done."

Some others had entered the room behind Mari, and she turned to see Bev standing close by. Bev had her eyes fixed on the row of Senior Mechanics, her face rigid.

She brought the barrel of her rifle up and started walking toward the captives. Mari almost flung out a hand to stop her, but Alain shook his head. "She must handle this," he said in a very low voice.

"What's going on?" S'san whispered to Mari.

"I don't know exactly. I assume it has something to do with when Bev was an Apprentice at Emdin," Mari whispered back.

"Blazes! What is she going to do?"

Mari looked at Alain again. "She must know she has the power to shape her world," Alain said.

Her rifle in a ready position, Bev halted directly in front of one of the Senior Mechanics, a man Mari didn't recognize. Nobody was saying anything, the silence almost oppressive.

Finally Bev spoke, her voice sounding almost as dead as a Mage's. "Senior Mechanic Sodo."

Sodo, a man of average height and a bit too much weight, stared back at her wordlessly, his terrified eyes going from the barrel of the rifle to Bev's face and back again. The Senior Mechanics next to him were edging away, plainly almost as frightened as Sodo.

"Aren't you happy to see me again, Senior Mechanic Sodo?" Bev asked in that same emotionless voice. "Aren't you?"

With shocking suddenness, Bev swung the butt of the rifle around and forward, slamming it into Sodo's groin. The Senior Mechanic gasped in pain, his legs giving way.

"Aren't you?" Bev demanded, her voice finally tinged with rage. She brought the rifle barrel forward again and jammed it against Sodo's teeth, forcing the Senior Mechanic's head back against the wall and preventing him from falling to his knees.

One of the Mechanics standing next to Mari looked to her for guidance, his face anxious, but Mari just shook her head and made a restraining gesture. From what Alain had said and the little Mari knew of the events at Emdin, she understood what was going on. "Mechanic Bev decides how this ends."

Bev paused as she heard Mari's words, then leaned in closer to Sodo, her eyes blazing. "Don't you have anything to say, Senior Mechanic Sodo? No lectures on an Apprentice's duty to the Guild? No instructions on the importance of an Apprentice doing anything that she is ordered to do? No threats of what might happen if an Apprentice spoke out of turn? *Now* you have nothing to say, Senior Mechanic Sodo?" She jabbed with the rifle barrel, drawing a grunt of pain from Sodo and a trickle of blood from his lips and gums.

"How does it feel, Senior Mechanic Sodo? How does it feel to know that I can do whatever I want to do to you? How does it feel to be helpless?" Bev's lips drew back in a snarling smile. "But you know what, Senior Mechanic Sodo? Not only are you a sorry excuse for a Mechanic, not only are you a sorry, pitiful, and pathetic excuse for a *man*, but you're also a lousy teacher. Lucky for you, because if I had become what you tried to make me, you'd be dead."

Bev jerked her rifle away, letting Sodo drop to his knees as he grabbed at his mouth in agony. "Listen to me very closely, Senior Mechanic Sodo. You're going to live this time, because I won't let what you did to me destroy me. But if you ever, *ever* hurt anyone else, I will find you. You will never know what door I might be behind, what corner I might be waiting around, with a pistol and a knife, to ensure that you die a slower and more painful death than you can possibly imagine. Do you understand, Senior Mechanic Sodo?"

Sodo nodded frantically, and Bev turned away, walking back to Mari, leaving the Senior Mechanic on his knees.

Bev reached Mari and nodded to her, breathing deeply and looking oddly relieved. "Thanks, Mari. Thank you, Mage Alain. I'm good now."

Mari reached up to squeeze her shoulder. "We trust you."

Bev put her own hand over Mari's. "More importantly, you just showed everyone that you trust me. Do you want me to beat up anyone else?"

Mari couldn't help glancing at Professor T'mos, who was staring at Sodo in shock, but she shook her head. This was…too pleasant. Getting revenge, being in control, scaring people who couldn't fight back… She saw an ugly path ahead, a path that would lead to her becoming like the Senior Mechanics she now faced. Unless starting right now she made a major effort to turn her course in another direction. "Once we've taken all that we need from this Guild Hall," Mari told the Senior Mechanics, forcing her voice to sound in control but not threatening, "we'll leave. No one will be harmed if I can help it. I am truly sorry it came to this. I don't want bloodshed, I don't want fighting. If the Guild leaves me alone, I won't attack any more Guild Halls. If the Guild attacks me, then all bets are off. Tell the Guild's leaders that. They have a choice."

"More lies! You'll hang in Palandur when your lunacy and pride take you back there!" shouted another of the Senior Mechanics. "You're a traitorous slave of the Mages, you filthy—" His voice broke off as his face suddenly flushed red and sweat sprang out on his forehead. The Senior Mechanic seemed to have trouble breathing for a moment, staggering back against the wall.

Alain spoke softly, but his voice held the dead quality that was terrifying to anyone who heard it. "That was a warning, just enough heat in the air to make you very uncomfortable. Speak of Master Mechanic Mari again in such a fashion and the air around your head will set you aflame."

"Alain," Mari said, "their words can't hurt me." Which was a lie, but she knew she had to get used to being called worse than a slave of the Mages.

"But why should they be allowed to speak those words?" Alain asked.

"Because not allowing someone to speak is what they do," Mari insisted. "Because I can't say I'm doing to this to free everyone and then act as though I have the right to tell everyone what they can and cannot say. Even if what they say is about me."

Alain hesitated, then nodded. "Your wisdom exceeds mine." Then he frowned slightly, looking over to one side as if seeing through the walls between him and the outside.

That didn't look good. Mari eyed the Senior Mechanics, thinking that no one with any brains would try anything while being covered by rifles and with the Guild Hall occupied by a hostile force. But these were Senior Mechanics, used to being able to do what they wanted with impunity. Overestimating their ability to judge the situation might be a mistake. "Bev, I want you in charge of watching these guys until we leave." Mari addressed the Senior Mechanics again. "I'd be on my best behavior if I were you. As you have already seen, Mechanic Bev wouldn't mind shooting any Senior Mechanic who gives her trouble."

Mari turned to go, passing close by Bev. "Try not to actually shoot any of them, all right?" she muttered.

"Can't I shoot just a few?" Bev asked loudly, her eyes glinting.

"If you have to," Mari replied just as clearly.

"I can maim them if they make me shoot them, right?"

"If you want to." Mari lowered her voice. "I hope you're kidding."

Bev nodded. "I think so. But I'm having fun scaring them." She gave Mari a rueful look. "After this I need to be good, though. The last thing I want is to fall into the habit of being cruel to people who are at my mercy."

"I know exactly what you mean," Mari agreed.

Beckoning to Alain and Professor S'san, Mari left the room, oddly deflated by what should have been a triumphal experience. At least none of the Senior Mechanics had noticed the promise rings she and Alain were wearing. She was getting tired of explaining them, especially to a hostile audience. "Did you sense something while we were in there, Alain?"

"A spell—" he began.

Mage Asha came running down the hall, long hair flowing behind her in a way that caused male Mechanics to stop and gape. "Fortunate that I could find you quickly," she advised Mari. "Mechanic Dav says you must be told. We have sensed a mighty spell being cast. Mage Hiro and Mage Dav both believe the spell is one to create a dragon."

CHAPTER TEN

Alain followed as Mari ran for the entry, Professor S'san and Mage Asha right behind him. He tried to order his thoughts despite his fears for Mari. "From the size of the spell I sensed, this dragon will be larger than the one we fought in Dorcastle," Alain told her.

She glanced back. "How much larger? As big as the one in the Northern Ramparts?"

"No. But still large."

Alain almost slid into Mari as she came to a sudden halt in the entry area. All of the other Mages were present and gazing out into the city. So were Mechanics Alli, Calu, and Dav, as well as a few other Mechanics wearing Mari's armbands.

"Mari?" Alli said. "Just in time. There are some very agitated commons outside."

Alain stayed close to Mari as she rushed to the massive main entrance door, which was ajar. Just outside, two common soldiers and another common waited. "Daughter! We need you!" one cried.

"There is a monster in the city!" another said. "A Mage dragon!"

Alain saw Mage Dav point. "It approaches from that direction."

The commons shrank back as they saw Alain and Mage Dav.

"You can tell where it is?" Mari asked Mage Dav. "Then we can go out there and stop it."

"Mari," Alain said, "this is a very dangerous dragon."

"Every dragon I've met has been very dangerous!"

Professor S'san was outside now as well, peering about. "If we have to deal with a threat from the Mages—"

"Other Mages," Mari broke in. "My Mages will help us."

"Very well, Mari. As I was saying," S'san began once more, "we would be well advised to seal this Hall. We can shoot at it from the inside, and it shouldn't be able to reach us."

The commons looked stricken as S'san gave her advice.

"We can't do that," Mari said. "There's a dragon out there, coming through the city, and it's going to kill and destroy anything in its path. It's there because of me. The Mage elders want me dead. I'm not going to sit safely inside this Guild Hall while others face death because of me!"

Alain did not want to back Mari in this. He wanted her safe. But he looked upon her and saw the woman who had insisted on saving him, a Mage, when every rule she had ever been taught would have justified leaving him to his fate. "Master Mechanic Mari speaks wisdom," Alain said, wishing he did not have to say so.

"Then let her Mages deal with this problem!" Professor S'san insisted.

"We will confront the dragon if Master Mechanic Mari says wisdom dictates it," Mage Dav said, his emotionless statement sounding totally calm. "We are unlikely to stop it."

"And likely to die?" Mechanic Alli asked. "Mari, we can't send Mage Dav and Mage Asha and the others out there alone." She offered Mari a rifle.

"Mari!" S'san said, growing angry. "You have said yourself how critical you are to the success of your plan! How can you risk yourself like this?"

"How can I not?" Mari said, taking the weapon from Alli. "Professor, only two people here have ever fought a dragon. Me, and Alain."

"I have fought one," Mage Asha said.

"All right, three people. The point is, I know what I'm doing. No one else does. What kind of leader sends others out to do a job she knows how to do and they don't? And there is another important factor. If a Mage monster attacks this Guild Hall, it might break apart the fragile coalition of Mechanics and Mages that I am building. The Mechanics who have just joined with me might turn on the Mages out of habitual suspicion. But if we defeat this threat with a band of Mechanics and Mages working together, it will be a powerful example of what cooperation can do."

Calu nodded. "It will also show that Mages and Mechanics can risk their lives for each other."

A sound drifted toward them across the city, an inhuman scream of anger that Mari remembered all too well.

One of the common soldiers looked pleadingly at her. "Lady... daughter, the monster must have encountered our forces. We will defend this city, but with only our weapons, our numbers will mean little."

Alain felt something similar to what he had experienced when the Alexdrians had been ambushed by an Imperial legion. A sense of sadness and a resolve to do what he could. "Do not waste the lives of your people to no purpose. If the monster can be stopped, we will stop it."

Shocked to be directly addressed by a Mage, the commons had trouble for a moment understanding what he had said. Then the one who wasn't a soldier bowed his head to Alain. "The daughter's Mage. We have heard of you. The Mage who stood between death and commons in the Northern Ramparts."

Mari looked over her weapon. "Professor, you and Master Mechanic Lukas are in charge here until we get back. Alli, help arrange a defense of the Guild Hall—"

"Alli ain't staying here," she replied.

"Neither am I," Calu said.

"If Mage Asha goes, then I'm going," Mechanic Dav added.

Mari cast an aggravated look at Alain, who gestured at her friends. "It would be wise to accept their help, Mari."

"Stop telling me I'm wise when I do what you want me to do,"

Mari grumbled. "Mage Dav, you told me that only Alain can cast fire. None of you other Mages can create that kind of destruction? There's no sense in all of you coming, then."

Alain shook his head. "They must come."

"Because...?" Mari demanded.

"The path of wisdom lies in following you," Mage Dav said.

"The path of wisdom does not lie in risking your life for no reason," Mari insisted.

"We must go with you," Mage Hiro said, somehow sounding insistent despite the lack of emotion in his voice.

"I thought nothing mattered and nothing was real!" Mari said.

"Nothing is real," Alain agreed.

"It's been a while since you said that, and I haven't missed it."

"But this must be done," Alain continued, not knowing how to explain it. "No Mage would stay behind. That would mean that shadows had forced a Mage to treat the shadows as real, that the illusion of the world had frightened a Mage from taking a course the Mage would have chosen. These things would mean leaving the path of wisdom."

Mari stared at Alain, frustrated. "It's a *dragon*, Alain!"

"It is the illusion of a dragon on the illusion of the world."

She threw up her hands in surrender. "All right! All right! Let's all go out and get killed so everyone will know how wise we are!"

"Mari!" Professor S'san cried in anger and despair as Mari ran down the steps accompanied by Alain, the commons, the other Mages, and her three Mechanic friends. "This matter requires more thought!"

"No time!" Mari called back.

"We will return," Alain called to Professor S'san.

"Is this thing flying toward us?" Mechanic Dav asked.

Mage Asha gave him the slightest of puzzled frowns. "A dragon? How could a dragon fly?"

"Don't they have wings?"

"No."

"Why not?" Alli asked between breaths as they ran. "If you Mages make dragons, why can't you make one any way you want?"

"Because dragons do not have wings," Asha said. "And they are very heavy. Wings would not fit the illusion."

"What about fire?" Calu said.

"Do Mechanics know of dragons that cast flame?" Alain asked. "Mari asked me this as well when we were in Dorcastle."

"Real dragons don't breathe fire," Mari said.

"Nothing is real," Asha and Mage Dav said in unison.

"*I know!*"

"So what do dragons do?" Alli pressed. "How do we stop it?"

Alain considered the question. "Dragons kill and destroy. It is all they do. They are very powerful. Their scales are very strong armor. They are swift and require much damage to stop. The weak spots on a dragon are the eyes," he advised. "The eyes are well protected by heavy, armored brow ridges, but they are still the dragon's most vulnerable feature. The other weak points are under the arms and the inner side of the thighs, where the armored scales are thinnest. The dragon-killer weapon that Mechanic Alli gave Mari killed a dragon with a blow to its chest, though."

"Yeah, well, I don't have any more shoulder-fired, fin-stabilized rockets with shaped-charge warheads on me at the moment," Alli said. She held up something that filled her hand. "I do have some explosives with short fuses."

"How many?" Mari asked.

"Two bombs. Hand-delivered."

"Not ideal," Calu said.

The commons who had pled for help were running with them, gesturing and calling commands to other commons. Cavalry was dashing ahead to carry word and to clear the streets. Bells were ringing from towers, sending warnings across the city. Alain could see commons running into buildings and barring doors and windows. It was odd to think that he had once been able to convince himself that he believed as he had been taught, that those commons, and the Mechanics with him, were shadows of no consequence. Perhaps when all was said and done they were only shadows, but Alain watched them with worry and knew that for him they would always have importance.

"Where do we want to meet this thing, Alain?" Mari asked. "In the middle of a street or in one of these courtyards where streets meet?"

He jerked his attention back to the current problem. "A courtyard," Alain said. "Large but not too large. We must have enough room to move around the dragon, but the dragon must not have enough room to move as it desires."

"How close is it, Mage Dav?" Before Mage Dav could answer the question, another dragon scream cut through the air like a knife.

"Pretty close," Alli commented.

"We need a courtyard!" Mari yelled to one of the nearby cavalry.

The soldier appeared to be in her early thirties, with the look and bearing of a veteran. "About two hundred lances up ahead, Lady. The Court of Dyers. There's a plaza another six hundred lances beyond that."

The sound of fighting came to them as the street opened out into a court a few hundred lances across, substantial but much smaller than the plaza around the Mechanics Guild Hall. Streets entered the courtyard from all four sides, and the buildings surrounding it rose for three or four stories. As in the rest of Edinton, the buildings and galleries around the court combined the clean, straight lines of northern architecture with the curves and arches of the south. The railings and balconies were draped with drying fabrics in a rainbow of colors, and the air was filled with the smell of the makings of dyes, some pleasant and some pungent. Alain held out a hand. "This should be large enough. We should fight here."

The Mechanics took deep breaths, looking around as they rested. "I love that purple, Mari," Alli said. "See it up there?"

"It's beautiful," Mari agreed. "But it's really expensive. What do you think of those reds?"

"Nice! Mage Asha, you'd look great in that one."

The first thing Alain had done as they entered the courtyard was to look at the stone paving to see if it matched that in the frightening image his foresight had shown. Relieved to see that it did not, he reminded himself that the vision didn't mean that Mari could not be badly hurt or die in a different place if her or others' decisions led her there. "Mari," Alain said, trying to understand why she and Alli were talking about fabrics and colors, "the dragon will try to choose one target to attack. If it is confused, it will keep trying to settle on one target."

"There's our tactic," Mari said. "That's the right word, isn't it? Can dragons see color?"

Alain hesitated at the question, looking at the other Mages. All shook their heads very slightly to indicate ignorance. "I do not know," Alain said. "Is that important?"

"We might have used some of the colored fabrics to distract the dragon," Mari explained. "That's why Alli and I were checking them out. But since we have no way of knowing whether it would work, we'll have to depend on most of the Mechanics and the Mages hitting the dragon from all sides so that it is constantly having to deal with new threats. Based on the way my pistol's bullets bounced off that smaller dragon in Dorcastle, I don't think our rifles will be able to penetrate this one's armor, but maybe the impacts will still raise a few bruises and shift that thing's attention. Alain, Alli, you two have the best chance of really hurting the dragon, so the rest of us will support you by keeping it confused and hopefully in one place. We Mechanics will try to hit the eyes or maybe the underarms, you aim for whatever looks good, and the other Mages...how do you guys fight dragons?"

Asha and the other four Mages all produced their long knives from beneath their robes.

"Are you joking?" Mari asked in a shocked voice.

"Mages do not joke," Alain reminded her. "They will use their concealment spells to get close to the monster. A well-delivered blow to the back of the knee joint can hamstring even a dragon."

"It is not easily done," Asha added, her face an emotionless mask. "But it is a worthy test of a Mage's ability to focus, to concentrate on a spell while also aiming to strike the dragon and evade its blows."

Mechanic Dav stared at her. "Please be careful."

Asha said nothing, but one corner of her mouth twitched in a tiny Mage smile as she reached out one hand to touch his cheek.

Mari turned to Alain, but before she could say anything another dragon scream sounded close by, this time accompanied by shouts and yells. "Over there!" Mari cried, directing Alli to one side. "You stay on this side near me," she told Alain. "But move back a little so you'll be able to spot a good shot at the dragon and make it happen. Everybody else, disperse along these three sides of the courtyard so we'll have that thing surrounded when it enters."

Everyone was still moving into position when three cavalry bolted through the courtyard from the direction the dragon was coming, the soldiers making frantic and unsuccessful attempts to regain control of their terrified mounts.

The shouts were rapidly growing louder. Alain saw common soldiers racing into the courtyard as well, some running all out like the panicked horses and others supporting injured comrades. Some of the soldiers still carried crossbows, but many had lost theirs in the retreat.

Behind them came a larger group of soldiers still under the control of their officers, who were yelling commands as the soldiers fell back fast. The rear rank formed a line just inside the courtyard, the soldiers aiming and firing their crossbows as their comrades staggered back.

Mari waved her Mechanic weapon over her head, her shout carrying over the commands of the officers and the thudding sound of steps from something very large that was very close. "Get behind us! We're going to stop that thing!"

The formation of soldiers paused in disbelief, then a quick-thinking officer began crying out commands to send them to the sides of the courtyard. "Fall back!" he called to the lone rank at the entrance to the courtyard, who were reloading their crossbows.

The rearguard loosed a final volley, then broke and ran for all they were worth.

Alain heard the dragon's scream again at the same moment he caught sight of it. It towered high enough for its head to rise above the surrounding buildings, wicked rows of teeth as long as a person's arm catching the light of the rising sun. Long claws gleamed on the end of its forearms. Crossbow bolts bounced off of the dragon's scales with dull thuds as the monster bent to slash at the fleeing soldiers.

One small group of soldiers was flung in different directions as the dragon's blow swept through them. Moving with amazing speed for something so large, the dragon entered the courtyard, one massive, clawed hind-leg raised to squash a wounded soldier who was lying stunned on the paving.

"Fire!" Mari shouted to the other Mechanics. The booms of the Mechanic weapons echoed from the buildings around the courtyard, startling the dragon so that it fell back one step. Bullets sparked from the dragon's head as the Mechanics tried to hit its eyes, flying off with high-pitched keening sounds instead of bouncing away as the crossbow bolts had.

All of the Mages except Alain disappeared as they used concealment spells, under cover of which they would be moving in to attack the dragon as well.

Standing slightly back, Alain felt like an observer to the fight rather than a participant. It frustrated him because he wanted to be among those in front, but he understood the wisdom of Mari placing him far enough back to be able to act immediately if a good target presented itself.

But as the dragon shook off the first volley of Mechanic rifle fire and refocused on the fallen soldier, Alain was too far back to stop her as Mari suddenly ran forward.

She was firing her weapon as fast as possible, but something appeared to stick on it. Mari wrestled with the rifle for a moment, then hurled it away, drawing her pistol. Standing over the fallen soldier as the dragon bent to strike, Mari unleashed a stream of bullets that caused the dragon to flinch up and back.

"Somebody help me here!" Mari cried as she reloaded her pistol.

Mage Dav appeared next to her, dropping his concealment spell to grab the soldier by one arm and pull him quickly back to where some of the soldier's comrades were forming ranks behind the Mechanics.

Mechanic Alli dashed out to help get the man to the small relative safety that existed behind the screen of the other soldiers.

Alain knew he should not waste strength on an attack that could not seriously harm the dragon, but it had recovered from the shock of Mari's attack and was now fixing on her. He imagined the heat above his hand, using the power available in this spot along with his own strength to feed the illusion. Not waiting for the illusion to build to the maximum he could manage, Alain imagined the heat no longer above his hand but next to the dragon's head.

The dragon screamed again, the sound deafening so close and confined in the courtyard. It sidestepped, its huge tail sweeping around to strike at Mari, who was running backwards. Alain's distraction, on top of that caused by the Mechanic bullets continuing to strike the creature, slowed the beast enough that the tail barely missed striking Mari. She was able to make it back among the others so that she no longer stood out as a target for the dragon.

"I am angry at you!" Alain yelled over the cacophony of combat.

"Save it for later!" Mari shouted back. "Get that thing!"

"I cannot see a place to strike!" The dragon twisted and lunged, making abortive strikes that kept breaking off as hits from other directions caused it to forget its original target.

The common soldiers had formed up behind the very thin screen of Mechanics, those carrying pikes which looked ridiculously small against the dragon planting their weapons to protect the remaining crossbow wielders, who were shooting out bolts as fast as they could. But every crossbow bolt glanced harmlessly off the dragon's scales.

On the other side of the courtyard Alain could see Mechanic Alli, carrying one of the bundles she called explosives, also frustrated by her inability to use it. "It won't hold still!" Alli cried to Mari.

The booming of the Mechanic weapons had slowed, Calu, Dav, and Mari taking time to aim each shot. But the creature's darting head presented a poor target, and none of the bullets succeeded in hitting an eye. So far no real damage had been done.

"I've only got so many bullets, Mari!" Calu called.

"Only fire often enough to keep the dragon from fixing on one target!" Mari yelled back, firing her pistol a moment later.

The dragon twisted, its head lunging toward Mari, who scrambled to one side as both Calu and Dav fired. Both shots hit the dragon's head. The creature halted its lunge, shook its head, then looked around for some other enemy to fix on.

The ring of metal on scales sounded in the interval between the crashes of the Mechanic weapons. The dragon jerked its leg forward, then back. Mage Asha appeared suddenly, her long knife flying from her hand, stumbling to one side as the dragon's leg brushed her with bruising force. Seeking its latest attacker, the dragon pivoted, its tail slamming into Asha hard enough to hurl her across the courtyard.

Mechanic Dav gave a cry of mingled rage and distress as she rolled to a stop, rushing to stand next to Asha and fire his weapon again and again. The dragon screamed its own challenge in reply, taking a step toward him as bullets sparked off its muzzle.

"Over here!" Mari yelled, running toward the dragon and firing rapidly again.

"My rifle's jammed!" Calu shouted, working frantically at the inert weapon.

The dragon jerked its head back to focus on Mari. Alain saw the light of recognition fill its eyes and knew the creature had finally realized that Mari was the one it had been sent to destroy.

The dragon would not be diverted from its target again.

He had only moments left to stop it.

As the dragon pivoted to face Mari, Alain saw the flash of one of its inner thighs, the scales thin enough there for the difference to be clear. He knew he did not have time to create a fire spell and place it on that part of the dragon before the beast moved again and left him unable to see the spot. He did not have time. It was impossible.

Mari was about to die.

He never knew how it happened, how he achieved something that could not be done. The fire appeared above his hand and was exploding next to the most vulnerable part of the dragon in a single instant. The scales on the dragon's inner thigh blackened and melted from the intense heat.

The dragon's scream was louder than ever, this time wracked with pain. The beast's right leg crumpled under it and the dragon began falling toward Mari, who was racing back toward Alain.

The dragon hit the pavement with enough force to make the ground jump under the feet of everyone facing it.

Alain, barely able to stand after the sudden expenditure of so much of his strength, felt himself falling.

Mechanic Alli was running forward, one arm drawn back. As the dragon opened its mouth to snap at Mari's retreating figure, Alli hurled her burden into it.

Alain fell to his knees, trying desperately not to collapse entirely.

Alli had skidded into a sliding turn that brought her just clear of the monster's jaws. She ran all out toward Calu. "Everybody get down!" she shouted loudly enough to carry over the choking scream of the dragon.

Mari leaped and hit Alain, knocking him to the pavement and covering his body with her own. He had a confused image of the common soldiers obediently dropping to the ground, the other Mages appearing and going flat as they saw Mari doing so, and Mechanic Dav falling to protect Mage Asha.

No more weapons were firing. The dragon had broken off its last scream. For a long moment, the only sound was the scrabbling of the dragon's claws on the pavement as it struggled to rise.

Alain heard it make an odd gagging sound, as if something were stuck in its throat.

Something exploded with a sound that dwarfed that of the Mechanic weapons, the noise reverberating from the buildings around the courtyard. Alain felt a hail of small objects pelt him, the ones that hit his skin striking hard enough to sting.

And then silence made all the more profound by the vast noise that had preceded it.

Despite Mari being on top of him, Alain managed to twist his head enough to see the dragon.

The monster's body lay in the courtyard, twitching.

Nothing was left of the dragon above its shoulders.

Mari staggered to her feet, helping Alain up, then wrapped her arms around him in a tight hug. "Thank the stars you're all right. Alain, when Alli says get down, you get down."

"I will remember," Alain said.

She looked up at him, frowned, and reached to touch something on his cheek that felt wet. "What is—" Mari's eyes widened and she combed the fingers of one hand through her hair. "*What* is in my hair?"

"It is pieces of the dragon's head," Alain said. Once he had seen that the dragon's head was gone, the answer had seemed obvious. He did not mention that similar pieces speckled her face and clothes.

"I've got little pieces of dragon brain in my hair?" Mari asked, horrified.

"Yeah," Mechanic Alli said, running her fingers through her own hair and gazing distastefully at the results as she got to her feet. "Little pieces of dragon brain, little pieces of dragon skull, little pieces of dragon snot—"

"Euwwww!" Mari cried. "Could you have used a little less explosive!?!"

"I didn't know how much I'd need to blow off a dragon's head! Excuse me for ensuring that thing won't get up again!"

"The pieces will dissolve in several days as the power that created them dissipates," Alain offered.

"Several days?" Mari asked. "No. I am washing my hair as soon as possible. We're just lucky no one was hurt—" She broke off, turned, and ran over to where Asha lay with Mechanic Dav kneeling beside her. "Asha. How is she, Dav?"

"I don't know," Mechanic Dav said, frantic with worry.

"The healers," Alain said, pointing to where Cas and Pol had entered the courtyard. He found it hard to look at Asha as she lay there, as if he could feel the pain of her injuries just as he once had felt a blow to Mari's head.

Cas examined Asha carefully. "She's very tough, which helped. Her muscles were able to absorb some of the force of the blow. It feels like a couple of broken ribs. I'm not sure whether her arm is broken or not. She's going to have some serious bruises on this side of her body."

"What does that mean?" Mechanic Dav demanded. "Is Asha going to be all right?"

"I think so," Cas said. "We should get her to one of Edinton's hospitals so specialists can look her over, though."

Alain looked at Mage Dav. "Is this acceptable to you?"

"It is," Mage Dav said. "My niece believes in the wisdom of Lady Mari."

Mari shook her head wearily at Mage Dav, then turned to the common soldiers who were watching. "We need a stretcher and someone to carry it."

"We have healers on the way," an officer replied. "We have many injured."

"I'm sorry," Mari said.

Alain heard the regret in her voice, and knew without asking that Mari was blaming herself for the dragon having been unleashed.

"Sorry?" the officer said. "Lady, you killed the monster. You and yours stood between us and the death it carried. I have never heard of such a thing."

"The only reason Corporal Rik is still alive is because you stood over him," another soldier said. "We saw it. The dragon lunging and you not giving way until Rik was safe. Lady, we have heard rumors. I have long ceased believing in myths and legends, but now I see one before me and I know the stories are true."

As if an order had been given, the soldiers all knelt before Mari.

Alain saw her dismay as she looked upon them.

"Not the kneeling!" Mari said. "What is with the kneeling thing? Stand up, all of you! I don't care how you…do homage to your own rulers, but no one should be kneeling to me. Ever."

The soldiers climbed to their feet, looking sheepish. "We do not kneel to our city councilors," the officer explained. "Or any official of the Confederation. It is a rule among us that even the least deserves the same dignity as the greatest."

"That's a very good rule," Mari said.

"It came down from Jules herself," the officer said. "Small wonder the daughter of her daughters feels the same. We thought perhaps— We were wrong."

Cries of welcome marked the arrival of a large group of new soldiers carrying stretchers and several healers who hastened to assist Cas and Pol.

Mari slumped against one wall, her eyes distant, as Asha was carefully placed on a stretcher by soldiers who seemed terrified to be touching a Mage. Standing next to them, Mechanic Dav looked helpless and afraid.

Alain leaned closer to Mari. "You cannot rest yet."

She nodded, drawing in a deep breath, her eyes refocusing. "What—? Asha." Mari took in everything at a glance. "Dav? Mechanic Dav? Someone is going to need to guard Mage Asha. Protect her and ensure she gets safely back to our ships. You do it. Stay with her."

Mechanic Dav blinked at her in disbelief. "Seriously?"

"Seriously," Mari said. "You have your instructions, Mechanic. Get the job done!"

"Thanks, Mari! You really are the greatest." Dav walked alongside the stretcher as the soldiers carrying Asha followed one of the local healers toward the nearest hospital. He still held his rifle, and looked ready to battle another dragon singlehandedly if one showed up and threatened Asha.

Mari gazed after them, her expression tragic. "Why did she— Why did *anyone* have to be hurt?" Her face changed, growing stiff and angry. She looked at Alain, her eyes blazing. "Alain, didn't you tell me that one of the new Mages was the type who could send messages to other Mages?"

"Yes. Mage Dimitri." Alain gestured and Mage Dimitri came up, eyeing them both impassively. A long cut in Dimitri's Mage robes marked a slash from the dragon which had narrowly missed him.

"Mage Dimitri," Mari said, breathing hard, "I want you to send a message to the Mage Guild in this city. To the elders in the Mage Guild Hall."

"What is the message?" Dimitri asked.

She had to pause, staring at Asha's stretcher as it was carried out of the courtyard, before speaking in a voice that quivered with anger. "Tell them, tell the elders, that we've destroyed their dragon. Tell them that if any more attacks are aimed at me or at this city I will lead everything I have against their Guild Hall, and I will reduce that Guild Hall to a lifeless pile of smoldering rubble that will make the ruins of Marandur pale by comparison. The world illusion will be changed, and changed for all time, in a way that leaves none of them alive in it. Tell them that."

Dimitri's Mage composure, as good as it was, was obviously tested by Mari's words. He looked at Alain.

Alain nodded to Mage Dimitri. "Tell the elders, and tell them that you saw no falseness in the words of Master Mechanic Mari. She is not making a threat. She is making a promise."

"This one understands." A common or a Mechanic would have seen no emotion on Mage Dimitri's face, b ut Alain saw traces of elation there. This was one message Mage Dimitri would be pleased to send.

Dimitri went off to work his spell. Alain saw Mari rubbing her face with one hand. "I hope the elders listen," she mumbled so that only Alain could hear.

"If nothing else," said Alain, "your message should cause the elders to debate what wisdom dictates in this case. It will delay any further action by the Mages in the Guild Hall."

"I hope you're right." Mari sighed and faced a common soldier who approached them.

"Lady?" The officer came to a stop before Mari, saluting. "Corporal Rik asked that he be allowed to thank you personally."

"He's awake? Come on, Alain." Mari followed the officer until they stopped at another stretcher.

Corporal Rik looked as though he had been used as a kickball by a giant, but his bruised and scratched face bore a smile as he saw Mari. "They told me what you did, Lady. I have nothing. I am nothing, except to my wife and children, but on their behalf I cannot thank you enough."

Mari knelt next to the stretcher. "Who told you that you were nothing? Everyone is something. Even my Mage agrees with that now."

"Your Mage." Corporal Rik's eyes went to Alain. "They said a Mage pulled me to safety. A Mage and a Mechanic, holding onto my arms. What sort of miracle is this, Lady, that those who think the least of us would risk themselves for us?"

"From now on," Mari said, "you'll meet more and more Mechanics and Mages who aren't like the others. Do you see this armband? I have it. Mage Alain has it. All who follow me will have it. If you see the sign of the new day, you will know that whoever bears it, Mechanic or Mage or common, is someone who will help those who need it. If we're going to free this world, we're going to have to work together."

"I will be well enough to help soon—"

"You must wait until it is time," Mari said. "All of you," she added, looking around. "Wait until it is time. It won't be that long now if I can get done what I need to get done. But not today, and not tomorrow. Understand? If you trust me, then wait."

Corporal Rik, big and bluff, seemed ready to cry. "I did not believe it could be true, but it is. You are the daughter, for who else could lead or would lead Mechanics and Mages in the defense of common folk? Take my sword, Lady! It is yours!"

"Use it to defend your city," Mari said. "That's what I need from you now." She stood up again as Corporal Rik's stretcher was carried off. "Hey, Calu. How are you doing?"

Calu rubbed his forehead, wiping away sweat. "You've already killed two of those? One was more than enough for me."

"I'm not exactly looking for them, Calu, and now you and Alli can claim one as well."

Alli, busy trying to comb gobbets of dragon out of her hair, just grimaced in reply.

Mari suddenly looked at Alain, as if seeing him here for the first time. She leaned in and kissed him, holding the kiss uncaring of any spectators. "You are a gift, my Mage. Even when there aren't any dragons around. In case you're wondering, I saw that you were the one who crippled that dragon badly enough to give Alli a good shot at it. I owe you another one."

"We have discussed this before," Alain said, feeling oddly put out by Mari's phrasing. "You owe me nothing. I do not ask for payment or repayment, and that is not why I did it."

"I know, you silly Mage! I'm going to have to talk to Mechanic Dav so he'll know how you Mages take things." She cocked her head at him. "Does Asha like him as much as he obviously likes her?"

Alain nodded. "She has feelings. She has asked me about some of them."

"*What?*"

"Asha has asked me about some of the things she is feeling," Alain explained, wondering why Mari was acting so surprised. "These emotions are things we Mages have denied and been denied, and so it is hard to deal with them. I have been able to help her because I understand how love changes the entire nature of the world illusion. And it is sometimes difficult to comprehend the words of Mechanics."

"It is, huh?" Mari looked around at the doors and windows being unlocked around the courtyard, fearful commons looking out on the scene of the recent battle, many of the drying fabrics still fluttering in the breeze like a rainbow broken into fragments. Practically all of the fabrics bore speckles of dragon head, but Alain knew those would vanish without a trace within several days. "Are you saying that you have trouble understanding me, Alain?" she added.

Alain gazed back at her. Something about the question made him wary. There were questions, he had learned, that it was best not to answer, or at least to answer with care. "No," he said.

"Liar." Mari smiled slightly. "Like a Mage. But you're learning more about being married. We need to get back to the Mechanics Guild Hall. Is everybody ready?"

The Mages did not answer, of course, but Mechanics Alli and Calu nodded. Alli had picked up Mari's discarded Mechanic weapon and was fiddling with it. "There. I cleared the jam. Here it is."

"I don't need it now," Mari said.

"A pirate queen should have a rifle," Alli said. "Right, Calu?"

"Right," Calu agreed.

"When did I become a pirate queen?" Mari asked, accepting the rifle as she walked beside Alain.

Alain saw that the common soldiers, unasked, had formed lines to keep a clear path before Mari and their companions. More soldiers were rushing into place ahead, doubtless called in to confront the dragon but now facing a much less hazardous task.

Mari began pushing the pace as they walked, doubtless wanting to return to the Mechanics Guild Hall as quickly as possible. Alain suspected, though, that she was also uncomfortable with the growing number of commons who were lining the streets, all of them pointing at her or raising young children to see Mari.

His speculation was confirmed when Mari looked over at him with worried eyes. "What if I let them down, Alain? The task I'm facing is nearly impossible. What if I fail?"

"Should we fail," Alain said, "neither of us is likely to remain in this dream long enough to have to face the disappointment of others. The Great Guilds would want to seal a victory with our deaths."

She rolled her eyes at him. "That is so very pragmatic and so very not comforting, my Mage. I just hope we get out of Edinton without any more—"

They had just reentered the vast plaza surrounding the Mechanics Guild Hall, where the soldiers of Edinton had cleared a wide area ahead of them. Mari broke off her words as the high-pitched screech of an enormous bird of prey sounded right over their heads and they were suddenly shadowed by the sweep of immense wings.

CHAPTER ELEVEN

Mari cursed and aimed her weapon as the Roc came to ground directly ahead of them, the Mage on the back of the giant bird gazing toward the group of Mages and Mechanics.

Alain put himself between Mari and the Roc, his hands out. "Mari, it is not attacking."

She glared at him. "I don't have good experiences with giant birds. You do remember that, don't you?"

"If the Mage riding the Roc meant to harm you or me, the Roc would not have alighted on this plaza. It would have remained in the air and struck at us."

"Mari?" Alli called. Her own weapon was leveled toward the Roc. "What's the deal with this one?"

Mari shook her head at Alain as she called back to the others. "Hold your fire. Alain thinks *this* giant bird isn't out to kill me." In a lower voice, she spoke sharply to him, indicating the Mage on the Roc. "Well? What do we do?"

"I will speak with the Mage," Alain said.

"You will not get within reach of that thing's beak or claws!" Mari objected.

"I will take care," Alain said.

He turned to face the Roc and advanced several paces, then waited silently in Mage fashion.

The Mage riding the giant creature patted the Roc's neck. The immense bird lowered its head so that the Mage could slide off onto the pavement. Dropping the cowl of her robes, the Mage walked up to Alain, expressionless face giving no clue to her motives.

"You are Mage Alain of Ihris," the Roc Mage said.

"I am," Alain said.

"I am Mage Alera of Larharbor," she said. Her eyes shifted from Alain to Mari. "The daughter is here."

"Why are you here?" Alain asked.

"I am one of several Mages sent by the elders in Julesport to search for the daughter and report on her location to the nearest Mage Guild Hall." Mage Alera's gaze went back to Alain. "Instead, I have come to warn you. A Mage in Julesport had foresight of the daughter coming to this city. The elders did not trust in the foresight, but thought it wise to send me and others to search the south. They also thought it wise to inform the Mechanics that the daughter might come here."

Alain was sure his surprise had shown despite his efforts to look as emotionless as Mage Alera. "Elders of the Mage Guild spoke with Mechanics?"

"No. The elders sent one they respected least to speak with the Mechanics." Alera's own impassivity cracked as she spoke, revealing anger and resentment. "The message was given, then this Mage was ordered to search."

"Why do you warn us?" Alain asked.

Mage Alera did not answer for a long moment, then looked back briefly toward her Roc. "This Mage tires of disrespect and poor treatment. This Mage has seen her Roc ended early by orders of the elders. This Mage seeks a new wisdom, and whispers among the Guild are that Mage Alain and the daughter are finding such a path."

"I will speak with the daughter," Alain said. He walked back to Mari, who had lowered her weapon but was still pointing it toward the Roc. "Mage Alera came to warn us. The elders in Julesport learned by foresight that you would come here, and they told the Mechanics."

Mechanic Calu stared at Alain. "Mages told the Mechanics?"

"I guess wanting me dead is making my enemies cooperate," Mari said. "She's telling the truth?"

"Mage Alera does not lie. She was sent here to search for you, but instead wishes to join us."

"Alain, what are we supposed to do with a giant bird?"

"Like all illusions, the Roc will cease to be when the power put into it is exhausted," Alain said. "I sense it has little time left. Have I told you that the elders have little liking for those Mages who create Rocs? The elders distrust the emotional connections those Mages have with their creatures, for every time such a Mage creates a Roc, it is the same Roc. That is one reason for Mage Alera's desire to join us. She says the elders have sometimes forced her to end her Roc before the spell would have been exhausted."

"They're like a pair?" Mechanic Alli asked, lowering her weapon and gazing at the Roc with a growing smile. "Like a rider and a special horse, or one of those people who work with a rescue dog?"

Mari's face reflected growing alarm. "The Mages told the Mechanics Guild that I might be here. If the Senior Mechanics took that warning seriously, they might be sending reinforcements to Edinton."

"Wouldn't they have used the far-talker to warn the Senior Mechanics in Edinton?" Calu asked, then answered his own question. "No. They would have assumed there was too big a chance of some malcontent at Edinton hearing and passing a warning to you, and they never would have dreamed that you could capture the Guild Hall."

"A ship could not arrive quickly," Alain began.

"There's a rail line, Alain! The regular train isn't supposed to arrive until tomorrow, but if the Senior Mechanics laid on a special express—"

"It could be getting close now," Alli said. "We have no way of knowing how much time we have left."

Alain pointed back to Mage Alera. "There is a way to see if one of your Mechanic trains approaches this city."

Mari gave him a skeptical look. "The bird? We're going to send a Mage we just met on a giant bird to see if there is a train getting close to Edinton?"

"Yes."

"How far can she see?" Calu asked.

"It depends on high the Roc flies," Alain said.

"Yeah. Like somebody on top of a mountain looking out across the land." Calu grinned at Mari. "This is an amazing capability, Mari. If Alain says we can trust this Mage, why not use it?"

"Because you and me and Alli all know a bird that big cannot fly!"

"The Roc creates the illusion of flying," Alain said. "Or rather, the Mage creates the illusion of a Roc that creates the illusion of flying."

"Oh, well, why didn't you explain that before? Now it all makes sense!" Mari said in what Alain thought of as her sarcasm voice. She sighed. "I'm never going to get used to this stuff. What's her name again?"

"Mage Alera."

Mari walked up to her, Alain at her side. "Lady Mage Alera," Mari said. "Thank you for your warning."

Alera looked back blankly.

"She does not know what thank you means," Alain murmured to Mari.

"Right. Lady Mage Alera, would you do something for us?"

"You do not order? You…ask?" Alera said.

"Yes. I ask. Do you know what Mechanic trains are?"

Alera shook her head. "I do not know this word. I know nothing of Mechanics."

"You have seen these trains," Alain said. "They move more swiftly than anything that runs, and put out smoke from their front."

"Yes," Alera said. "I know those. The smoke snakes. They follow the shining lines across the land. Sometimes we have heard them scream."

"Scream?" Mari asked. "Oh. The whistles. Um, we can explain that later. Could you…fly…up and see if one of those is coming toward this city from the north?"

"My Roc and I can do this." Mage Alera paused, her head lowered, then looked at both Mari and Alain. "Does your wisdom permit my Roc to have a name?" Even though Alera did her best to hide any feeling in her voice, a note of yearning came through in the question.

"Yes," Mari said, her attitude finally softening. "You are welcome with us, Mage Alera. You and your Roc."

"He will cease soon," Alera said. "But he will be again, and then his name will be Swift." She ran to the Roc, vaulting up as the huge bird bent his neck once more. As soon as Mage Alera was settled, the Roc spread his vast wings, raised them, and leaped into the air with a push of its legs and a downward sweep of wings that sent a powerful gust of air to stagger everyone nearby.

Alli watched the Roc rise into the sky. "For the first time in my life, I wish I was something other than a Mechanic," she whispered.

Mari had broken into a trot, heading for a group of Mechanics and commons visible near the Mechanics Guild Hall. Alain caught up with her, the others trailing, as Mari reached the group.

"I see that you survived," Professor S'san said. "I hadn't seen this side of you before, Mari. Reacting to a crisis, taking charge, giving clear orders, and leading by example. I knew that you had moral courage to spare, but it was nice to see you demonstrating great personal courage as well."

Mari laughed incredulously. "Oh, please, Professor. Courage? Do you have any idea how scared I was?"

"And you fought anyway. Just what do you think courage is?"

"I...never mind. There are more important issues."

Alain listened as Mari explained to the others what they had learned from Mage Alera. "How soon can we get out of here?" she finished.

"There is a problem that must be resolved before we can answer that," Captain Banda said. "I've sized up what Mechanic Ken and the others want to take, and there's far too much for the *Pride* to carry."

"We can't easily choose what to leave," Master Mechanic Lukas added. "We need it all. Lathes, punches, small forges, drill presses, you name it. We need them."

"Can we buy another ship?" Calu asked. "How much money was in the Guild Hall treasury?"

Professor S'san shook her head. "Not that much. Contrary to

rumor, Guild Halls rarely have large amounts of currency on hand, especially out-of-the-way Guild Halls like this. It all gets forwarded to headquarters in Palandur or to the Guild offices in Longfalls."

"Do any of you have any idea," Mari asked, "what the Guild might have sent if they took the Mage elders' warning seriously?"

"The assassins, if they could get some in time," S'san said.

"Maybe common soldiers," Lukas suggested. "As many as they could get their hands on. Mercenaries or loaners from anyone wanting to ingratiate themselves with the Guild. I doubt the Senior Mechanics would use commons whose loyalty might shift to Mari."

Alain saw several commons standing nearby, obviously waiting but equally obviously not wanting to interrupt a discussion among Mechanics. "Mari, perhaps these officials have information."

She looked. "Maybe they do. Are you waiting to talk to me?"

The officials walked forward, then as one began to kneel.

"Don't!" Mari said. "*Don't!* That's better," she added as the officials straightened again.

"Lady," said one of the richly dressed officials, "we are in your debt. But we hope that you understand our ability to aid you is hindered by our obligations to the safety of our city and our people."

"But we still want to help!" another said, looking daggers at the first to speak.

"We have been told that you intend leaving Edinton very soon?" a third asked.

"Yes," Mari said. "We need to load this equipment, which requires another ship."

"It also requires more heavy wagons and more laborers to get the equipment down to the docks," Lukas said.

The officials bent into a whispered discussion and debate that was ended by one woman yelling at the others. "You fools! Here we are being threatened by a pirate whose forces are strong enough to capture a Guild Hall of the Mechanics and to defeat a monster of the Mages! If she takes a ship as well, what can we do? Our military is not capable of resisting such a force!"

Alain studied the woman, trying to understand her words and her tone. "Is she speaking a lie or does she believe this to be the truth?" Alain asked Mari.

"It's the kind of lie that everyone knows is a lie but can pretend is the truth," she replied.

"I do not understand."

Another official nodded, speaking with mock grimness. "And if this pirate also demands our cooperation in providing wagons and laborers, how can we deny her? We must do as she demands. The safety of the city requires it."

"No one is going to believe this!" the first official to have spoken insisted.

"They will when they see that dragon! And even the Mechanics will know that their own Guild Hall fell to this pirate!"

"I would not want to fight the Lady's forces," a woman in uniform with gold shining on the collar said as she approached the group. "My soldiers are in awe of the Lady, of her Mechanics, and of her Mages."

A man with her, in a different uniform but also high-ranking, pointed to Mari. "She wears a knife. May I see it, Lady?"

Mari pulled the sailor's knife from the leather belt sheath that the crew of the *Pride* had crafted.

The man examined it, nodded, then looked to the officials. "A sign of the fellowship. The pirates of these seas have accepted her as one of their own. My cutters are not adequate to confront this pirate's forces, and the warships of the Confederation that are in port would require orders to act."

"Where are the Confederation's representatives?" demanded the first official, still reluctant. "What do they say?"

"They cannot be found," the uniformed woman said with mock regret. "It is most distressing."

"No one will believe any of this!" the official insisted again..

"But it is true," Alain said, his impassive Mage's voice demanding everyone's full attention. "A pirate with a strong force entered this city. You could not stop her. Her force captured the Mechanics Guild Hall.

Her force defeated a Mage dragon. Her force will take another ship with them, and she requires of you laborers and wagons. You can say all of that, and not even a Mage will see a lie in you."

"We do not need lectures on truth from a Ma—" The reluctant official suddenly realized that he was about to insult a Mage to his face. His mouth twisted in a frantic attempt to let no more sounds escape.

The man in a blue uniform gazed toward the harbor. "It is unfortunate that the pirate is demanding...the *Worthy Son*. I will ensure that the ship's crew is replaced with volunteers, and that the ship is brought next to the dock for loading. How quickly must this be done?"

"How quickly can it be done?" Mari asked. "Here is Mechanic Captain Banda. Please work with him."

"Please? I have never before heard a Mechanic use that word in my presence." The officer saluted. "It will be my honor to do as you say, Lady. Under duress, of course."

"There may be Mechanic forces on their way to Edinton," Alain told the woman in the red uniform.

"We cannot fight them," she replied. "Not unless the daughter wants us to rise up now."

"Can you remain uninvolved even if the Mechanics Guild demands assistance?"

"It would take time to respond to the Guild's demands," the woman said. "Perhaps a lot of time. My forces have been greatly stressed by the pirate attack and the dragon."

"Thank you," Mari said, awkward with gratitude. "I need to talk to my people about some other things."

"We will be nearby until you depart," one of the officials assured her.

As Alain and Mari walked away, Alain heard argument break out again, at least a couple of the officials terrified of what might happen to the city if its cooperation with the daughter was discovered or even suspected by the Great Guilds.

"It's almost a relief to have some of them disagree with me," Mari said to Alain. "I'm beginning to worry that I might start liking being surrounded by people who will agree to anything I say."

"I do not think that will ever be a problem," Alain assured her. "The more people are in awe of you, the less you like it."

Mari choked out a brief laugh. "I've always been a little resistant to being told who to be and what to do. I guess being seen as…her… feels like people trying to make me into something else. So if I ever start to act too high and mighty, just start worshiping me and I'll start being humble just to spite you."

"But I already worship you," Alain protested.

That earned him a full laugh.

Mari dove into the work of making decisions needed to loot the Guild Hall. Alain stood by, watching for signs of deception in those Mari spoke with. Mechanics Alli and Calu also stood ready to assist. Mechanic Ken came up with information and left with more instructions, while the older Mechanics like Lukas and S'san gave advice that Mari listened to intently. Open-bed wagons rolled up to the Guild Hall and large Mechanic devices were hoisted onto them. Every once in a while several loaded wagons would head for the docks, accompanied by Mechanics who appeared gleeful to be pillaging their Guild Hall.

Alain was not certain how much time had passed when he felt the presence of a now-familiar Mage and looked to the north. A black dot was visible in the sky and growing rapidly larger. "Mage Alera returns."

Mari stared as the Roc glided low above the plaza and came to a running halt nearby.

"A smoke-snake comes," Mage Alera said even before dismounting from the Roc. She slid off the bird's neck and inclined her head toward Mari. "Elder, the smoke snake is on the shining lines entering the far side of the hills beyond this city."

"Kasi!" Master Mechanic Lukas called to another Mechanic who was not yet wearing one of Mari's armbands. "Did you get any notice of a special coming in today?"

Mechanic Kasi ran up to Lukas. "No. A special? Why would the Guild have sent a special train?"

"They got warned that we might hit Edinton," Mari explained. "The train is just entering the hills north of here. How much time do we have?"

"From there, if they come in at the best speed they can manage on those stretches, maybe two hours."

"That's not nearly enough," Lukas said. "We'd have to abandon almost everything."

"Is there a place where we could blow the track?" Alli demanded. "Some spot where it would really slow them down?"

Mechanic Kasi nodded. "Where the trestle crosses the river north of town, on the near side of those hills. That's the only good spot between here and there. Blow the trestle and they'll have to climb down, cross the river, climb up, and walk along the track to get here. That'd take several hours at least. But you çan't do it. There is no way to get to that trestle before the train does."

"Horses at full gallop—" Calu began.

"Not even close," Kasi said. "The train is too near and that trestle is too far. Nothing could get you there fast enough."

Everyone had forgotten Mage Alera, but now she spoke as dispassionately as ever. "If a Mechanic can do a spell at this place, my Roc and I can take the Mechanic there."

"Fly?" Alli said, then broke into a broad smile. "Yes! She can fly me to the trestle, I can blow it, and we'll be fine."

Calu waved both hands at Alli. "Whoa. Wait. We have to think about this."

"Why?" Alli asked. "I'm going to fly on the back of an imaginary bird to plant an explosive charge in front of a train loaded with heavily armed, hostile Mechanics. What could possibly go wrong?"

"Then I need to go, too," Calu insisted.

Mage Alera shook her head once. "The spell forming my Roc grows old and fades. He cannot carry three to the river and back."

"Alli..." Mari stared at her helplessly.

"The suggestion of Mage Alera and Mechanic Alli is a good one," Alain said, knowing that Mari did not want to hear that but needed to regardless.

"Do I get a say in this?" Mechanic Calu asked, his eyes on Alli.

She stepped close to him and whispered, then kissed him. "It'll be all right," Alli added as she stepped back. "How much can I carry, Mage Alera?"

Alera looked at her Roc. "He grows weak. Carry as little as needed."

Alli tossed her rifle to Calu. "I've already got the fuse I require, but I need several blocks of standard explosive compound C. Who can get it for me really fast?"

Mechanic Kasi and Mechanic Ken ran off. Alli pulled a small packet from a pocket of her Mechanics jacket, placed it carefully in one pocket of her pants, then peeled off her jacket before kicking off her boots.

"Do you want my pistol?" Mari asked.

"I'm good," Alli said. "I just need those boom blocks."

Alain saw the look on Mechanic Calu's face and felt the need to say something. "I am sorry," he said to Calu.

"Don't be," Calu said. "This was Alli's idea, and it is a good idea. I just wish it wasn't Alli doing it. But she's right. I shouldn't stop her from doing what she's best at. You and I really made some choices in women, huh? Never a dull moment."

"I do not think I have experienced a dull moment since meeting Mari," Alain agreed.

Mechanics Kasi and Ken came running back with what looked to Alain like several bricks, though the material seemed softer. Alli pulled her shirt out of her pants and wrapped the blocks into the front, then nodded to Alera. "Tell me what to do, Lady Mage."

Alera helped a visibly nervous Alli onto the back of the Roc, the bird eyeing her with the vast orb of his right eye. As soon as Alli was settled, Mage Alera climbed on in front of her, leaning over to whisper into the ear of her Roc.

The bird shuffled about, then ran across the plaza, hopping into

220 ♦ *The Pirates of Pacta Servanda*

the air just in time to clear the crowds and the buildings around its margin.

Mari stared after it, blinking hard. "Alain, what else should we do?"

"Even if—" Alain saw the effect of his first two words on Calu and quickly changed them. "After Mechanic Alli succeeds, the Mechanics from your Guild will still come on, though they will need more time. You will need armed Mechanics to slow them further. It is called a rear guard."

"I'll—" Mari started.

"No!" came simultaneously from Professor S'san, Master Mechanic Lukas, Mechanic Calu, and Alain.

"I'll take command of this," Calu said. "You stay back for once, Mari. How many Mechanics do you think we need, Alain?"

"It has to be enough to slow the attackers, but not so many that the rear guard is slow to retreat and cannot escape," Alain said.

"Twenty?" Calu suggested.

"I'll ask for volunteers," Mechanic Kasi said. "They'll all have rifles?"

"Yes," Calu said. "We'll take up positions near the railyard and see how long we can hold them up."

Master Mechanic Lukas held out a blocky Mechanic device. "You'll need a far-talker. This is Guild junk, but it's all we've got."

"The attackers can listen in on those," Mari objected.

"We'll use a code like when we were Apprentices," Calu said. "Let's go, Kasi. I'll be real happy to have something to do to take my mind off of other things."

"I should—" Alain started to say.

"Uh-uh," Mari said. "If I have to be smart, so do you. Stay with me. No matter what anyone says, I will not leave for the ships before we've gotten everyone else off safely."

Alain had thought the activity around the Guild Hall had been moving quickly before. But now it sped up, everyone working at a frantic pace. The Mages could do little except occasionally make part of a wall vanish to ease the removal of large Mechanic items.

He felt the return of Alera and called. "Mari!"

She turned with a growing smile of relief as Mari saw that Alain was pointing to the north.

The Roc glided in very low, barely clearing the buildings about the plaza, and came to a long, stumbling landing that ended near the Guild Hall.

Alli as much fell as dismounted from the Roc, followed by Mage Alera. While Alli staggered up to Mari, Alera knelt next to the lowered head of her Roc. She placed both arms on the Roc's neck, embracing it as the Roc rubbed her with his head.

The power put into the spell completely used up, the Roc disintegrated into a shower of dust that itself vanished before reaching the ground. Alera was left kneeling on the empty pavement.

Alain saw Mari wiping away a tear as she spoke to Alli. "How did it go?"

"No problem," Alli said, sitting down heavily on the nearest step. "My legs are a little wobbly. You would not believe— That's for later. The important thing is that when we landed on this side of the trestle we could see the smoke from the approaching train. Mage Alera put us down right on the edge, so all I had to do was get down, run onto the trestle, find the best spot, plant my charge, set the fuse, and run back."

Alli inhaled deeply. "Which I did. The train was coming into sight when the charge blew and knocked half the trestle into the river."

"Were we right?" Mari asked. "Was the Guild sending someone on that train to reinforce Edinton's Guild Hall?"

"Judging from the number of rifles that fired at us as Mage Alera and I flew off, I'd say the answer is surely yes. We had a lot of bullets chasing us before that bird got us clear." Alli looked around. "What happened to the bird?"

"It has gone," Alain said. He walked to Mage Alera, hearing Alli asking another question of Mari.

"Where's Calu?"

"Commanding the rear guard," Mari said.

"He's—" Alli threw up her hands. "Isn't that like a man? You risk your life, so he figures he has to risk his life. What is the matter with men?"

Alain offered his hand to Mage Alera. "Let me help you stand."

She looked up at him, impassive and tragic at the same time. "Help?"

"As you helped Mechanic Alli do what she must." Alain got Mage Alera to her feet, not surprised to discover that she was completely worn out, having put what strength she could into keeping her Roc going as long as possible. He put a spare armband on her sleeve. "Do you see the Mages over there? You can rest among them. We will leave this city tonight on ships."

"Is it worth it, Mage Alain? Is…helping…the daughter a path of wisdom?"

"It is," he said. "May you soon ride Swift again."

Alera looked at Alain. "You remembered his name. But he is even less than a shadow."

"Not to one who believes in him."

❖ ❖ ❖

It was very late in the afternoon when Alain heard the rattle of Mechanic weaponry firing in another part of the city.

Professor S'san listened on a looted far-talker, then nodded to Mari. "Mechanic Calu says the Mechanics he is facing are professional fighters. He is not trying to defend any spot, but is only having his Mechanics take stands long enough to cause the attackers to have to stop and advance cautiously afterwards."

"Alli will kill me if Calu is hurt," Mari said. "Where is Alli?"

"With Calu," Alain said. "She told me to tell you."

Shaking her head, Mari yelled at those still working. "Drop anything we haven't already loaded! Get the loads down to the dock and get yourselves and your loads onto the ship. Master Mechanic Lukas, inform Captain Banda that he needs to get all of our ships away from the dock as soon as possible, and have all of our boats waiting to take the rear guard and others to the ships."

She paused. "Come on, Alain."

Alain followed as Mari ran into the Guild Hall, moving through the hallways with the ease of someone familiar with the building. Reaching the Senior Mechanic conference room, Mari waved to the Mechanics guarding the door. "Get down to the docks."

Entering, Alain saw most of the captive Senior Mechanics sitting against the far wall, looking subdued and dazed. "They've been kind of nervous around me for some reason," Bev explained. "What the blazes is going on?"

"Mechanic attack force entering the city," Mari murmured to her. "You and the other two in here get out, lock and bar the doors to this room, and head for the docks."

"Got it. You've got something in your hair," Bev pointed out. "Right there."

Mari shuddered as she pulled out another fragment of dragon. "Don't waste any time. I'm going to make certain no one else is left in the Hall."

Alain followed again as Mari ran, stopping by numerous rooms to look inside and racing off again. She stopped to order the Mechanics guarding the Guild loyalists in the dining hall to seal the doors and then run for safety.

The far-talker Mari still carried began making noise. She listened, then shook her head. "Calu is falling back really quickly. He says if he doesn't, the other guys will cut off the rear guard."

They burst out of the front entry, Alain seeing that the sun had fallen so low that its rays were grazing the rooftops of Edinton. At the bottom of the stairs, Mechanic Bev waited along with several other armed Mechanics. "I didn't get to go up against the dragon," she said, "so I'm staying for this fight."

In the midst of the erratic crashes of the Mechanic weapons, much louder now as the fight neared the Guild Hall, Alain heard a deeper boom.

"Alli must have set a bomb to slow them down," Mari said. She ran, breathing heavily, to where the Edinton officials still waited. "Get out of here. Get all of the commons who aren't already at home into shelter. If those Mechanic assassins see you they might kill you out of sheer meanness."

"We'll see you again, daughter!" one called as the officials took to their heels.

"Everyone else is heading for the docks," Professor S'san said.

"Why are you still here?" Mari demanded. "Go!"

S'san hesitated, then nodded, joining the tail end of the fleeing procession.

Alain saw a patch of darkness appear on one side of the plaza, then moments later saw Mechanics wearing Mari's armbands running toward them. "The attack comes," he said.

Bev and the others knelt to aim their weapons, Mari standing beside Alain and counting as more Mechanics ran into the plaza, heading for the shelter offered by the Guild Hall. "Where are Alli and Calu?" she whispered.

A small group of Mechanics burst out of a street, pausing to fire a volley behind them, then bolted for all they were worth across the plaza.

Before the last of Mari's rear guard had reached the Guild Hall's walls, while they were still in the open, a larger group of Mechanics appeared and swung their weapons up to fire, ignoring the long-range shots of Bev and the rest of Mari's Mechanics.

CHAPTER TWELVE

Alain had been gathering strength to himself, preparing his spell, and now he placed the strongest heat he could on the pavement in front of the attacking Mechanics. The stones of the pavement shattered into fragments and dust, creating a boom that rivaled the sound of Mechanic Alli's bombs.

The attackers reeled back, seeking cover.

More Mechanics appeared to the right of them.

Alain placed another ball of heat in front of that group.

The sun sank below the buildings, putting the plaza into shadow.

The first group of attackers was firing on the rear guard from the shelter of some of the buildings.

Alain, feeling his strength draining rapidly, put a third globe of heat just inside the window of the largest structure the attackers were using as cover, causing the nearest windows to blow out.

He took a faltering step, nearly falling, but Mari caught him. "This day must have taken more from me than I realized," Alain told her, startled that his strength had given out so quickly.

The rear guard was reaching them now, racing past Bev and her force as Bev waved them onward. "We'll form a line at the buildings," one Mechanic yelled as he went by, his face streaked with smoke, sweat, and blood.

"Mari, you and Alain ought to get out of here, too," Bev urged, pausing in her firing across the plaza.

"Not until the rest are clear," Mari insisted.

"Then send Alain ahead! From the looks of him he can't run very far!"

Mari gave Alain an anguished look, then focused on Bev again. "Make sure Alli and Calu make it past before you fall back."

"You got it."

Alain, angry at being so weakened, did his best to move quickly as Mari helped him toward the line of buildings ahead. "Like Marandur all over again," Mari gasped. "Or Altis. Why do we keep ending up like this?"

Just ahead of them, one of the rear guard stumbled and fell forward, blood appearing on her back where a bullet had hit. But two other Mechanics grabbed her, one on each side, and carried her on. "Get her to the boats!" Mari ordered.

Alain looked back as they reached the shelter of a building, able to stand on his own once more. About a dozen members of the rear guard and Bev's force were intermingled in the plaza. He saw Mechanic Alli stop, turn, aim carefully, and fire. Moments later, one of the attackers came to a sudden halt and fell as her bullet struck.

Spurts of dust and fragments were flying from the buildings around them, marking hits by the attackers' bullets.

"Keep going! Keep going!" Calu was yelling. He jerked from a bullet hitting one arm, but kept on his feet.

Unable to see any targets worth using another fire spell, Alain could only fall back again with the others.

Alli stopped nearby, reloading her rifle. "Alain, the only thing that will keep Mari from insisting on being the last out will be if you keep her moving. Don't you be a hero or she'll do the same."

"I understand," Alain said. He felt a strong reluctance to follow Alli's advice, but he knew it was wise. Wisdom this day seemed to involve telling someone else something that they did not want to hear. "Mari! This way!"

Without waiting for her to argue, Alain once more began moving back with the rear guard.

Mari caught up, glaring at him, but stayed at Alain's side.

Despite the way parts of the rear guard kept halting to cover other members as they retreated, Alain found he had trouble keeping up as the Mechanics hurried down the long way they had marched through just the night before. It only slowly occurred to him how long he had been up, moving, and often fighting and casting spells. Little wonder three fire spells had exhausted him.

Fortunately, this time the journey was downhill toward the harbor, not uphill into the city, and fear lent wings to everyone heading for the boats they hoped were still waiting at the docks.

With all the commons in the city in hiding, no one had come out to light the streetlamps. The streets grew increasingly dark as the sun set, the buildings to either side dim shapes.

Alain paused in a darker patch of shadow, looking back down a long straight stretch of a wide street. Mari leaned against the wall of the building, breathing heavily, her pistol ready in one hand as she used the other to pull out the far-talker Professor S'san had given her. "Ditch the far-talkers!" she said into it. "Don't forget that the Guild can track their locations. Get rid of them now if you haven't already."

Mari dropped the device onto the pavement, raised one boot, and slammed it down repeatedly on the far-talker. "That felt good."

Several shots resounded from the far end of the street. Alain saw the shapes of Mechanics running toward him and Mari. It was obviously time to force Mari to fall back as well, but Alain paused, remembering an abandoned draft wagon they had passed at the head of the street. He could still barely make it out.

More shots as more Mechanics appeared, these firing at the rear guard. Alain measured his strength, then built heat above his hand. A moment later he placed that heat on the dimly visible form of the wagon.

The wooden wagon erupted into flames which sharply revealed the shapes of the attacking Mechanics. The rear guard fired at the clear targets, causing three to drop while the others scattered for shelter.

Calu stumbled up to them, his wounded arm dripping blood that formed tiny, dark pools on the street. "Move!"

"You, too!" Alli ordered as she joined them. She shoved Calu towards Mari and Alain. "All three of you, get to the boats!"

"Where's Bev?" Mari demanded.

"With the other section! Get out of here, Mari! And take my idiot husband with you so the healers can patch him up!"

Alain grabbed Calu's uninjured arm and pulled him along. Mari, muttering something angry under her breath, followed just behind, covering their back trail with her pistol.

They staggered out onto the open area along the dockfront. Alain saw three boats in the water, two of the large ones from the Pride and the largest boat from the Gray Lady. Sailors were at the oars, and Mechanics in each boat were gazing anxiously toward the sounds of battle.

"Alli…" Calu fought being handed down into a boat, but he was weak from loss of blood.

Alain turned to Mari, who was standing on the edge of the dock and staring into the city. The sound of rifle fire was coming closer, and Alain heard one bullet strike the surface of the dock not far from them. "We must go," he told Mari.

"Not yet!" Mari cupped her hands around her mouth and yelled as loudly as she could. "Everyone in the rear guard! Fall back to the boats now! We are leaving!"

Dark shapes appeared, racing over the short remaining distance, some of them lurching with fatigue or injury.

"Get in the boat, Mari!" Alli shouted as she appeared. She turned, fired again, then came running their way.

Alain saw Bev reaching one of the other boats and helping in some of the others before kneeling and firing at other Mechanics who were darting from the buildings. He reached out, took Mari's arm, and pulled her toward the boat as Alli came charging up.

They all got into the boat at about the same moment, Alain dropping in, pulling Mari with him, and Alli diving off the dock to land on the oar handlers as bullets tore by overhead.

"That's all of them! Shove off!" Mechanic Deni ordered from her post at the stern of their boat.

Deni tossed off the line holding the stern to the dock, then used a pole to help push off as the sailors got their oars in the water and began pulling with the vigor of those hearing bullets headed their way.

"Asha," Mari gasped, staring around frantically. "Did we get Asha to a ship, or are she and Dav still at a hospital?"

Alain pointed toward the shape of the *Pride*, which was growing in size as the boat approached it. "I can sense Asha on that ship. Mechanic Dav is surely with her."

"Thank— Oww!"

Alain spun to look, alarmed, and saw Mechanic Alli hit Mari again. "Stop risking yourself like that!" Alli stretched far enough to hit Mechanic Calu as well. "You, too! I cannot be the only adult in this crowd!"

"I'm glad that you're safe, too," Calu said in a worn-out voice.

"Thank the stars that Alain listens to sense!" Alli sagged back, still holding her weapon, gazing at the flash of rifle shots from the dock. "You did an amazing job commanding the rear guard through most of the retreat, Calu. I love you. When we get nice and safe, I think I'm going to cry a little. I'm kind of stressed."

"Me, too," Mari said. "I'm going to slug you back once we get on the ship."

They came alongside the *Pride*, sailors helping everyone up the ladder. Alain saw the boats being hooked up and hoisted out of the water, while other sailors brought up the anchor and unfurled sails that looked ghostly in the light of the rising moon.

"They'll be looking for other boats in order to follow us and attack again," Mechanic Deni commented to Alain as she passed. "Those killers, I mean. But the commons took every boat but ours and tied them up out on the water. We'll be clear of this mess before you know it, Sir Mage."

The *Gray Lady* led the way out of the harbor, out between other vessels that sat silent as she and the *Pride* wove their way toward open water.

Alain leaned on the railing as they passed the breakwater. The swells came stronger as the ships entered the open sea, the *Pride* rolling and twisting as she put on more sail and gained speed.

"Go west until we're out of sight of land," Mari told Captain Banda. "Then turn south."

"South?"

"Yes, south. We'll hold a conference tomorrow, or is it today now? In the morning." Mari came over to Alain. "We made it. Do you think anyone will pay attention to me any more after that near disaster?"

"You may be surprised," Alain said.

Mari woke to the rolling motion of the *Pride* and a sense of relief mingled with dread at the conference that had to be held.

She got out of the bunk carefully, somehow untangling herself from Alain without waking him despite the tight quarters.

Asha was in the other bunk, looking beat-up but otherwise all right. Mechanic Dav slept on the deck beside her bunk, still keeping guard.

Mari went out on deck, squinting against the light of the sun and a brisk wind that carried salt spray with it. The day looked beautiful, all four ships sailing together with the sun nearly overhead—

Four ships?

Mari shaded her eyes, staring. Each of the four ships flew the square banner of the new day from its highest mast. The *Pride* she was on, the *Gray Lady* was bounding along to starboard, and one of the other two must be the ship that Edinton had provided.

Captain Banda came up next to her, smiling. "A fine sight, isn't it? Nothing beats a tall ship with the wind in her sails and a fair sea."

"Where did we get four ships from?" Mari asked.

"That large one there to port is the *Worthy Son*, which was pirated out of the Edinton port itself in a daring raid and is now loaded with many rare and valuable Mechanic tools." Banda pointed astern. "And that ship with all the boats is the *Dolphin*, a Confederation transport used for landing soldiers. Lost at sea, I was informed, fate unknown. It's possible it was also captured by pirates."

"Are there soldiers aboard it?" Mari asked, aghast.

"Aye. I'm not certain how many."

"The Confederation isn't supposed to be getting directly involved in anything yet! Captain, we need to hold a conference. I'll give you a list of everyone who has to be there. They're probably scattered on all four ships."

Banda nodded. "No problem, Lady Master Mechanic. We'll all bring in sail so we're just drifting, and use boats to ferry anyone needed to the *Pride*."

Mari gave Banda her list, then went back to the cabin. She found a tray of food and drink on the table and barely managed to avoid wolfing it all down. Alain woke up as she was eating and joined in, managing a smile which was almost perfectly done. From someone who had once been forced to forget how to smile, it was very nice to see.

They left the cabin quietly to avoid disturbing either Asha or Dav. The ships had all furled their sails. Now they rocked in the swells without moving forward, four stationary objects in a vast expanse of water. Mari could see boats already headed for the *Pride*.

Banda had offered his cabin for the meeting, since it doubled as a dining room for the Mechanics aboard and thus boasted a decent-sized table and multiple chairs and benches. When Mari finally entered she saw one seat left empty at the head of the table—the place Captain Banda usually sat—and another empty seat beside it. Everyone else was either seated or standing around the edges of the cabin.

Feeling awkward, Mari walked to the head of the table, steeling herself for the criticism she felt certain would soon be hurled at her. Would these Mechanics, Mages, and commons continue to listen to her after the mess which Edinton had turned into?

She reached her seat and paused while seeking words.

Master Mechanic Lukas began softly pounding the table with the palm of one hand. The others picked up the applause, some smiling at Mari and others just giving her looks of approval.

She wondered if her mouth had fallen open in astonishment.

"Well done, Master Mechanic," Lukas said as the applause ended. "I wouldn't have believed it possible."

"There—" Mari began. "There were mistakes—"

"No plan goes perfectly," Mechanic Ken said. "But every time something went amiss, you knew what to do. How did you get Edinton to give up a ship so easily?"

"And that Mage who warned us," Professor S'san said. "You sized her up, knew how to use her, and gave the right orders."

"Those were Alli's, and Calu's, and Alain's ideas!"

"You obviously listened to them," Mechanic Kasi remarked. "And gave the right people the right jobs. What now, Master Mechanic?"

"Um…" Thrown off by not having to defend or excuse her actions in Edinton, Mari took a moment to gather her thoughts. "You are?" she asked a man in uniform.

"Major Sima," he replied, standing up and saluting. "On long-term leave from the Confederation military to deal with family issues."

Captain Banda smiled. "Exactly how many members of the Confederation military on long-term leave for family issues are aboard the *Dolphin*?"

"One hundred and three, counting my officers and me," Sima replied.

"You're not here representing the Confederation?" Mari asked.

"No. Anything I happen to do while on leave is strictly unofficial, unsanctioned, and unapproved." Sima paused. "We had little time to find volunteers with long-term family issues, or there would have been more of us, daughter."

"All right," Mari said, managing not to flinch this time at the use of the title. "Two things. First, we'll need to have my Mages check your soldiers to ensure none are spies for the Great Guilds. Or the empire."

Sima nodded. "I understand. Since I do not want to attempt to lie to a Mage, I will confess freely that my superiors have asked me to keep them informed about your actions, daughter."

"You'll need to keep that information vague for the time being,"

Mari warned. "Anything the Confederation learns might reach the Great Guilds, and we are going to need time before the Great Guilds muster an effort against us."

"I understand, daughter."

"Which brings up the second thing. I am...really...uncomfortable with being addressed as...her. I would prefer just Lady Master Mechanic."

"But there are other Lady Master Mechanics," Mechanic Kasi pointed out.

"Perhaps just Lady?" Major Sima said. "Or Lady Mari? Stories from the Northern Ramparts say you used that title there."

"Lady Mari will be fine," Mari said. "How many Mechanics do we have now with everyone who joined us at Edinton?"

Senior Mechanic Gina answered. "One hundred fifty-six. Mechanics and Apprentices. None of the Senior Mechanics at Edinton were sympathetic, but we picked up ten more Master Mechanics among the hundred fifty-six."

"You're kidding." Mari took a deep breath.

"Mage Dav told me that an additional twelve Mages joined us as well," Alain said. "Three are Mages who can create Rocs."

"So, that's four counting Mage Alera? Mage Dav says all the new Mages are all right?"

"He does. I have told him the new Mages must not mistreat anyone and must not deliberately insult Mechanics. I will also speak to them of this," Alain said.

"Where are you taking all of these people?" Professor S'san asked. "What is your plan from here on?"

Mari gestured to Captain Banda, who unrolled a chart. "Tiae," she said. "The Broken Kingdom. We're going there, where no one will expect us to go, where we can find commons to train, and where we can begin fixing the problems of this world at the place where they have done the most damage."

She had expected the first reaction to be an outburst of protests and objections, but instead Mechanic Kasi laughed. "I kept telling the Senior Mechanics that we should send a strong force into Tiae and rebuild things! It would be like melting down scrap metal and reforging it! But all they could think to do was try to seal off the break."

"Where in Tiae?" Lukas asked. "If what I know is even remotely accurate, there are warlords and bandit gangs everywhere. How could we keep them off our backs?"

The captain of the *Gray Lady* cleared his throat. "If I may, honored Mechanics and honored Mage, I do have some information regarding Tiae."

Captain Banda raised a disapproving eyebrow at him. "I was informed that you had spent much of our time in Edinton prowling the waterfront taverns."

"Aye, that I did. How better to learn what could be learned?" The captain stood up and gestured to the chart. "I posed as a member of the fellowship, you see, one who had become too well known in the north and was seeking safer waters to ply the old trade until things cooled off in the waters I normally sailed."

"You posed as a pirate?" Banda asked. "That must have been difficult," he added sarcastically.

The captain of the *Gray Lady* smiled in response. "There were those I spoke to who had been south of Confederation waters in the last several years. Not many. Few ships go to Tiae now. There are the pirates along the coast, and the embargo."

"Embargo?" Professor S'san asked.

"Aye, Lady. The Confederation, the Alliance, the Free Cities, and even the Empire have all banned the shipment of arms and armor to what used to be Tiae. To control the violence, you see. It was demanded by the Great Guilds."

"I guess that's something most Mechanics were never told. How has that embargo worked?" asked Calu. His arm was bandaged, but he looked weak and had a seat at the table instead of standing.

"How has it worked? Not at all."

"Pirates along the coast?" Banda asked. "How bad is that?"

"Not as bad as formerly," the captain replied. "Too little prey, you see. But I was warned that any ship sailing off the coast of Tiae, especially off the cities, will attract pirates coming out in small boats, usually at night. The cities are shadows of what they once were, great empty monuments of the past with few people left, but some still find homes in them."

"What happened to the people?" Professor S'san asked in a low voice.

"Most went into the countryside," Major Sima said. "They scratch out survival on tiny farms. It was their only hope once food stopped coming into the cities as the roads became unusable due to bandits, warlords, and deterioration."

"Not many refugees in the Confederation itself?"

"Some. Not many made it across before the Great Guilds ordered the Confederation to seal the borders. I was told that the Confederation was still debating what to do when the decision was taken from our hands. I will confess that is a source of guilt among many of us."

"Like trying to block the spread of a plague," Captain Banda remarked.

"We're going to fix things," Mari said. "Not just try to seal off what we don't know how to fix. We can avoid the pirates just by sailing out of sight of land. Right?"

Banda shook his head. "Not if you want to know where you are. The Mechanics Guild has limited the navigational equipment available to us. I have no idea why. But sailing out of sight of land, unless a ship is following clear sailing directions in well-known waters like the Sea of Bakre, is a good way to become lost at sea. Out here I know I can sail east and find the coast, but where on the coast? That I can't say."

Mari grimaced and shook her head. "The Guild probably limited navigational methods to prevent anyone getting to the Western Continent. There's no telling what might be there. It might be something the Guild doesn't want anyone to know about."

Everyone except Alain stared at her. "The Western Continent is real?" Banda asked.

"Yes. Alain and I have seen it on…a map. An absolutely reliable map."

"I've always wanted to sail out looking for it," Banda murmured, his eyes distant.

"We're not going there now," Mari said. "It might be completely barren. What else did you learn?" she asked the captain of the *Gray Lady*.

"I was advised that piracy was unlikely to pay but that if I cared to risk it, running weapons past the embargo might gain some valuable goods in trade. However, just about everywhere on the coast is controlled by bandits or warlords who would more likely slit your throat and take what you have rather than make an honest trade."

The captain leaned and pointed to one place on the coast of what had been Tiae. "Except here. Pacta Servanda. It's a town with a decent harbor, on the coast about halfway between Minut and Tiaesun. Somehow it has held out against the warlords. The sailors I talked to claimed that it is the only place along the coast where the old flag of Tiae still flies. They are civilized—they'll make an honest deal if you don't try to cheat them—but you still must be very careful with them."

"Why?" Mari asked.

The captain sat down again, his eyes hooded. "It was explained to me so, Lady. Have you ever seen a dog, one that had been mistreated, beaten, starved, for most of its life? If you saw that dog, would you go to pet it?"

"Such a dog would bite your hand off," Master Mechanic Lukas said.

"Aye, he would. And if you offered him food? Would the dog wag his tail and be your friend?"

Lukas shook his head, looking grim. "No. He might take the food, but he'd still be ready to bite, because to him everyone is an enemy."

"And just so are the people of Tiae," the captain said. "Pacta Servanda has held on to the rule of law, but the people of Pacta Servanda have been marked by too many years of dealing with a world that is full of hurt and death."

Mari nodded, feeling hurt inside herself as she thought of Tiae and its people. "We'll have to talk to them. Approach them very carefully. Hopefully we can convince them that we are willing to help, long term."

"If anybody can do it, you can," Lukas said.

"I'm not—"

"Oh, stop it, Mari," Alli said. "How many Mages do you have taking orders from you, listening to you, calling you elder? How many people even talked to Mages before you decided to do it?"

"Even Mages talk to Mages only when they have to," Alain said.

"There!" Alli said. "See? And you got the locals in Julesport to help us, and the locals in Edinton. Commons listen to you. You know how to talk to them."

"And Mechanics," Professor S'san said. "I know of no rebellion that has ever occurred within the Guild. No matter how badly things went, no group of Mechanics ever arose to fight against the Guild. But you are leading such a group. The commons and the Mages may listen to you because of the daughter prophecy, but Mechanics are another matter. Even before the daughter connection, the Senior Mechanics feared your ability to lead and inspire others."

Mari couldn't sort out how she felt as the others spoke. Was it discomfiture at the praise? Happiness at being told she was doing a good job by people whose opinions she respected? Fear of letting down them and so many others? "I…I'll do my best. I assume everyone agrees that we should go to Pacta Servanda? What else do we need to decide?"

Senior Mechanic Gina spoke up again. "As far as I can tell, things aren't really organized. Everyone just listens to you. But you shouldn't be deciding everything, or having to deal with everything, especially if we keep gaining people."

"That's a very good point," Professor S'san said.

"I would recommend that Master Mechanic Lukas and Professor S'san be put in direct charge of the Mechanics, reporting to you and passing on important decisions to you," Gina added.

Mari looked around for objections. "That sounds like a good idea. But I also want Mechanic Alli designated in charge of arms production. She is going to need that authority."

Lukas nodded judiciously. "Alli would be an excellent choice for that job. If I had my wishes, we'd work on other things first, but we're going to need weapons to give us time and space to work on other things next."

"Thank you," Alli said, smiling. "I've found a design in one of Mari's forbidden texts. It's a rifle that's simple and rugged. It uses a clip and semi-automatic feed like Mari's pistol, so it would have a much higher rate of fire than the Guild's lever-action rifles, and the barrel is longer and has better specs, so it would also have a significantly better effective range."

"Sounds like it would need a lot of ammunition," Mechanic Ken commented.

"It will," Alli said. "We'll have to look at mass production of small-arms ammunition."

"And far-talkers," Calu said. "Another one of Mari's texts has some designs that would let us build far-talkers smaller, lighter, and a lot better than the current Guild models. Hey, Mari, do you have any idea why the texts call the far-talkers rah-dee-ohs?"

"No idea," Mari said. "Those sound like good first priorities."

Mechanic Kasi waved toward Calu. "I don't know what his specialty is, but this guy did a great job on that rear guard command. If we need someone to work with the common militaries, I recommend him."

"My specialty is theory," Calu admitted.

"Ha! Well, you got your hands dirty in Edinton, theorist!"

"What about the Mages?" Professor S'san asked. "Do they report to Mage Alain?"

"That would mean Alain was reporting to me," Mari objected.

"Is that a problem?"

"He's my partner! We've made every decision together, and his have equal weight with mine! Alain should be seen as…as…"

"Your executive," Senior Mechanic Gina said. "The invaluable co-worker who helps get everything done."

"Then who deals with the Mages on everyday matters?" S'san asked. "Assuming that everyday and Mages belong in the same sentence?"

"Mage Dav," Alain said. "He has shown a gift for speaking to other Mages."

"Mage Dav is cool," Alli agreed.

"That's settled, then," Mari said, hoping that Alain had taken well what she and others had said. It had proven unexpectedly difficult to put a title on the role he played for her and with her. "What else?"

Professor S'san pushed a piece of paper toward Mari. "I went through the Guild Hall Supervisor's files before we left Edinton and found this. It's the latest warning the Guild sent out about you, a few days before you showed up in Edinton. I would advise you not to bother reading the parts about your mental, emotional, technical, and moral failings."

Mari picked up the paper, skimming through the first part despite S'San's warning. "Clearly insane, huh? Fanatical. Paranoid. Pro—*promiscuous*?"

"You didn't think they'd avoid saying that about you, did you?" S'san asked.

"I didn't— *Unqualified*?!" That stung worse than the charge of promiscuity.

"Nobody who knows you would believe any of that," Alli said.

"Yeah, but first the Mage elders claim I'm some seductress trying to ensnare Alain, and then—" Mari stopped talking, realizing too late that she had never told even her friends about that embarrassing charge. "Let's just forget that last part."

"Fat chance," Alli murmured.

Mari did her best to focus on the last part of the report. "Seriously? The Guild leadership is reporting that I may be in Altis again, and in Syndar, and in Amandan en route to Kitara, and off Daarendi, and in Gullhaven, Kelsi and Jacksport. The Guild also has reports that I've got armies in Amandan, Kelsi and Jacksport."

"Wow," Alli commented. "You sure get around, don't you? Why didn't you tell us about all of these armies of yours?"

"It must have slipped my mind." Mari read the final paragraph out loud. "If Mari is seen, she is to be shot on sight. Take no chances, as she is murderous, ruthless, and deranged, and will show no mercy to any Mechanic who crosses her path. Any Mechanics, Mages, or commons who are near her are also to be killed without hesitation because they may well be part of her evil plots against the right and proper role of the Mechanics Guild as the supreme power in Dematr."

It was quiet for a moment after Mari had finished, then Calu shrugged. "No surprises there. The Guild first tried to kill you just on suspicion that you were doing something wrong or might do something wrong someday. They would have done the same to us, eventually. Mechanic Dav told me about the evidence of Guild purges that he found in old records."

"There is good news in that report," Captain Banda said. "They're not thinking about Tiae. The Guild is seeing you behind every tree, but they're still not imagining that you'd be going to Tiae. It doesn't occur as an option to the Senior Mechanics."

"That's good for us," Lukas agreed.

"May I ask something?" Mechanic Kasi spoke up. "Mechanic Calu is suffering from a bullet wound. So are some other Mechanics. I understand that one of the Mages was badly hurt in the fight with the dragon. Why haven't the Mages healed any of them?"

Mari indicated Alain. "He can explain."

"Mages," Alain said, "can do nothing to another directly. I can create heat in the air which will burn someone, but I cannot set a fire inside them. I can create the illusion of a hole in a wall, but I cannot create the illusion of a hole in the heart of another. No Mage can."

"Why are there so many stories about Mages doing those kinds of things to people?" Banda asked.

"Because the Mage Guild has encouraged such stories," Alain said. "They served to increase the awe and fear with which shadows regarded Mages. But the truth—and you must understand I was taught that there is no truth but have rejected that—is that no Mage spell can directly change another, for good or for ill. Mage elders claim that the reason for this is because no Mage has ever been able to totally disassociate themselves from others, that even in the wisest Mages to date there has always been a trace of belief that others are real and not just shadows who mean nothing."

"What do you think?" Calu asked.

Alain remained silent for a moment. "I think it is because all others are real. The world is an illusion and may be changed. But others *are*, they are reality amid the illusion, and cannot be altered. Perhaps we all create the illusion together. This is my theory."

Master Mechanic Lukas smiled. "I hope you're right, Sir Mage. If we're real, then that might mean there's more to the story even after we die."

"We go from this dream to another dream," Alain said. "The story never ends."

Senior Mechanic Gina gazed at Alain with a shocked expression. "I wondered how you could have fallen in love with a Mage," Gina said to Mari. "Now I know. Are there any others like him?"

Mari grinned. "There is no one else anywhere like him."

Later, alone, she held Alain close. "What am I doing giving orders to the likes of Professor S'san?" Mari asked, resting her head against his shoulder.

"They do not have to obey you," Alain said. "They have made a choice to obey you."

"Was Edinton as messed up as I thought it was? Because everybody else seems to think it went great."

"You achieved everything you set out to do," Alain pointed out. "Despite some major threats which surprised everyone. I have seen an experienced and talented military commander in the face of such a surprise, Mari. You did as well as he did."

"You are so delusional!" Mari drew back a little and shook her head at Alain. "I'm sure General Flyn would love hearing that I'm as good a commander as he is!"

"He is already sworn to your service."

"And I wish he was here! If we face any fights in Tiae, everybody is going to look to me, aren't they?" Mari stepped away from Alain, rubbing her face with both hands. "Where is this going to end, Alain?"

"With the overthrow of the Great Guilds," he replied.

"And then what? What happens to me if I'm still alive at that point?"

"I do not know," Alain said. "But I will be with you, wherever you are."

Somehow, that made everything feel all right.

Two days later, in the late afternoon, Captain Banda led Mari's small fleet past the city of Minut. "It's necessary to fix our position here before we turn south again," he insisted.

Mari stood on the deck of the *Pride*, gazing on what had once been one of the largest cities in the Kingdom of Tiae. From a distance it looked all right, if oddly pristine. "Marandur was like that," she said to Alli, who was standing beside her. "Cities always have this cloud of smoke and dust above them from fires and people and everything. But Marandur had nothing above it but blue sky. It looked so clean from a distance. Because Marandur was dead."

"How do you sleep?" Alli asked. "You've seen more than your share of nightmares."

"Sometimes I don't sleep," Mari said. "Other times I don't sleep well." She raised her far-seers to her eyes and scanned the city. "I can see some people, not nearly enough for a city of that size, and a lot of the buildings are still intact but some are beat up and falling apart. It's like the city is on its way to becoming like Marandur." She passed the far-seers to Alli.

"Everywhere is going to become like Marandur if we fail, right?" Alli asked as she studied Minut.

"Yeah."

"How long exactly do we have?"

"Not very long. That's as exact as I know." Mari paused. "Alli? Why are Mechanics like you and me and Calu leading this? All right, I know why I am, but why you two when we have people like Professor S'san and Master Mechanic Lukas also with us? They're in charge of Mechanics, but you and Calu are running the two most important projects almost independently. And why are Alain and Asha playing leading roles with our Mages? Mage Dav guides the other Mages, but he does what Alain says."

"You want to know why older and wiser heads aren't calling the shots?" Alli lowered the far-seers and shuddered. "That is an awful sight, isn't it? My theory, Master Mechanic Mari, is that the Great Guilds are at least partly designed to operate like lathes. Over time they grind down Mechanics and Mages alike, taking off the hard edges and the other parts that stick out, and eventually shearing away anything like rebellion and free thinking and initiative. Mechanics like S'san and Lukas are smart and capable, but when faced with something bad they look around for someone to tell them what to do. You and me and Calu haven't been under the lathe too long. We've still got all our nonconforming and inventiveness attached to us."

"I actually wasn't expecting an answer," Mari said, "but that's a really good one."

"Want another?"

"I love your answers, Alli."

"And I love your humility, your daughterness." Alli went on speaking before Mari could finish getting her glare on. "Everybody is like, whoa, Mari has figured out how to get Mechanics and Mages to work together! Isn't that totally amazing? But for me, what's amazing is how you get us young types to work well with the older-and-wisers. You remember how yesterday I came to you all ticked off because Master Mechanic Lukas was telling me something about the production process for the new rifles and I am Mechanic Alli and I already know everything about weapons? What did you do?"

"Umm." Mari had to think. There had been a lot going on that day. "I asked you…"

"'Is there something we're missing because we're not seeing it?'" Alli quoted. "And I thought, how can I miss it if I can't see it? And then I realized that I can't notice a problem I've never seen or thought about. But Lukas is older than dirt. He's seen all kinds of stuff. And he's willing to talk about it. At great length. Which can be annoying. But I went back to him and listened and, yeah, I was missing something."

"It just seemed like the right thing to ask ourselves," Mari said. "Alain has really made me think more about our assumptions and how we shape what we see by how we expect to see it."

"You're starting to sound like Calu and his observer-effect stuff," Alli commented. "Not that I mind. I do love him. But that stuff is weird."

"How is Calu doing?" Mari asked, taking back the far-seers and looking at the harbor of Minut. There were forlorn masts rising out of the water where ships had sunk, some rotting wrecks still tied up to the piers, and a long stretch of brownish water that Captain Banda said probably marked silt from the river which was slowly choking the decaying harbor.

"He'll be fine. Complains that his arm hurts more now that it's healing than it did when he was shot." Alli squinted at the city. "How is Mage Asha doing?"

"Half of her is a glorious tapestry of blacks and blues," Mari said. "She must hurt every time she breathes. But not a word of complaint. The healers say she's doing well, but it'll be a while before her ribs mend."

"I had no idea Mages were so tough," Alli said. "Hey, what's that?"

Mari had spotted it too and was focusing on the distant activity. "People running to some boats. I think I see sun glinting off weapons. They're pushing off from the pier. One…two…three. Three boats. All three are raising sails."

"These are ugly-type pirates, right?" Alli asked. "Not nice daughter-of-Jules pirates like us?"

"That's what I understand," Mari said. "Do you have to keep using that word?"

"Yes. Yes, I do. Is there any chance we could just wait here until those three boats catch us and then show them how bad a mistake they've made?"

Mari stopped to think, lowering the far-seers and gazing at the sad remnants of Minut. "That's tempting. I've noticed something, Alli. Whenever something is tempting, it turns out to be something I shouldn't have done or tried to do."

"How can it be wrong to take out those pirates?" Alli asked.

"I don't know. But it would be…well, we'd kill them, right? Not because we had to, but because we wanted to. We can get away from them easily enough. If we wait here just to kill them when they get close…" Mari shook her head. "It feels wrong."

Alli gave her a searching glance. "You've got a good feel for that sort of thing, Mari. Maybe sometimes when your gut tells you something is wrong, what it's really saying is that something is more dangerous than it looks."

"That could be," Mari said.

The *Gray Lady* shifted course, swinging closer to the *Pride*. Mari saw the *Lady*'s captain raise a speaking trumpet to his mouth. "Those boats are bait!" he yelled across to the *Pride*. "I was warned of this. They'll provoke us with crossbow fire in hopes we'll chase them and end up closer to shore. They'll prolong the chase until the sun sets, then under cover of the dark many of their friends will swarm out in other boats to overwhelm our crews."

"It's amazing what you can learn in waterfront bars," Alli commented. "Maybe I should spend more time in them."

"You're joking, right?" Mari said as she waved an acknowledgement to the *Lady*'s captain.

"We're all pirates, aren't we? And I know Calu would love to show off his scar and boast about it. *Aye, there we were at Edinton, dragons on all sides and assassins charging from the front. I'll hold them off, I said, while the rest of you get to the ships with the loot.*"

"Aye, the spirit of Jules was with us that day!" Mari said, and laughed. "Let's hope that spirit is also with us at Pacta Servanda. Jules managed to found a city and help cobble together the Confederation. We're going to need those kinds of skills."

She stayed at the rail for some time after Alli went below decks. She watched the pirate craft come closer, loose a few crossbow bolts at long range, then lose ground increasingly as the *Gray Lady*, the *Pride of Longfalls*, the *Worthy Son*, and the *Dolphin* put on more sail and left the pirates of Minut in their wakes.

Three days later the small fleet arrived off the town of Pacta Servanda. Mari saw everyone on the ships staring at the land of Tiae as the ships wore into the small harbor. For as long as she could remember Tiae had been the Broken Kingdom, a place of anarchy and violence. Like everyone else on the four ships, Mari had never expected to see Tiae, let alone choose to go there.

She raised her far-seers, spotting the green and gold banner of Tiae still flying over the town. "Our information was correct. Pacta Servanda still considers itself to be part of the kingdom."

"A kingdom that no longer exists except for this town," Captain Banda commented. "What is happening there on the left?"

Mari swung her far-seers to view that part of the defensive wall. Pacta Servanda occupied a small peninsula which both shaped the town's harbor and limited the land approaches to the town. The wall guarding the town was still intact, but where Banda had indicated Mari could see a mass of armed fighters surging at its base, trying to put up ladders that would get them to the top. Behind them a single ballista was hurling rocks against the city and the wall. "Pacta Servanda is under attack," Mari said.

Captain Banda had been studying the situation through his far-seers as well, and now shook his head. "There aren't nearly as many defenders on that wall as there are attackers trying to get in. It looks bad."

Alain declined Mari's offer of her far-seers as he always did, having a Mage's discomfort with Mechanic devices, instead shading his eyes to view what he could from this distance. "We may have arrived just in time."

Mari took another look at the battle, and at the attackers in a variety of cast-off armor and clothing swarming at the walls. This was no army deserving of the name. One of the warlords who had caused so much suffering in Tiae was trying to extinguish the last vestige of the kingdom. "Or we may have arrived just too late."

CHAPTER THIRTEEN

W e have a hundred soldiers with Major Sima," Mari said. "If we send them into the city to reinforce the walls… what?"

Alain shook his head. "The people here know nothing of us. If they see us landing soldiers on the waterfront, they will assume we are also attacking the town."

Captain Banda nodded in agreement. "And if they think they need to defend the waterfront, they'll strip some troops from the walls, weakening their defenses there and possibly ensuring the city falls."

"We've got to do something!" Mari said. "We can't just sit here and watch that town fall because we didn't arrive a half-day earlier!"

"We have the *Pride*'s deck gun," Captain Banda said. "It's a light-caliber weapon, but still ought to impress anyone we fire on."

"Your gun has enough range to reach the attackers?" Mari asked hopefully.

"We'll have to get closer to ensure accuracy, but yes." Banda grimaced apologetically. "We are low on shells, though. The Guild has allowed us only ten rounds."

"Ten?" Mari felt like yelling in frustration. "If the Senior Mechanics were going to pay to put a light gun on this ship, why wouldn't they pay the much smaller sums to provide it with a decent amount of ammunition! What else can we do? Alain, can you or the other Mages do anything without getting close to the fight?"

Alain frowned in thought. "We are still on the water and have access to little power to change the world illusion… An illusion. That is something that can be done without the use of Mages. We do not have enough soldiers to assault those who are attacking the town. But the attackers do not know that. If the ship *Dolphin* moves as if preparing to land soldiers outside the town, and our soldiers are seen on the deck, it will look to anyone watching as if we are readying a powerful strike against those attacking the walls."

Calu had joined them, his arm still bandaged. He nodded. "They'll have to break off the attack. Have the *Pride*'s gun go after that ballista first, and if we knock it out drop some shells on the guys just outside the walls."

The *Pride* and the *Dolphin* moved slowly closer to the coast, feeling their way through an unfamiliar harbor, while Mari tried not to scream with frustration at how long it was taking. She kept hauling out her far-seers to check on the defense of the town, seeing the thin ranks of those on the wall repeatedly throwing back attempts by their attackers to reach the top.

"The guys holding that wall are tough," Calu commented from the rail to Mari's right. "They're not giving any ground at all."

"But there aren't enough of them," Alli said. She was standing next to Alain, who was just to Mari's left. "Just imagine what those guys could do if they all had rifles. If they all had the new rifles we're going to make!"

Mari, worriedly watching the fight near the town wall, was surprised when a sudden boom announced the firing of the *Pride*'s deck gun. She could see the shell fly out in a flat trajectory toward the ballista that was firing on the wall. The shell struck and exploded, throwing up a fountain of dirt and grass a dozen lances from the ballista.

She saw Mechanic Deni making adjustments to the deck gun while it was reloaded. Deni stood back and pointed at the gunner, who fired again.

This time the shell struck only a few lances from the ballista.

Those attacking the wall had been absorbed in the fight, but the sounds of two explosions had drawn their attention. Mari saw some of the attackers edging away from the wall, pointing out to the ships in the harbor and shouting words impossible to hear from this far away.

A third boom, a third shell flying out, and an explosion right next to the ballista that sent its crew flying away. Some of the ballista's crew got up and ran, but others lay still.

"Shift your target to the soldiers in front of the wall!" Captain Banda called from the quarterdeck.

The next shell exploded in the rear ranks of the attackers, blowing apart a new ladder being brought up as well as those carrying it.

"Dud!" the gunner yelled.

Mari watched the gun crew yank open the breech and hastily pull out the shell that hadn't fired. Two carried the shell to the edge and tossed it as far from the ship as they could, the unexploded shell making only a large splash as it hit the water.

"Only five rounds left," Mari said.

"The *Dolphin* is in position," Alain pointed out.

From this angle Mari could see how thin the ranks of soldiers on the *Dolphin*'s deck were. But from the shore those ranks should look deep and solid. The *Dolphin*'s crew was making an elaborate production out of preparing the ship's boats for lowering.

Another shot from the *Pride*'s gun slammed into the force outside the town wall.

The attack collapsed, those who had been trying to breach the wall now running away from it in a confused mass.

"Cease fire!" Banda called. "Well done! That will teach those scum not to mess with Mechanic artillery!"

"It's a good thing they don't know we only have four shots left," Alli commented. "Now what? Pursue the beaten enemy?"

"I would not advise that," Alain said. "There is too much we do not know. The size of this warlord's forces, the nature of the land, what other threats might be near, and how the townspeople would react to us landing soldiers even outside their walls."

"I'm with Alain," Calu said.

"Far be it from me to argue," Alli said.

Mari nodded and turned to face the quarterdeck. "Captain Banda, tell the *Dolphin* to break off the fake landing and move back into the harbor. I'm going to need a boat to take a group ashore to talk with the town's leaders."

"Yes, Lady Master Mechanic," Banda replied. "I hope you are not assuming the town's leaders will be grateful."

She looked through her far-seers at the section of wall that had been most fiercely attacked and most fiercely defended. The men and women atop the wall were not celebrating victory, not cheering or raising weapons high. They stood, weapons at ready, all facing toward the four ships that had entered the harbor of Pacta Servanda.

The warning she had received from the captain of the *Gray Lady* came back to her. The defenders of Pacta Servanda looked uncomfortably lean and wolfish as they unflinchingly faced what they must see as another threat.

Mari had kept the landing party small but hopefully impressive. Herself. Mechanics Alli and Calu. Master Mechanic Lukas and Professor S'san. All of the Mechanics were impossible to mistake in their dark jackets. Alain, Mage Dav, Mage Hiro, and Mage Alera in their robes. Major Sima and a couple of his soldiers. The captain of the *Gray Lady* and a few sailors.

The only sound as they were rowed to the town landing was the splash of water as oars dipped and rose. Mari could see abandoned buildings along the waterfront. She could also see groups of people silently watching the approaching boat. Something about the way they stood waiting made Mari grateful for the pistol holstered under her jacket.

Calu shifted his grip on his rifle as he stared back at the silent watchers. "This feels like one of those stories where everyone is yelling at the characters, 'Don't go into that town!' Doesn't it?"

"No one warned me of any cannibalism in Pacta Servanda," the Gray Lady's captain remarked cheerfully. "I'm sure they would have mentioned that if it was anything to worry about."

A detachment of soldiers awaited the boat as it reached the landing. The soldiers wore the green and gold of Tiae on their uniforms, the colors faded and the fabric worn and patched from age and use. Their armor and the weapons they carried were battered, but in good repair and without a trace of rust.

"These soldiers remind me of some others," Alain murmured to Mari.

"I was thinking the same thing," she replied. The inhabitants of the university in Marandur, holding things together within their small portion of the world but showing the strain of being under constant threat and having to make do with the leavings of the past.

The officer in command stood at the edge of the landing, waving off the sailors on the boat who tried to tie up. The sailors took one look at the soldiers behind her, their weapons drawn and ready, and settled back to wait for their superiors to handle things.

Mari didn't blame them. The soldiers had the grim look of professionals who combined experience with fatalism. Facing a pack of wolves would probably have been less intimidating.

"Why are you here?" the officer demanded, her voice as harsh as her expression.

Mari stayed seated in the boat as she tried to sound both confident and nonthreatening. "We want to meet the leaders of Pacta Servanda."

"If you seek ransom or an opportunity to pillage, you are wasting your time. The only things of value left in Pacta Servanda are our weapons, and those we will only give you point first."

"We don't want a ransom," Mari said. "We just helped drive off the people assaulting your wall. We are here to help this town. We are here to help Tiae."

The officer smiled incredulously. "To help Tiae? Are you not a few years late in that task, Lady Mechanic?"

"Yes," Mari said. "But hopefully not too late. Do you speak for the town? We have an offer for your leaders. Not threats. An offer. Are you authorized to reject that offer?"

As Mari had hoped, the officer had vast experience with confronting physical threats but not much familiarity with diplomacy. "Your ships fly the flag of no country. I will not allow pirates to land in this city."

"Don't you want to know whose flag they do fly?" Professor S'san asked, unintimidated.

"Let us talk to the leaders of Pacta Servanda," Mari insisted. "It doesn't take a genius to tell that this town is on its last legs. Our help can make the difference for you. But what we bring is an offer, not any type of ultimatum."

Alain spoke up, using his Mage voice. Mari knew he was aware of how little she liked that voice, so he must be using it for the effect it had on the officer and her soldiers. "If you want to change the fate of this town," Alain said, "and the fates of everyone in it, and the fates of everyone in Tiae, you will not stand in our way. The choice is yours."

The officer eyed them, slowly lowering the blade of her sword as she did so. "I know what those are," she said, using the sword to point at the rifles held by Alli and Calu. "I have never seen one in use, but I have heard what they can do."

"Then you know," Mari said, "that if we wanted to we could sit here and kill you and all of your soldiers without risk to ourselves." That was an exaggeration, given how close the boat was to the landing and the crossbows carried by some of the soldiers, but Mari thought the white lie was justified in this case. "We're not here to threaten or harm you. We are here to offer a deal that will benefit you and us."

"A deal?" The officer nodded, as if finally understanding. "We are familiar with trade-offs, Lady Mechanic. You will leave those—" she said, using her sword to point again at the rifles held by Alli and Calu—"and come with me."

Apparently the officer's knowledge of Mechanic weapons did not extend to pistols, which wasn't surprising given how long it had been since the Mechanics Guild had a presence in Tiae. No one suggested searching Mari or the other Mechanics.

But from the way the officer and her soldiers watched the Mages, they had heard plenty of stories about them. Mentally, Mari sighed, hoping that the worst of Mage excesses had been forgotten in the years since the Mage Guild had abandoned Tiae.

The boat tied up and most of Mari's group disembarked, Sima's soldiers and the sailors remaining at the dock. The officer led the way into the town, her soldiers forming two lines, one on either side of Mari's group.

The walk through Pacta Servanda showed Mari more of the town. As at the waterfront, some buildings were empty, usually those devoted to businesses. Living accommodations tended to be occupied, though. The commons she could see wore a variety of clothes that implied both townsfolk and refugees from the countryside. Mari had the overwhelming impression of a town that existed only to survive. Trade and business and crafts had all given way to the most basic need.

Professor S'san leaned close to Mari. "There is no trash in the streets," she murmured. "Just like in the Empire."

Mari nodded in silent reply. The Imperial government kept the streets clean, which was a sign both of how efficient the Imperials could be and of how much emphasis they placed on maintaining order. The leaders of Pacta Servanda were also keeping it clean, displaying an obvious sign of a government which had the power to fulfill basic functions.

The city hall they eventually reached was a stout building with a worn but well-built façade. Graceful curves marked doorways and rooflines, and vines grew along the front, almost masking the ravages of too many years with too few repairs. The commander of the soldiers escorting them brought Mari's group to the doorway. "You must wait here." She entered the building, leaving Mari and others guarded by the soldiers of the town.

S'san glanced around, annoyed. "Waiting on the whims of commons," she grumbled just loudly enough for Mari to hear.

A crowd was forming at a small distance, silently watching Mari and her companions. "Even the babies aren't crying," Mari heard Alli whisper to Calu.

Mage Dav and Mage Hiro walked to Mari. "There is no fear in them," Mage Dav said. "Not even when they look on Mages."

"Something has been burned out of these shadows," Alain agreed in a murmur.

"Can it be relit?" Mari asked.

The Mages looked at her, even Mage Hiro revealing a tiny degree of surprise at the question. "I do not know," Mage Dav said.

"We'll have to try."

The officer stepped out of the building, her eyes sweeping across the group. "You will be allowed to enter," she said, making the concession sound like a warning.

Mari followed the officer, leading her group into the city hall. Just inside the door was a big entry area with a high ceiling. The entry was vacant of furnishings or decoration, but traces on the walls and floor showed where such things had once been found. After ascending a wide staircase, Mari and her companions were brought into a large room dominated by a long table. In some ways it echoed the room in which Mari and Alain had met some of the city leaders in Julesport, but here there were ample signs that the past glories of Tiae had been sacrificed to today's necessity. Darker areas on the walls marked where tapestries had doubtless once hung before being sold. Aside from the table, there were very few furnishings for such a large room, leading Mari to suspect most of those had been sold off as well. She knew what kind of prices furniture and tapestries from Tiae were commanding around the Sea of Bakre these days, and wondered how much of those inflated prices had actually gone to the people here who needed the money the most.

There were no weapons displayed on the walls, either, even though some alcoves seemed designed for that. Every available weapon had been pressed into the defense of the town.

The near side of the long table was bare, but on the opposite side three men and three women sat facing Mari and her group. Mari ran her gaze across them as she walked forward, trying to read their attitudes and determine who would be most open to her proposals. The three women ranged in age from an elderly common with a sharp face and a sharper gaze to a young woman who looked only several years older than Mari. One of the three men was also old, the other two middle-aged like the remaining woman. All were keeping their expressions composed, betraying little, but their eyes were suspicious and wary. They were all lean, even those with stouter builds betraying years of barely sufficient food. Aside from a sword one man wore at his side, none of the city leaders were armed with anything more than a dagger. Mari wondered whether other weapons were hidden beneath the table.

Mari stopped a couple of paces from the table, standing opposite the leaders of Pacta Servanda. She felt her youth more keenly under the gaze of the older commons, but with her jacket on and other Mechanics at her back as well as her Mages, Major Sima, and the captain of the *Gray Lady*, Mari also felt confidence. She nodded toward the group, trying to address all six of the commons without seeming to single any one of them out. "Greetings. I'm Master Mechanic Mari of Caer Lyn."

The elderly woman nodded back, her eyes glinting. "Greetings, Lady Mechanic. Were you sent to bring us a message from your leader?"

"Lady *Master* Mechanic," Mari corrected. "I am the leader."

"Then explain your presence at Pacta Servanda," the oldest man demanded. "Why did you sail your ships into our harbor, flying a pirate's banner?"

"It's not a pirate's banner," Mari said. "It's the banner of the new day."

"You are not pirates?"

"Technically…yes. But our only targets are the Great Guilds."

The old man made a scoffing sound. "The Great Guilds left Tiae a long time ago. If you have come for payment from them or from us, you will be disappointed."

Payment?" Mari asked.

"For aiding in the repulse of the barbarians attempting to breach our wall."

They were being blunt, so Mari decided to do the same. "If you'll forgive me for saying so, anyone seeing this town would know you don't have spare money lying around. We did not aid you in the expectation of payment."

"Then what do you seek?" the middle-aged woman asked. "There is nothing of value in Pacta Servanda."

Out of the corner of her eye, Mari saw Alain and the other three Mages shake their heads. A lie? What could be here that was of value? Perhaps some artifacts of the kingdom, maybe even some jewels or whatever remained of the crown of Tiae. Nothing that mattered to her, Mari was certain. "There is something here of value to us," Mari said, "but we demand nothing. We want to discuss what we can give you in exchange for what you can provide us."

"Words are cheap enough to exchange," the youngest woman said. "And what do the Mages seek?"

Alain indicated Mari. "The Mages follow Lady Mari."

The oldest man spoke again, despair apparent in his voice. "The Mage Guild and Mechanics Guild have openly allied?"

"No," Mari said. "We are not here as representatives of our former Guilds. We are dedicated to overthrowing those Guilds and bringing change to this world."

Her words didn't seem to reassure the leaders of Pacta Servanda at all. Another of the men spoke, his voice rough. "You wish to change the world, so you came here? Lady *Master* Mechanic, whatever you seek, Pacta Servanda does not have it."

"On the contrary," Mari corrected, keeping her voice commanding but polite, "your town has exactly what we seek. We want—"

The youngest woman's voice was low but firm, her face as hard as that of the officer on the landing. "What you want matters little to us who have so little. We will fight before we will allow any outsiders to enslave us. We will destroy this town fighting from every building before we give it to you. Every one of us will die trying to kill one of you. You would conquer only ruins inhabited by the dead. Do not doubt the price you would pay to seize Pacta Servanda, Lady *Master* Mechanic."

Mari gazed back at the young woman, seeing the suspicion and anger in her, but also the strength and determination. "I don't doubt you at all. I have seen such a place. My Mage and I have been to Marandur. I don't think even you can imagine the horror of that city. It is our goal to avoid such a fate for any other place in Dematr."

"Marandur?" the third man asked. "Is it no longer forbidden? Why did the Emperor permit you to visit?"

"He didn't," Mari replied dryly. "He's actually really upset about it, which is why Mage Alain and I have avoided every opportunity to personally discuss the matter with Imperial authorities."

"You're under an Imperial death sentence?" the oldest woman asked. "And seek to hide here? You've made a poor choice."

"Looking at you, and listening to you," Mari said, "I am convinced that we made a good choice. I hope you will also make a good choice: to accept what we can offer."

The youngest woman answered her again. "Beware the gifts of Mechanics, for their price will always be beyond your means. Have you heard that saying, Lady *Master* Mechanic?"

Mari gave her a flat look, annoyed by the way these commons were deliberately overemphasizing her full status and grateful that that level of sarcasm had never infected the ranks of unimaginative Senior Mechanics. "I've heard worse than that. Why not listen before you make up your minds? This town is clearly a bastion of order and decency in a land where such things have become rare. Tiae was given too little aid and too little consideration by the Great Guilds, who were more concerned with trying to limit the spread of anarchy than they were with helping those who needed it. But alone you can't hold out forever, and alone you can't return Tiae to what it once was. We're prepared to offer our weapons and our skills and our power to help you defeat your enemies and expand the area you control. We will help you to return order to Tiae."

"And in exchange?" the oldest man inquired in the silence that followed Mari's words.

"In exchange you give us what you have, and what we need. A secure place to operate from, a place to set up workshops, access to raw materials, and a labor force willing to work for us."

The oldest woman nodded slowly. "Now I grasp why you're here. The Great Guilds are beginning to crumble just as the Kingdom of Tiae did. You seek a place where you can build up enough strength to challenge your Guilds."

Mari wasn't sure she liked the way that sounded, but she had to admit the truth of it. "Yes."

"You wish to place the people of Pacta Servanda, the people of Tiae, in the middle of a struggle between the Great Guilds and renegade members of those guilds? Has Tiae not suffered enough?"

Mari liked the way that sounded even less. "The people of this town, the people of Tiae, won't be in the middle." How to say it right? "They'll be alongside us."

"Alongside?" the youngest woman asked with broad skepticism.

"Yes. We'll defend you just as we'd defend ourselves."

"As you rebel against the authority you were sworn to obey," the oldest man said. "As you lead forces against them and overthrow them and…then what? We have seen this. We have lived through this. Many others did not. Why should we aid any warlord, even if she wears the jacket of a Mechanic and has Mages at her command?"

Mari wondered if her expression conveyed how much the charge had shocked and hurt her. She stood wordless for a moment, struggling with anger.

Alli's voice rang out. "How dare you? Mari's trying to gain freedom for this world, she's trying to gain freedom for every Mechanic and Mage and common, and you accuse her of being a warlord?"

"She's never asked anything for herself," Calu added, his voice brimming with outrage.

"Lady Mari," said Alain, his Mage voice revealing a cold fury, "does not seek gain or glory. She does not seek to harm. Her goal is to

prevent the Storm that approaches this world, a Storm which has been foreseen by the Mages and which will turn all of Dematr into a place of death and ruin. Tiae was the forewarning of the Storm that the Great Guilds have tried to ignore. If the Storm is not stopped, Tiae represents only the beginning of the destruction to come."

"I would follow no warlord," the captain of the *Gray Lady* spat. "I follow her. I follow the daughter. You know not who you insult."

"The daughter?" The oldest woman blurted out the name, her eyes wide. "Impossible. She did not come when Tiae needed her. She will never come."

Mari's anger faded as she thought about all of those who had waited, and hoped, and died. "I'm sorry. I…I was born when I was."

The youngest woman leaned forward, studying Mari. "You claim to be the daughter? What insight led you to know that about yourself?"

"The sight of Mages," Mage Dav said. "We see her, and we know. We see the Storm approach, and we know."

"She did not want this of herself," Alain added. "She did not want the burden."

"The burden." The young woman looked at Mari again. "Is that how you see it?"

"Yes," Mari said. "It's a very tough job, and a great many people want to kill me, and quite a few of them have already tried. I wouldn't have volunteered for the job, if that's what you're asking."

"And yet you are a Mechanic," the oldest woman said. "And you partner with Mages. Neither have been friends to common folk. Mechanics consider us beneath contempt. Mages do not consider us worthy of any concern or notice."

"We're different," Mari said. "Do you think that if I felt that way I'd be here talking to you? That I'd be giving you an offer for a deal that will help Tiae instead of an ultimatum to do what I ask, or else? And my Mages have spoken to you. Have you noticed? They admit you exist. Well, not all of them yet. But we're working on that. I have commons here who can tell you that they are treated with the respect they deserve, because all of us, including me and Mage Alain and even

Master Mechanic Lukas and Professor S'san and Mage Dav and Mage Hiro and Mage Alera and Mechanics Alli and Calu, we have all been treated with contempt by others. Those others are the leaders of the Great Guilds. And we realize that the only way to earn real respect is to really respect others."

"I could believe it," the middle-aged woman said. "It could be her."

The young woman was resting her chin on one fist as she eyed Mari. "Tiae has no ruler. The royal family has been wiped out."

Mari once again saw Alain shake his head slightly. The woman was lying. But why?

"You come seeking to help," the woman continued. "Suppose every word you say is true, suppose you provide the means to rebuild Tiae. Then what?"

"Then we defeat the Great Guilds," Mari said.

"That's not what I mean. Who is in charge of Tiae?"

Mari shrugged. "I don't know. Whoever you decide should be in charge."

"You?"

"Me?" Mari physically recoiled at the suggestion. "No. Absolutely not."

"But the daughter could unite our people again," the oldest woman said. "You could found a new royal family. The daughter of Jules would bring a proud and mighty lineage to replace that of the old royal family, which was destroyed in these years of revolution and lawlessness."

"I said no," Mari insisted. "That will not happen. Tiae finds its own leaders, and its choices do not include me."

"Suppose we insisted, as a price for cooperation?"

Mari shook her head. She wanted to look back, to gain some insight or advice from the expressions of Professor S'san and Alain and her other friends, but that would be too obvious. And her own feelings were clear to her. "Then we have no deal. We'll go elsewhere, try to find another place where we can begin to rebuild Tiae and stave off the Storm. My job, my only job, is to build up enough strength to overthrow the Great Guilds, free the common folk from being vassals to the Guilds, and allow change to come to this world so that the Storm won't destroy it. What commons and their governments do with their freedom is their decision. I will not be a party to substituting one set of rulers for another, even if one of them is me. No, that's not strong enough. *Especially* if one of them is me."

"Your words are full of promises and ideals," the young woman said. "But they are words. Mechanics have been known to lie. Mages are infamous for lies. Is there any proof great enough to demonstrate the truth of your words, Lady Master Mechanic?"

Mari nodded. "I understand why you would be skeptical. Someone once told me that nothing he could say would convince me he was being truthful. All I could do was judge his actions. And I do have that kind of proof available." She turned to Alain and reached out. He gave her the text she had asked him to carry, and then Mari carried it to the table and set it down in front of the young woman. "Do you know what this is?"

"No," the woman said, puzzling over the words on the cover. "Demeter Projekt?"

"This a text of Mechanic technology," Mari said. "Technology that even the Mechanics Guild has for centuries banned Mechanics from seeing or using. Now I show it to you. Go ahead and read it. You may read anything in it. You may copy it and share those copies with anyone."

The woman's gaze dropped to the book again, her expression shifting to amazement. "I don't believe it."

"You wanted proof," Mari insisted. "There it is. We're ready to teach Mechanic skills to any person in this town. *Any* person in Tiae. We're ready to install equipment here and build workshops. To build Mechanic devices faster and in larger quantities than anyone has seen before. Better devices, too. What would you say to a promise to provide every single one of your soldiers with a Mechanic rifle that fires faster, farther, and more accurately than anything the Mechanics Guild has offered? Along with all of the ammunition they can carry? And small devices that let those soldiers talk to each other across long distances. And medical devices that can save those who now die of their wounds. We will give you the means to rebuild Tiae. We're ready to help, if you'll let us."

"Why would you do this for common folk?" the woman asked. "Why would you do this for anyone?"

"Because the chaos the Storm will cause began here, and we will heal that damage where it began to keep it from spreading. Because the Mechanics with me believe that our Guild has done a disservice not only to us but to everyone. They believe we'll all, Mechanics and common folk alike, benefit from change. They don't want to run the world. They want to be able to build and design new things. They want to be free, too."

"And the Mages?"

"The Mages believe that the wisdom they were taught is lacking. They're looking for a new wisdom which has more room for...well, for being human."

The young woman looked at Mari, looked down at the text, then passed it to one of the middle-aged men.

The man looked it over slowly, page by page, then nodded and spoke in a wondering voice. "It looks real. This all looks real."

Master Mechanic Lukas spoke for the first time, looking at the man. "You're a Mechanic."

"I used to be," the man said. "When the Guild pulled out of Tiae, I...I had a family here. A woman I loved. One of the common folk. I decided that this was my home, and I stayed where my wife and children were." He shrugged. "I stopped wearing the jacket when it became obvious how big a target that made me. I've done what I can to help people, but that hasn't been much."

"You can do more now," Mari said. "You can call yourself a Mechanic once again, if you wish. If we can reach agreement."

The young woman leaned back, tapping her chin with one finger as she thought. Mari realized that the dynamic in the room had shifted. When she and her friends had entered, the six leaders of Pacta Servanda had seemed to be equals. But now Mari felt a strong sense that the young woman was the true leader, with the others deferring to her and following her lead. "There would have to be someone in charge," the woman observed. "You say that we will command Tiae? Then who directs the larger effort?"

"Only the daughter can do that," Alain said. "Only she can command Mages, as well as Mechanics, and has the trust of the commons throughout Dematr."

"Your words are wise, Sir Mage. I've never talked to a Mage before. I can barely remember seeing any. But I know of their reputations, which are unpleasant to say the least. Except in one case." The young woman looked closely at Alain. "A small ship from the north visited us months ago, carrying mostly weapons and armor but also rumors. Rumors of the daughter appearing in the Northern Ramparts, slaying dragons, and accepting no payment for saving commons. The rumors said a Mage accompanied her, a Mage who was willing to sacrifice himself to save commons. Are you that Mage?"

Alain nodded.

"What makes you different?"

Alain gestured toward Mari with one hand. "She has changed me."

"Because she is the daughter?"

"Because I love her."

The young woman took a long moment to reply. "I…see. But I also see that she wears a promise ring. How does her partner feel about your love for her?"

"He is my partner," Mari said. "Mage Alain is my promised husband."

This time the silence lasted longer.

"I find myself lacking for words," the young woman finally said.

The elderly man had been silent for a while, but now pointed at Mari's armband. "You're all wearing those, and your ships fly banners with the same design. We thought it just the emblem of a pirate, but you called it the banner of the new day. What does that mean?"

"The new day," Mari answered. "The new day when knowledge will no longer be banned and the grip of the Mechanics Guild on science and technology is ended. The new day when Mages are free to see others as real. The new day when all the people in the world will be free if they choose."

"That banner will fly over Tiae?"

Mari glared at the man. "That banner will fly over my forces. The green and gold of Tiae will fly over Tiae. How many times do I have to say this? I will not rule Tiae. I want Tiae as a partner in bringing about the new day. That's all."

The young woman looked around at her comrades, judging their feelings. "Against all of my preconceptions, I find myself believing you. Perhaps I am even beginning to believe in you. Tiae has had no hope for so long that it is hard to recognize it even when it stands before us. I believe that you do not want the crown of Tiae, Lady Master Mechanic, and that is well, since you would never be offered that crown."

"It is you," Alain said, surprising Mari.

The young woman smiled slightly. "It is me. Lady Master Mechanic, daughter, I will offer to place the forces of Tiae, the resources of Tiae, at your disposal, following your direction just as these Mechanics and Mages do, with the understanding that you will use everything to further the goal you have promised—the rebirth of Tiae as a unified and peaceful country—and that you will allow Tiae's people to rule themselves. In return, Tiae will offer the home you seek to challenge the control the Great Guilds exercise over the world. And to prevent the Storm you fear. The world would not help Tiae, but Tiae will help the world."

"*You're* personally committing everything in Tiae?" Mari shook her head in bafflement, turning to Alain. "What did you mean, *it is you?*"

"She is the ruler of Tiae."

"But they're all dead..." Mari stared at the young woman.

"One survives," the young woman said. "And as long as one survives, Tiae survives."

The others behind the table stood up and bowed to the young woman as the old woman spoke with quiet formality. "May I present Her Royal Highness, the Princess Sien of Tiae." The old woman's expression reflected both pride and tragedy. "The last surviving member of the royal family of Tiae."

Mari wondered how she was supposed to acknowledge the introduction, finally settling for a half-bow toward Princess Sien. "You don't look like a princess," was the only thing that Mari could think to say. She had always imagined princesses to be pampered, fragile things. This princess looked like a battle veteran resting briefly between campaigns.

"My survival has often hinged on not looking like a princess," Sien said. "And what title should I use for the daughter?"

"Not *the daughter*, please," Mari said. "I prefer Lady Master Mechanic or just Lady Mari. That's who I am."

"Then, Lady Mari, we have the deal you wished for. The details can be worked out, but I freely admit what you surely already know. The defenses of Pacta Servanda are being sorely stressed by the so-called army of a warlord who styles himself General Raul. Any assistance you can immediately provide to our defenses would be most welcome." Sien looked down, then back at Mari. "Understand this. If I have erred in my trust of you, then my life is finally forfeit, and Tiae's last hope is gone."

"I have my faults, Princess Sien," Mari admitted. "Plenty of them. But I never break a promise, and I never abandon anyone."

"Not even a Mage," Alain said.

That night Mari and Alain walked along the wall of the town, looking out at the fires that marked the encampment of "General" Raul's "army." Accompanying them as both bodyguard and escort was the female officer who had first met them at the landing. "Half of Raul's fighters are scum," she told Mari. "The other half are men and women forced to fight, or be killed."

"Can he be reasoned with at all?" Mari asked.

The officer spat over the wall. "No. Nor would anyone want to. Ask around about Raul's victims. He's not human."

Screams suddenly came drifting on the winds from Raul's encampment. Mari felt her blood chill at the sound.

"We hear that sort of thing most nights," the officer remarked, staring into the darkness as if her gaze could deal death to Raul and his minions.

"Prisoners from this town?" Alain asked.

"No, Sir Mage. Raul tortures prisoners from the town in daylight, where we can see them. Those screams might be some poor soul who got caught in the countryside and was brought back for the amusement of Raul and his officers. Or one of Raul's fighters who ran during the last fight and is being made an example of. Or just someone picked at random."

"There is a Dark Mage at the warlord's camp," Alain said. "The Dark Mage has power, but little skill at hiding his presence. I did not sense him earlier this day. He must have arrived recently."

The officer glared into the night again. "We have little defense against Mages."

"You *had* little defense against Mages," Alain corrected. "Lady Mari's Mages can surely stop whatever the Dark Mage intends."

Mari had not been happy about having to make an attack on Raul a priority. She had considered just waiting out the warlord by repelling attacks until Raul gave up and went away.

Not anymore. She felt the chill in her blood replaced by a growing heat. "Alain, how soon can we take him apart?"

Alain pondered the question, gazing out across the land. "How will Raul respond if attacked by many Mechanics with their weapons, supported by Mages?" he asked the officer.

"Do what damage he can, then run," the officer replied. "Or maybe just run. He'd head for some other place, maybe a village, tear it apart for the fun of it and to keep his scum happy."

"We have to trap him, then," Alain said.

The officer gave Alain an appraising look. "Raul has survived a lot of fights."

"He has not fought us."

CHAPTER FOURTEEN

The sun had barely risen before Mari called a planning meeting. She had slept poorly. If Mari had not already guessed that she looked as irritable and upset as she felt it would have been obvious from the cautious attitudes of everyone around her. Calu and Alli were suppressing yawns. Alain appeared to be tired but ready to keep going for as long as necessary. Three officers from the forces defending Pacta Servanda also sat around the table, which had a map spread across it.

"How many reliable rifles do we have?" Mari asked Alli.

"Forty-eight," she replied before stifling another yawn. "And there's plenty of ammo. A lot of the stuff we got out of the armory at Edinton had corrosion on the brass, but Apprentices have been cleaning that off since we left the city."

Calu studied the map. "Raul's just encamped out there, huh? No fortifications?"

One of the officers shook his head. "Raul's forces don't build, even to defend themselves. They only destroy."

"I've heard," the female officer added, "that Raul thinks building defenses would cause his fighters to think defensively. So he just depends on attacking. Or running."

"Does he keep sentries posted?" Alain asked.

"Only facing the town," the third officer said. "That we know of."

"The training I received in military matters encouraged the idea of striking an enemy from the side," Alain added.

"In the flank," the first officer agreed. "Yes. But there's no way to get around to the left of Raul's camp without being spotted well in advance, and his right is protected by this swampy, wooded area that runs right down to the harbor." The officer ran one finger across a brownish patch on the map. "A force could get through there during the day, but their boats would be seen by Raul's sentries out front as they passed along the coast."

"What about at night?" Calu asked.

"It would be pitch black under those trees. There's no way to orient yourself at night. We've tried sending in scouts, and they all report that finding your way forward in the night is impossible."

Alain leaned forward suddenly, his eyes on the map. "Last night, as we watched the camp of Raul, I sensed a Dark Mage there."

"You told us. That's another problem," Mari said, sighing with aggravation.

"It is an opportunity," Alain said. "Remember that Mages can sense other Mages who do not have enough skill at blocking their presence."

Mari realized what that meant while the others were still puzzling over it. "You could use that Dark Mage like a compass? Tell where he was and by that know what direction it was to Raul's camp?"

"Yes," Alain said. "Mages could lead the Mechanics through the darkness."

"Is this the best we know about Raul's camp?" Calu asked. "That's a pretty rough drawing."

"We couldn't afford to lose scouts just to get a nice picture that we did not have the means to make use of," the third officer commented bitterly.

"Why can't we send up Mage Alera?" Alli asked. "Can she make her Roc here, Alain?"

"There is much power," Alain said. "Mage Alera is rested and should have no difficulty."

"Great! We send her up to look around, and she can tell us everything we need to know."

"Mage Alera has a Mage's view of the world," Alain said. "I have learned that Mages do not always see the same things as Mechanics or commons. We see some things they do not, and do not recognize other things they see easily."

"That's not a problem," Alli said. "Calu can fly up with her. He'll spot anything important."

Calu stared at Alli. "I can what?"

"Get up on the Roc and fly with Mage Alera and tell us what you can see of Raul's camp," Alli explained.

"In the air? High in the air? Above a bunch of murderous thugs? On the back of an imaginary giant bird?"

Despite her lack of sleep, Mari found herself smiling. "Calu doesn't appear to be too enthusiastic about your idea, Alli."

"No, Calu is not enthusiastic," Calu said. "Isn't it traditional for new wives to wait a little longer than this before they shove their husbands into life-threatening situations?"

"I've done it already. I guess I could go this time too..." Alli said.

"What? No! You are not going to guilt me into this, Alli!"

"Or maybe Mari could go. If you don't feel up to it," Alli added with exaggerated concern.

"I— You— All right!" Calu slumped back, looking cross. "Does the condemned man at least get a decent breakfast?"

Alli gave him a smile. "Actually, dearest, having been up there myself, I'd kind of suggest not having a full stomach when you fly on the Roc. You might not be able to keep that breakfast down."

Alain stood beside Mari as Mage Alera prepared her spell. He knew that Mari had never seen a spell-creature illusion come into existence and covertly watched her expression, taking a secret pleasure in Mari's astonishment, as the air suddenly shimmered with dust that coalesced into the huge shape of a Roc.

"This really is impossible, you know," Mari said to Alli.

"Yeah."

"But you're sending your husband up on that bird anyway."

"Yeah."

Many of the inhabitants of Pacta Servanda were watching from a distance, enjoying the spectacle. Word had apparently raced through the town that these Mechanics and Mages and commons had come to help, and the people were no longer as sullen and silent.

Alain saw Calu trudge up to the Roc with the expression of a martyr, climbing up with the assistance of Mage Alera.

"Don't look so gloomy!" Alli called. "I know you've been wanting to do this! It'll be fun!"

"Hey, Alain!" Calu called back. "Could you do me a favor? If I don't come back, would you remind Alli at least once a day for the rest of her life that those were her last words to me?"

Alain barely had time to nod before Mage Alera gave the Roc a command and the bird leapt skyward. He had a brief glimpse of Mechanic Calu hanging on with a terrified expression, then the shapes dwindled too quickly to make out faces.

"I'm going to go to the wall and watch," Alli said. "Are you coming?"

"I'll wait here," Mari said. "I'd be too nervous if I was watching them fly over Raul's camp."

Mari waited until Alli had gotten out of earshot, then took a deep breath before turning to face Alain. "I'm going along tonight. I'm going to lead the force that attacks through the swamp."

Alain realized that he had been expecting to hear just that ever since the meeting, but had managed to suppress his certainty. "Mari, it will be extremely hazardous—"

"I know."

"It would not be wise for one so important—"

"All right, first of all, I am not more important than anyone else," Mari said, her voice low and intense. "I can never afford to believe that of myself. Everyone is important. Secondly, you know I don't like that kind of wisdom. I'm going to be employing a different wisdom, the wisdom that says I should not be sending people to do things that I would not be willing to do myself. The people of Tiae will not respect me if they think I'm the sort who refuses to run the risks I demand of others."

"But Princess Sien—"

"Princess Sien! Alain, did you look at her? That girl is as tough as nails. I will bet you anything that Princess Sien has been on the walls of this town helping to fight off attacks. I want her to respect me as well."

Alain sought another argument. "The daughter of Jules—"

"Which *you* are never supposed to call me to my face," Mari said, pointing an angry forefinger at him. "Jules, Alain. Did she sit in her palace and send other people out to fight for her? To stop people like Raul?"

"Jules did not have a palace," Alain said.

"So not the point, Sir Mage! I'm going. End of discussion."

He considered her arguments and her attitude and realized that further debate would be useless as well as possibly misguided. "You may be right about the need to demonstrate your leadership in this way, Mari."

She folded her arms across her chest and gave him a flat look. "I may be right? I'm your wife."

Alain realized his mistake. "You *are* right."

"Better. You're planning on going along with the attack force tonight, too, aren't you? Uh-huh. I knew it. Because you're needed. So am I."

"You must get some sleep before then," Alain said, sure of his ground this time.

She hesitated, then nodded. "As soon as Calu gets back and we hear his report, I'll try to sleep through the afternoon. I probably ought to stay up to monitor bringing our Mechanics and equipment ashore, but Master Mechanic Lukas and Professor S'san are running that, so they don't need me. And Mage Dav is making sure the Mages are finding places. It's more important that I be ready for tonight."

"I will wake you in time to prepare for the attack," Alain said.

Mari smiled at him. "I know you will. I knew I didn't have to remind you, or warn you not to try to let me oversleep. One of the nice things about knowing how much my husband respects me is that I don't worry about whether or not he'll respect my decisions."

"Do you know how much he worries about you?" Alain said.

Her expression softened. "Yeah. I'm sorry. It's the whole 'daughter of Jules, everything is going to be destroyed, got to change the world' thing. If not for that, we could just go somewhere and be happy. And that's what we'll do, Alain." She enfolded him in a hug, speaking gently. "When this is all over. When we've won and everyone is safe. We'll find a quiet place to live and be with each other and try to forget everything bad that happened."

"We will do that," Alain said, his voice steady but his mind remembering the awful foresight vision of a motionless Mari with blood on her jacket. "We will survive, and we will find a good place." He said it as a promise to her, and as a vow to himself.

Alain could not sleep that afternoon. He waited for some sign from his foresight, but nothing came. He knew that meant nothing, that the foresight might not warn of even the greatest dangers, so the lack of warning brought no comfort.

His restless steps took him to the town wall, where he looked across the fields toward the camp of the self-styled General Raul. Mechanic Calu, his legs wobbly and his stomach unsettled but smiling nonetheless, had provided more information about the layout of the camp and where sentries were posted. Mage Alera had confirmed that there was only one Dark Mage in the camp, expressing her contempt for the Dark Mage's inability to conceal himself. "He was surprised when Swift and I flew over," Alera said, making a point of saying the new name of her Roc. "His sense of other Mages is very poor."

From there Alain went to the waterfront. Most of the buildings there had been dedicated to the trade which once flowed through Pacta Servanda. With that trade nonexistent for so many years, those buildings were vacant, to Alain's eyes standing like grave markers for the hopes and dreams of those who had once built them. It was not nearly as depressing a sight as the ruins of Marandur, but sad enough as a sign of how much had been lost when the government and society of Tiae had collapsed.

The *Pride* and the big merchant ship *Worthy Son* had tied up to the town's long-disused pier and begun disgorging the supplies and Mechanic equipment they had brought from Edinton. Many of the Mechanics had come ashore and were working around the ships and their equipment, engaged in activities that Alain found incomprehensible.

Alain gazed outward across the water, watching the boats ferrying items and people between the shore and the two other ships. The whole process reminded him of ants laboring, each individual unable to accomplish much but together creating impressive works. It was hard for him to believe that the illusion surrounding Mari had grown so much in so short a time. They had arrived in Altis as just the two of them, seeking the tower where the past of Dematr might be learned. Leaving Altis, their party had grown to include Mechanics Alli, Calu, Dav, and Bev, as well as the Mages Asha and Dav.

And now there were so many. He did not see Mechanics Alli, Calu, or Bev, and knew that Mechanic Dav must still be watching over Mage Asha aboard the *Pride*. Alain watched the Mechanics and Mages who were here, trying to spot the Mechanics Lukas and S'san or Mage Dav. But other tasks must have drawn them away from this place, where so many Mechanics and Mages who did not know each other and had been long taught to detest each other were now intermingling.

It did not take foresight to be worried about what might happen.

As if in answer to Alain's concern, angry voices broke into his reverie. Alain turned to see a small group of Mages confronting a larger group of Mechanics. Everything about the way the two groups faced each other caused alarm to rise in Alain. He walked quickly toward them, certain that there was no time to summon Mari, Lukas, S'san or any of the others to help deal with these Mechanics.

As he got closer, a large male Mechanic was leaning in toward a Mage who stood at the head of her group. The big Mechanic yelled again. "Just get out of the way!"

The Mage did not react at all. It was typical Mage behavior to ignore the actions of the shadows around them, as they had been taught others were only illusions. Those Mages who had joined Mari had been told to behave differently, but a lifetime of experience was not so easily set aside. Especially when it involved Mechanics. Every Mage knew that the best way to infuriate arrogant Mechanics was to ignore them. That old tactic was working all too well at the moment.

The big Mechanic tried to shove the Mage aside but she slid away from his shove without apparent effort or even taking notice. The other Mages in her group moved to face the Mechanics. The Mechanics stepped closer, the two groups only a short distance apart. "I'm only going to tell you one more time," the big Mechanic said in a threatening voice.

"There is a problem?" Alain used his full Mage voice, which drew the attention of the Mages who would have disregarded anyone else, and of the Mechanics who were already keyed on Mages.

Alain could read the traces of stubbornness and anger in the faces of the Mages, who no doubt looked impassive to the Mechanics. The pride and resentment of the Mechanics was much easier to see.

The big Mechanic turned a furious eye on Alain. "Oh, so *you'll* talk to me?"

"I am Mage Alain of Ihris," he said.

"I don't really care. What I do care is that these Mages are deliberately blocking us!"

"Hold on," said one of the other Mechanics. "Mage Alain. He's Master Mechanic Mari's Mage."

"Then he ought to understand why we're unhappy!"

Alain looked around the dock area. "I see a large place, and two groups arguing over a very small patch of it."

The big Mechanic looked angrier, pointing to a small building standing nearby. It sat near the waterfront and was separated from the structures on either side by access roads leading onto short piers. "We need that vacant building. The Mages won't get out of the way."

Alain looked to the Mages. "Is there a purpose?" he asked.

The woman leading the group of Mages spoke as emotionlessly as Alain had. "There is no Guild Hall, and Mages should live apart. That place will serve our needs."

"*We* need this building!" the big Mechanic insisted. "It's empty, it's in the right place, and it's the right size. And you should be grateful that I said that much, because we don't need to justify what we do to anyone!"

"Mages care not for the imaginary needs of shadows," the female Mage responded, her impassivity seemingly designed to further goad the Mechanics.

"That does it," the big Mechanic snarled. He clenched his large hands into fists and stepped forward. The other Mechanics did the same.

The Mages gave no ground, but their long knives appeared in their hands.

In another moment blood would surely be shed, and the stain of it would lie between Mages and Mechanics whom Mari wanted to work together as one.

And Alain could not strike at the Mechanics, or he would be one more Mage acting as an enemy. Nor could he attack the Mages, who would regard him as a Dark Mage if he aided their enemies.

His eyes fell upon the place the groups both wanted and in that moment, as he eyed the illusion of a building, he realized that it had become something else. Not just a structure, but a symbol to each of these Mechanics and Mages. None of them would have risked injury or death for such a building. But they would for that symbol, which represented their own pride and status.

Alain cast his arms wide, his robes flaring around him, and shoved his way between the two groups just before they clashed. Startled, both groups backed up slightly. Facing the building they were prepared to fight over, Alain rapidly summoned the heat over his palm, then placed it within the structure.

A muted roar sounded, followed by fire billowing out from the windows. Alain rapidly placed two smaller fires within it, spending his strength recklessly, so that within moments the entire building was a roaring mass of flames.

Trying not to let his weakness from casting the spells so quickly be apparent to either group, Alain turned to face them. "Mages. You would fight with shadows over an illusion. Look upon it. It never stood and does not burn, for all we see is false. Yet you would have let that falseness control your actions. I have destroyed nothing. But seeking that illusion above all else would have destroyed our hopes to find a new wisdom, one free of the dogmatism of the Guild elders.

"Mechanics. You know these Mages have powers that are real." Alain pointed at the bonfire which had been a building. "They are worthy of your respect, for they can do as I did. Master Mechanic Mari has shown me that a person does not need to understand something to respect it. I do not understand what you do. No Mage does. You create things with your hands as Mages do with our minds. Accept that we also can do things beyond your understanding, as I will try to teach Mages to accept the very different wisdom of Mechanics."

Alain pointed to the building again, already collapsing into itself. "Mechanics. Mages. Look upon this. If you wish to fight over nothing, then nothing will remain. To create something new, to change what was, requires minds willing to see what could be, not simply the illusion of what was."

He stopped, breathing heavily from the exertion of the spells and then the speech.

An alarm bell was ringing frantically, and commons were bringing a wagon designed to pump water onto fires while many others stared in the direction of the blaze.

The female Mage nodded to Alain. "A young Mage, and yet he knows wisdom better than those who have studied it longer. I sought a battle over nothing. I will not fight over an illusion given greatness only by one's own lack of wisdom."

The big Mechanic shook his head, then laughed. "You're crazy, you know that, Mage Alain? But you've got guts, coming between us like that. And you're right." He looked at the flames dancing over the ruin of the building and shook his head again. "That building wasn't worth what it could've cost all of us. Stubborn pride won't bring us freedom or change this world to what we'd like it to be." He switched his gaze to the female Mage. "I don't know how to talk to you. I'm willing to give it a try."

The Mage considered those words. "This one listens."

"She does not know how to talk to you," Alain told the Mechanics. "It is something Mages must learn."

"I don't understand that," another Mechanic said. "How hard is it to talk to somebody?"

"Extend your arm from under your robes," Alain told the female Mage. She did as asked, showing an arm laced with numerous old scars.

"What happened to her?" the big Mechanic asked.

"This is how Mage Acolytes are taught," Alain said. "This is how we were made to forget how to talk to somebody not a Mage. The price for doing wrong was a painful one."

The Mechanics exchanged embarrassed glances as the water wagon finally arrived and began hosing down the neighboring buildings to cool them. Little remained of the building Alain had set afire. "All right," the big Mechanic said. "That's…rough. It's not like Mechanics are experts at social skills, either. We'll…handle things differently while we figure out how to get along."

Mechanic Bev ambled up, looking relaxed but carrying one of the Mechanic weapons and, to Alain's Mage eyes, inwardly tense. "Any problems here?"

"Not anymore," the big Mechanic said. "Do you know how to talk to Mages?"

"Sure," Bev said. "One of my best friends is a Mage." She nodded to Alain.

Reassured that Bev would handle matters from this point on, Alain began walking back to where he and Mari had been given a room, feeling worn out from the physical and emotional effort. He saw Master Mechanic Lukas approaching quickly, a thundercloud on his brow, and Mage Dav also hurrying in the same direction. "It is dealt with," Alain said. "There was no conflict."

"Whose fault was it?" Lukas demanded. "That hothead Mechanic Len?"

Alain paused to think, assuming that Len was the big man he had spoken with. "The fault lies with those who founded our Guilds and set us on paths of mutual distrust and contempt. Mechanic Len has seen another path, as have the Mages he argued with."

"You got Len to listen to you?" Lucas said with a snort. "You're a better man than I am. Thank you, Sir Mage. I should have been watching these goons but got called to handle something else."

"I should have been present as well," Mage Dav said, as Lukas walked onward at a more sedate pace, the Mechanic's eyes searching for more trouble. "I neglected my duties to check on Mage Asha."

"Mage Asha is your niece," Alain said. "It is right that you care for her. But now is perhaps not the best time. Is she well?"

Mage Dav looked back at the *Pride*. "Our Guild insists that happiness is an illusion and love cannot exist. You know this. Like you, I have spent years trying to put aside feelings the wisdom of the elders declared were not real, and yet I could never find the answer to one question. Why do such things have so much power if they do not exist?"

"It is a worthy question," Alain said. "But not one the Guild elders would ever accept."

"I look upon my niece Asha and I feel something I cannot describe," Mage Dav said. "It is more than satisfaction in her skills. There is a concern for her welfare and a pleasure in seeing her." Mage Dav gave a most un-Magelike sigh. "Asha's mother is my sister. A shadow. One of those the Mechanics call commons. Like you with your parents, Mage Alain, I could never in my innermost self believe that my sister was nothing. Asha's father died before Asha was taken by the Guild. He was a soldier. Her mother still lives. If the opportunity should come, I will take Asha to her mother. I do not know why I am resolved in this, but I know it feels like wisdom."

"I believe it is wisdom," Alain said. "What of Mechanic Dav?"

"What of him? Mage Asha's wisdom must decide her path with Mechanic Dav. I think Mechanic Dav has already decided on his path with Mage Asha, but she will doubtless take more time to consider which road is the right one for her." Mage Dav paused again. "Do you go to battle tonight, Mage Alain?"

"This one does."

"I will find more Mages to accompany you. We cannot let the Mechanics claim the victory as their own."

Surprised, Alain was about to remind Mage Dav that such rivalries must end, when he spotted a hint of amusement on Dav's face. "You speak a joke."

"Was it done well?"

"Well enough. I understood." Alain could almost see Mari rolling her eyes. "*Mage humor*," she would say.

He hurried back to where Mari still slept.

Mari sniffed the air as they approached the docks, where the setting sun was painting red long-abandoned buildings now bustling with activity. "Was there a fire?"

"At the waterfront," Alain said.

"What burned?"

"Only one building that meant nothing."

"Was anyone hurt?" Mari pressed.

"No."

"Good." Mari gave Alain a suspicious glance. She had the sense that he was hiding something, but whatever it was probably wasn't as important as what was going on now. "Thanks for letting me sleep. I really needed it."

"Hey, your daughterness. Have a rifle," Alli said as Mari approached.

"Alli, I swear, if you don't—" Mari took the rifle, looking at it and thinking that soon she would be using it to shoot at people.

At "General" Raul's people. Before they could torture anyone else.

She checked the safety and sighted out into the harbor, getting a feel for the weapon.

Calu came up, carrying his own rifle. "Hey, I had an idea. If those Rocs can carry a couple of people, they could be used to ferry soldiers someplace behind the enemy. Think of that! Just go right over the enemy defenses!"

"One soldier at a time?" Mechanic Bev said as she approached. "Slow way of attacking."

"And not very inconspicuous," Alli said. "You know, giant birds going by overhead. Somebody might think to check on what they're doing."

"There are a few bugs to work out," Calu conceded. "Alain, is there any chance any of the Mages who create dragons would join us?"

"I don't want them," Mari said before Alain could reply.

"It is unlikely they would join," Alain said. "The…temperament?… of Mages who create the illusion of dragons is…somewhat like that of a dragon itself."

"Say no more," Alli replied. "I agree with Mari that we don't need that kind of help. Here come the last couple of guys I've been waiting for. I've think we've got your whole Mechanic army assembled, Mari."

Mari looked around in the growing darkness. Forty men and women, most of them Mechanics but a few older Apprentices as well. Each carried a rifle, and with Apprentices authorized for this night mission to wear dark jackets like the Mechanics, the entire group blended into the gloom. In addition, eight Mages counting Alain stood on the waterside, their robes wraithlike in the night.

"The other eight good rifles are with Mechanics on the town wall, like you ordered," Alli added. "Just in case that warlord tries a night attack against the town while we're getting into position to kick his butt."

"Great." Mari spoke to the others in a low voice that carried. "We're going to get to the edge of the swamp and then break into eight parallel columns, each led by a Mage. The Mages will head toward the Dark Mage they can sense in Raul's camp. Each Mage will hold a length of line, and the Mechanics behind them will hold that line to keep from losing contact with the Mage or each other. Mechanics, if the Mage leading you tells you something, *listen.* Calu thought he spotted some sentries near the edge of the swamp. If they are there, the Mages will take them out before they can sound any alarm. We'll form into a line once we clear the swamp and get ready to give Raul and his scum an unpleasant wake-up call. The locals here have given us a salve they say will repel insects and recommended we apply it very liberally, so make sure you follow their advice before we get to the swamp. Any questions?"

One Mechanic raised his hand. "I heard those screams last night. Are we taking any prisoners?"

"Yes," Mari said. "The officials of Pacta Servanda say about half of Raul's people are being forced to fight for him. It might have been one of them being tortured last night as a lesson to the others. We'll accept surrenders, then turn them over to the people of Tiae so that anyone forced to fight can be sorted out from the real criminals. Remember, everyone be as quiet as possible, and make absolutely certain that your safeties stay on until you get the order to fire. A single gunshot could ruin everything."

They moved to where the boats from the *Pride* and the *Dolphin* waited, sailors with muffled oars already seated and ready to row.

Bev sat near Mari and Alain in one boat as they waited for everyone else to load. "I hear we're doing this for a princess?" she whispered. "A for-real princess?"

"Who told you?" Mari asked. "As few people as possible are supposed to know."

"Alli told me. So we really are rescuing a princess?"

Mari couldn't help smiling. "Sort of. Helping her out, anyway.

She's a pretty hard-core princess, though. You know, this is like the sort of games I used to play as a little girl. I had a friend. Dina. We had a rule that there could only be one princess, so one of us would be the princess and the other would be the hero coming to save her."

"Why couldn't you both be heroes?"

"I don't know. We were little girls playing a silly game." Mari stared into the darkness, feeling almost as if she could see those little girls at play. "I haven't seen Dina since the Guild came for me when I was eight years old and took me to the Guild Hall for training. And you know what's funny? Here I am, and I could become a princess, or I could become a hero, but I don't really want to be either one. I just want to be free to do what I enjoy, instead of being forced to do what I must."

"Did it ever occur to you that you already are a hero?" Bev asked. "What do you think, Alain?"

"Mari has saved me many times," Alain said.

"Ha ha," Mari whispered. "Quiet, everyone. Here we go."

With all of the Mechanics, Apprentices, and Mages seated in the boats, the sailors cast off and began rowing away from the landing, north and west to gain a little distance off the coast, then straight north to where the swamp jutted out into one side of the harbor. Behind them lanterns flickered low on the waterfront of Pacta Servanda, invisible to Raul's sentries on the other side of the town wall but providing navigational references so the sailors could tell whether they were going in the right direction.

Mari, staring into the night with dark water surrounding them and the vague blackness of land off to the right, realized just how important those lights were. The stars above gave a little light, but they were screened by a layer of high clouds, while the crescent moon would provide little illumination even after it rose. Without the lights on the waterfront, she would not have had any idea where she was, let alone which direction she should go.

Rags had been stuffed into the oarlocks, but nevertheless the muffled creaking sounds made by the oars sounded far too loud to Mari, as did the faint splashing of water as they rowed. Normally the oars would be lifted between strokes, making it easy to draw the oar back through the air for another sweep through the water. But oars breaking the water's surface repeatedly would have made a lot of noise, so the rowers kept the oars in the water, twisting them for the return stroke so the flat paddles met little resistance, then twisting them again so the paddles were upright and propelled the boats forward on the sweep. It was a lot more work, but a lot quieter.

Mari jerked with surprise as something darker than the night obscured the sky just above her head. She looked around, realizing that her boat must be nosing into the swamp, feeling its way forward through partially submerged trees and other obstacles.

The swamp stank of salt and decaying matter. Mari had to suppress an urge to cough.

The boat she was in slid to a stop. "That's as far as we can go and still get out again," Mechanic Deni whispered to Mari.

"Thanks." Mari passed along the word to the others in the boat, then nerved herself and swung her legs over the side.

Her legs sank into water and loose mud. Mari blessed the loan of high boots from the ships and Pacta Servanda's supplies. As it was the water felt icy through the boots and her trousers, and the sucking mud felt as if it was trying to pull her down.

Alain placed a length of light rope into her hands and Mari passed one end back to the next Mechanic in line, working by feel since she could see almost nothing. The Tiae officer who had warned of the darkness here at night had if anything understated the problem.

Mari felt a light tug on the line and began walking. Or trying to walk. She could see nothing before her. The water held her back, the mud refused to release her feet without a prolonged, slow pull at each step to break the suction, and branches, trees, stumps, and numerous other objects blocked her every move. Insects were beginning to swarm around her and the others, invisible in the night but filling her ears with high-pitched buzzing and threatening to alight on any patch of bare skin.

Edinton had been stressful. This...this was a nightmare.

CHAPTER FIFTEEN

Mari had no idea how much time passed as she and the others struggled through the swamp. She grew worried about whether they would make it to the edge of the warlord's camp before dawn. But the mud gradually became less gooey and less deep, the water shallower. The insects did not let up, but the salve the locals had provided seemed to be effective enough to keep their torment within endurable limits. The obstructions in their path thinned out.

It took a little while to realize that she was walking on nearly solid ground amidst trees which grew fairly straight, few bushes or other undergrowth blocking their progress.

Alain stopped abruptly so that Mari bumped into him and the Mechanics behind her bumped into her. "Wait," he murmured in the barest whisper, then Mari felt the rope she held grow slack. He had let go.

Having no choice, Mari stood still, trying to see into darkness so thick that she wondered if it was solidifying just beyond her reach.

"I am back," Alain said. "There was a sentry ahead."

"Was?"

"He will not trouble us."

Mari inhaled slowly. She knew what had happened. Alain had used a concealment spell, if one was required on a night like this, to get close to the sentry and kill without warning. Because she had given orders to carry out this attack. Mari remembered the screams last night and tightened her resolve to see this through.

They reached another natural barrier, brush on the ground and vines dangling from the trees, picking their way through with the best care they could and still setting off what sounded to Mari like a bedlam of noise. But those sentries who would have heard and called warnings to Raul's camp were already dead from the blows of Mage blades.

After the pitch blackness of the woods, the starlit night beyond seemed almost bright for a moment before it became obvious how little could still be seen. Mari ensured the Mechanics with her were all out of the woods. "Everyone spread out. Stay right at the edge of the woods, keep low and keep quiet. Bev? Go down the line until you meet up with Calu and tell him to bend the line outside the woods so we block all the paths of retreat from Raul's camp."

Mari's stomach felt as if it had tied itself into a knot so tight even the sailors on the *Gray Lady* wouldn't have been able to untangle it.

Bev came back. "Everybody is out of the woods, all Mechanics within sight of each other, and the Mages right behind them. The line is bent where Calu is, extended out of the woods to the east."

"All right. Good. We're going to advance slowly. Ten paces at a time. I'll pass word down before anybody walks. Got it?"

"Got it." Bev ran down the line, passing the word.

Mari stood in a crouch, holding her rifle, trying to control her breathing. "Ten paces. Pass it down."

She took the ten steps with care, watching ahead. Raul's encampment wasn't in sight yet, so Mari ordered another ten paces.

A low ridge loomed just ahead. Mari told the Mechanic next to her to wait, then moved in a crouch to look over it. Directly in front of her, about two hundred lances away, was a large open area. As Calu had described, tents were set up helter-skelter except for a spot near the center of the camp, where a large tent sat by itself. The fires outside the tents had subsided to beds of glowing coals, giving little light. Mari checked the time. The attack was supposed to start at dawn, when there would be enough light for the Mechanics to see their targets.

Alain moved up beside her. "The Dark Mage is moving."

"Where?" Mari fought down an urge to curse at the unwelcome development.

"There." Alain pointed, and Mari spotted a figure next to one of the tents.

Mage Tana spoke in a whisper just loud enough to carry. "I sense a Dark Mage at work."

"So do I," Alain agreed. "He is preparing a spell. A powerful one."

"A dragon?" Mari hissed. She had thought she was worried before, but if a dragon appeared—-

"I do not think so," Alain said.

"Not a dragon," Tana said. "Another spell creature."

Mari pulled out her far-seers to try to get a better look at the Dark Mage, then flinched as they became superfluous. A large, hulking shape had appeared in front of the Dark Mage. It was at least half again as tall as the Dark Mage and much broader, a being whose crude lines suggested a half-formed imitation of a human being.

"A troll," Alain said.

Mari stared, remembering the troll that had attacked them in Palandur and taken a good portion of an Imperial legion to destroy. "We're supposed to wait until dawn to attack, but that thing just forced a change in our plans. Alain, is there any way to stop that troll?"

"Do enough damage and it will cease."

"I'm looking for other options!" Mari said. "The Dark Mage and the troll are just standing there looking at each other. What's happening?"

"The Dark Mage is instructing the troll on what it should do. If the task is complicated, the instructing will take some time. Trolls are not very bright," Alain added.

Mari inhaled sharply as an idea came to her. She didn't like the idea, but she liked the alternatives much less. "What if something happened to the Dark Mage before he finished giving directions to the troll?"

"It would simply attack the first thing it saw," Alain said, looking to Mage Tana for confirmation. She nodded in agreement.

"And it's in the middle of Raul's camp." Mari looked back. "Alli? I need Mechanic Alli up here as fast as possible."

Only a few moments later Alli ran up to Mari and dropped down beside her. "What's the job?"

"See that troll? It's not the target. The guy talking to the troll is a Dark Mage. He…he needs to be killed. Fast."

"No problem." Alli eased her rifle into position, resting it on the ground and aiming carefully.

Mari looked back again. "Pass the word down the line that we're going to have to change the plan and attack earlier. There will be one shot, maybe two, from here. Everyone is to advance to the edge of this ridge when they hear the shots, but wait to open fire until they hear me call the order."

Several long moments passed, while Mari felt increasing fear that the Dark Mage would finish and dart away. She wanted to hiss orders to Alli to go ahead and shoot already, but she knew that distracting Alli would be a mistake.

The crash of Alli's shot sounded cataclysmic in the silence of the night, startling Mari so much that she almost dropped her own rifle.

The Dark Mage turned his head to look toward the sound, but suddenly jerked sideways, staggering.

Alli had levered in another round and now fired quickly a second time.

This time the Dark Mage jolted backwards as if he had been punched, falling to the ground and lying still.

The echoes of the shots faded into the night as the troll stood staring down mutely at the figure of the Dark Mage.

Aroused by the sound of Alli's shots, the warlord's soldiers started running out of their tents with weapons at hand, hastily buckling on whatever armor each one owned. Some skidded to frantic stops at the sight of the troll, while others who were scanning the woods for threats didn't yet seem aware of the hulking figure nearby.

The troll roared, its voice slurred and impossible for Mari to understand. But its gestures were unmistakable as the troll raised its arms threateningly at the sight of people with weapons and charged forward. Within moments the open area had turned into a horrible brawl as the soldiers fought to subdue the monster, their weapons doing little damage while the troll's hammering blows wreaked havoc on the warlord's troops.

Mari could hear murmurs of grim satisfaction as those with her took in the battle. "How much damage can that troll take?" she asked Alain.

"It depends on the troll," Alain said.

"Of course it does." There were times when Mages could be just as particular as engineers.

The former silence of the night had given way to a cacophony of yells, shouts, screams, clashes of metal on metal, and over all the roar of the troll. Mari saw Raul's soldiers form into ranks and volley crossbow fire at the troll. To one side others were wheeling the warlord's ballista into position. "Alain, we need some light down there, and that ballista needs to be taken out."

"I understand." She saw Alain tense with concentration, and a moment later the wooden ballista erupted into flame, those who had been loading it falling away with cries of dismay. "What about some of the tents?" he asked.

"Yes. Set some of those on fire, too."

Mari nerved herself again as two tents blossomed with fire. Between them and the burning ballista the fights in the warlord's camp were well illuminated. *General Raul is a monster. He needs to be stopped just like a rampaging dragon or that troll.* She raised her rifle, remembering the faces of those she had been forced to kill in Marandur. Then Mari looked up to see the warlord's soldiers being beaten into formation to face the troll. She remembered the screams and wondered how many nights had been like that, how many victims had suffered. "Mechanics! Aim at anyone giving orders and at anyone with a crossbow! Open fire!"

Entire common armies might muster only twenty rifles because of the cost the Mechanics Guild charged and because the Guild deliberately kept the supply of rifles very limited. Ammunition was so expensive that soldiers might as well be firing gold coins every time they pulled a trigger. But Mari had forty rifles that suddenly erupted in a ragged volley to pour fire into the warlord's camp, and plenty of ammunition looted from Edinton.

A dozen of "General" Raul's officers fell under the hail of bullets. A few others tried to rally or threaten Raul's fighters, only to fall as well as the Mechanics targeted them.

The troll stomped around, smashing everything and everyone within reach, but a thick dark substance was oozing from numerous wounds and its ponderous movements were slowing.

A company of the warlord's troops in matched armor and armed with crossbows came running into the area, stopping to work the levers to draw their bows. "Get the new guys!" Mari yelled over the sound of gunshots and battle.

Mari raised her rifle, sighting on a fighter with a crossbow and feeling once again a sick turmoil inside. Mari's target fell as she levered another round into her rifle, trying not to think about what she had just done, then leveling the gun again and firing at a second crossbowman. The crackling of Mechanic rifle shots rose in an almost continuous roar and their muzzle flashes lit the field in a riot of light. Mari's shot missed her target but apparently hit someone nearby, who screamed and clutched her arm, dropping her crossbow.

Mari blinked in surprise as her latest target seemed to disappear. Then she realized the troll had stumbled close to the crossbow wielders and was slamming them right and left so hard that they were flying through the air for some distance before crashing to the ground or into other fighters.

Mari tried to lever in another round and realized her rifle was empty. She dug out bullets from her jacket pocket and fed them in as fast as she could, wondering how much longer it would be before her Mechanics themselves came under attack. The warlord's soldiers couldn't miss the barrage of rifle fire, but in their dark jackets the Mechanics were hard to see, and the troll was occupying the attention of almost everyone in the camp.

She felt a curious exhilaration mingling with the dread that still filled her. Alain was by her side, she was facing danger and overcoming it, she was righting all of the wrongs done by the warlord and his thugs, and it felt good, it felt right, and that scared her, too, even as Mari saw one of the warlord's officers brandish a sword to threaten a reluctant batch of Raul's fighters and with an angry snarl put a bullet in him.

A tight group of soldiers carrying pikes came marching into the battle, leveling their weapons at the troll and advancing with steady discipline. General Raul's bodyguards, Mari guessed. The keystone of his little army. "Take out those people with the pikes!" she yelled.

A moment later she heard and felt a whoosh of air past her head. Puzzled, Mari suddenly noticed one of Raul's fighters gazing directly at her and setting another bolt onto his crossbow.

Mari brought her rifle to her shoulder again, but as the soldier raised his crossbow it caught fire. He dropped it and ran. "Thanks, Alain."

The pike formation had lost quite a few soldiers before reaching the troll, dissolving under the hail of Mechanic rifle fire like a block of salt left out in the rain. The troll, spotting the large group of enemies, shambled toward them. Ignoring the pikes that tore into it, it waded into the formation. The fighters scattered, dropping their long weapons, which were worse than useless once the enemy was among them.

"It is time to call in the others," Alain said.

Mari stopped, aghast at realizing she had been so caught up in events that she had forgotten about other responsibilities. She dug the far-talker looted from Edinton out of one of her jacket pockets. "Master Mechanic Lukas! Tell Major Sima it is time for his soldiers to move in!"

"…move?" she heard in reply.

Cursing Guild technology, Mari tried again. "Major Sima! Attack now!"

"…under…Sim…now…"

Sima and his one hundred volunteers from the Confederation should be leaving the town now, sallying from one of the gates and moving against the front of Raul's camp to pin the warlord's army between Sima's force and the Mechanic rifles.

"There he is!" Mari heard Alli cry. A moment later, Alli's rifle barked again. Down in the camp, a big man in an ornate breastplate spun about and fell. Alli fired again, then a third time, and the man stopped moving.

Mari could hear trumpets sounding in the direction of the city. Sima's soldiers. But in addition, she heard the sound of drums. "What's that, Alain?"

He paused to listen over the sounds of battle. "Tiae. The battle drums of Tiae. The soldiers of the city come to join the fight."

"They've got some scores to settle," Mari said.

The troll staggered into the last organized body of fighters in the camp, and a moment later the survivors of the warlord's army fell apart into a mob trying to escape.

Mari went to one knee from weariness as she stared down at the camp, seeing common soldiers from the Confederation and Tiae sweeping in to take prisoner men and women who had dropped their weapons and were begging for mercy. Others kept running until they collided with the line of Mechanics or with other soldiers from Pacta Servanda.

"General" Raul's army had ceased to exist.

Mari got to her feet, leaning on her rifle for support. "Is anybody hurt?" she yelled.

"Tesa took a crossbow bolt in her hip," a hail came back.

"Jorge got grazed. Nothing serious."

Realizing how lucky they had been, how much they owed the troll for the damage it had done to the warlord's army, Mari shouted again. "Somebody stay with Tesa until the healers get to her! The rest of you, let's move in!" She waved the Mechanics forward.

They advanced slowly, pushing the broken remnants of the warlord's fighters ahead of them until the common soldiers took them prisoner. Mari stopped when they reached the armored man she had seen Alli kill.

"It's not a pretty thing," Alli said. "But I'm glad I nailed that guy. He didn't get away to cause more hurt."

Mari didn't know what she had expected the warlord to look like. Monstrous, maybe. But Raul looked distressingly average. A little tall. A little heavy. Nothing in his face or in the eyes staring sightlessly up at the sky that would indicate this was someone who took pleasure in inflicting pain.

That was more frightening than if he had appeared hideous. "Monsters should look like monsters," Mari said.

"His sort of monsters do not," Alain said.

Before she could speak again three men came running out of a tent, holding their hands high. None of them wore armor or carried weapons. "We surrender! Don't turn us over to the commons!" one pleaded.

"But aren't you commons?" Bev asked.

"We're part of the Order! We know Mechanic skills!"

Mari glared at the three, thinking of the evil they had abetted by helping Raul. The presence of these Dark Mechanics explained how Raul's ballista had been repaired after the damage inflicted by the *Pride*'s deck gun. But the idea of ordering the deaths of the Dark Mechanics repelled her. "We will turn you over to the authorities of Tiae. They can decide what punishment your crimes merit."

"There are no authorities in Tiae!" one of the Dark Mechanics protested.

"Yes, there are, and you'd better be prepared to beg mercy from them." Mari took a step away from the three and stumbled slightly.

Alain was right there, grasping her arm to steady Mari. He eyed her closely. "How are you feeling?"

"Sick," Mari said, feeling an odd buzzing in her ears. "Sick to my stomach, sick at heart, and sick of death." The surge of excitement that had kept her going during the battle was fading, replaced with weariness and something that felt like depression. Then she heard a strange sound filled with anguish, which yanked her out of her mood for a moment. "What's that?"

Alain looked in the direction of the sound. "The troll. It is not yet dead, but it is no longer a threat."

Mari got to her feet, pushing past Alain, drawn to the noise even though she wasn't sure why. Looking past the bodies of the warlord's fighters littering the ground, Mari saw the shape of the troll, not lying in the dirt but seeming shorter than it should and not moving.

Despite a reflexive burst of fear at the sight of the monster, Mari walked closer and stood watching the troll in the light of the burning ballista. The creature was on its knees, arms hanging uselessly, its thick blood coating heavy, rough skin ripped and torn by the weapons of the soldiers it had fought. The troll was so badly hurt it could no longer move, but it kept moaning. Mari could easily hear the pain in the inarticulate sounds coming from the troll's malformed mouth.

"There is nothing we can do," Alain told her, standing beside Mari. "If anyone gets within reach it will still attempt to kill. That is all it knows. It will cease in time."

"Alain, it is in pain. That creature hurts and it doesn't understand why, it doesn't understand anything except that it's in pain." Mari still held her rifle, but she rubbed tears roughly from her eyes with her free hand. "It didn't ask for this. It didn't choose this fate. That Dark Mage created it to be nothing more than…than a monster. It couldn't be anything else."

Alain stood next to her, searching for words. "There is nothing we can do," he finally repeated.

Mari shook her head. "I will never believe that there's nothing to be done." She walked toward the monster again, hearing Alain following, and stopped near it, so close it could almost reach her with one of those long arms. So close, a short lunge from the troll would have doomed her. But the troll was beyond lunging. It just stared at her, its eyes dark with pain and, Mari thought, perhaps puzzlement. The creature had just enough intelligence to kill, but not enough to understand what it had done and what was happening to it. "This is so wrong, Alain. To create a living creature as a weapon."

"It is not truly living, Mari."

"It lives enough to feel pain!" She raised her rifle, aiming at one of those eyes. Her hands trembled, making the rifle wobble, but she steadied them. "I'm sorry," she whispered, "this is all I can do." Then she squeezed the trigger.

From this close she couldn't miss her unmoving target. The bullet went into the troll's eye. It stiffened and the moaning sound finally stopped, then it fell forward, its bulk slamming to the ground at Mari's feet to lie silent and finally bereft of the illusion of life. She looked down at it, then shook her head and turned away, pausing to stare at Alain. "It's wrong," she repeated, tears coming again. She rubbed them away, flinging the tears from her hand so that they fell to the ground, mixing with the blood everywhere.

Alain nodded. "I understand."

Late on the afternoon of the next day Mari entered the grandly named, sparsely furnished, and slightly cramped suite of the Princess of Tiae on the third floor of the city hall.

Princess Sien stood next to a window, gazing out over the town, her back to Mari. From the streets below muted sounds of celebration could be heard. "Please be seated."

Mari, still worn out from the exertions of the previous night, did not object. She took a comfortable-looking chair and sat back, wondering why the chair looked and felt familiar.

"Your Captain Banda provided us with a number of chairs," Sien said. "He said that he understood we had need of them, and that those who had once used them no longer required them. Are you displeased?"

So that was why the chair felt familiar and was so comfortable. It had been one of those made for the Senior Mechanics and looted from the Mechanics Guild Hall in Edinton. Mari took another look, realizing that this particular chair must have come from the Guild Hall Supervisor's office. "Displeased? Not at all. I'm glad that Captain Banda found them a good home."

The Princess turned to face Mari, her expression somber. "It's odd how hard it can be, accepting charity even there is almost nothing left to us. Where is your Mage?"

"Alain is helping make sure no one from Raul's army got away. We don't want any of the scum who terrorized people to hide in the woods or elsewhere and go on to cause more trouble."

"A wise measure," Princess Sien said. "You've won a notable victory. Raul has been terrorizing this area for a long time. With him dead and his army destroyed, a major threat to the surrounding area has been removed, and other people in this region will be more inclined to deal with us rather than hide and hope to avoid further danger. I'd wondered if you could really help us, if you would really risk yourself to help Tiae, but you've proven that you can and will."

Mari just nodded.

"Why aren't you celebrating, Lady Mari?" Princess Sien asked.

This time Mari shrugged. "I don't particularly feel like it. We have a Mage who can send messages. I've asked him to contact a General Flyn, who operates around the Free Cities."

"You think that this Flyn will come?"

"He's, um, already sworn himself to my service," Mari said. "He's a good commander, and I'll be more than happy to turn over fighting battles to him. I'm not actually that good at it."

Princess Sien raised a questioning eyebrow. "In that case I would hate to go against you in something you think you *are* good at. You've every right to feel proud of this victory. You've helped ensure the safety of this town and eliminated a warlord who has done great harm."

Mari let her distaste show. "And all I had to do was kill a lot of people."

"I see. You don't like causing deaths."

"No. Even when it's totally justified. Even when it's the only good option."

"But you do it anyway," Sien observed.

"I don't have any choice, Princess. How else do we stop people like that? If you know another way, please tell me."

Sien watched Mari for a little while without speaking. "As you say, we have no choice. But I understand you participated in the combat, in firing your Mechanic weapon at the warlord's soldiers. As commander, you didn't have to do that."

"Maybe not." Mari gave the princess an angry look. "But how could I tell somebody else to do something I wasn't willing to do myself?"

The princess nodded. "I see more and more why people follow you, Lady Mari."

"Feel free to explain it to me sometime," Mari offered, feeling irritable.

Sien's lips curved in a wry smile. "It's not my place to do that. I will say that the choices we make define us to the world. You seem to make difficult choices for the right reasons."

Mari laughed. "I wish I had choices, Princess Sien. It seems more like I've got lots of things I have to do, and then whatever choices exist are between bad or worse."

"Really? I understand you even granted a merciful death to a troll. That was a choice."

Mari looked away, agitated and angry over feeling defensive about her action. "Why not? Why shouldn't I have done that?"

The princess's expression was impossible to read. "You felt sorry for a hideous creature whose only function in life was to kill."

"That wasn't the troll's fault," Mari replied with a scowl. "It had to die. I know that. That didn't mean it had to suffer. It wasn't like Raul. It didn't choose to be what it was."

"You speak truth." Sien glanced out of the window again. "Tiae has suffered at the hands of those who care nothing for the pain others endure. Yet we came to this state in part because of those who hesitated to punish, even those who most deserved it."

Mari leaned back again, watching the princess's face. "Alain knows a lot of history, but I don't."

Sien gave Mari a startled look. "You depend upon a Mage for knowledge of the world?"

"Well…yes." Mari couldn't suppress another sudden, brief laugh. Mages believed the world to be an illusion and most knew practically nothing of it, let alone any history. "I know that's a little strange. But Alain's not a typical Mage, either."

"Obviously," the princess observed. "The entire history of Tiae's troubles is too long and complicated to force upon you at this time, but in short, my parents were well-meaning but naïve. So I've been told by those who knew them well and who I trust, for my memories are those of a very young child." Her face was shadowed by old grief. "They would not act against those who were acting against them, and they would not take steps needed to stop those who defied them. Perhaps they were already trapped in this Storm you and your Mages spoke of, helpless before the fate that had come to Tiae in their time."

"What happened to them?" Mari asked.

"Eventually, one of those they would not confront brought about their deaths. My brothers and sisters and I were all too young to assume the throne, so a regent was appointed.

"The regent," Sien continued, "was my uncle, a man as hard as my parents were soft. Where they would inflict only the mildest of punishments, and then only reluctantly, he dealt death as a common remedy for wrongdoing. And my uncle greatly expanded the list of those things considered wrongdoing. He killed many enemies but created far more in the process. One of them ended his life and his regency. By then Tiae was in great turmoil after the combined excesses of kindness and harshness. But there were other problems, mostly the rage of our people against the Great Guilds and the repression the Great Guilds ordered as punishment. There are few records surviving from that time, but I suspect the Great Guilds had demanded many of the most severe actions my uncle took against his own people."

"I'm very sorry," Mari said.

Princess Sien eyed her. "If you still represented the Mechanics Guild whose jacket you wear, your words would mean nothing. I would regard you as just one more agent of those who helped destroy Tiae."

Mari nodded. "I had to decide whether I would keep defending that Guild. I realized that I couldn't."

Sien sighed. "After my uncle was killed, the next regent died within weeks. Then my eldest brother, who was close to reaching the age at which he could rule, was slain by poison, for by that point many others thought they saw the way to power over Tiae."

Mari looked away, not wanting to see the sorrow on the princess's face. "I guess it just got worse after that."

"It did," Sien confirmed. "Full-scale riots erupted in the cities. The army fell apart as officers and politicians vied for control. The Great Guilds unleashed spasms of violence that fed the chaos instead of suppressing it. Trade collapsed as the roads became unsafe. In the midst of that, my brothers and sisters and cousins and I became pawns. Powerful people, or people who wished to be powerful, wanted to control us, and to kill the ones they didn't control. Tiae broke into two parts, then three, then shattered completely. The royal family died person by person. I was traded for a while among captors wishing to use my royal status, narrowly escaping from the last thanks to some still loyal to Tiae itself. Those brave men and women died to save me. I hid. I fought. I survived. I learned how to judge who I could trust and who I could not. A single mistake would have doomed me."

"How did you survive?" Mari asked. "I've only gotten this far because of Alain."

"I had no Alain," Sien said, averting her eyes from Mari. "I did have those who still believed that Tiae meant something. Who were willing to run the greatest risks in what seemed a hopeless effort to keep one small part of Tiae alive." She paused, staring out the window. "I eventually ended up here. I have done all I could to help Pacta Servanda hold out, to remain Tiae, while the rest of my country sank further into barbarism."

The Princess looked at Mari again. "Why did the Great Guilds do nothing? They left what had been Tiae. They left us to suffer. Why? Did they no longer wish to rule the commons here, or consider us not worth the effort?"

Mari shook her head. "They were afraid. Every tool they were used to using to control the commons had failed. Trying something else would have required them to change, and both the Mage Guild and the Mechanics Guild are dedicated to not allowing any change."

"That is...stupid," Sien said. "They control the world. Shouldn't that be their priority?"

"They control the world because they haven't allowed any change," Mari said. "The Great Guilds have long since made that tactic into their whole reason for being. Change must not happen. Yet change did happen in Tiae, and anything else the Guild did would open the door for greater change. What would happen to the world's stability if the Bakre Confederation restored order in Tiae with the help of the Guild and then decided to stay, thereby doubling its size and power? What would happen if the Confederation moved into Tiae and instead of restoring order the social collapse in Tiae spread into the Confederation? So the Great Guilds did nothing, because the Great Guilds feared doing anything else."

Mari leaned forward, resting her forearms on her legs as weariness struck again. "That's why I'm here. Why my Guild decided to kill me even before I knew I was...that person. Because I thought that kind of reasoning was terrible and I want it to stop. I want to fix things, not let them go to blazes because I'm afraid change might undermine the way things are."

The princess watched Mari a little longer, then shook her head. "Would that you had been born twenty years earlier. Perhaps you could've prevented much suffering here."

Mari shook her head in turn, closing her eyes for a moment. "No. I don't think conditions would've been right twenty years ago for me to get the support I've needed. Besides, it's not me alone. I wouldn't be here now if not for Alain. He's kept me alive and kept me going. Without him, without his skills as a Mage, I'd be lost. Actually, I'd be dead. And I know a lot of people look at us and think we couldn't possibly really be in love, but we are. He's my partner in every way."

"Your partner." Sien nodded. "A nice thing to have. Can he then take your place if the worst happens? You told me the others would follow only you."

"I'm afraid that's true." Mari sighed, raising both palms in a what-can-I-do gesture. "Don't ask me why. They listen to Alain because they think he's telling them what I want. Even though he's smarter than I am. Probably has a lot more common sense, too."

"Success depends upon you," Sien noted. "As it depends upon me for Tiae. I'm all my country has left to rally around, Lady Mari. There should be an elected parliament to exercise some authority. That disappeared long ago and will need to be recreated, but even when the government has been rebuilt my status will stay the same in one very important way. I literally *am* Tiae, by the laws and beliefs of Tiae."

"I've got enough trouble with being the woman of the prophecy," Mari said. "I can't imagine being a country."

"If I fall, all will be lost. There is no one and nothing else left that all of Tiae could look to. It would be generations, or never, before Tiae was whole and happy again."

"If the Storm hits as the Mages keep warning, it'll be a lot longer than that," Mari said. "Why does it have to be me? I'll bet you've wondered the same thing plenty of times."

The princess nodded at Mari. "You may be the only other person in the world who understands how I feel. And I may be the only one who fully understands how you feel." She blinked, smiling sadly. "I remember as a small child playing in the palace in Tiaesun. Tiae was whole and at peace. It seems an impossible memory now, a dream of a place that never really was. I've spent so many years hiding, trying to stay alive, trusting in only a few. Even within this town only a trusted few know my true identity, because if it became widely known that the last princess was here, the warlords would flock to capture or kill me. There has been no one I could share the burden with."

"I'm sorry you never found your own Alain," Mari said.

Sien lowered her head, the smile changing into something that Mari couldn't interpret. "I have had three men who intended to marry me. The first was when I was ten years old."

"What?" Mari asked, thinking she couldn't have heard right.

"He was much older. He claimed he would protect and love me

and help me save Tiae when, with my help, he became ruler of Tiae. Wasn't that noble of him? But he was killed by rivals, and I changed hands. The second man gained control of me when I was fifteen, holding me prisoner and swearing that I would marry him and do exactly as he demanded so that he could become king someday. Are you seeing a pattern?" Sien paused, her eyes shadowed by memory.

Mari swallowed before she could speak. "What happened to him?"

The princess smiled again. "I had hidden a knife on myself. Only a small knife, but I had learned enough of the ways of violence by then to kill him with it when he attempted to attack me in the bedroom that was my cell. With his keys I was able to escape." Her expression changed again, becoming wistful. "And then, at seventeen, I met a knight in shining armor. Faris had defied the embargo of the Great Guilds, coming south from Danalee in the Confederation to try to learn the fate of relatives who had been trapped in Inser when the kingdom was broken. He was twenty, and he believed in good things and meant all the best, and I believe to this day that he truly loved me. But he thought that if we wed we should be equals in all things, and I told him that was not possible, that I would always be Tiae and he could not be. He did his best to understand, I think, and perhaps in time he would have been able to accept that. But our small group was ambushed, and he died as valiantly as any hero could have wished, holding off the bandits until I and a few others could escape. It has been almost ten years since he died, and there has been no one since, for I would not again put myself at the mercy of another, and I could not put enough trust in anyone."

"I...don't know what to say," Mari confessed. "Except that I don't know that I would have survived what you have, let alone come out of it as...as well as you have."

"I have my demons, Lady Mari," Sien said, looking at Mari again. "They come in the night, usually, but sometimes in the day, to mock me and frighten me and attempt to warp me into something that would harm Tiae and all who believe in it. Maybe being Tiae is what has kept me sane."

A soft knock sounded on the door, then the old woman looked in. "The Mage is here asking after Lady Mari."

"Send him in," Sien said. "Mage Alain. You are welcome, and I thank you as I thanked Lady Mari for your service to Tiae."

Alain nodded, moving to stand next to Mari. "One of the first things I learned from Mari was the need to do the right thing."

"Is there no end to the good that Lady Mari does in this world?" Sien asked with just the right amount of humor in her voice. "I now face the need to live up to her example."

Mari couldn't help smiling. "Yeah, that's me. Absolutely perfect, and a model for princesses everywhere. Do *not* nod, Alain. Did you find any more of Raul's people hiding out there?"

"About twenty in various locations," Alain said. "But none of them lied when they said they had been forced to join the warlord's army. The commander of the town's forces let them go. Most of them. Four said they had nothing left and asked to join the town's defenders."

Sien finally sat down, looking at Mari and Alain. "You have given us much. What can Tiae give you besides workers and soldiers?"

Mari bit her lip, hesitant to bring up what she really wanted. "Princess, I'm a Mechanic. I have a lot of training in how to fix things and build things. Machines. And the nice thing about machines is that even though they are often temperamental in their own ways, and each can have its quirks, one machine of a certain type is just like every other machine of that type. But I've been, more and more, having to work with people, and people are…really complicated. Alain can tell me if someone is lying, but what about people who think they're being truthful when they tell me something that isn't right? What about people who know how to twist the truth?"

"You're talking politics," Sien said. "I imagine that every ruler of the common folk, no matter how elected or appointed, has greeted the news of the daughter's appearance with thoughts of how they could use the daughter to their own ends. If you're claiming that you have no skills to motivate and inspire, I must disagree, but if you are worried about those who will try to manipulate you for their own power and profit, you have every right to be concerned. I'm afraid that I have far too much experience in dealing with that."

"Can you help me?" Mari asked. "Alain and I? Help us with the politics?"

"The Princess of Tiae become political advisor to the daughter of Jules? How can you trust me, Lady Mari? Do you not realize I would do anything to help Tiae?"

"No," Mari said. "I don't think you would do anything. I can see what this town is like. I've also seen places like Marandur, and I've dealt with the Senior Mechanics. I know what people who would do *anything* are like, and what their works are like. You're not one of those people."

Sien did not answer for a long time. Finally, she nodded. "Thank you. I often fear what I could become. What I could become for the best of reasons. Yes, Lady Mari, I will be happy to advise you in matters political, and perhaps help keep the vipers from whispering in your ears those things that benefit only them."

"Can you just call me Mari, Princess?"

"Can you just call me Sien, daughter?"

Mari laughed, finally feeling her depression after the fight lifting a little. "That's a deal."

"And what does Sien call Mage Alain?" the princess asked.

"To friends of Mari," Alain said, "I am Alain."

"Then, Mari and Alain, let us go down to the streets and join the people who are celebrating the beginning of the rebirth of Tiae. It is a lean celebration, given how little we have, but no less sincere for that. And afterwards we will speak with each other of the impossible things we are going to do together, restoring my country and bringing peace to its people."

"And overthrowing the Great Guilds and bringing the new day," Mari said.

"And stopping the Storm before it causes more grief," Alain said.

Princess Sien shook her head. "You two don't dream small. I don't know if I'll be able to help you as much as you will help me. Can you change the entire world alone, Mari?"

"No, of course not," Mari said. "But I don't have to do it alone. Alain's helping me get it done."

ABOUT THE AUTHOR

"Jack Campbell" is the pseudonym for John G. Hemry, a retired Naval officer who graduated from the U.S. Naval Academy in Annapolis before serving with the surface fleet and in a variety of other assignments. He is the author of The Lost Fleet military science fiction series, as well as the Stark's War series, and the Paul Sinclair series. His short fiction appears frequently in *Analog* magazine, and many have been collected in ebook anthologies *Ad Astra*, *Borrowed Time*, and *Swords and Saddles*. The Pillars of Reality is his first epic fantasy series. He lives with his indomitable wife and three children in Maryland.

*CONTINUE THE STORY
IN...*

THE SERVANTS
OF THE STORM

PILLARS OF REALITY
BOOK 5

AVAILABLE NOW

FOR NEWS ABOUT JABBERWOCKY BOOKS AND AUTHORS

Sign up for our newsletter*: http://eepurl.com/b84tDz
visit our website: awfulagent.com/ebooks
or follow us on twitter: @awfulagent

THANKS FOR READING!

41992529R00192

Made in the USA
Middletown, DE
28 March 2017